SIGHT LINES

CARA CARNES

HEARTSCAPE PUBLISHING, LLC

COPYRIGHT

The characters are productions of the author's imagination and used fictitiously.

Cover Models: Elaine Monville and Paul Steiger
Photography by: Shauna Kruse @ Kruse Images & Photography
Cover Design by Freya Barker at RE&D
Editor: Heather Long
Proofing: Ink It Out Editing

For the latest information, subscribe to my <u>newsletter</u>.

1

Viviana "Quillery" Chambers secured the wrist control into position and activated HERA. Drones rose and zoomed to their pre-programmed positions. Palms sweaty, pulse racing, she forced a deep breath and exhaled through the unease. She'd participated in hundreds, no thousands, of ops through the years. This one was different, though. She was in the field on this one because it was personal.

"Hey, we've got this." Addy Rugers slapped her on the back and smiled. "We've run through every possible scenario damn near a hundred times."

The kickass operative wasn't lying. Every muscle in Vi's body ached from the hours upon hours of "dry runs" her new boss insisted on doing. Marshall Mason and his brothers didn't mess around. It was one of the ten thousand reasons The Arsenal was the best private paramilitary organization around.

"I'm good. I'm just sick of waiting." Vi adjusted the earpiece in her left ear and stared out across the street. Apartment 6E held their quarry. He damned well better have the answers she wanted.

"Shake it off or you'll get benched," Addy warned. The redhead motioned to the vehicle in front of them, a black SUV with darkened windows—a twin to the one they had just exited. "Say the word and Cord'll step in."

"No. This is mine. I'm lead." She punctuated the last two words as she channeled the anger, the seething rage she'd kept contained, unseen. Nervous energy was expected, an acceptable display, one she'd allowed the past few minutes.

No more.

If her new boss knew how emotionally vested she was, they'd bench her. She'd spent damn near every hour of the past two weeks scouring the Deep Web and every other crevice of humanity to unearth the asshole in apartment 6E. The Arsenal didn't mess around, but they didn't put their people in trouble's sight lines, not if they were too deep in their own heads to focus.

Today's objective was simple: breach apartment 6E and get answers.

She summoned the calm: the no-holds-barred confidence which had translated to nothing but successful missions for her and her partner, Mary, aka the Edge. Together they'd been the Quillery Edge ever since freshman year at MIT. Today was for Mary.

Her *and* Addy.

Vi looked over at her redheaded friend, the one who'd lost so much and hadn't batted an eye. Fierce operatives like Addison Rugers took whatever blows life dealt and came back stronger. She deserved a break. It was the least Vi could do, seeing how she failed them both so miserably when the Hive nightmare started. They deserved answers.

Justice.

Closure.

Her wrist apparatus chimed, signaling the start of the mission. Drones were in position.

"Hallways are clear and secure," Mary offered through the com.

"Roger," Vi replied.

"Be careful," Mary whispered in reply. "Listen to Addy if things go wrong. Cord and I have your back."

Mary had insisted on coming, being alongside Vi. Thank goodness Dylan had talked sense into her.

You'll be better backup here in Command. She and Mary had received limited field training when they started at their former employer, Hive. Thus the "refresher courses" Addy and the other team leaders at The Arsenal had made her go through. Fortunately, she'd done well enough for them to flag her as active for field work.

They had no choice. Although they'd gotten most of those responsible for kidnapping Mary, the ring leader was still in the wind. Her friend wouldn't be truly safe, able to move on until every single person with a hand in what happened paid. This entire thing was Vi's mess and she was going to clean it up.

"We're going in," Vi stated.

A drone maneuvered up the stairwell to the left when they entered the lobby. Huntington Apartments was in a part of Chicago where most people wouldn't care to live. But it was within a quarter mile of the pizzeria Arnie Mulligan worked at thirty hours a week. The minimum wage position and shitty one-bedroom kept him off Uncle Sam's radar. Too bad he'd hit Vi's in a big way.

Addy's long-legged stride chewed up the stairs two and sometimes three at a time. Vi cursed her short and much fuller body, but remained radio silent. She didn't need to breathe to kick Arnie's ass. She wouldn't be kicking his ass at all. That was Addy's job.

Addy remained five to six stairs ahead of Vi the entire way up to the sixth floor. Two drones hovered near Vi. One in front of

Addy. They'd only used two in the last hostage recovery mission they'd undertaken last week. Needless to say, the entire Arsenal was personally vested in the objective.

Vi pulled out the Sig Sauer she'd been issued. Just holding it made her feel a bit more bad ass and a little less fat ass. Then Addy nodded, lifted a leg and kicked the door to apartment 6E. Wood splintered. The redhead didn't miss a beat. She disappeared through the entry. Vi remembered the instructions. Duck and to the right.

Easy enough.

Penetration of the target's domicile wasn't difficult. He was a three-hundred-seventy-pound idiot savant with a penchant for kiddie porn. Addy had her gun pressed against Arnie's temple. Arnie was staring at Vi as she entered. His large, brown-eyed gaze flitted between her and Addy.

"Hello, Arnie," Vi said.

She set the gun down on the kitchen table, one he'd converted into a workstation of sorts. Computers in assorted stages of completion or deconstruction were strewn about the area. Gnats flitted about and landed on half-finished food and paper plates. Super-sized drinks from the corner convenience store laid in a heap in the corner.

"Jesus, the bastard's a cliché geek," Cord spat through the com.

Arnie gasped as the drone hovered inches from his face.

"Back off. This is my op," Vi commented. She waited as the drone backed away a few inches, hovering near her ear. "We need to talk, Arnie."

"I ain't got nothing of any value. Take whatever you want." His lower lip quivered. "Just don't hurt me."

"Please. You'd probably enjoy it too much," Addy replied, her voice low and lethal.

"You disappoint me, Arnie." Vi forced his attention back to her.

"Lady, I don't even know you." His shaky voice rose an octave. "Don't hurt me."

Vi pulled on a pair of gloves, more for effect than necessity, and waited until his eyes widened. "What am I going to find on your computer, Arnie?"

Lower lip trembling, he remained quiet. She'd dreamed of this moment for days. He wasn't supposed to cry, not this soon. He needed to suffer for his part in Mary's abduction. Arnie was messing with her pissed-off mojo.

It wasn't fun squashing a bug if they didn't offer at least a little fight.

She'd seen what the bastard got off on. Studied what he sold to pad his secret bank accounts. He deserved far more than her wrath.

"You've been a bad, bad boy, Arnold Harry Mulligan. You would've gotten by with it if you hadn't gotten greedy." Vi went around the table to stand at his other side. "See, you're one of a million cockroaches scurrying when the lights go on. When I purge the Deep Web, I move right past you because you aren't worth the effort. I'm going for the snakes, the vipers."

She reached down and banged the table. Gnats flew for cover, unfinished drinks teetered. Arnie trembled.

"Talk to me about your voice alteration programs. Who hired you to duplicate my voice?"

Recognition flared his eyes wide and for a flash, barely a breath, Vi tasted something other than failure, guilt. She heard something other than her best friend's voice screaming in the middle of the night. Screaming her name over and over and over. It'd been weeks since Mary had bad episodes, but Vi remembered. Every time she closed her eyes she remembered those screams.

"Oh God." Arnie squeezed his eyes shut. His bladder let loose. "I didn't know. I swear, I didn't know what they were gonna do."

"But you agreed. Did the deed, took the money and ran like

the cockroach you are," she whispered angrily. "You knew whose voice you were cloning. You aren't a dumb troll, just lazy. You knew there'd be consequences. You knew who I was."

"Y-Yeah, I knew. Quillery, the bitch who culls the Shadows."

Vi culled far more than the Shadows. The one sight was a frequent pit stop for her personal quest to clean up the cesspit in the Hidden Web. While many people had heard of the Dark Web, there were far worse, seedier areas. Those were her hunting grounds. "I'm surprised they let little piss ants like you in, with your paltry few credit card numbers you lift from the pizzeria."

Pander to his pride, piss off the peacock and he'll preen. She backed up a step when his face reddened. Addy eased the gun away and shook her head. Vi allowed her revulsion to show in her expression. Arnie had cracked too fast, too easy.

"You stupid cow. You think I pawn digits? You're the idiot. I'm the best damn coder in the Shadows. No one's better." His chest swelled. "I can make anything if the price is right. Everything I create is genius."

"What was the price?" Addy demanded.

Arnie gulped.

The redhead's eyes glimmered and she smirked. Taking a step back, she aimed and fired at the biggest monitor with her silenced weapon. The 4K television serving as a monitor shattered.

"Here's what's gonna happen," Vi whispered. "You're going to tell me everything, and fast. My friend here is short tempered and has a lot of bullets. The next one's going into your hard drive."

"I'm not telling you a damn thing. They'll kill me."

"I won't let them because that'd be too easy." He needed to suffer, scream endlessly night after night feeling phantom horrors. "First, I'm going to put you in a cold, dark hole and make you listen to what they did to her. Make you listen to your *genius*. Then you'll take her place, experience everything she did as you listen to your *genius*."

"Vi, ease off," Cord whispered through the com.

To hell with easing off. Those bastards hadn't eased off when they'd had Mary. Hurt Mary. Made her scream.

Made her think they were hurting Vi the same way. All because of Arnie.

The *genius*.

"I didn't know," he cried out. "I swear."

"Actions have consequences, Arn. Today you get yours." Vi motioned toward the computer. "Call up your genius. Show me."

"I-I don't keep a copy, it's part of my agreement."

Like hell he didn't keep a copy.

"Show me," Vi thundered.

"O-okay."

His fingers trembled as he got to work on the keyboard. Vi watched, noted passwords as he keyed them in, and observed his security measures and protocols as he bypassed them. The drone hovered, recording each keystroke, each move. "H-here it is."

He motioned to the screen. Vi grabbed the keyboard. She called up the source files, the ones he'd been given with her voice. No date or time stamps. Oh well. She'd figure out where they came from, narrow suspects down. Likely Peter himself had recorded them, which meant they were at another dead end.

"Where did the payment you got come from?"

"Untraceable wires, pinged through four banks. I trace payments. Knowledge is power," he offered lamely.

"How did they contact you?"

"On the Shadows, said a friend recommended me. I didn't ask who."

"Of course you didn't," Addy commented dryly. "Afraid the hard drive's eating a bullet, Arnie."

"No, no, no. Wait. I-I may have recorded a conversation or two. He used an app to disguise his voice, but I got passed it."

"Right. Cause you're the genius," Vi supplied. "Call it up."

He looked up nervously at Addy, then back at Vi. With a nod, he got to work. Moments later a thickly accented voice droned on through the computer's speakers.

"Middle Eastern," Mary commented through the headset.

HERA could trace the voice, possibly. She snagged the keyboard and entered a few commands, uploading the data to a secured network and downloading a virus to obliterate Arnie's operation. It'd take forty-eight hours for the worm she'd written to duplicate all his data and send all incriminating evidence to the FBI. Just enough time for her to have what she needed without government suits getting in her way.

"Anything else you want to offer up, Arn?" Addy asked.

"I cooperated. I need security. He'll come after me."

"Doubtful. You aren't worth the effort," Vi commented. "Besides, remember what I said about consequences? Making stupid decisions gets you in trouble."

Vi turned, picked up the weapon she'd set on the table and headed toward the door. She wanted to put two rounds in his forehead, but the bastard would get his comeuppance courtesy of the alphabet soup. Until then, he could marinate a couple days. "Don't get on my radar again. I won't be so nice next time. You owe me."

Each step away from Arnie Mulligan quickened her pulse. She remained silent as Addy fell into step alongside her. Drones zoomed past them as they exited the building and headed across the street to the vehicle.

Addy grabbed Vi's wrist and removed HERA's controller, the one she hadn't even considered using because Mary and Cord had handled the drones from the compound. Vi sat in her seat as Addy removed both their ear buds and sealed everything into the case. She slammed the door shut behind Vi, then went around the front of the SUV. The vehicle slid away from the curb less than a minute later.

A shrill ring sounded overhead.

"We're clear," Addy replied upon answering.

"Mary and Cord are working on the data," Marshall replied. "We'll talk in the air. Transport is waiting. We're wheels up in forty minutes."

Vi didn't want to talk. Not now. Not in the air. Not anytime soon.

"He's worried," Addy offered unnecessarily when she hung up the call. "Vi, the things you said back there. You aren't past what went down with Hive."

"And you are?" Vi laughed and shook her head as she stared out the window. Chicago whizzed by as they headed toward the private airstrip they'd landed at less than three hours ago. "I'm not anymore messed up about what went down than you are."

"You're right. I'm not over it." Addy locked gazes with Vi when she turned her head. "But I've spoken with Doctor Sinclair. I'm working through it. So is Mary."

Her stomach clenched. Seeing a head shrink wasn't on Vi's agenda. She didn't need help, not that kind anyway. She should've been there to keep Mary safe. She should've gotten them out of Hive sooner. It was her fault they'd remained too long. Mary had wanted to leave weeks before she was taken, but Vi wanted more dirt on Martin Driggs, Peter's co-owner.

They'd both suspected Driggs as being dirty.

Neither had considered Peter, mainly because the bastard had faked his death.

Vi couldn't undo her foolish decision, a decision Mary suffered for.

She squeezed her eyes shut and forced a deep breath. Her fingers moved in time to invisible code scrawling through her brain, but the stress management technique she'd taught herself didn't ease the ache in her chest. The regret lodged in her throat.

I won't let you down again, Mary. I won't let any of you down. I swear.

The vehicle signaled another incoming call. Addy answered before Vi could say otherwise.

"Vi." Mary's voice was soft, hesitant. The Edge wasn't ever supposed to be soft.

And sure as hell not hesitant.

Vi had done that, added those cracks in a once unbreakable armor.

She forced a cleansing breath and focused on the task at hand. "Any luck with HERA tracking the voice?"

"She's working on it," Mary replied. "Are you okay?"

"Okay, I'll see you soon."

"See you."

The line went dead. Addy shook her head. "You can't avoid her forever. She's worried."

Vi didn't need to avoid Mary forever, just long enough to track down the bastards who funded Peter's betrayal. The ones who got away. Once Vi found them, everything would be good. She would fix everything. Better late than never, right?

2

___

"They're out. Quillery kicks ass in the field." Jacob looked over at him. "What now?"

Judson Jensen looked over at his nephew, unsure how to respond. For the first time in a long time he had no clue.

A contract was in play—terminate the Quillery Edge. The payout was huge, huge enough to awaken all the sharks. The bastards behind the payday added chum to the already bloodied waters with a triple the reward offer—kill them and secure HERA. Six million dollars.

He'd received numerous phone calls about the recent contract —one he had a personal stake in ensuring didn't happen. The two women saved his nephew's father fifteen years before. It'd taken more favors than he cared to expend to find their new location.

The Quillery Edge had taken down Hive, their former employer, after they realized it was dirty. That action alone made a lot of people nervous, including Jud's employer. The fact they'd created the most sophisticated offensive and defensive security system around added chum to the already shark-infested waters.

No matter how much he might want to stay out of the situation, he didn't have a choice. They'd saved Danny. He owed them. "Time to make a call. Stay quiet, bud."

"Like I'm an idiot," Jacob muttered.

The phone rang in the vehicle's speakers. "Jud, what a pleasant surprise."

"Cut the shit, Jian. I got your message." Jud watched Viviana Chambers, aka Quillery, and her team pull out. "What's with the contract on the Quillery Edge?"

"My message was pretty clear. Two million for them, four for their program." Amusement glinted in his voice. "If you take it, I'm prepared to extend an additional incentive."

He'd taken a lot of jobs, operated in the shadows his entire career. "I don't take unjustified contracts, not anymore."

"We all have our lines, Judson. I'm thinking you'll move yours for this particular...situation."

Jian Chen was a bastard, one who'd stayed alive because he was useful to Jud's employers. The Collective had turned the man into a puppet over the years, one who acquired anything and anyone as long as the price was right.

"You know better than to piss me off, Jian. I'm not interested in the contract and I'd advise you to withdraw it. Going after the Quillery Edge is highly inadvisable."

"That's a shame, because I have some connections who could help with your little problem, assuming they're ordered to do so."

"I don't have a problem." Jud's sixth sense kicked in, the one that'd kept him breathing in impossible situations. "Cut your shit and get to the point, Jian."

"I'm afraid your brother's convoy had some unfortunate problems last week and has been declared missing." *Son of a bitch*. Jud settled his hand on Jacob's mouth. Tears formed in his nineteen-year-old nephew's eyes. "I'm sure you'll be notified soon enough. You know how slow these situations sometimes unfold. I have some assets in position to help...expedite his safe extraction, should I have reason to do so."

Son of a bitch.

"I take the contract and you'll make sure he's released unharmed. Is that how this works?"

"It's rather unfortunate this little incident happened, but friends do look out for one another, yes? Secure the program and eliminate the Quillery Edge and I'll make sure Danny is returned without harm." Jian's voice dropped. "Don't take too much time to decide. Six million is a big payday, one many are bound to seek."

"It'll take some time to get into position. They're aligned with The Arsenal now. Only an idiot would think this is a simple contract."

"I'm well aware of their recent employment shift. It's unfortunate they betrayed their former employers like they did."

Yeah, right. Their former employers, Hive, had kidnapped Mary, aka Edge, and tortured her to gain access to their security system. The Arsenal had mounted a rescue and gotten the two women safely. Jud was of half a mind to go after the rest of the bastards behind the kidnapping himself, but it was obvious Viviana, aka Quillery, had her partner's back. She had the entirety of The Arsenal looking for whomever hired Hive to betray them and go after the program.

"I'll need a week to get into place."

"Unacceptable."

"You know damn good and well I'm the only one capable of pulling this off. Warning, Jian. Don't piss me off more than I already am," Jud growled.

"I'll expect frequent updates. My employer for this matter is quite...impatient."

His employer. Disgust rolled through Jud. Few had the balls or the finances to bankroll a high-value contract. Only one came to mind. Jud's employer, The Collective.

Son of a bitch.

"I'll be in touch." He clicked off and released his steely grip on Jacob's mouth.

His nephew screamed and wailed, more rage than surprise. Jud held on, let the young man vent the emotions stealing his control a couple moments, then he pulled away. "Gotta get it together, bud. I know it sucks, but we need to verify what Jian said and make some decisions."

The teen grabbed his computer. Tears streamed down his face. "He was lying. Right, Uncle Jud? Dad's okay, right?"

"Wish he was, bud. He wouldn't lie about something I can verify."

Danny had taken an overseas training mission even though he had zero business in the field. The man was determined to do right by Jacob and help him pay down his entry into a doctorate degree program at MIT. The brilliant kid had already gotten his bachelor's and was halfway through with a master's. Jud's waste of space sister had walked away from them fifteen years ago, when Danny narrowly escaped his last captivity.

"Dad can't survive that again, Uncle Jud. He's in a wheelchair. They wouldn't hurt a paraplegic, would they?"

Jacob had somehow maintained a naive view on many things, including what people would and wouldn't do. He'd recently started delving into the seedy black ops world Jud had lived in the past couple of decades. The kid knew the answer to the question. "I don't ever bullshit you."

He turned ashen as he pointed at the screen. "There's...there's a message."

"Play it."

Jud squeezed his nephew's shoulder and bit back the rage rising in him as he watched the video play. Danny was beaten, bloodied but alive. There was no message, no audio whatsoever. The short ten second clip offered little in the way of insight into where he was being held or by who. Very few could find out those details from what little was known.

"This is bullshit," Jacob clipped.

"Yeah, it is."

"He thinks you'll take out the Quillery Edge, that he can control you. Make you." Jacob's hands fisted in his lap. "This is bullshit."

"Yeah, it is."

"Dad wouldn't want to keep breathing if it meant they weren't." Tears flowed down Jacob's face. "What are you gonna do?"

"The only thing I can, get into position and make certain no one else takes them out."

"You're doing it? You're going to murder the Quillery Edge, after what they did for Dad. They saved his life, Uncle Jud. We can't...you can't."

"You and your dad are more important to me than anyone," he replied. "This wouldn't be the first shitty contract I've taken."

"There's gotta be another way."

"We'll figure it out, bud."

"There's gotta be another way," Jacob repeated. "They'll help us, you know. The Quillery Edge will help us. We can help them. You and them together would be unstoppable."

The kid idolized the two women. Danny had regaled his son with stories of how the two brilliant women so much like Jacob had kept him alive. Jud couldn't imagine taking either of them out, which meant he'd have to stand between them and anyone else who tried to take the contract.

But what about Danny?

Refusing the contract was a certain death sentence for his brother-in-law.

"Get us tickets to Texas, bud. We're going to have a chat with the Quillery Edge."

"So you'll help them?"

"No one's touching them. You saw the group they're with now. They're good. Secure." He looked over and navigated the vehicle onto the busy highway leading toward the airport. "You looked into The Arsenal, bud. They're good. The best."

"No. You're the best," his nephew shot back angrily. "You're so good no one knows you even exist. You can help The Arsenal go after those assholes. She needs you. They wouldn't dare go after her or The Edge if you were involved. And they can rescue Dad without breaking a sweat."

"It's not that simple. Walking onto their compound and announcing there's a contract on their head will earn me a bullet in my brain, especially once they figure out who I'm with."

The Arsenal was a relatively new operation, one already respected within the paramilitary arena as the best around, mainly because of the six brothers who'd formed the operation. The Masons. Jud had only worked with one of the men, Dallas. He doubted the man would appreciate him showing up at their compound, but Jud wasn't seeing much of a choice.

"If they kill her, we never get Dad out of there. She saved him once, she can do it again. You're in a perfect position to help keep her breathing, Uncle Jud. Or should I call you *Judge*?"

Jud clenched his jaw and looked out the window. Jacob was a brilliant pain in the ass. He'd stumbled across Jud's second life, the one he'd carefully kept hidden for over two decades. But his nephew had figured out the quiet, barely operable investigation company he ran out of Boston was more than it seemed. "Bud, you've got to ease off on plunging into the cesspit I'm in. Now isn't the time for you to swim around, not when everyone's nervous about what went down with Edge and Hive."

After The Arsenal rescued Edge from her captivity, she and Quillery partnered up with the new private paramilitary organization and brought the bastards who'd taken her down. Hard. Hive had been a force within more than just the private paramilitary arena. Tremors from its collapse rocked Jud's world, one very few knew—a world where knowing too much got you killed. His nephew danced the line daily despite Jud's insistence he back off.

"This has nothing to do with The Collective." Or so he hoped.

Jian was a puppet controlled by The Collective, but he had more clients. Jud couldn't ignore the fact his employer was probably involved, however. The security system the Quillery Edge created would be a huge boon for them. If The Collective was behind Jian, then Jud had a much larger problem on his hands.

His employer was the largest, most formidable organization in existence. It operated in the dark shadows of the underworld, where unknown individuals controlled entire empires.

"No, but no one in The Collective would go against their very best. You stand between the contract and the target and they'll back down. Then Quillery and Edge will owe us and they'll help us save Dad." Jacob clenched his laptop tight. His lips thinned into a grim line. "Besides, we already owe them."

Fuck. He'd maintained a firm grip on the reins of his two worlds and kept them separated. Only his brilliant MIT graduate nephew had connected them. "Jacob, I can't cash the debt in, not against this."

"Why not? Is it too hard? Too dangerous?" Jacob's voice rose. "What if Quillery had thought that? And Edge? Yeah, if they'd thought that, Dad wouldn't be breathing. We owe them, Uncle Jud. It's not your debt, though. It's Dad's and mine, so I'll help if you won't. Either way, I'm keeping them breathing and getting them to help me save him."

"I'm thinking they need a different skill set than you can offer," he replied calmly. Tension coiled within the vehicle, a viper poised to strike. He recognized the gleam in his nephew's eyes. Fiery determination, the same drive that made Jud the best available within The Collective.

"Courage doesn't come from winning the battle," Jacob whispered, his voice tight and threaded with anger. "It comes from looking impossible in the eyes and kneeing his nuts."

"You're still throwing that quote out?"

"Every chance I get." A smile spread on his face.

"Your mom's not a fan," he commented. "I promised her I'd keep you safe and happy."

"I'm not a fan of Mom's."

"Bud..."

"Leave her out of this, Uncle Jud. She left. She doesn't get a say in what I do. I'm an adult now and get my own say and I'm in. Whatever it takes to rescue Dad and keep the Quillery Edge breathing, I'm in." His fierceness maligned the moisture in his eyes. "We don't get to walk away because the impossible is big, Uncle Jud. They didn't."

"You're right. We don't." He gripped the steering wheel and breathed the decision in deep, until it filled him with the calm, the same calm he thrived in. "No one touches the Quillery Edge, bud."

"So you're in?"

"I'm in, but only if you're out." He kept talking when Jacob's head shook side to side. "You're on the sideline, helping when I ask for it. Nothing more."

"Just like Quillery and Edge," he said.

"Yeah."

"Though, she really kicked ass in the field today," Jacob commented.

"Yeah, she did."

Viviana Chambers had trouble written all over her. She was the worst decision he could make. Add in The Arsenal and Jud had zero business heading to Texas and walking onto that compound. But Jacob was right. A debt was owed, one he'd honor and keep them breathing because it was the right thing to do.

More importantly, he needed to get Danny secure and teach Jian and whoever was behind his decision a lesson.

No one fucked with his family.

He was a bit surprised Jacob wasn't more freaked out by what Jian had just told them. Then again, Jacob never gave up, never quit. He was resilient and determined. Headstrong. Brilliant. He was all those things because of his dad, and the two women who saved his life fifteen years prior. Jud stared into his nephew's determined face. The kid had kept him going the past year and didn't even know.

Jud had bathed in carnage and shady decisions a long time, too long. Jacob had waded into the muck and straddled the ravine between reality and hell. He was a hell of a kid. "Book us a flight to Texas."

Jacob grinned big. "I'll get us a flight, express. Quillery and her team are leaving in half an hour on a private jet. We don't want to waste time. I've got to pack my stuff and get my lists and..."

"Breathe, bud." He squeezed his nephew's shoulder. "We don't have to chase them. We know where they're going."

"Yeah, okay." Jacob swallowed, looked down at the keyboard. "You think they'll like me?"

The question was a punch to the gut, one Jud took deep. Though he was nineteen, the little boy Jacob had once been, the one impacted so heavily by the Quillery Edge, remained steadfast, a permanent part of him. He'd established the framework of his entire future around them. He hoped to hell they were worthy of that level of devotion, especially since he'd just put himself between them and a six-million-dollar contract, one likely issued by The Collective.

"They'd be crazy not to," he replied. "Make sure you pay for those tickets, bud."

"But Uncle Jud..."

"We talked about this." Jud and Danny had worked on curtailing Jacob's tendency to appropriate items without paying.

It'd been a big problem a few years before, one somewhat curbed the past few years.

"Okay." Jacob's shoulders drooped a couple notches. "I hope Dad's okay."

"Your dad's the strongest person I know, and Jian won't do anything more than he has. That was shock and awe to get my attention." Jud hoped so. The man wasn't usually an idiot.

"You think they'll help us free him?"

The two women had been through hell the past few weeks. The last thing they probably wanted was a contract killer guarding their six with a scrawny geek in tow. A scrawny geek dead set on enlisting their help rescuing his father.

"Just remember they're dealing with a lot. They won't know you, bud. And Edge is..." Jud didn't know what the hell to say.

"I know." He shrugged. "Never wanted to meet them like this. It sucks. Still, it's gonna be wicked."

More like complicated. People didn't just walk onto a secured compound like The Arsenal, not when they were on full alert, which they likely were. He'd get onto the compound and in a position to assist.

He had an ace in the hole he could play if necessary. Jian was mixed up in what'd gone down with the Hive, which meant Viviana and Mary, aka the Quillery Edge, had an even bigger reason to hunt him down than Jud did. The bastard underestimated the two women's tenacity. It'd be fun to watch them kick the man's ass and destroy his scuzzy trafficking ring, one that'd operated within the safe shadows of The Collective's protection too long.

But giving Jian's info to the Quillery Edge meant potentially pissing off The Collective. It was a see-saw, one he'd have to keep carefully balanced. Fortunately, he was good at doing the impossible.

While a lot of lone wolves operated within Jud's niche world, he'd established himself as the best around, which meant everyone knew who he was. When he weighed in, the message would be loud. Swift.

"Put together everything we have on Jian. His involvement with what went down with Hive is our way into the Arsenal."

"Right." Jacob glanced over at him. "Does that mean we can finally do something about him selling kids?"

Jud cursed. "Told you to stop digging in my shit."

"Your shit stinks."

He wasn't wrong. "Jian's side business is a battle I had to ignore. He's painted a target on himself by mediating that contract. I can't turn a blind eye on him anymore. If we're giving the Quillery Edge a warning about him, we can give them whatever we have on his operation."

"Good. They'll kick his ass and take down the whole operation. We can help." Jacob tapped on his computer.

"When you're done, I want you to send a message." He started up the vehicle. "Blast it everywhere."

"What am I saying?" Jacob glanced at him.

"Go after the Quillery Edge and I'll go after you."

3

The situation was worse than Vi expected.

Someone had put a contract out on her and Mary—a two-million-dollar payout that went up to six if HERA was acquired. She sat back and glanced at the screen. The contract hadn't concerned her. Been there, done that.

It was the communication in the Shadows in response that startled her. The message echoed swiftly within the Dark Web and everywhere else she looked.

Go after the Quillery Edge and I'll go after you —The Judge

Who the heck was the Judge and why was he involved? She rubbed her temples and expended a weary breath. She'd figure out the Judge issue later, after she figured out the Arnie mess. Mess being the operative word.

It'd taken six hours of hard scouring to get a hit on the recordings. Arnie's mysterious buyer was Adil Al-Abadi, an Iraqi extremist and former informant of Peter Rugers. He lived on the seventh story of an apartment in Harlem, so she'd called in a couple of favors and had the NYPD haul his ass in on outstanding arrest warrants.

That was two hours before. Now she paced, to hear if they had him in custody. Once he was secured they could send a team to get him, and she could get some answers.

The door to the operations area opened. Her best friend entered. The compulsion to share what she'd learned about the contract was on the tip of her tongue, but Mary had enough to deal with. Vi needed to look into the situation closer, assess the severity. A multi-million-dollar hit might seem pretty damn serious. If it didn't have the monetary backing, it was a flaming pile of bogus, which meant it wasn't worth worrying Mary over.

"You need to get some sleep," Mary said. She set a cup of coffee down beside Vi. "I've never seen you like this. When was the last time you slept?"

"I'll crash as soon as our guy's locked up tight downstairs." She halted her pacing and noted the worry lines on Mary's face. "Have you slept? Where's Dylan?"

"He's on patrol. Believe it or not, we do separate on occasion." Red tinged her friend's cheeks as she took a sip of coffee.

Dylan Mason and his family were the best thing to happen to either of them in a long time. He'd given Mary the calm she needed and stood at her side as she recovered from what'd happened. Vi admired the hell out of the man—he understood Mary needed to fight her own battles. He just made damn sure she'd never do it alone, not again.

He wouldn't fail her like Vi had.

"If I had a man that fine and awesome, I'd never come up for air." Vi smiled. "How are the wedding plans?"

"No clue. Momma Mason has full control. Dylan and I don't care what she does as long as it's soon and we're married when it's over."

Vi couldn't be happier for her friend. At least she'd moved on from what happened, thanks to Dylan and his family.

"You know it's not your fault, right?" Mary asked.

Damn. She'd avoided the conversation up until now, but Dylan had warned her days ago it was coming. The new psychiatrist had worked miracles with Mary. Miracles which translated to her verbalizing her thoughts about her capture and subsequent torture.

Rape.

"I'm the reason we stayed too long. I'm the one who believed the bullshit mission to Bogotá was real. I should've seen something was wrong the day those orders came through," Vi whispered into the room. Eyes averted, she let the guilt surface for the first time.

"Why..." Mary settled a hand on Vi's arm and forced eye contact. "You seriously believe that? Why?"

"Why? Mary, we've worked together since we got out of MIT. We've never, ever been separated. I should have known. You'd been wanting to leave Hive for weeks, had already looked into Dylan and The Arsenal."

"And for all we know my digging got us flagged. Don't you get it? We'll never know why they chose to grab me." Mary squeezed Vi's arm. "I thought I got taken because I was the weak one."

"What?" The breath swooshed out of Vi's lungs. "You're nuts. Why would you think you're the weak one? I'm the one who screwed up, not you. It wasn't your fault. Don't you dare think that."

"I don't," Mary whispered. "Not anymore, and I want you to get there, too. They were monsters. Monsters don't play by the same rules. We'll probably never know why they took me, why they thought I'd break easier."

"We're getting answers. Fallon will make Adil talk." Vi grasped her friend's shoulder. "You and Addy are getting closure."

"I don't want closure if it means losing you in the process."

"I'm right here, Mary. I'm not going anywhere."

"You've been so lost in your head, you've been gone since we got here." Mary's eyes shimmered with unshed tears. "Dylan says I need to give you time, says you'll work through it on your own, but you aren't. I'm terrified you aren't going to, either. Hive's gone. Peter's dead. I have the only closure I need every night when a good man, the very best man, wraps his arms around me and I sleep easy knowing everyone I love is safe. For the first time in my life I breathe easy knowing you, Addy, Bree, Rhea, and I are okay. We aren't alone, not anymore. We have something good here, and we're going to make it great. We can make this a real home, Vi."

Home.

Vi squeezed her eyes shut. They'd agreed long ago not to bring up the past. Neither of them had a spectacular upbringing. MIT had been a new start for them both, one they'd both desperately needed. Then they'd gotten mixed up with Peter. Hive.

She prayed The Arsenal was the fresh reboot they'd wanted long ago. A real do-over that'd last.

"We can't let the ones who got away keep breathing. You know backlash from laziness gets people every time."

"There's no way in hell anyone here's going to let them get away with it, Vi. No. Way. In. Hell." Mary emphasized each word with the bone-deep confidence she'd used for years during operations. "You aren't the only one in the hunt. They won't get away. Take a deep breath and let everyone around you help. This isn't your fight to handle alone. We're a team. Every single person on this compound is on the team, Vi. You going lone wolf undermines everything Marshall and Dylan and everyone else is trying to do here. It's an insult to everyone, especially me."

Vi tightened beneath the accusation. Her mind processed the words, analyzed the facts, but her friend didn't understand.

"Team trusts one another. If you aren't sharing, that means you don't trust them." Mary's voice lowered. "Or me."

"You know that's not true. I trust you, with anything and everything." She hugged Mary close. "I'm not undermining you or anyone else. I'm doing my job."

"No, you're doing yours, mine, Marshall's and everyone else's. Take a moment away from your mission lists and think. Step back and self-evaluate your actions since we've been here. Ask yourself this one question. If the roles were reversed, would you be okay with me doing what you are? Would you stand here and say it's okay if I take the blame for what those bastards did?"

Vi tried to shut down what her friend said, but the words hammered away at the niggling doubt, the small worm in a cesspool of guilt and anger she'd wallowed in. She was right. Vi couldn't have singlehandedly prevented what happened.

But she still shouldn't have left them at Hive so long.

That was a guilt she'd carry because there was no refuting the cold, hard truth she was the reason they stayed too long.

"Now, I swear this isn't a setup to get you to talk to Doctor Sinclair." Mary's eyes turned pleading. "She wants you to come to a session or two with me. I-I'm working through some issues. She says it'll help if I have a few group sessions with the people I work most with. It's part of the healing process."

Sure it was. Vi didn't doubt the honesty in her friend's voice. They'd never lied or done the half-truth thing with one another. That didn't mean the new psychiatrist wasn't pulling one over on them both. "Sure. Just tell me when."

"Great." Mary sat and motioned toward Vi's seat. "Sit and tell me what's wrong. Something was eating at you when I came in and it wasn't Adil."

Vi chewed on her lower lip a moment, then sat. Mary's words from earlier echoed in her brain. She had been hoarding intel and working the op without Mary and the others. She called up what she'd stumbled across and ran through the information, including the mysterious warning.

"Weird. He must be an operative we helped," Mary guessed.

"Maybe, but why wouldn't he come in like all the others?"

"Guess that's another mystery we'll have to solve." Mary grinned. "Together. I'll let Dylan know about the contract. He and Nolan already have new security parameters established for when we need to raise the threat level. They have color codes. It's awesome."

A knock sounded at the door. They both turned in time to see Riley walk in and throw herself against the closed door. She fanned herself as though she were about to swoon.

Riley Mason was a loon. Vi suspected she was like that because all six of her older brothers were ultimate bad ass commandos. Having that many overprotective siblings was bound to have an impact.

"Are you okay?" Mary asked.

Vi sat back at her station and got back to work mining data on Adil, but she turned her head to make sure the woman was okay.

"Oh, yeah, more than okay." Riley's gaze narrowed and pinned Vi. "We're friends, right?"

Vi's fingers hovered over the keyboard.

"Leave her be, sis." Cord shoved his way through the door. "Whatever you're up to, it can wait. It's been a long day."

Riley crossed her arms. "You realize you aren't the boss of me just because Mom spewed you out a few years earlier than me, right?"

"Jesus," he muttered. Exhaustion aged his otherwise handsome face. "Now is not the time."

"He's right, sweetie," Mary whispered. "What's up? Is Rachelle okay?"

"No, actually. She's far from okay, but we'll sort her out on another day because I listen. I'm a friend and recognize now is not the time. Now, back to my question. We're friends. Right, Vi?"

"Uhm, sure." Vi shoved the pencil back in her mouth and kept tapping.

"Friends share things with one another."

"Okay." Mary stretched the word out. "What's this about?"

The perky blonde smirked. "Viviana has a guest up front, a very sexy, nuclear smile flashing guest."

What? The pencil tumbled from her mouth. She whirled the chair around. Mary's eyes were narrow, concerned.

Cord stood. "What's wrong?"

"I don't know any sexy, nuclear smile flashing people," Vi argued.

"Erm, yeah you do." Riley crossed her arms. "Fallon."

Oh, right.

"Gage," Mary added. "Dylan."

"And me," Cord added.

Pfft, right.

"Logan," Riley added into the silence.

Vi's heart clenched. Mary's face softened. Logan had gotten shot saving Mary. He was on the road to recovery—a very slow, painful road. "Right."

She stood. Some Hive operative had probably scoped out The Arsenal and decided to come out of the cold, check out the operation and apply. Almost every one of them had thrown either her name or Mary's out to whichever poor, unfortunate soul was manning reception. The fire hydrant of visitors had slowed to a trickle the past week. Getting through the front gate was damn near impossible now.

Yet someone managed and asked to talk to her.

She sighed in frustration.

The last thing she needed was to trudge to the other building and look some poor has-been operative in the eyes and tell him—

or her—"You aren't good enough for The Arsenal." She knew the route of the conversation because she and Mary had personally tracked every operative worth a damn down themselves. They'd all said hell yeah because they weren't dumb. They recruited five. Five out of hundreds. To say they were selective was an understatement.

She hadn't studied the backside of her eyelids in two and a half days. She had enough caffeine flowing through her system to fuel the entirety of NASA. Her stomach rumbled. Oh, yeah. Food. At least the useless trek to the other building took her by the cafeteria. She wandered in, flip-flopping her way to the back counter. Although it was well past dinner, the majority of the tables were filled with people, most of them former military personnel taking part in the Warrior's Path Project.

Vi admired the hell out of the Mason's for starting the project, which gave those coming out of military service a safe haven to decompress and acclimate to civilian life. The people helped by the program may have hung up their fatigues and turned in their guns, but that didn't mean they'd sloughed off the excess baggage of military service. Post-traumatic stress, injuries. The extensive list rolled through her mind as she opened the first of five industrial-sized fridges and snagged one of the pre-made sandwiches Momma Mason made every morning. She grabbed an icy Coke from the door and headed toward the chips.

"Late night snack?" Dallas asked. Amusement glimmered in his gaze as it swept past the sandwich. "Tuna. Excellent choice, though Mom's egg salad is to die for."

Dallas was unlike Dylan in many ways. Though he was younger, he had a darker edge to him, one she and Mary had analyzed the whys of ad nauseam. He wore the requisite dark Mason hair longer than his brothers. It hid his upper ears. The eyes set Dallas apart, a lush blue instead of green.

"I've never seen one of those," Vi commented.

"Probably because it's my and Jesse's favorite." He looked down at the chips and motioned.

"Sea salt and vinegar, please."

"Where you headed?"

"Up front. Someone has the nerve to show up and ask to see me," she grumbled. "It's almost nine in the evening. This isn't a freaking twenty-four hotel. And now I'm schlepping my tired ass to reception rather than waiting on the call saying the NYPD has Adil Al-Abadi in custody."

She blew stray hairs out of her face and noted the surprised expression on his face. "Interesting, I got a call from the guards saying someone was on their way who used my name. I'll carry the chips, escort you up there."

"I'm good."

"Yeah, but you'll be better if you let me walk you up there," he replied. "It's been a rough day on us all."

Vi learned to pick her battles a long time ago. Sometimes you just had to let a bad ass be a bad ass, even if it was unnecessary.

"Fine," she added into the silence as she flip-flopped through the cafeteria and out the door. Down the walk toward the main visitor area in the other building. "We need golf carts."

"I'll mention it to Nolan," he commented dryly.

Vi was serious about the golf carts, but didn't figure operatives thought much about having something with an engine cart them between buildings. By the time they entered the visitor's building and spilled into the lobby, she'd worked up a full head of steam. She didn't appreciate her name being bandied about without permission. The nerve.

Dallas tightened beside her. He settled the chips atop her sandwich. "Stay here. Call Marshall and Nolan."

What?

She tracked his progression across the lobby. The scent of freshly installed carpet filled her nostrils. Pale beige melded with soft blues along the walls. The massive man looming just inside the door commanded her attention. Riley was right. He was nuclear.

Thick waves of light brown hair tumbled around a strong jawline that hadn't seen a razor in a couple days. He exuded control. His gaze trekked the room like a hunter seeking prey. Her pulse quickened when he pinned her with a look. His eyes flared. Lips set in a grim expression, his attention settled on Dallas, who stepped into the man's personal space.

Vi set her food down and snagged the reception phone.

"Yeah, what's wrong now, Riley? I know it's boring, but it's your shift." Marshall's exhausted voice filled the line.

"Dallas and I are up here. He's in some guy's face. Not sure who, but it's intense and he said to call you and Nolan."

"Fuck." The line went dead.

Vi powered forward, closing the distance between her and Dallas, who was pointing at the man.

"You have a hell of a lot of nerve showing up here." Dallas clenched his teeth.

"Not here for you, man. Used your name at the gate, though." The man shrugged off any apology.

He didn't strike Vi as the sort who apologized for anything. She swallowed as his gaze settled on her again.

"Viviana," he greeted. "I'm sorry for the late arrival. It took longer than I expected."

"Erm, I don't know you," she responded.

His attention swept behind her a brief second, but returned. He offered a smile. "I'm Jud. Or, The Judge."

"The Judge, as in 'go after the Quillery Edge and I'll go after you'. That Judge?" She air quoted the message and studied his face, his bone structure. A lot of operatives were masters at disguise, but there was only so much they could do to hide bone structure. Still nothing memorable. "I've never met you."

"What's this about?" Dallas asked.

The security panel on the wall chimed as the door coming from the rear hallway opened. Reinforcements had arrived. She kept her gaze locked with the stranger's as he smirked and crossed his arms in front of his body.

"There's a hit on Viviana and Mary," Jud replied. "A two-million-dollar one with a four-million-dollar rider that guarantees anyone with half a shot will come after them. I'm here to make sure they don't succeed."

The confident, smooth delivery settled around her like a warm blanket. His gaze remained on her, but he'd strike anyone in the room who got too close. How she knew that was more instinct than observation, a sixth sense she'd developed over the years in dealing with his kind.

"As you can see, The Arsenal has all my security requirements more than met," she replied. "And I don't need anyone fighting my battles."

"I'm glad the Quillery Edge landed on their feet. Hell of a shit storm, lots of fallout. Buzzards are circling, too many for your new crew to handle alone, Viviana."

"And you're going to close the gap, one man?" She crossed her arms and allowed her doubt free reign.

"Get the hell out while you still can, man," Dallas said. "We had an agreement, one I've upheld."

"Why would you involve yourself in this? I don't even know you." Vi hated mysteries, especially those who set trained operatives like Dallas on edge.

"I suspected you'd reject my offer for assistance." Jud reached behind him.

Dallas, Marshall and Nolan shoved her back. The latter drew a weapon. The stranger didn't halt like a sane person would. He smiled, holding out a sheaf of folded papers toward her.

"For you. Let me help with your contract negotiations," he

paused with a smirk, as if she hadn't picked up on an important, but amusing fact, "and I'll help you with your other problem."

Dallas grabbed the papers before she could. "We don't need your kind of help."

Jud prowled to the door. Stopped. Did a half turn of his head. "Let me help me out, Viviana, and I'll hand deliver the bastard to you. Whether he's breathing when I do is up to you."

He left.

She stared at the door, her heartbeat thundering in her ears. She took the papers before Dallas could destroy them. He paced.

"Who was that?" Nolan asked.

"No one important." Dallas whirled and pointed at the papers. "You aren't in whatever his bullshit is."

Curiosity drew her toward the papers. She unfolded them. Shock activated her brain, scraping off the dregs of exhaustion. What the hell?

Jian Chen. Who the hell was Jian Chen and why would Jud offer to hand deliver him?

Why would Jud offer anything at all?

"Who the heck was that?" Vi demanded.

"Leave it alone, Vi," Marshall suggested. "We'll discuss it tomorrow. Give him time."

Right. Time. Great idea. She shoved the papers under her shirt and flip-flopped back to where she'd deposited her food. She snagged it all and headed out the door. The sooner she got back to Command, the quicker she could figure out who the heck that was. HERA would've already done facial recognition on him.

She exited the visitor's building in time to see taillights turning onto the main road. Jud had left without argument. Weird. Most operatives were stubborn to a fault.

She added two items to her list of things to do before she slept. Find out who Jud was and investigate Jian Chen. Dread settled in a dull ache at her temples, through her neck and down her spine when she entered Command and she saw Mary's pale expression. She dropped the food and grabbed her com. Her NYPD contact offered a chin lift, no smile.

"There was a problem," she surmised.

"Adil Al-Abadi is dead. ME is doing an autopsy, but it'll take a while. Two shots to the head. No evidence found on scene."

Vi flopped in her chair and groaned. Could this day get any worse?

4

"And he just left?" Riley sat on the sofa.

Vi sighed and nodded. Bree and Rhea were curled beneath blankets on chairs bookending where Riley and Addy sat. "Where's Mary?"

"She's on her way," Bree replied.

Vi looked around the small bungalow-style house. Everyone had pitched in over the past couple of weeks. Who knew you could get a house built so quickly? Apparently the Masons could do anything they put their minds to.

Home.

She shook the sentiment off. Mary may have found a home, but Vi hadn't settled. Her stuff remained strewn about the small two-bedroom home she now shared with Addy.

"So who is Jian Chen?" Rhea asked.

"I was about to fire up HERA and find out," Vi replied as she reached for the laptop.

"To hell with Jian. I want to know who the hot guy was," Bree said.

"Uh, yeah. I'm with her," Riley replied.

Vi had to admit the idea had merit. Fortunately HERA was a brilliant multi-tasker. "Jud. Or, The Judge."

"Like that's a lot to go on," Addy commented.

"We've gotten loads with less," Rhea said. "Besides, HERA caught his image, right?"

"Yeah, so we already have a full name and everything." Bree leaned back and chomped on her chocolate chip cookie.

Vi was about to call up HERA's security reports when the front door opened. Mary bustled in with a huge smile on her face, a smile that faltered when her gaze settled on Vi. Damn. Her stomach lurched. They'd had a heart-to-heart, but her BFF was still worried. Dylan offered a supportive smile. Vi was sure it was more for Mary than her, but she took it nonetheless.

"I heard about New York. That sucks, but we'll get another lead," Dylan said as he sat and Mary settled beside him. "I had a chat with Dallas before we came over here. I figured you all would be digging into our visitor today. He's politely asking you all to back off."

"Not happening," Vi replied.

"Some things are best left alone," Dylan said.

"Like hell they are. We're mired in chaos right now because of Hive and Peter and Martin Driggs. The last thing we need is some unknown walking onto this compound and making demands of our time like he owns us. No one bandies my name about without me knowing the person. It's that simple." Vi called up HERA and accessed the images from earlier.

"He wasn't making demands of your time," Bree argued. "He was offering to help keep you and Mary safe from the contract. That's loads sexier."

Only Bree would find a man putting himself between a woman and a bullet sexy. Her friend had a thing for alpha males in a big way, one Vi typically didn't share, but she had to admit the fierce protectiveness radiating from Jud earlier was...interesting.

Okay, it was hot, but she didn't have time for hot. She had a best friend and a new team to keep safe. Vi sat, grabbed her laptop and got to work, but hit a roadblock faster than expected.

"Weird," she commented.

"What's weird?" Riley asked.

"HERA couldn't identify Jud." She stared at the "Not Found" prompt, one she'd rarely seen. "He's not in any of the databases."

"None of them?" Bree asked.

"None."

"Dallas knew him," Mary said. "They worked together, that much was obvious."

Right. She was all too aware of the missing years in Dallas's file, the years she'd been unable to fill in despite her best attempts. He'd been in the SEALs then went off grid. So Jud was a big question mark for the time being. She'd leave it be for tonight. She was too tired to tackle a deep hack to find info on Jud. HERA may not have found anything, but everybody had some kind of trail out there.

Which shifted her focus on what she could easily research. Who the heck was Jian Chen and why did Jud think she'd care?

She thumbed through the rest of the papers and froze. Jian Chen's background, specialty. She passed it over to Mary.

"Okay, so this is the best lead we've gotten so far." She held up a photograph of an unknown man and Peter Rugers. "Okay, so this is definitely a credible lead."

"One that just walked into the front door," Addy muttered. "Convenient."

Vi agreed. She didn't like convenient. Ever. "Still, it's more than we've had, and I'm not passing it up. If Jian knew Peter and Jud knew Jian..."

"Then Jud knew Peter," Rhea finished. "That doesn't sound good."

"It's not," Mary said. "All the more reason for us to get some answers from our mysterious new friend."

"Dallas doesn't want you mixed up with Jud. I got the message on that one loud and clear when he called me," Addy commented. "He ordered me to sit on you in case Dylan didn't handle you."

"Wow, Vi, you need to take a look at this."

The poor misguided Mason men thought they could handle her. It was almost cute. She took the papers Mary offered and ignored Addy. She knew good and well finding Peter's backers was her top priority.

Disgust soured her stomach as she read through a sheet she'd accidentally bypassed, one toward the front. Jian trafficked kids. She'd dedicated a considerable chunk of her personal time battling pedophiles on line, consulting with authorities whenever possible. She didn't let those sick monsters slither away, which meant Jian was now in her cross hairs for more than one reason.

"Son of a bitch," she spat. "Whoever this Jud is, he's got a lot of nerve."

"What?" Riley asked.

"Jian's overseeing an auction of a five-year-old Russian boy named Mico in four days." She opened her web crawling program and typed in the data at the bottom of the sheet. "I've never found this spot."

"Spot?" Bree asked.

"In the Deep Web," Mary answered as she nestled in beside Vi to watch the screen. "Crap, it's legit, isn't it?"

Dread settled in a dull throb in her head, behind her eyes. She waited a few minutes for her program to do its thing and ferret out what information it could, which was sadly far less than it normally was. The operation Jian led was deep and heavily secure.

"Yeah, it's legit. He traffics children, women, weapons and other exotic collectibles."

"And HERA would be a hell of an auction item," Dylan growled. "Gather what you can about Jian and how to move once we get back from the application testing tomorrow."

Ugh. Vi had almost forgotten that was tomorrow. The Arsenal needed more boots on the ground and more brains behind the screens. She and Mary couldn't handle everything alone, and Cord was needed more in the field. They needed more operatives and back office personnel. She and Mary both detested the idea of noobs mucking around in HERA, but what choice did they have?

She thumbed through the final pages she'd gotten from Jud, which appeared to be investigative notes into Mico's abduction and Jian's operation. She scanned the data, which was well organized. The investigation had been methodical and extremely detailed. Excellent notes with dates, times, locations. Names. If this was Jud's work, she was suitably impressed—which left her even more determined to find out who the heck he was and, more importantly, how he knew her.

Operative?

More than likely.

But whose?

Dallas was the key. Specifically, his dark years, the ones not in his service record. Where had he been? Did Mary know? If Dylan mentioned his little brother's background, her friend likely wouldn't offer up the details, not without permission. If Vi wanted answers there was only one surefire way to get them.

"Fire up a truck, Riley."

Riley grinned. Eyes gleaming, she stood. "Where are we going?"

"On a man hunt."

"You're not going alone," Dylan stated.

"I'll go with them," Addy offered. "We're only going into

Resino. He's likely at the bed and breakfast or Bubba's. I'll call for backup if needed."

"Dallas doesn't want you mixed up with him, Vi."

She looked up at Dylan as she stood. "I know, but we need answers more than he needs his secrets."

"It's not about him keeping secrets. He says Jud is dangerous."

Which meant he was probably far, far worse than dangerous. They nibbled on danger for dessert. "I'm not doing this alone. This is a team mission. The lead's good, Dylan."

Dylan looked at her, then over at Mary, who nodded. He chuckled and swiped his hand through his hair. "You two are going to keep us hopping."

"You know it," Vi responded. "You wouldn't have us any other way."

~

"Eyes on your plate, bud." Jud forked some beans into his mouth.

Resino residents were too curious for their own good. The small eatery was more bar than restaurant this late at night, and busier than Jud expected. Although the grill was closed, Bubba had graciously pulled out some leftovers. He ignored the pointed looks they'd gotten from the locals when they sat at the only vacant table earlier.

"I can't believe the Quillery Edge would be in such a remote place. There's not even any WiFi." Jacob motioned to the laptop open on the table. "It's gonna be a slow connection at the bed and breakfast."

Jud was a bit surprised a town as small as Resino even had a bed and breakfast. It was a short walk, about half a mile down the road nearer the town square. So far Resino was what he'd expected for small town Texas. He'd paid for two nights. If he didn't hear back from Viviana by then, he'd move on. He wasn't the type to sit on his ass and wait on anyone, though, which was why he'd continue chasing down leads while he waited.

He'd sworn to keep her breathing, which didn't require her permission or knowledge. He operated within the shadows easier than the light of day anyway. His first order of business was busting Jian's ring up. The bastard pushed Jud to take the contract on the Quillery Edge. Jud was about to push back. Hard.

But that left Danny in trouble, which was unacceptable.

There was always an answer. Jud would find it.

"We'll get some shuteye tonight, then get to work. I've got a couple leads I could use your help with." He took a sip of his beer and waited for his nephew's eruption. He'd been fairly subdued and quiet so far, but that'd only last so long given the fact he'd been within spitting distance of his idols and hadn't met them.

"What was she like? What'd she say?" Jacob's voice lowered. "I can't believe you just walked out. Did you mention Dad?"

No. The much-needed reality check about Danny was barreling around the corner, but he'd hold it off for the next day. That'd be soon enough to crush his nephew's hopes. He hoped to hell they weren't dumb enough to kill Danny, but if Marla was involved the chances of him being recovered were slim. She was a psychopathic bitch on a power trip who had a hard-on for making Jud hurt whenever she could—mainly because she'd never gotten him to heel like the other operatives.

"I should have waited until morning. She had every right to toss my ass out. It was a disrespectful, crap play, one I'm betting lots of people they worked with at Hive have done." He looked over at the bar, where Bubba watched them while he wiped down the bar.

"You should have made her look at the papers," Jacob argued.

"I'm not a fan of making a woman do anything she doesn't want."

"We don't have time to be polite, Uncle Jud." Jacob slammed his drink glass on the table. "Dad needs help."

He'd kept Jacob from that world as much as possible, the one where he exerted his will on others. Eliminated those who stepped too far out of line. Now that Jacob had graduated from MIT and was aiming for Quillery Edge notoriety within the same arena, Jud had adopted a side mission—keep his nephew in the light, like The Arsenal.

"We give respect if we want to earn it. More importantly, we practice patience. That's the most critical asset for this type of work."

"Waiting around sucks," Jacob replied. "At least the food's good."

Sullen described his nephew's attitude. He'd expected an open-arms welcome into The Arsenal. Jud shouldn't have brought him along, but leaving him alone wasn't exactly an option since he didn't know who all was in play.

Whispered murmurs drew his attention. The long-haired blonde from The Arsenal's reception area entered, drawing everyone's attention. Everyone's except his, which latched onto Viviana and Mary. Jacob gasped. Jud grabbed some napkins and wiped his hands as the procession of women headed their direction. The redhead carried herself like a soldier. Her gaze swept the room. Another blonde and brunette closed off the group.

"Sorry, you and your boy are gonna have to move. House rules. This is the Mason table. Riley's here, so you've gotta move." Bubba's voice boomed from beside Jud. "I'll make room for you and the boy at the bar. Best I can do."

"It's fine, Bubba. We're here to see him anyway," the blonde replied. She looked down at Jud, then over at Jacob. "Hi, I'm Riley Mason. I was working reception when you came in."

Right. He remained silent, watching Vi take a seat beside Jacob. Mary sat on Jacob's opposite side. Jacob's gaze swept from one to another. Mouth open, eyes wide, face bright, he sat. Stunned.

"You want a beer? Something to drink?" Bubba asked the group as they sat.

"Bottle, shots. Glasses." The redhead sat beside Jud.

"Beers all around, Bubba. Thanks." Riley dragged a chair over and sat at the edge of the table. "So..."

"Who's Jian and how do you know him? Who told you about this operation? How do you know Peter?" Viviana asked.

Straight to the point. No bullshit. His kind of woman. She tapped a folder for emphasis, one much fatter than he'd expected. She'd done some homework before hunting him down. That was a good sign. He looked over at Jacob, who'd yet to move. He hoped the kid remembered to breathe.

"Jian and I cross paths on occasion, but I've left him be because he proves useful to my employer at times. As for Peter, we've also crossed paths. Unfortunately." He continued eating his meal, glancing at his nephew. "Eat your food, bud."

"Your research is first rate, well organized. Methodical," Mary offered.

"Wicked." Jacob breathed the word.

"Jacob here is the brains behind the papers. He keeps me organized and methodical." He smiled. Jacob's body trembled, damn near hummed with excitement.

"Is he okay?" The brunette whispered the word gently as she sat on the other side of the redhead.

"He's not a fan of crowds." Jud didn't want to get into the fact his brother-in-law was just kidnapped. Or Jacob's hero worship of the two women bookending him. That'd be awkward at best. "I'm Jud. You are?"

"Right. I'm Addy Rugers." The redhead motioned to the brunette beside her. "This is Rhea. Bree is the blonde across from us and to the far left. Then there's Viviana, who you apparently know. Mary's on the other side of your nephew. And that's Riley."

Jud offered a nod to the women and wiped his hands and mouth. "Introduce yourself, bud."

"Jacob." The boy breathed the word. "I-I work with my uncle. Back office work mostly, nothing exciting."

"I wouldn't say that. Back office work is sometimes way too exciting," Mary commented. "Vi and I do back office work at The Arsenal, computer stuff mostly."

"You're The Edge," he whispered.

Mary visibly tightened. Code names were armor in the covert ops world, a way to keep a protective layer between who you were and what you did in the name of duty, honor, or whatever other contrived excuse got rammed down your throat.

"Funny how you and your nephew know the Quillery Edge, but they don't know you. My two girls don't forget faces or names. Neither do I, and I knew everyone connected to Hive." Addy shifted beside him.

"Not everyone, Princess, just those your brother wanted you to know. There were lots of dark corners and shadows, people skulking about," Jud commented.

"So you were Hive," Viviana guessed.

"No. Peter wanted me to be, but I was hooked up with a different operation, one that colored in black. Hive worked mostly in the gray." He took a sip of his beer and met Viviana's curious gaze dead-on. The woman was breathtaking. Long hair so dark blonde it shimmered like pale brown in the darkened lighting grazed her shoulders. Her wide, expressive, almond-colored eyes studied him behind red wire-rimmed glasses. "I know you by reputation. I'm glad you two have moved out of the gray and into the light."

Not exactly the truth, not exactly a lie. He took another long drink and let the silence hang a moment.

"The Arsenal has no problems coloring in the gray when necessary," Vi said.

Jud knew the Masons wouldn't have issues going into the black if necessary. Dallas had been a hell of an operative. He concentrated on his beer and waited through the silence. Sometimes what you didn't say was more important.

"Tell us about Mico's abduction," Mary ordered. "How did you connect it to Jian's operation?"

"I didn't, not at first. Jacob found his auction while we were investigating Jian."

"And why look into Jian in the first place?" Addy asked. "You said you'd crossed paths before and left him be. Why change that now?"

"I didn't appreciate him trying to push my buttons. I decided to get some leverage to push back. I started looking into him recently." A few hours before if he were being precise. He'd pulled old surveillance footage from The Collective's records to substantiate a connection between the now-deceased Peter Rugers and Jian. The rest fell into place easily enough, thanks to Jacob's mad computer skills.

Bubba appeared at the table. Beers were handed out. A bottle of liquor was settled nearest Addy. The burly man set stacked shot glasses on the edge of the table.

"You girls want anything to suck all this up? I've got some grub left from lunch."

"We're good, but thanks." Riley smiled wide. "I wouldn't mind taking some of it to go, though. I heard Marshall and the guys had a long day."

"Sure thing, doll. I'll even throw in extra desserts. I know your mom has a sweet tooth."

"I know Mom loves your peach cobbler," Riley teased. "Add it to our tab."

"Your money's no good here, not for grub." Bubba motioned

toward the beers. "You girls drink anymore and you're eating. I'm not liking the idea of calling Marshall and Nolan and having them come get your drunk asses."

"We'll go slow," Bree promised.

Jud swallowed the food he'd shoved in his mouth. Resino respected the Mason brood. It'd been smart to set up shop here. Upon initial inspection it appeared to be a foolish mistake, but he grudgingly admitted there was a lot of mileage in respect that deep.

"I'm not here to stir up trouble. I'm sure that's what Dallas assumed. My apologies, I should have made my approach in the morning. Late night visits aren't ever a good idea without permission."

Vi's mouth quirked into a confused cross between a glower and a smile. "If you want us to take this request seriously, you need to give us some answers. Tonight."

"Fair enough." He looked around. "Ask your questions. I can't guarantee an answer."

"You worked with Dallas. Where?" Mary asked.

So much for starting off simple. He should've expected hard questions straight out of the gate. These women didn't mess around, which was why they were the most sought after assets around.

"Did he tell you where he worked?" Jud knew the answer.

"Not exactly," the woman replied.

"Then let's keep it that way. It's best you not know," he replied. "I'm still there. This is a favor, personal time. Anything else isn't up for discussion, not here."

"Why help us? We don't know you." Mary crossed her arms. "Why care if we get hit?"

He didn't want the 411 to shift to his nephew, why the favor mattered. He hadn't been lying when he said crowds were an issue for Jacob. Add the fact he was bookended by the two most influential people in his world and Jud suspected the kid was about to lose it. He noted the widened eyes and red complexion, the clenched hand around his fork.

"You helped someone close to me a long time ago. He's not in a position to help you, but I am."

"Who?" Vi asked.

"Do you always look a gift horse in the mouth?" he asked.

"Yep, every time. She's not stupid," Riley replied.

"It's my dad," Jacob blurted. "You helped him once and he needs your help again. We have to keep you breathing so you'll help us keep him breathing."

"Your dad?" A softness settled in Vi's voice as she looked at his nephew. "How does he need our help? Do we know him?"

"Jian had him kidnapped to force Uncle Jud to take the contract on you." Jacob's voice rose. "No one messes with family. That's the rule. Jian broke it, so now he's gonna pay, but Uncle Jud can't go alone. He needs the Quillery Edge. You saved Dad once. You can do it again. I know it."

The two women visibly recoiled beneath the voracity in his nephew's words. Tension sliced through the room as Addy and the other women focused on him and Jacob.

"You didn't mention anything about an abduction," Vi said through clenched teeth. "You dangle Jian in front of us to get our help with a rescue mission? Is that it?"

"Pretty much." Though he suspected it'd be more of a recovery mission than rescue at this point. "My other option was to take the contract and kill you both. I figured you'd prefer this option."

The two women looked at one another, then their gazes settled on Jacob, who sat silently between them, tears in his eyes.

"No one touches my family and lives."

"How do we know you aren't here to take the payday Jian's offering?" Mary asked.

"Uncle Jud's between you and a bullet because you can rescue

Dad." Jacob's voice was icy cold, malevolent. "He wouldn't hit the Quillery Edge. Ever. Anyone gets close to you, he'll take them out because he's the best."

"And we're supposed to believe you," Addy said.

"Believe me or not, help or not." Jud shrugged. "I'll keep everyone off you either way. I can't get Jacob's dad freed without your help though. That's not a lone wolf operation."

"I don't want or need you between me and a bullet," Vi replied.

"What you want isn't what you need, not in this instance. I won't ever stand between you and anything, Viviana. I'm keeping everyone off you, but I'll do it at your side, or behind you. I know this is your fight. But it became mine, too, when they took my family."

"You'll do that so I can help rescue him," she whispered.

"Hopefully. Whether you take that on or not, I'm helping you take down whoever issued the hit."

"Even if it's your group?" Mary asked.

The women were brilliant, quick minded. They'd put two and two together. They didn't know who his employer was, but he doubted it'd matter. They stared impossible in the eyes and kneed it in the nuts every day.

"Even if it's my group," he replied.

"Then we'd better get busy," Mary said.

"You're in." He leaned back in his chair, a bit surprised they'd made a decision so quickly. "Dallas and the guys okay with that decision?"

"We have operational governance over back office," Viviana said. "As for your desire to keep Mary and I safe, it's appreciated but unnecessary. We are protected, but you can stay at The Arsenal while we work on the Jian angle."

"Thank you, Viviana."

"It's Vi," she replied. "We'll postpone the application exercise tomorrow morning. We'll white board your intel and see what HERA spits out."

"White board?" Jacob asked.

"It's so cool. Vi and Mary enter all the data into HERA and data gets spit out into all these categories based on whatever parameters they establish. Then we all get to work filling out the white boards," Bree explained.

"Cool."

Jud watched his nephew shut down beneath the pressure, the anticipation and curiosity were too much when combined with his dad's kidnapping. His shoulders drooped, his gaze swept downward. Mental lockdown. No matter how much he might want to work with the Quillery Edge and their group white boarding with HERA, he wouldn't ask. Risk rejection.

"What time do we start?" Jud asked.

The women looked at one another.

"You want to white board?" Vi asked.

"Sure. Why not? It makes sense. Jacob's got a real knack for technical stuff and knows the details almost better than I do," he supplied proudly. "He'd be an asset, and I promise not to get in the way."

Addy chuckled. "You have no idea what you're stepping into. Their process takes hours. Hours and hours of brainiac genius at work."

"I can't wait," he replied, gaze locked with Vi.

"A word," Viviana repeated as she pushed her chair back. "Alone."

"Vi," Mary said.

Addy rose. Vi held up her hand. "I've got this. We'll be back in a minute."

Addy unholstered a weapon and set it on the table beside her beer. She motioned toward the hallway heading to the bathrooms. "Where I can see you."

Riley and Bree exchanged wide-eyed looks. Rhea and Mary both chuckled as they took a sip of their beers. Vi didn't reply, she simply headed toward the hall. Jud smiled, watching her progression. All sass and attitude, just like she'd marched into reception.

The moment he entered the narrow hallway, she shoved him back against the wall with more force than he expected. Her forearm pressed against his throat. He looked down, noted how she stood on her tiptoes to accomplish the grip. He could have her pinned in under a second, but that'd probably get him a bullet in the brain for his trouble. He looked over at Addy, who raised her eyebrows in a silent dare.

He took Viviana by the waist. "I think it's too soon for us to be alone. Your chaperon isn't happy."

"She's not my chaperon and I'd pay more attention to me and less to her if I were you," she clipped. "I'll make this quick. Nothing about anyone or anything remotely connected to what went down with Mary, Peter Rugers or Hive is mentioned around her. I field everything."

Protective. Fierce. Way more than superficial sass like most women. A fire rumbled in him, a flicker of appreciation born from something more than her operative reputation. This wasn't just Edge's partner shoving him against a wall. This was a friend. Someone who cared about those around her and would do anything to keep them safe.

"I'm not here to stir trouble. I'm more than happy to work one-on-one with you."

Her eyes narrowed, tiny slivers of glimmering brown. "You'd be better off sniffing around my chaperon if you're looking for more than taking Jian down and getting your brother freed."

"I'm only here to help, nothing else." He grabbed her arm and settled her into a constricting hold within a couple seconds. Her eyes widened. She tugged and twisted, but he held her firm. "Just to say, if I want more than that, I think I know my taste better than you."

"Chasing after the others will get you in a heap of trouble, Jud."

He settled a hand on her cheek and smiled when she glared up at him. "And throwing all that sass will get you in a bigger heap of trouble."

"Why is that?"

"Because I've got a sweet tooth for sass, babe, and it's been a long time since I've met a woman who could satisfy it." He released her from the hold when he sensed Addy's approach. "I'm here to help, but that doesn't mean I'm blind or dead."

"You will be if you don't back off," Addy warned. "Not tonight, Romeo. There's a bathroom down the hall. Go satisfy yourself without her."

Vi gasped.

Jud laughed and headed toward the table. Jacob was sitting there staring at the women as they chattered on about drones and new weapons. "Let's go, bud."

He waited as Jacob grabbed his backpack. Vi stood a couple feet away, her gaze curious and gleaming sass. Her brain likely fired words like an automatic weapon—so fast and intense it'd knock you down if you weren't prepared. "Text instructions for tomorrow and I'll be there."

"Bring data on Danny. He'll be our first priority," Vi declared.

5

V i tapped on the door and waited. Her pulse hammered hard, but she didn't have a choice. The door opened silently, much like the man inside. She took a few steps in as Dallas wandered back toward the bed. Clad in a pair of jogging pants and shirtless, he swiped his hand down his face and turned. Resignation reflected in his gaze.

"This couldn't wait until daylight?"

"I'm thinking you already know the answer," she said. "He claims he's here to keep me breathing. His nephew's dad needs a rescue. What do you know about him?"

Her pulse still quickened from the brief time Jud had her pinned against the wall. No one had ever stirred her curiosity or incited her desire so fast, which made sense because he was clearly wrong for her in every conceivable way. Vi had a taste for bad boys, always had. She'd never scratched that itch. She might've liked bad boys, but she certainly didn't turn their heads.

Because I've got a sweet tooth for sass, babe, and it's been a long time since I've met a woman who could satisfy it.

God, she was beyond pathetic. She knew nothing about Jud at all. Oh, except he was being coerced into killing her to save Danny. Yeah, that was a great reason to be attracted to someone.

Idiot.

He wasn't taking the contract, though. He was going to take the assholes down instead.

Or so he said.

"What do you know about him?" She repeated the inquiry into the silence as Dallas prowled toward his bed.

"More than most. Nothing." He sat on the edge of the bed. "Jud isn't someone you know. He's someone you survive."

"He said he'd take down anyone who goes after us, even his employer," she said.

Dallas shook his head in disbelief. "No one takes them down, but I guess he'd get closer than anyone else. I sure as hell wouldn't go after him."

"Dallas, Mary and I have respected your need to keep those years blacked out, but I can't risk not knowing, not when it's come and knocked on our door. Literally." She knelt on the floor and took the man's hand.

He'd gone through hell during those years; that much was obvious. He'd come home and fallen into a deeper rut of problems because of Dylan's manipulative ex. The two brothers had barely reconciled. While Vi didn't want to push, she didn't have a choice. She wasn't letting anyone or anything get near Mary or her teams. Failure wasn't an option, not again.

"Jesus, you're worse than Riles," he muttered.

"I'll keep it under wraps," she promised. "I can't let that dark patch in your life jeopardize everyone here, not if it's about to rain hell down on us."

Dallas expended a breath and ran his hand down the back of his head and neck. Gaze averted to the floor, he pulled his hand away. "You're right. We can't let that happen. Marshall knows who I was with, but not how deep I'd gotten."

Few operations were so dark Vi couldn't find them. Dread seeped into her as she waited through the silence. Each second deepened her certainty that what she learned wasn't good—not for her. Mary. The Team.

Or Dallas.

"The Collective."

The two words swooshed the breath from her lungs. She leaned back on her heels and sealed her eyes closed. The Collective. They were the monsters under the bed in the Deep Web, the urban legend bandied about to terrify the worst of the worst. An unstoppable force capable of doing anything at any time with zero repercussions because their influence was marrow-deep within any and every governmental organization. Some believed they controlled the world's empires from the shadows.

Because men like Jud and Dallas made it so.

And now one of their operatives wanted to stand between her and them. God. She wanted to shove her head in the sand and ignore the fact The Collective was probably behind everything. The contract. Mary's kidnapping. Hiring Peter.

Everything.

A thousand questions listed in her mind, but the haunted depths of Dallas's eyes warned her she wouldn't get answers, not tonight. She reached out and grasped his hand. "Thank you."

"Did..." Dallas cleared his throat when his voice broke. "Did he say they'd issued the contract?"

"No, but Jian was pushing him to take it. He said the man thought he was the best one to fill it."

"He is." Dallas squeezed her hand. "The Collective operates in layers. I started off on the outer shell, sank a couple layers deeper over the years. No one ever penetrates to the center, the core of who makes the decisions and runs the organization. Rumor within the group was that the Judge was their personal henchman, the one they trusted to do whatever they needed. He served the core."

That didn't sound good. Vi swallowed and nodded.

"I didn't know him very well, obviously. My last operation was a disaster. The operative I was paired with was out on a personal vendetta and set me up to take the fall. Jud was dispatched to handle the situation. To handle me."

"The core ordered a hit on you?" Anger raised her voice. *Oh hell no.*

"He assessed the situation and reversed the decision." Dallas snapped his fingers. "Just like that. He told me I was clear to walk away."

"He gave you an out."

"You don't get it, Vi," Dallas said. His voice lowered. "There is no out, not with The Collective. But in the space of an hour I went from being in their sight lines to breathing free, all because of Jud."

Wow. Vi added another hundred or so questions to her mental tally and took a couple deep breaths. Jud was the real deal then, the veritable monster in the shadows.

And he wanted to protect her.

"I guess you don't have a full name or anything to offer about his family."

Dallas chuckled. "I'm surprised he has family. The Collective doesn't operate in the light of day."

"Thank you for trusting me," she said.

"Don't dig, not into his mud pit. Leave the still waters alone, Vi," he warned.

She nodded, though she suspected he knew the impossibility of his command. Digging was tantamount to breathing for her. She wasn't happy if she wasn't mired in muck. "Get some rest. We're white boarding the dad's abduction, then Jian."

"I'll let everyone know to be there," he said.

"That's not necessary. We're more productive working alone." We meant her, Mary, Bree, and Rhea. Addy and Riley assisted by keeping them sufficiently hydrated and supplied with whatever they needed. They were a female brain trust jokingly called The Pentagon, but they'd recently expanded to six, which made the name even funnier. Dylan was the token male, mainly because he enjoyed watching Mary work. They didn't need all the rest of the Mason squad involved.

"If Jud's there, we're there," Dallas announced. "No option on this one, Vi. He said he's here to help, but six million is a lot of reasons to change someone's mind."

Whatever. She'd sort out the chaos in the morning. "Let Marshall know we're postponing application testing tomorrow."

"He won't be happy."

"That's why you're telling him and not me." Vi waved. "See you in the morning."

The Collective. Vi had a name. With a name she could bring down anyone and anything if given enough time. She had all night to dig. She should have asked for Danny's last name. Hell, she should have asked for Jud's full name. And Jacob's. At least he was in town and not under the same roof for now. Trusting a veritable stranger—one who fully admitted to being the best assassin to fulfill the contract on her—was a huge risk, one she wasn't necessarily okay with. But she'd learned long ago the best way to handle the enemy was keeping them close.

Vi called up HERA when she arrived back at the small cottage she now called home. Though the hour was late, Addy had left a lamp on in the corner. Vi sat and called up the surveillance cameras they'd put up in Resino a couple weeks ago. The small bed and breakfast was a new addition to the town, a welcomed one everyone hoped would bring tourists to the area. She didn't think there was much to draw tourists to the area, but she admitted she hadn't exactly nosed around with a tourist mindset.

A rental vehicle sat out front of the small establishment. She ran the plate, and hacked into the rental company's records.

Judson Jensen.

Talk about a fake name. Ha. She smiled at the screen as she started her search. No matter how good someone was, there was always, always a footprint. It might not be anything more than a whisper in the wind, but it would be there. And she would find it.

Someone was out for blood and Jud was an unknown.

Not for long.

~

"Kabul, Afghanistan is sixteen and a half hours from San Antonio by plane," Jacob offered. "Flights are pretty limited."

Jud looked over at his nephew. He'd started a master's program at MIT a few months before, which had spurred his dad's decision to take the contract gig overseas. Danny's sole focus was providing for his son, making sure he had everything he needed to continue his trek toward a bright future.

Gotta take this contract, man. It's only a couple weeks over in the sandpit. I'll show the newbies what's what and be back with enough bank to get Jacob through graduate school.

Jud remembered the conversation well—it'd been the last one he'd had with his brother-in-law. The only time they'd ever argued. Danny left the next day.

Jud and Jacob had spent the morning going over whatever intel they could get on Danny's disappearance, but information was sparse.

"I'm thinking they'll use different means to get there than commercial flights, bud." He turned the vehicle into the entry road leading to The Arsenal. Two armed guards flagged him through without conversation. Unlike the previous night, he was expected.

Dallas and one of his brothers stood outside a patch of parking spaces cordoned off for visitors. He took the one nearest the building. Jacob had his backpack in hand and jumped out before he could stop him. To say he was a bit excited to be in the hallowed work area of the Quillery Edge was an understatement. Add that to his determination to find his father and Jud worried the kid would have a panic attack any moment. It'd been a few years since he'd had them, but they'd been an ongoing problem since Danny's capture the first time fifteen years before.

He left the keys in the vehicle and placed himself between Jacob and the Masons. Dallas's jaw twitched as he tracked the move.

"We aren't thrilled about you being here, but we wouldn't hurt a kid," Dallas said.

"I'm not a kid," Jacob argued. "I'm nineteen and working on a master's at MIT."

The kid puffed his chest up and met Dallas's gaze dead-on. "I'm gonna be just like the Quillery Edge in a few years."

"That's good," the man beside Dallas said. "They're the best in the business. I'm Jesse, let's head inside so you can meet everybody. Vi and Mary are going to be along in a bit."

Jud let Jesse guide his nephew into the building since there was clearly a divide and conquer mission of some sort going down. Jacob looked over his shoulder.

"You good, Uncle Jud?"

"I'm fine, bud. Head on inside. I'll be there in a bit." The lanky kid plodded alongside Jesse, matching his long-legged stride easily.

"What's your play here, man?" Dallas asked. "Vi and Mary are off limits."

"I'm not here to fill the contract if that's what you're wondering," Jud said. "No one's going to mess with them as long as I'm around. Beyond that, we'll know soon enough."

"They involved with the hit?"

"Probably, but they'd be stupid to take Danny. The only thing I have is that kid and his dad, my family. Them still in my life was a reward I earned a few years ago, one I protect fiercely and they know that. The Collective also knows I've got a connection to the Quillery Edge through Danny. Them messing with those connections wouldn't be smart, but they've done dumber things."

Jian was neck deep the contract, but he was the middleman for a lot of people. The situation stunk.

"You care to explain that connection?"

"I figure it'll come out in a few minutes. The kid's been through enough. I've gotta get inside, see to him. Panic attacks are in his history." He glanced at the doors Jacob entered moments ago. "Whatever beef you have with me, contain it around him."

It was the only warning he'd give. Dallas grunted, but motioned toward the building. Jud followed the operative he'd put his ass on the line to save once. Apparently what'd gone down back then wasn't a bullet point on the agenda today, which was fine with Jud. He never cared for trips down memory lane anyway.

So far The Arsenal was impressive. It was set far enough from town to spotlight strangers wandering where they shouldn't. Drones circled in seemingly randomized patterns overhead, something he'd noted from his reconnaissance mission a few days previous—one he did via long distance across the highway. Smaller drones lurked in the corners of the hallways when they entered. None of the doors were labeled and all hallways resembled one another to the point a layman would get lost in the winding mess.

Slick.

Jud followed Dallas down a shorter hallway then followed him left. The area opened up into a series of what he assumed were meeting rooms. The doors weren't as close together. The one on the right was a frosted glass offering a hint at shadowed bodies in the interior. Dallas opened the door and motioned him inside. A rumble of disapproval rose in him as his gaze swept over the crush of people—fifteen including him and Jacob. The large standing style table had a dozen high-backed leather stools around it. Addy stood with two men book-ending her in the far corner.

"Okay, everyone. Grab a seat, we've got a lot to go over," Vi ordered. "For anyone who hasn't met him, this is Jud, aka The Judge, and his nephew, Jacob Ralters."

He froze hearing his nephew's last name, one he hadn't shared yet. A grin spread on his face. She'd been digging. The woman avoided eye contact as she introduced everyone in the room. He expected most of them to be present, except for Addy, Gage and Fallon—who were apparently Arsenal team leads—and Bree and Rhea. He made a mental note to dig up some more background on them as he sat beside Jacob at the table.

His nephew drew his laptop out of his backpack. Jud doubted he'd have reason to use it, but knew it was more of a security blanket in a group of strangers than anything. Cord smiled at him and offered a connection across the table. Jacob's grin was a mile wide as he plugged into The Arsenal like a part of the team.

Fuck. This was going to go sideways fast and he couldn't control the spin, not on something like this.

Jacob glanced at him. Wariness reflected in the kid's eyes, but Jud didn't have much in the way of comfort to offer. He'd never been in a situation where this many people were discussing or debriefing anything. He operated lone wolf style most of his career. Team was a foreign, four letter word.

Vi caught his gaze, moving her own between his and Jacob as if reading his worry. Her lips pursed, but she kept going with her conversation.

"We have several notable bullet points for today. First, and not on the agenda for this meeting other than this mention, there's a two-million-dollar contract for my and Mary's termination. It goes up to six if HERA is secured in the process. Compound security is advancing two levels. Nolan and Dylan will have more on that in a sidebar meeting with you all. For now, we progress to the second and third agenda items. Item two came as a result of said contract. Jud arrived last night offering his..." The pause was obvious and tense. "Protection. We have some information he's provided, which we'll review in the final agenda item. Jacob's father was taken to coerce him into taking the contract, but he's chosen to approach us for assistance in handling the situation instead."

All attention settled on him and Jacob. His nephew cast his gaze on the computer in front of him and folded his shoulders and body inward. Jud settled a hand on the kid's back and took the lead. "Daniel Ralters is my brother-in-law and works for a private contractor offering services in Afghanistan. He stopped field work almost fifteen years ago after being captured. His employer, on occasion, asks him to go overseas to either meet with clients, facilitate new deals or train new personnel. The latter was why he went over recently."

Vi and Mary were both typing on their laptops. The two froze, looking at one another. Color leeched from Viviana's face.

"What did we miss?" Marshall asked.

"I..." Viviana stared at the screen. "I hadn't connected the dots. Sorry, we need a minute. We'll be right back."

Jud watched as the two women rose and left the room. Dylan was hot on their heels.

~

I've got a boy, a brilliant, beautiful boy who scares the crap out of me, Quillery. He's smart, way too good to have an old man like me. He's only four, but so smart. It scares me. I know he can light up the *world just like he's lit up my life. I'm so scared of screwing him. What the hell do I do with a little genius?*

Don't feed him the fear. Fuel the genius, let him soar. Be there if he falls, but don't hold him down. Teach him it's okay to stumble as long as you get back up and keep trying. Show him courage doesn't come from winning the battle, it comes from looking impossible in the eyes and kneeing his nuts."

Vi squeezed her eyes closed. God. God. God. It'd been years. So, so many years. The conversation was one of many that looped in her brain, when the darkness of the night creeped into her thoughts and spread like a virus. He was one of her personal failures, one of the missions that'd gone wrong along the way. It'd been hailed a success because there were no casualties, but Vi knew better. She may have succeeded in the mission, but she'd failed one man that day.

Danny.

"You okay?" Mary asked.

"No. I..." She looked down and paced in the narrow nook leading into the large war room. "I can't believe this."

"What am I missing? What's wrong?" Dylan asked.

Concern filled his gaze as it settled on her. He wasn't out here solely for Mary. He was genuinely worried about her. Vi took a deep breath and drank in the calm he exuded. "Ghosts from the past. We helped rescue Danny and his convoy back then. I still remember the conversation, how I failed to keep him safe. I should have put the dots together, but I hadn't."

"No." Mary squeezed her arm. "No, that's not on you. You did nothing wrong. At all. He was already blown up by the IED before we were even on the com to help with an exfil. It's like you weren't even in the same theater as me. All these years and you still think you failed him? You kept him breathing. Alive."

Alive. What a crock of horse shit. There was a sliding scale of what alive meant. He may have been hauled away from hell "alive", but he wasn't the man he could've been if she'd reacted faster, done more.

"I should have done more," Vi whispered. "Sorry, it all hit me again when I glanced at my notes from the mission. It was like I was there again."

"There's a kid in there chomping at the bit to figure out if we can help him find his dad." Mary grinned. "Again. I love you, but you need to shake this off."

Mary was right. It was why she was The Edge. She never quit, never surrendered to the overwhelming emotional fallout of mission after mission after mission. Though they'd done hundreds of ops, Vi couldn't shake some of them loose. Ghosts. Danny was one of hers.

"I know." Vi forced back the memories and focused on the current situation. "Let's get back in there and figure out what the hell's going on."

"If this gets to be too much, let me know and we're done. Nothing and no one is more important than you and our new crew here." Mary motioned toward the room. "Let's go."

Vi followed her friend and Dylan back into the room and sat down. "Sorry, I needed to take a breath for a minute. Some missions feel like they just happened yesterday, and this was one of them."

Jacob's gaze was watery. Son of a bitch, she hadn't handled that well. The kid needed the calm, quiet confidence she and Mary offered as the Quillery Edge. He didn't need an emotional mess, not with his dad missing again. She called up the mission records from the last time, hacked her way into the organization's database and pulled up the data they had on Danny's last orders.

"He works for Palmetto," she said.

"Of course he does," Mary muttered.

"There a problem with that?" Jud asked.

"Palmetto is on the up and up for the most part," Vi replied.

"They have a side division called Palmetto Pointe that operates in the grayer areas. It was partially owned by Martin Driggs, one of our former bosses at Hive."

Several of the pieces clicked into place as to who orchestrated this mess. Someone was dishing up a big stew of coincidences. Clearly whoever took Danny was also behind Peter and Martin betraying them and trying to steal HERA. Now that she and Mary had dismantled and systematically destroyed the two bastards, they'd put out a hit on them.

Now that they had the why, Vi wanted the who.

"It's dirty," Jud said.

"No way, no way Dad is dirty," Jacob shouted. "No way. You're wrong."

"Easy, bud. They aren't saying he's dirty. The contract was likely issued because they took down Hive and everyone associated with..." His gaze darted to Mary, who tensed beside Vi. "The recent incidents. That takes someone with a lot of clout to pull off."

The Collective was probably behind it all. Vi's chest squeezed as the shock and pain flashed through Jacob's face. Guilt and rage harshened Jud's face. His employer had kidnapped his nephew's dad. He'd likely already put the pieces together, but it was becoming more abundantly clear. If he had any doubt. She didn't exactly have room to throw stones. How long had she and Mary denied the fact Hive was dirty? That everything they'd worked so hard to achieve had been tainted by corruption and greed?

Yeah, it was easy to look at a situation from a bird's eye view and cast judgment, call bullshit on what seemed obvious from a distance. But when someone was in the trenches, mired in the bullshit for so long it was hard to smell it any longer—especially when someone you supposedly trust and rely on was the one crapping on what you care about. She glanced around the room and noted the matching expressions of empathy and patience.

Anger and determination.

"The Collective did this?" Tears trekked down the boy's face. "Why would they do that?"

"Leverage," Vi said. "Someone familiar with your uncle's track record wanted leverage to get him to do what they wanted. Your dad is their ace in the hole."

Jacob shook his head. "No. They wouldn't use Dad because it'd piss Uncle Jud off, and no one smart ever does that. Not if they want to keep breathing."

Vi couldn't help but smile at the conviction within Jacob's voice. He had no doubt his uncle was the best.

"Let's take a few steps back and start at ground zero. Then we can get to the questions of who and why," Mary suggested. "Tell us about Danny's work with Palmetto."

"I have his bio," Jacob said. He yanked his notebook from the backpack and thumbed through it. "It's more of a list of assignments he's had over the years. Will this help?"

He slid the notebook across the table. Cord reached over and grabbed it. He grinned.

"Nice lists, man. You'll fit in good with these two. They have lists for their lists."

"Wicked," Jacob replied. "They help me sort my thoughts."

"Me, too," Vi admitted.

Jud helped fill in the holes of the Palmetto data she'd unearthed. Danny went missing on a stretch of highway deep within the Golden Crescent, one of the heaviest areas of opium growers and suppliers in the world. The area was rife with political unrest and in the middle of highly sought-after terrain. Local drug lords controlled growth over around ninety percent of the world's opium production.

"Naturally Peter and Martin took a cut of the profits for their assistance in easing any trafficking concerns with their connections, but how does Palmetto Pointe play into this?" Addy asked.

Vi noted the tension in her friend's voice. She couldn't imagine how Addy'd gotten through all she had. Finding out your only brother was a scum-sucking leech on humanity was bound to be difficult. "Palmetto and their counterpart, Palmetto Pointe, are the primary contractors in the area. They offer engineering and logistical support for a lot of the local building initiatives."

"Dad's an engineer, the best."

Which would explain why he was dragged over to the region despite what'd happened in the past. *I'd do anything for that kid.* The words from years ago haunted Vi as they ran through the data. She and Mary unearthed what little documentation there was.

"Someone's scrubbed records," Cord surmised.

"Pretty much," Mary said.

"The question is who," Jud said.

"I'm thinking you already know the answer. He's been gone a while now, long enough for someone to reach out and yank that chain, extend an offer you couldn't refuse," Dallas said. He leaned back in his chair and pinned Jud with a malevolent glare.

"I figured they were involved when Jian phoned. He has other clients, but it takes a big bank account to fund an operation of this magnitude." Jud's voice offered no emotion, no subtext.

"And we're supposed to believe you'd not only pass up that much money, but offer protection?" Marshall chuckled. "This isn't Hollywood. We're not dumb enough to fall for that scripted crap."

"Never thought you were." Jud crossed his arms. "I've operated in the shadows a long time, done things so black it's in my marrow. I had one rule going in. My family stays clean. Someone broke that rule. That's why I'm here. No one jerks my chain, especially the one tied to my family."

Silence descended a few moments. The Mason brothers looked at one another. Vi sensed the shift in their mindset. With the few sentences Jud had climbed up a few pegs as far as most of the operatives in the room were concerned. Family was the most important thing to the Masons.

"I'm not bending over for anyone. Ever. Someone breaks my rule, I break them in a way that sends a message no one forgets."

"Someone had to be close enough to know you had that string for them to pull," Nolan commented. "I'd imagine the list is narrow."

"It should be," Jud admitted. He pulled out a phone and slid it across the table. "Let's see what we can find out."

Vi looked at Mary, then at the phone. Cord snatched it first.

"It's a burner. Hit number two," Jud said. "It'd be best if everyone stayed quiet."

Cord hooked the phone to the overhead speakers. Unease filled Vi as the device started ringing. A velvety, feminine voice filled the speakers.

"Why, Jud, this is a pleasant surprise. You weren't due to check in for another month. Are you sick of your little investigation firm already?"

"No." Jud's jaw twitched. "I need some answers, Marla. I'm hoping you have them because I'm not in a good mood."

"You don't sound happy."

"Got a call. Danny's disappeared, Jian's behind it and pushing me to take the Quillery Edge contract. I'm not happy, Marla."

"How unfortunate. Looks like you don't have much in the way of options. It'll be an easy six million for you."

"What does The Collective have to do with the contract on the Quillery Edge and Danny's disappearance?"

Marla sighed. "Honestly, Jud, it's like you haven't been paying attention. Hive was...an important ally. Losing them undermines us. I'm afraid decisions were made to neutralize the risk. They were outsourced to other interested parties. You should really stay out of that mess, Jud."

"Hard to do since Jian dragged me into it by taking Danny."

"Well, that's true. You know Jian. He's like the eager puppy bouncing around in the corner to get attention."

"You know the rule, Marla. The Collective stays away from my list. Danny and his kid were at the top."

"Now, Jud, we can't control what others do. You know how many vie for our attention. It's not our fault if they get overly enthusiastic." She sighed again. "I warned him it was a terrible idea to get his little buddies over there to take Danny. It's not like you'll negotiate with anyone. But you know how Jian gets."

"He's pulling my string," Jud declared. "You're letting him pull my strings, Marla. I've got problems with that, problems guaranteed to make you and everyone you report to very uncomfortable."

"We're staying out of this one out of respect for you, Jud. We couldn't stop Jian from making his move, and we can't stop you from making yours. We stayed out of it when he got involved with Peter and Hive, too. Really, kindergarten politics are beneath us."

"Yeah, right. You said earlier you were nervous about Hive going down." Jud tapped the table. "I'm thinking you're spewing lies so fast you can't keep them straight."

"I said decisions were made to neutralize the threat. I never said we made them, Judson. Now, enough with the boring drama." Marla sing-songed the words. "I miss you, lover. It's been rather dull around here without you."

Vi tightened beside Mary. Everything was connected.

"You should've kept him away from my family, Marla. You may not have issued the order, but your silence ensured its success. For that, you and The Collective will pay," he warned.

"You know better than to make threats. I let you get by with more than the rest of my toys, but don't forget that's what you are. Don't upset me by being stupid, Jud, or I'll be forced to punish you."

"I've never been your toy, Marla, and I don't make threats. Clean this mess up. Get Danny back and the contract against the

Quillery Edge withdrawn now, or there will be consequences. I don't make threats. That's a promise."

"Ordering us around is a mistake, Jud."

"No. The mistake was going after my family. This discussion is done." He made a cutting motion.

Mary flicked the phone off. Tension corded the room. Jud's gaze swept the area. "In case you missed it, I just declared war on Jian Chen and The Collective."

Yep. Vi was pretty sure everyone in the room figured that out.

6

Jud chased after Jacob when he fled the room. He'd collapsed in a small alcove outside a set of double doors. Tears trekked down his cheeks. "They took Dad. The Collective is behind all this."

"It's looking like it," he admitted. He looked up and saw Viviana hovering nearby.

"We aren't going after him tomorrow, are we? This is going to take some time to sort out, plan." Jacob sniffed. "Is he going to be okay? I want to go and kick their asses now."

"Your dad is more useful alive," he answered. "As for going now, you know better."

His nephew was far from stupid. He read between the lines. So did Vi. Her gaze narrowed, her lips thinned. Hands on her hips, she gave every indication of a woman pissed. He was screwing this up.

"There's a lot we don't know, not yet. I do know one thing. The two women who pulled your dad out of hell once are in the room and they need our help to find him. They're hooked up with the best organization around. If anyone can stand against The Collective it's The Arsenal." He glanced at Viviana. "I don't give a shit who's after them and who took your dad. All I know is they fucked up. They shouldn't have ever touched my family. Or the Quillery Edge. They will rot in hell, even if it means I have to drag them there myself."

"Hey, Jacob, I think Cord and Edge could use your help inside. We're looking through all the information you helped put together on Jian," Vi said.

"Oh, right. I'd better get in there." Jacob jumped up and froze when Viviana got closer. "Thanks, Quillery, for everything."

"We'll find him," she promised. "We'll be inside in a minute. I need to talk to your uncle alone for a little while."

He almost wished the kid would hang around. His pulse quickened as she sat on the floor. Her legs grazed his in the small niche, but he didn't make any attempt to move. The slight contact arced awareness between them as her gaze latched onto his. Her lips pursed.

"You have issues," he guessed.

"More concerns and rules than issues, but yes. We need to clear the air about a few things." She crossed her arms. "First off, I don't trust you. I don't trust you with my teams, around Mary, or anyone else here. Marshall just said you'd be put on an operational team. We had words about it, words I lost. He'd rather keep you close to a team that can take you out than have you running amok alone. Dallas wants to double tap you now and save everyone the effort of keeping you contained. Either way, when teams are in the field, I'm in charge. You do what I say. Teams don't have room for lone wolves with attitude."

"Understood." Amusement filled his voice. "Though, just to point out, I haven't agreed to be on a team."

She leaned forward. Determination filled her gaze. "If you

cross me, my team, or anyone else while you're in the field, I'll put a bullet in your brain."

She meant every word. He leaned back against the wall and let the torrential downpour of her anger settle to a raincloud. Viviana definitely stirred his interest. Sex had become a commonplace afterthought, kind of like hauling trashcans to the curb. He did it when it was necessary, when the pent-up need became too much to ignore.

He loved women. Sex.

Physical contact.

He reached out and feathered his fingers across her exposed ankle. She twitched, narrowed her gaze, but didn't draw away. He deepened the contact, relishing the glide of her soft skin beneath his callused hand. "You've got it in you to gut my boy in there. You, Edge or anyone else take your frustrations with me out on him and you'll feel the full weight of my anger. Trust me, you don't want that. He walks away clean from this, no matter what."

"We don't hurt kids." She uncrossed her arms and leaned back against the wall. "Where's his mom? Is there more family?"

"Judith didn't handle things well the last time, back when Danny got back. The recovery was a long and painful process. Rehabilitation, reconstruction of the house."

"She left." Anger edged the two words.

"She left." Shame and bitterness filled him. "My sister didn't want to deal, so she left. Mom and Dad pitched in to help, moved closer to Boston to help with Jacob when he graduated early and got into MIT. Keeping up with him became a family mission."

One he hadn't carried his weight in most of the time. He'd been away on assignments and handling problems before they could touch his other life, the life where everyone was clean, whole. Good.

"He admires you," she whispered. "His eyes light up when he talks about you."

"Nah, that's love. You should know. You and Edge...you two are his idols." Doubt reflected in her gaze when she looked up at him. "Danny came back a different man. He showed Jacob intelligence mattered just as much as brute strength, that you could be a superhero with your brain instead of muscles."

She swallowed and looked away.

"He learned that from you and Edge," Jud said. "I didn't believe him, not at first. The stories he told sounded more like comic book tales. There wasn't any way two women like that existed. But you did."

Little guns decorated tight leggings that ended just below her knee. He ran his hand up her naked calf. Stroked.

"You are his superhero, Viviana."

"Don't, don't call me that," she said. "I'm Vi."

"Two letters and one syllable don't do you justice. You're definitely a Viviana." He stood, looking down at her shapely legs. He'd always been more of a knife man, but she came close to converting him with the little guns. "We'd better get inside."

Two letters and one syllable don't do you justice.

What the heck did that mean? Viviana tried keeping her mind from wandering back to the comment, but the damn thing kept burrowing through her defense system to revisit Jud's compliment. She and Mary had led a white boarding session to end all white boarding sessions. Jud and Jacob turned over whatever information they had on Jian and his operations. The process was slower than she would've liked.

"Why aren't we heading overseas? What's all this for?" Jacob asked.

Vi glanced up and waited for someone else to field the questions. When no one volunteered, she waded in. The young man had been helpful and quiet for the most part, but it'd been hours. Any teenager would be crawling out of their skin by now. Vi figured he was entitled to a few answers. He wasn't a typical teen, though. He'd graduated MIT already and was only nineteen. He was more like her and Mary than the highly trained operatives in the room. Like his uncle.

Jud regarded her from across the room, as if sensing she was about to tackle Jacob's questions.

"I'm going to shoot straight with you on this, Jacob, because we're running low on time and I know you can handle the truth, the entire truth—not just the watered-down version." She waited for him to nod his head and focus on her. An awkward silence descended as everyone else in the room tuned in. "If we send teams overseas before handling whatever this stateside connection with Jian is, he could go to ground and we'll never find him. The little boy would get killed. If Jian's network is large enough to be watching your uncle and you, they'd know you're here. If we mobilize and go wheels up to get your dad, he could notify his people over there and the rescue mission becomes a recovery mission."

Translation—your father would get killed while we're over an ocean.

"So we're going after the boy first? Wouldn't Jian warn whoever has my dad when he realizes we're going after his trafficking operation?" The boy shook his head. "That's not fair. Dad deserves a rescue, too."

"And he'll get it, Jacob," Vi assured. "We're cutting both heads off the snake at once. Teams will move on his stateside operations, while the majority of the teams converge on wherever your dad is held. But we need information before we can do anything."

She glanced at the clock. Judson had provided a location for Jian three hours ago. Without letting him or, well, anyone else in the room know, she'd sent Addy and Gage to shadow the bastard in case HERA couldn't come up with his resources overseas. Who did the bastard trust? Which rock did they crawl under? The computer chimed as two streams of data erupted from the device. Lines of information flowed across the large table's surface. She and Mary leaned forward and started organizing the important bits. They'd get color-coded and settled on whichever wall they pertained to. Then Bree and Rhea would hopefully have enough to extrapolate connections, the network.

Two hours later, pain radiated from her shoulders and down her arms. Her neck was tighter than a drum. Were drums tight? She had no clue.

"You two women need a rest. You've been at it nonstop for hours," Marshall declared.

"I'm fine," Vi argued.

"I'm thinking he's right, Viviana." Jud's voice boomed behind her.

When the heck had he gotten behind her? And how? The man was a stealthy ghost.

"Lean forward, head on your outstretched arms," he ordered. A firm hand settled on her shoulders. "Trust me."

Whatever. Head on her arms sounded phenomenal, like a short nap without the time commitment of real sleep. One of these days she'd have to give a full five or six hours at a time a go, but she'd managed with two or three here and there so far. Once Danny was safe and they had Jian in custody, she'd sleep. She rested her head between her arms.

Deft hands massaged her neck and shoulders. She tried not to tense beneath the ministration, mainly because the man doing it was an unknown assassin and there was a six-million-dollar bounty on her head. Dying might almost be worth it, though, if she got a few more minutes of his fingers kneading the tension away. He angled downward, working the tired muscles in her back. Then upward to her arms. Then back to her shoulders and neck. The contact alternated between light and deep, so she remained fully focused on it, never quite knowing what to expect.

Her pulse quickened, her breathing turned erratic. Anticipation beaded along her skin in tiny goosebumps she hoped he couldn't see along her arms. It'd been forever since anyone touched her like this. She still remembered him touching her ankle in the hallway. The man was impossibly tactile. Was he like that with everyone?

"Come on, Viviana. Time to walk around some."

She lifted up and realized fifteen minutes had passed. How the heck had that happened? Wait. "Where did everyone go?"

Though it appeared she and Jud were very much alone, they weren't. Cameras observed in the corner.

"The mess hall to eat," he answered with a smirk. "Come on, Sleeping Beauty, let's get some grub then we'll walk you a bit."

"Walk me? I'm not a dog, Judson Jensen." She kinked up her nose. "That's insulting. I'm not a dog person. I'm a cat girl. I think."

"You think?" He turned her to face him. "No pets?"

"No, it doesn't seem fair to them, you know. I work all the time. But, I'm settled in here with The Arsenal." Or sort of settled. Did unpacked boxes count? "I figured a cat wouldn't mind. They're kind of anti-social animals like me, right?"

"Dogs are curious and intensely loyal. Protective." He bumped her nose with a finger. "That's more like you than a fur ball with attitude and whiskers, though I have to admit you have a lot of sass."

Okay, he really was comparing her to animals. That was... adorable. Insulting. She see-sawed between the two reactions as she looked up at him. An awareness pebbled beneath her skin, she could still feel his hands on her even though he was a good foot away. He prowled closer, an uncaged hunter. His hand settled around her waist. She trundled alongside him as he guided her down the hall like he'd been at The Arsenal for years.

"You're very tactile," she blurted.

"Does that bother you?"

"Depends."

"On?"

"On why," she admitted. "You aren't touching all the others. Are you hoping to get the perfect opportunity to snap my neck or something?"

He turned, guiding her backward until she was against the wall. He leaned forward, settling both hands around her head like muscular bookends. "I'm not going to hurt you, Mary, or anyone else here at The Arsenal, Viviana. I touch you because I find it impossible not to. It's been a long time since a woman stirred my interest for something more than some quick fun between the sheets."

Vi thought any fun with Judson between the sheets wouldn't ever be quick. That'd be a downright travesty if it were true. She must've blurted the thought or done something equally embarrassing because his laughter echoed through the corridor—the very empty corridor. His handsome face really did turn nuclear when he smiled full-on. Riley hadn't been wrong.

Vi reached out and caressed his face. He liked touch. Did that mean he craved someone's in return? "Were you always in contact with your family?"

He leaned toward the contact, but tension corded in his arms. "No. That was recent, a perk I demanded because I'd earned it with a bigger graveyard than most of their operatives combined. I'm not a good man, Viviana. I never will be."

"That's not true," she argued with a whisper. "A bad man wouldn't have put himself on the line for a woman he didn't know, a team he wasn't part of, because his nephew wanted him to. A bad man would've put a bullet in my brain and demanded his nephew's dad be cut loose."

Jud looked down, as if unwilling to concede the point he'd

made. Vi ran her hand down to where his face met his neck and squeezed until he looked at her again. The fiery intensity within his gaze silenced the voice in her head a moment, the one demanding she walk away from whatever the awareness between them meant.

"That was never a consideration for either you or Jacob, was it?"

"No," he admitted.

"It'd be a lot easier. It's not like you know me or Mary."

"That's where you're wrong," he argued. "I know the women Danny knew you to be, the Wonder Women who yanked him out of hell and refused to ever let go, ever give up."

Vi's chest squeezed, twisted. "Don't. You make it sound like we're perfect, infallible. Mary is. She's never made a mistake, never failed on a mission."

"But you think you have. You've run missions without her?"

"A few. And, yeah, I've failed. I failed Danny," she admitted. Heat rose in her cheeks when he dragged his feet closer. Heat from their bodies mingled, creating a furnace of awareness between them. Cocooned within it, she let the words she'd held onto tumble out. "I keep remembering the op, what went down. I didn't do enough for his injuries. Maybe if I'd done more he would've..."

"Don't," Jud growled. "Don't take that as your strike. I wasn't there, but I've heard Danny's recount. There's no way in hell you did anything that hurt him. He was already dead before you and Edge came into play."

She shook her head. He didn't understand. "I failed Mary, too, you know. I should have known the mission Driggs sent me on was bogus. If I hadn't gone, they wouldn't have taken her."

"No, they would've probably taken you, too. Then they would've made you both break."

"You're wrong. Mary wouldn't have ever broken. Me neither," she said.

"Alone, you're right. Neither of you would break," he admitted. "But had it been my op, had I been tasked to make you break."

He paused. His gaze swept down her face. His fingertips stroked her cheek, the contact so slight it was a flutter against her skin.

"Had I been tasked with making you break I would've used her to make you break, and vice versa."

"They did, you know," Vi said. "They ran fake recordings of me being tortured. Raped. Screaming. When she first got back, when Dylan saved her, she'd scream my name, so loud and strong the entire building could hear. I still wake up hearing those blood curdling screams. I should have been there."

He settled her head against his shoulder and drew her into his arms. She suckled the confidence, the power he exuded and let the guilt and regret she'd carried escape a moment, long enough to vent some of the pent-up emotions. She didn't understand why it was easier to share the darkness consuming her with him. He was a stranger.

An assassin.

Maybe that was why. No matter how dark her dark was, no matter the failures she'd reaped, he'd always be darker. It was rather ironic. The deadliest assassin in the deadliest organization around, The Judge, was the perfect confidant.

"I'm not an expert, Viviana, but I'm thinking you need some help sorting through what you think. Someone's done a number on you," he whispered into her ear. "Someone has you thinking perfection is your responsibility."

Shock muted her a few moments. No one ever made the connection, except Mary and the girls. Even then, they'd never said it outright. Certainly not that quickly. "My parents were a bit...exacting. I wasn't ever what they envisioned or wanted. I kind of did my own thing."

"That's their problem, not yours. From where I'm standing, you're pretty damn perfect, Viviana Chambers." He drew her away so their gazes locked. His lips feathered across hers, slow and soft at first.

The hesitancy burned away any insecurities she had. Whoever the hell Judson Jensen was, he was a damn good kisser. A frustrated moan escaped her as she deepened the contact, dared a foray of tongue along his lips. He repeated the motion, then added in a tantalizing seduction of tongue tangoing with hers. One hand cupped her face, the other remained at her waist. Hers roamed, ran along hard ridges of abdominals, up a sinewy back and across impossibly large biceps.

"Well, it looks like she started with dessert first." Mary's amused voice fractured the moment.

Vi scurried away like a teenager caught with a boy on her mom's sofa. She'd never experienced burning shame until now. Mary and Dylan wore matching grins, but a hardness reflected in the latter's gaze as he regarded Jud.

"We brought you both some food." Mary motioned to Dylan, who held two platters heaping with potato salad, beans and barbecue. "Momma Mason grabbed grub from Bubba's. There's even pecan pie."

"Pecan." Vi groaned the word as she snagged a plate and headed back into the debriefing room.

Food was the perfect distraction, mainly because it kept her mouth busy chewing food she shoveled into it rather than blurting out the things her brain was processing.

She was attracted to Judson Jensen. It was the worst possible deduction and one she couldn't refute, not after that kiss. Her entire body still hummed with need. Jud smirked as he sat across from her at the table. The bastard knew he'd knocked her for a loop with that kiss.

And then there was what she'd spewed before. Talk about verbal diarrhea. Yeesh. She shoveled barbecue and some potato salad into her mouth and chewed through the thought. It felt like someone had scraped her insides with sandpaper. Her gaze flitted nervously from Jud to Mary and Dylan. He wouldn't say anything, would he?

Ugh. The thought made her stomach revolt. She set her fork down.

"Eat, Viviana," he ordered. "The only thing you need more than food right now is sleep."

"He's right," Mary said. "You haven't been sleeping well, have you?"

"I'll catch some once teams are wheels up." She took another bite. "I'll have plenty of time to rest then."

"No, you and Mary will be handling the stateside teams and coordinating stuff. I know how you both are," Dylan said.

"It'll take another few hours for HERA to provide more data. Cord and I will keep working with what's coming out, but you need to get some sleep now. It'll be crazy later," Mary said.

She was right. Vi hadn't effectively time managed herself and now Mary and Cord would have to pick up her slack. Self-loathing seeped through her insides. Cord wasn't as good with the data as Vi, which meant something could be missed.

Mary shouldn't even be working with the data, not after what she'd gone through. What if she stumbled across something that caused a flashback or upset her somehow? Vi wouldn't be there to fix it because she'd screwed up and become too exhausted to function. She was hindering the team.

"There's a down room around the corner to the right. It's the last door on the left and has a small sign," Mary said. "Flip it over and people will know it's occupied."

"Appreciated." Jud's voice tumbled near her ear. "I'm thinking you need sleep more than food. Put your arm around me."

"What are you doing?" The question proved unnecessary. He'd obviously lost his mind.

Jud lifted her. One hand at her back and another under her knees, he carried her from the room.

"Put me down."

"I'll put you down in a minute. Relax."

Relax. The man was a loon. There wasn't time to relax. She had data to mine, operations to plan, teams to debrief.

"You'll be more good to them and me after you've had a few hours rest, Viviana. You don't know me, but trust me to care for you, just until you rest. Then you'll be back to caring for everyone else."

Viviana relaxed against him. Exhaustion settled in her now that her hunger had been somewhat sated. Jud paused in front of the down room. He pushed the door open and pale light from the automated system turned on, bathing the small area in pale yellow. He sat on one of the two comfy loveseats she and Mary had picked out. They were a manly brown with plush leather and enough padding to feel like you were floating.

He pulled a blanket from the table and settled it around her.

"You can go now. I'll rest," she said.

"I'm not going anywhere, Viviana," he whispered. "Those screams are haunting you, aren't they?"

God. God. God.

She squeezed her eyes closed and burrowed beneath the blanket and deeper into his arms. This was wrong on every level, she shouldn't trust him with anything. Yet the admission tumbled from her in a nod.

"Sleep. I'll chase away your nightmares."

God. God. God.

Deft hands moved along her arms and back, massaging the

tension wherever they settled. Her mind moved past the impossibly long list of problems to fix and disasters to avert. The hypnotic glide along her skin lulled her thoughts.

Sleep. I'll chase away your nightmares.

Vi smiled. For a few moments she had the biggest, baddest monster around to scare the others away. His name was Judson Jensen and he was trouble she didn't want to avoid, not anytime soon.

7

V iviana hadn't moved. Dylan had brought in a Bluetooth device for him to communicate with everyone in the other room three hours before, shortly after she'd fallen asleep. Jacob appeared a few minutes later with a tablet so he could see data as it streamed across. It took a while to navigate and figure out how to move between the various screens of information that were on the various white boards around the room, but Jud got the hang of it easily enough. HERA was a sweet system.

The computer ran data through endless programs, ones the brilliant woman passed out in his arms designed. Thanks to her and Edge's creation, Jud knew they had a crazy amount of data gathered—about Jian's operation stateside and Danny's situation.

"Okay, HERA's identified the boy. He's a five-year-old Russian, Mico Ivanenko. His father was supposed to testify against the Solov family, a new Russian crime syndicate carving out a presence for themselves in North, Central and South America," Mary said. "We gained access to the alphabet soup's assorted files on the operation. Connections and web identifying patterns are Vi's thing. I'm afraid we need our girl awake."

Three hours of rest was better than none he supposed. He glanced down at her head rested where it'd remained unmoving for the past few hours. The only thing that'd moved the entire time was her left flip-flop, which thudded to the floor a couple hours earlier. He smiled at her multi-colored toes. Adorable. Quirky.

"Give me a few, then we'll head in." He flicked the device off and put the tablet on the table.

He ran a hand down her silky, dark blonde hair and kissed her forehead. She sighed into the touch.

"Viviana, we need you awake," he whispered gently. Her hand burrowed under his shirt along the waist. She smacked her lips together, but kept sleeping. Amusement rumbled through him. She was the kind of woman who was all in once she made a decision. She held nothing back, even in sleep. He'd become her pillow and she wasn't surrendering her rest without a fight.

"Viviana." He added an edge to his voice, an urgency.

"What? What?" She popped up like a live wire. "What'd I miss?" She ran a hand down her face and looked around. "Okay, right. How long was I out?"

"Three hours, give or take." He held out the tablet. "Give yourself a couple minutes to wake, take a look at what HERA's pulled so far."

She flipped through the data quickly. Stood. Walked.

He followed, opening doors and steering her blind walk back to the debriefing room. Definitely all-in with everything she did. Her hair was rumpled from sleep, but he doubted she'd ever realize. He snagged her about the waist. "Hold up for a second."

"What? We have to get back in there," she said.

He knelt and wrapped a hand around her left ankle. "Lift."

"What?" She looked down. "Oh. Right."

He chuckled and put the flip-flop back on her foot. "When you get a dog, you'll need better footwear. Flip-flops don't make good chew toys for golden retrievers."

"No. Nuh uh. Flip-flops are perfect for cats because they don't care about shoes at all, but the noise they make when you walk is fun for their little ears. You should buy some for when you get a cat. I'm thinking one of those hairless ones."

He slid the flip-flop into place, stroked the soft skin around her ankle and then stood. "Not getting a hairless cat, Viviana. That's unnatural."

"They'd be easier to clean up after. Think of all the time you'd save," she clipped.

He wasn't sure why they were chatting about dogs versus cats, but he recognized the tactic—she wanted a step back from whatever trust she'd given when she'd fallen asleep in his arms, alone in a room with him. He should've left her sleeping and gone back to the debriefing area, but he didn't like the idea of her having a nightmare and waking up alone. How often did she have them? Did anyone know?

"True, but I'm a man, Viviana, a real man who doesn't mind getting dirty. I'm okay with cleaning up a mess. I love it dirty and messy and real."

"Hairless cats are real, Jud." Her gaze narrowed. "I found the name Judson Jenson on the car rental. Is that real? It sounds fake to me."

Laughter tumbled from him. "Afraid so. Judson Jason Jensen."

"Wow. I'm thinking The Collective did you a favor scrubbing that from databases," she muttered. "And your sister was Judith. They had a thing for J's. They sound like interesting people."

"They are, the best," he admitted. "It's been a while since we've seen them. They moved a year ago, decided to give warmer climates a try. Dad just retired, so he's driving Mom nuts."

A smile spread across her face. Then she glanced down at the screen and turned rigid, as if remembering why she'd woken.

"It's okay, you know," he commented.

"What's okay?"

"To turn off the operative side and live life a little."

"You don't know what you're talking about. Mary was the one who couldn't identify herself away from The Edge. I have a firm handle on that," she argued.

"Whatever you say, Viviana." He motioned down the hall. "They said they needed you, something about connections and webs."

~

hey'd lucked out. It'd taken Viviana a couple hours to assemble the pieces so she could glue them together into the complicated network the alphabet soup hadn't unearthed yet because they'd held everything close to their vests and shared nothing. Idiots.

She'd fallen asleep on Jud and he'd let her stay there for three hours. She was stunned, horrified, embarrassed and confused— all in equal measure. He'd taken care of her even when there was no reason. She'd slept.

Truly slept.

Though her body demanded a few more hours, she was more refreshed than she had been in a long time. She didn't understand why she'd fallen asleep so easily, or why she was drawn to Jud. He was attractive and a bad ass. Out of her league in a lot of ways. She dealt with so many hardheaded assholes running on more testosterone than brain cells at Hive, she'd gotten turned off muscled men in general.

But seeing Dylan with Mary shifted her mindset, and rebooted her internal processors when it came to men. Stereotyping all military men as hotheaded, walking testosterone wasn't fair. Jud wasn't military, though. Her brain labeled him as an assassin, but she couldn't toss someone like Jud in one category. He was...

Complicated.

Yep. There it was. She loved rooting around complicated. That's why she was so drawn to him. Tall, dark, handsome, mysterious and a bad ass. What wasn't there to like?

Assassin. Mysterious.

Ugh.

Marshall and Nolan had gone to the office to make a couple phone calls, see what they could do to involve the suits. Having their blessing to work the operations would expedite things and make cleanup a lot simpler. She helped Mary, Bree and Rhea complete the web while Cord and Jacob continued mining data. The kid was a natural. He'd taken to HERA like the proverbial duck to water.

Jud watched his nephew closely. Pride reflected in his gaze.

The door opened and the two eldest Mason brothers took their seats.

"Well?" Jacob asked impatiently.

"We're a go. After we got done laying out what we'd discovered, what we'd gathered from them, they were more than willing to turn control of the take down to us," Marshall said.

"Because they don't want to deal with the fallout," Nolan finished.

"Dylan and Jesse put together team assignments," Cord commented. "Where are they headed, Vi?"

She pulled up the map. "The Solov family has an extremely complex, and downright brilliant, network established, which is run by our man Jian. I'm not sure we've made all the connections yet, but we've gotten enough of them to establish patterns."

Red, green and orange lines appeared on the map, connecting cities and states to one another back and forth in a complicated web, a geographical one corresponding with a three-dimensional version connecting people.

"Data obtained from the FBI, CIA, and Homeland Security offered a patchwork of connections, layers of interlinked social media accounts. The guy running the operation in Philly doesn't know the one in Chicago, but they have a mutual friend on three different social media platforms," Mary explained.

"What does that have to do with it?" Dylan asked.

"It's layers of an onion," Jacob explained excitedly. "The guy running the trafficking operation in Philly ships to Chicago, but he doesn't know anything about Chicago because it's done through an intermediary."

"That way if the FBI or anyone else busts Philly, it doesn't spread to the rest of the network. Each location is isolated, except for the intermediary," Marshall said. "Insulation."

"And the mutual connections aren't around long. Bodies are piling up on HERAs lists as she links common MOs to unsolved murders around the country and some in Mexico," Vi said. "I'll forward the data to the FBI and let them run with that."

"So where's our man and do we need to worry about busting this up so we can tend to business overseas?" Jesse asked.

"What you see here is the Solov empire, one Jian runs. Jian's a busy boy, though, and has his own operation," Mary said. "We've found his contact in Afghanistan. He's running product through the Solov network. The product is produced in the region where Danny went missing."

"CIA intel marks the area as being controlled by Ahmad Zubair." Cord pulled up a grainy photo. "No one knows much about him or his group, it sprung up just under five years ago. They're heavily armed and have three base camps we have limited intel on."

"HERA's accessing satellites over the area in question so we can get detailed layouts. I'm going to contact a Delta team we've assisted a couple times and see if they'll do some recon for us. They have a slimmed down version of the field box," Vi said.

They hadn't been able to trust them with the version that included the biochemical agents as much as she'd wanted to. Although she trusted the team itself, she wouldn't trust HERA in the hands of any government run group. Everything the team had was easily destroyed via remote interface, something no one knew —not even Mary.

"Good. That'll give you and Mary time to work with us while we're wheels up."

"And we'll secure your use of the nearby military base. That'll give you somewhere slightly more secure to make thorough dry runs, hone the plans," Mary said. "Once you're in position and ready, the ground teams stateside will strike at the same time you do. We'll snag Jian."

"The alphabet soup gave us access to him for seventy-two hours," Marshall said. "That'll mean we need Sanderson or Graves stateside to handle interrogation."

Gage Sanderson and Fallon Graves were their two best assets for advanced interrogation. While anyone at The Arsenal was more than proficient, the two men were on an entirely different level. Neither of them, however, would be down with staying stateside while the majority of their counterparts were overseas freeing hostages. Taking down Jian would be considered the second-string. Vi studied both men, though everyone already knew which would be going overseas.

"Sorry, Gage. We can't risk not having Fallon's enhanced ordnance skills," Vi said.

"Understood," Gage said. "I'll let my team know we're cleaning up the streets stateside. We'll get the boy and anyone else there secure. And I'd be thrilled to go a few rounds in the box downstairs with Jian."

The containment facilities in the lower levels of The Arsenal were far more sophisticated than a box. They'd recently under-gone an overhaul, one she and Mary oversaw. Anyone who went down there wouldn't escape. Ever.

"I'll coordinate with local FBI offices at the other sites of Solov operations. Hopefully they'll work with us and strike with local law enforcement around the country at the same time we hit Jian's location," Mary said.

"FBI surveillance flagged Jian's operation in a trailer park on Roosevelt Avenue in Dover, but he's in a two-story Victorian half a click away." Vi called up the images HERA had pulled. "There's heavy tree coverage, lots of buildings and sheds. We'll need at least two teams."

"Understood. We'll iron out which will assist Gage's. The rest are wheels up for the sandbox in the morning. Until then, rest up. We've got a long haul ahead of us." Marshall rose.

Vi stood, intercepting him. "A moment."

He nodded as everyone filed out. Arms crossed, he looked down at Vi. "Is there a problem?"

"No, probably not." She took a deep breath and forced her thought out. "We need to make sure Jesse's cleared for this op."

"We've done a lot of extractions, Vi. Why would this be any different?"

"This one cuts closer to the grain than the others. Danny's a paraplegic who's been in captivity. Jesse might have issues remaining detached from this one."

"You want him stateside on Dover."

"I want him wherever he'll be least affected and okay with being there." She put a hand on her hip. "It might be my call or Mary's whether he's okay with going, but he's your brother. I figure you'd rather handle that."

"Appreciate it, I'll have a word with him."

Vi suspected he'd be overseas with the rest of the teams. She'd done what she could to make sure there wasn't any fallout for him after it was over. She glanced at the time and realized there weren't many hours left until sunrise. As much as she hated the idea, she needed more rest because, like Marshall said, there was a very long haul ahead.

"You okay?"

Judson's voice startled her when she exited the room. He shoved off the wall and closed the distance.

"Sorry."

"No, I'm fine. I was just thinking over what all needed to be done," she said. "Is Jacob okay?"

"The delays frustrate him, but he's starting to understand what'll happen if we don't plan ahead, take our time."

"I'm betting it's not easy on you either. You're used to being a lone wolf," she guessed. "It must be hard to have so many differing opinions."

"It is." His jaw twitched. "I could be in, have Jian and be out before Marshall has his plane in the air. But that's not the specialty we need for this operation. I haven't survived two decades in The Collective by being stubborn. I don't have a problem punting the ball to someone else as long as I'm still in the game."

"Good. That'll go a long way toward the guys trusting you on one of their teams. It's their call whether you're on one of the overseas teams, not mine." She chewed her lower lip and waited out the silence.

Jud opened the door leading out of the building. "Come on, I'll walk you to your place."

Her pulse quickened. Jud placed a hand at her waist. "I was raised in a working-class family. Dad was an engineer for the city. Mom was a college professor. We didn't have a lot, but we had each other and that's what mattered. I was raised with a strict moral code, one where you didn't put anyone above your family and you always kept your word."

Jud took her hand. Warmth spread where he rubbed his thumb into her palm, up her wrist. "That sounds nice."

And it did. Very nice. Family first was a concept her parents never quite grasped. She pushed back the thought of her family and focused on his, even though she wasn't sure how she'd earned the glimpse into who made Judson Jensen what he'd become.

"Leaving them, going into the life I led was hard, probably the worst decision of my life. I went years, over a decade without any contact. Jacob wasn't even a concept when I went in and Judith had left Danny and their kid by the time I reestablished contact. I had a brother-in-law in a wheelchair with a brilliant little boy missing his mom and two parents determined to make it right somehow. To fill the wound their daughter ripped into her kid." His jaw twitched. "It took a long time for Danny to recover, heal. But he never quit, he never let the pain take a second of his time away from Jacob. I asked him how he managed one night. As long as I live I'll never forget his words."

Vi took a breath. The emotion in Jud's voice spurred protectiveness in her. She wanted to wrap her arms around him and take away the ache, the pain they'd experienced back then. Maybe Jud and Mary were right. Maybe she hadn't done anything wrong during Danny's rescue, but that didn't make it any easier to see the fallout from the horrible situation. See how it ripped a family apart.

Jud turned so they faced one another. He cupped her face. "The Quillery Edge gave me a second chance with my boy. I'm not going to let them down by wasting a single second."

Breath swooshed from her lungs.

"I'm not going overseas, Viviana."

"You aren't? Why not? Jacob expects you to. The teams expect you to." Confusion muddled her brain. "Why aren't you going?"

"Because you aren't," he answered. "I said I'd stand between you and anyone who came after you. If you think for one second I'm leaving your side because everyone else is, you're crazy."

"They aren't leaving my side. They're doing their job," she shot back. "We can't let a contract on me, Mary, or anyone else neuter our ability to conduct missions."

"I agree. But I'm not Arsenal and my only mission right now is keeping you and Mary safe. The Arsenal is going after my family. While they do, I'm keeping theirs safe."

"I'm not their family," she argued. Thinking deeper than surface level on what he'd said was not happening, not now.

"You are." He squeezed her face between his hands and smiled. "Mary is. Everyone here is, but you're the one I'm protecting first and foremost. I'm not sure what this is between you and me, Viviana, but I want to explore it when all this is settled."

"Explore it? Wait, there's an it to explore?"

"You feel it." He ran a thumb across her lips. "I know you do. I've lived most of my life staring through the sight lines and making split-second decisions on whether someone lives or dies. I've learned to trust my gut."

Her heart thundered in her chest.

"It's telling me you're worth the risk."

"What risk?"

"Any risk," he whispered.

Pleasure assailed her as he pulled her against him and claimed her mouth. The kiss was hot, wanton and everything she needed rolled into one toe-curling moment. She followed his lead, then took over. The war was a duel of desire, a cat and mouse game promising carnal delight if they went further. He tasted of mint and danger.

Jud severed the kiss and offered a grin. "I'll see you in the morning, beautiful."

Beautiful? Ha.

An ugliness settled in her gut. He didn't mean it. She wasn't beautiful. She was average at best. Him declaring her beautiful negated everything else he'd said. One lie meant others, which made sense because he was an operative. They lived or died based on their ability to sell a lie.

He wasn't going overseas to assist with Danny's rescue because he was staying at her side. She scurried into her bedroom and closed the door before Addy wandered out of hers. The distant sound of a running shower offered her a bit of comfort in knowing she'd be alone with her thoughts for a while. She sat on the floor beside her new bed and yanked out the small ornamented box with her supplies. Her mind buzzed like a million command codes with nowhere to go. When her thoughts became too jumbled, or she was too confused or agitated, she had two recourses. Most of the time she ran simulated code in her head. She'd written entire programs in her brain over the years.

But when things got extra jumbled and her brain couldn't handle processing code, she went to the one thing that always worked, the one piece of her childhood she'd kept carefully guarded. The lone strand of goodness and love she'd carried forward into life after her family. Paper quilling.

As a child she'd often become overwhelmed by the data her brain absorbed. Sleeping and focusing proved impossible. After years of trying everything, her mother had finally sat her down and taught her quilling. At first Vi hated it. She'd rather study, read books or ask questions to figure out the why of everything around her. But a nine-year-old didn't have business being a know it all. Punishments never worked beyond the soreness or bruises. Confinement in locked rooms only made her mind twirl faster.

But quilling.

Quilling gave her a secret world, one where she could hide her fears and questions and hopes in tiny scraps of colored paper she folded and curled into any design she wanted. She typed up her dark thoughts from the past few days and sent them to the small printer on the edge of her desk. The paper cutter sat tucked away between the bed and the desk so no one noticed its existence. Tiny strands of colored paper in the wastebasket also went unseen.

She read each sentence as she cut the sheet into individual strands of dark blue, much like Jud's eyes. The white lettering was easily legible if you realized it was there. By the time it was coiled into a teardrop or one of the other shapes she often used in her quilling designs, no one would know the words were there, tucked away. Once they were spun into an intricate design and put away, hopefully they wouldn't haunt Vi anymore.

Quilling hadn't taken away her guilt and pain over what happened to Mary. Nothing would take that away.

Tears filled her eyes at the thought.

We're closer now, Mary. We'll get Jian and then we can get answers. You'll get your closure.

She forced a deep breath as she read the statements she'd wanted to give Jud earlier.

I don't know you, but I want to and that terrifies me.

Thank you for keeping the nightmares away so I could sleep. I wish you chased them away every night. Do you have nightmares?

The only thing that can matter in my life is protecting those I love. I have no space in my life for a man like you.

You look after those you love like I do. Who protects you?

Thank you for staying behind to keep me safe.

You make me feel things I want more than anything and that terrifies me.

I wish I was beautiful, then I'd believe you really wanted me and you could be mine.

Vi studied the narrow strips of dark blue and paired them with lighter shades. An arrow would be a good design to quill, a challenge, but masculine enough. It wasn't like anyone would ever see it anyway. She'd tuck it away in the box with all the others once she was done.

Tomorrow her mind would be ready for the tasks at hand. Save Danny. Secure Jian. Get Answers.

Protect her new family.

8

Vi shouldn't have stayed up as late as she had. The simple quilling design had turned into a complete mandala loaded with thoughts she'd spewed onto paper for the first time ever. There were so many it'd taken hours to cut the papers and curl them up. But her mind was sanitized, wiped clean for the missions ahead. She'd gotten a message from Mary saying the teams bound for overseas were wheels up. Her presence hadn't been required. It wasn't like she could fuel a plane or anything, and Mary could handle whatever else needed to be done from a logistics standpoint.

She paid homage to the coffee goddess Addy for leaving a full pot ready to consume and filled her mug. Her team was backing Gage's up in Dover, so she was around somewhere. The security panel beside her chimed as the door opened. Weird. Addy must've forgotten something. Daylight barely shown through the small kitchen window.

Jud wandered in wearing a pair of loose jogging shorts and a smile. A t-shirt hung over his otherwise naked chest—a very tan, very toned chest. There was less definition in her code lines, and those were very detailed. Her mouth dried as she memorized each ridge, each ripple of flesh and muscle. Each wound and scar. There were a lot.

"Morning," he offered. "Ran into your girl while I was finishing my jog. She mentioned coffee."

Right. Addy. No wonder he was all hot and sweaty. And naked.

Something in her gut twisted, an ugly vise that soured her thoughts. The woman was gorgeous, knew hundreds of different ways to get a man's attention. She was a good match for Jud in every possible way. Then again, he said he'd run into her. That didn't mean they'd...

Heat spread through her when Jud stalked across the room and settled in front of her, close enough for her to reach out and trace his abdominals with her fingertips. She swallowed and focused on where the distinctive groove along both hips disappeared into the band of his shorts. Heat raced up her cheeks when he touched her face and forced her gaze upward, to meet his amused expression.

"What?" She forced the word out despite the embarrassment burning her insides. He'd caught her ogling.

That wasn't ogling. That was outright visual molestation.

"You going to share?" he asked.

Share what? Before she could figure out an appropriate response, his hand settled against hers on the coffee mug. She watched, transfixed, as he brought the mug up to his lips and drank. She tracked the swallow along his throat, then downward to his glorious chest.

It was the single sexiest thing she'd ever experienced with a man. Talk about pathetic.

"Strong."

"I like it strong," she said, forcing her focus back to the coffee and not the man who'd just... Who the hell even did that? Jud was a total man whore. What other reason explained him walking in here barely dressed and drinking from her mug? "Get your own damn coffee."

"We need to talk," he stated.

"Briefing's in an hour. Marshall messaged us all." She motioned toward her cell. "I'll make sure he adds you. It'll be quick since service for them will be spotty at best."

"I've lived in the fast lane a long time now. I make decisions quick and don't look back."

"Good for you," Vi shot back. The last thing she was ready for was a conversation with Jud. She'd spent too much time going over every possible meaning for his words the last time they'd talked. He'd said she was beautiful.

"You think I'm playing you." He leaned forward, entering her personal space without pause. He put one hand on each side of her, palms down on the counter.

Awareness quickened her pulse. She wasn't the sort to back down from a challenge by looking away, but nowhere was safe to look where Jud was concerned. "You can't come in here half naked and decide we're having a conversation."

"Why?" His voice was husky velvet, coarse but smooth at the same time. She shivered as his hot breath fell against her cheek. "Am I bothering you?"

Yes.

"I mentioned this last night, but I'm thinking it didn't root, so I'll repeat myself. I want to see where this is headed."

"Where what's headed?" He was drunk. Or delusional.

"This attraction," he whispered against her earlobe. Her knees nearly buckled. Goosebumps ignited in a slight tremble along her skin.

Jud was lethal to the senses. A pine-scented soap permeated her nostrils when she inhaled. The aroma hadn't affected her when she'd smelled it on other men, but when combined with the rugged way he handled himself, she couldn't help but react. It was like a growly bear swiping his paw and knocking down a honey jar. She wasn't sure whether she was the jar or the honey in this situation.

In a lot of ways she wanted to be the honey. Have his tongue...

Woah. Where the heck was her brain going?

It'd been a while since she'd had any semblance of relationship outside work. The last couple of feeble attempts hadn't ended in more than boring romps in the sack with more sweating and grunting than toe-curling orgasms. Vi didn't think there'd be anything boring about going horizontal with Jud.

Not that she would ever get the chance, not in a million years.

"I'm not your type and you don't even know me. This is nuts," she argued. "I'm not an idiot."

"No, you sure as hell aren't. But you're wrong. I know you."

"Yeah, right."

"I know you spent eleven hours on the line with Jacob's dad when he and his group were stuck in a hotel being bombed by insurgents. I know you forced his convoy mates to patch him up even though they wanted to leave him behind, helped get everyone calmed and bunkered in the safest place possible—a place you scouted out while on the phone with him. I know you are a hell of a woman who puts everyone first and can't understand why anyone would even notice she exists."

Vi's brain ran through the words. She shook her head.

"It was Christmas and he was supposed to be at home, playing Santa for his little boy. He told you about the toys he'd gotten, and you convinced him to add a chemistry set, maybe a rocket or two. Feed the genius, let him soar. Those were your words," he whispered.

God, God, God.

I've got a boy, a brilliant, beautiful boy who scares the crap out of me, Quillery. He's smart, way too good to have an old man like me. He's only four, but so smart. It scares me. I know he can light up the world just like he's lit up my life. I'm so scared of screwing him. What the hell do I do with a little genius?

Don't feed him the fear. Fuel the genius, let him soar. Be there if he falls, but don't hold him down. Teach him it's okay to stumble as long as you get back up and keep trying. Show him courage doesn't come from winning the battle, it comes from looking impossible in the eyes and kneeing his nuts."

"Don't feed him the fear. Fuel the genius, let him soar," she whispered.

"You remember," he said.

"I remember the words. It was a long time ago."

"Fifteen years." Jud's thumb grazed her cheek. "Chemistry sets, computers. It was the stories about the two brilliant women who saved his life that enthralled Jacob. Hearing the things the Quillery Edge did to keep his old man alive shaped what he wanted to be, who he could be."

"That's how Jacob knows us."

"He doesn't know you. He idolizes you, like I said last night." Jud smiled. "MIT was his only focus. No other school was good enough because they weren't where the Quillery Edge went. The kid has your papers memorized."

Her papers? She almost asked which ones—her doctoral dissertation? The articles she'd published before going into Hive?

"I've had more than one conversation with him already, warning him to give you and Mary some space, but the kid's enthralled. If he gets to be too much, let me know. I'll have another word."

"It's fine. He's been through so much. I can't imagine."

"Yeah, he has. He's a great kid." Jud's lips feathered along her skin, so close to contact, yet too far away. "I know what type of woman you are. This is your notice I've set my sights on getting to know you, what makes you tick."

"I don't tick." She hadn't. Ever. Ticked. Ticking meant she was interesting, she had a life beyond the operations she led. Beyond her friendships with Mary and the girls. "I don't even have a cat."

"A cat, huh? We covered this ground before and I thought we agreed to a dog over a cat."

"People who tick would have cats because that'd make them interesting. Dog people are an entirely different level of ticking, a ninja level I'll never achieve." *Important. Worthy.*

His eyes drifted half-shut. Hers did the same thing of their own accord. "This goes anywhere, babe, I'm throwing down for a dog."

"You have a problem with cats?"

"No, but I'm thinking we're more dog people."

"If I've never had a cat, I can't jump straight to a dog. There's a hierarchy of responsibility and interest here, Jud. Dogs are way higher level than a cat. They're higher maintenance."

His lips upturned into a sexy smirk. "You've thought about this a lot. Is there a chart I could study?"

"Don't sass me, Judson Jason Jenson. I'm not a dog person. I'll never be a dog person because I'll never be that interesting." She huffed her frustration at his nerve. He didn't understand she didn't have time to be interesting. Her work was important, required her entire focus, because when she didn't focus she failed.

And people got hurt.

Mary got hurt.

"That's where I'm going to prove you wrong. You could teach a dog, he could be your assistant geek."

"Dogs get taken for walks and play Frisbee and lick their balls. They aren't geeks."

"You can make anyone and anything around you whatever you want them to be, Viviana. That's your superpower. I've got stealth and death in my arsenal." He smiled again. "And a dog."

Vi couldn't help but want to be the phantom superhero Jud

portrayed her as. He was so wrong, but she played along anyway. "What kind of dog? I'm not going for a yappy breed."

"You think I'd get a sissy dog?"

"Maybe. She'd balance you out." She swallowed as he shifted, nudging her back a step.

"I'd be okay with a sissy dog if she had as much sass as you," he whispered. One hand settled on her hip, holding her in place between him and the kitchen counter. "I'm thinking I could use a shot of sass with my morning coffee."

Vi licked her lips, imagining running her tongue along his. A low rumble rolled from him. The hand cupping her face tightened, settling in her hair. "You always such a demanding morning person?"

"Only when I see something I want," he replied as he leaned closer. His lips trailed on her cheek, then the edge of her mouth.

She groaned and turned, locking their lips together. She put a hand on his waist, savoring the rush of heat spreading on her palm like a brush fire. Damn, the man could kiss. She leaned into him and followed his lead, relishing the way he taunted and coaxed her surrender. Slow. Confident.

She forgot she was wearing a thin pair of pajama shorts with a spaghetti-strapped top. She remembered when she felt a pressure against her crotch. His thigh. Wow. She stifled a moan as he deepened the contact. His hands remained in place. He didn't grope or advance anything beyond the carnal kiss and the press of his leg between hers.

"I didn't realize that was on the breakfast menu today."

Vi startled. Addy's voice fractured the blissful numbness of her mind. Vi couldn't remember the last time her mind completely shut down. The entire world had slipped away when he kissed her.

Jud didn't move away. He remained settled against her, leg

pressed between hers. He licked her lips one more time and groaned. "Best damn shot of sass I've ever tasted."

Holy wow.

"I'll see you later. Thanks for the coffee." He snaked her mug and turned away. "And the sass."

She watched him leave, admired the way the shorts he wore molded against his firm ass. And those thighs...they could snap a...

"That was a hell of a kiss," Addy commented.

Yes, yes it was. It'd be smart to head him off at the pass, make sure he knew she wasn't interested. Or interesting. The nerve. She was so not dog owner material. He'd see. She'd make him see. Yep, that's what she should do. All she had to do was figure out how the hell to get uninterested in him.

~

"You didn't go."

Jud froze. Anger filled each word as Jacob fisted and unfisted his hands. He'd searched for his nephew earlier before his run, but the kid hadn't been in his room. "No, bud. I didn't go."

"He needs you. The bastards you work for are behind all this. Blame might be on Jian right now, but we both know they pull his strings. You need to be there to help get Dad out."

Jud sat on the bench and motioned for Jacob to have a seat.

Jacob paced.

Jud looked out at the compound. All six of the brothers went wheels up with their teams. Fallon took a seventh team. A total of thirty-five of the best-trained operatives around were on their way to pull Danny out of whatever hellhole he was in. A part of Jud agreed with Jacob. He should be there. But with the majority of The Arsenal over an ocean and hauling ass toward the sandbox and another chunk preparing to go wheels up for the stateside portion of the mission, the compound itself and those left behind were exposed.

Vulnerable.

"I'm not part of their teams, which means I'd be a liability to them."

"Bullshit. You're the best."

"Yeah, I am." He let the statement settle. He wouldn't lie to his nephew. Ever. "I'm the best when alone. Teams aren't my thing. There's a different mindset, an instinctual one born from years together. Hundreds, if not thousands, of ops. Those operatives going after your dad are the best in the business bar none. I'd pick them over anyone in The Collective, and they've got the Quillery Edge behind them. They've got you behind them. Someone has to keep Quillery and Edge safe, bud. Two more teams go wheels up in a few minutes, which leaves this place and them ripe for attack."

"You think someone's watching and will know they're vulnerable right now? Why didn't you say anything to Marshall and them before they left?"

"Marshall's not an idiot. Everyone in this compound knows what all of them leaving means. They're choosing to put your dad and anyone else being held above their own family. Even if someone isn't watching, an operation this big and all-encompassing is going to hit the radar of people The Collective have access to. They'll know something is in the works."

"They'll warn Jian," Jacob said. "You've gotta make sure they don't warn Jian."

"We've done what we can do. I need you focused on helping Vi and Mary. Get this place locked up tight, whatever it takes. They'll have their minds on Dover and Afghanistan. I know you're worried about your dad, but our focus has to stay on this compound and keeping it and everyone in it secure. You with me?" Jud waited, noting the war of emotions flashing across his nephew's face.

"Yeah. I'll run through the security, see if I see any holes." He looked down, then back up at him. "But you're wrong, Uncle Jud. Our sole focus isn't on keeping the compound secure. We've got to prepare for whatever The Collective's play is because we both know it's coming."

Jacob wandered off. The kid was right. Jud needed to move forward on a new end game—one that severed The Collective's jugular if they stepped over the line he'd drawn. Jud hadn't been lying when he'd said Jian was a puppet to many, but he was primarily The Collective's puppet. Like any good puppet, he was a methodical tool. Though The Collective didn't tolerate people keeping records, notes or anything else that could lead back to them or any operation, Jud knew Jian didn't take chances. He had data. Names. Locations. He'd seen it once, years ago.

Viviana could do a lot with data like that.

Maybe even take The Collective out entirely.

Jud wished he was going with Gage and Addy for the take down, but he wouldn't risk leaving the compound. He tracked the redheaded operative down. She was in the weapons room with her team. The four men all glared at him with a silent warning he'd eat more than one bullet if he stepped out of line.

"What's up?" she asked.

"Need a conversation, a private one."

"Anything you say to me, you say to my team."

"Fair enough." He crossed his arms before him and powered on. "Jian's office upstairs has a hidden safe behind the picture frame. That's the bogus one. It'll contain cash, passports and other important documents. There's a floor safe underneath the sofa near the window. Take whatever you need to blow the safe and secure whatever is inside. It'll likely be a laptop or hard drive, something to store data."

"And why should I believe you?" She tossed a rifle to one of the men and took a couple steps forward. She was tall for a woman but still a few inches shorter than him. "They're tolerating your presence here. If I had my say, you'd be downstairs where you belong."

"You'll believe me and get the documents because when push comes to shove—and we both know it will—they might keep Quillery and Edge breathing. Whatever he has in there shouldn't exist. It'll get the wrong people really nervous. There's too many outside people involved in this take down for us to share this side mission with anyone outside this room. Get whatever is there and don't let anyone know you're doing it."

"I don't ever keep things from Quillery or Edge," she snapped.

"I'll make sure they know."

9

Vi stood beside Mary in Command Central. All teams were wheels up. The briefing had been shorter than she would have preferred, but they'd regroup once everyone was in position. HERA snapped satellite imagery of the three encampments in Afghanistan and Jian's suspected location in Dover. Four simultaneous strikes with eight teams. Possible problems crawled through her mind like an army of unwanted spiders spinning hideous webs of calamity, chaos, and catastrophe.

The door to the room opened. Jud and Jacob entered. The latter set his laptop down where Cord typically sat and plugged in like he'd done it a thousand times. Vi raised her eyebrows and looked at Jud, hoping he got her what the heck look without her having to vocalize a harsh reality—his nephew had zero business in this operations room, especially for this particular mission. There was no certainty they'd find his father. If they did...

Well, sometimes it was better not knowing.

"You two will have your hands full. Jacob and I are running point on compound security. I'm ground operations, he's back office." Jud's authoritative voice rumbled into the room, delivering the first bit of calamity.

Vi looked at Mary, who raised her eyebrows. The truth was she hadn't considered compound security when every team they had went wheels up. She ran her hand down her neck and assessed the situation. Her first failure reared its head and snapped through the room.

"I sent a text to Bree and Rhea. They'll be here in a few minutes," Mary commented. Her gaze settled on Jud. "You think whoever is after us will strike while everyone's away."

"I would."

"Yeah," Vi admitted. "We've got new recruits not on teams here, along with one potential team leader. Marcus Salazar. He's a solid recruit out of the Rangers."

"I'll get everyone to meet us in the debriefing room. No one's wheels down for a while, so we'll sort the plan for here and then refocus on the missions." Mary typed away on her phone.

Vi set a hand on Jacob's shoulder. "Come on, let's get setup so you're ready when everyone arrives."

"So I'm ready?"

"Yeah, like your uncle said, you and him are in charge of compound security until everyone gets back." She forced a smile despite the unease consuming her thoughts.

She'd been so focused on the missions she hadn't seen the obvious. No, she'd gotten cocky. She had assumed HERA was good enough to hold anyone back. No wonder Marshall and the guys were all so growly earlier. They knew the compound would be weak once Gage and Addy went wheels up.

Marcus and nine new operatives arrived on the heels of Bree and Rhea, who both wore white lab coats when they entered.

"What's up?" Bree asked.

"Yeah, I'm afraid I'm low on time. Dallas and the guys cleaned me out of all the darts and juice I had. I need to get more made," Rhea said.

"Have a seat," Jacob ordered. "This won't take long. Uncle Jud, you want to start?"

Jud chuckled as he remained standing in the front of the small room. "I'm thinking everyone here knows all the teams went wheels up and will likely be gone for some time. Gage's and Addy's teams will be back first, but it'll be a while. That leaves this compound very low on security."

"Pfft, it's fine. Drones are flying and HERA will tell us if we have trouble," Bree said.

"I'm thinking he's expecting trouble and we're here for the when, not the if," Marcus said. "I'm not sure everyone in here's heard about the contract."

"Contract?" one of the men said.

"The details don't matter," Vi replied with an edge in her voice. "Jud's right. There's a high likelihood we'll get visitors, very unfriendly ones with their eyes set on getting HERA."

She didn't mention the primary objective of killing her and Mary. Most of the operatives in the room were green and spooked easier than the ones they worked with on a regular basis. Any firefight they might encounter before the teams returned would likely be their first, except for Marcus and a couple of the others.

She looked at Jud. The worrywart in her brain, the small voice doubting everyone and everything, screamed this was a bad idea. What choice did she have? They could have left Addy's team here, but that left Gage's going into a potential shit storm alone. She'd rather risk her and Mary's safety instead.

But The Arsenal facility was more than headquarters. It was the Mason ranch.

Civilians.

Retired soldiers in various stages of recovery and re-acclimation to society.

"Mary and I will have our hands full leading eight teams striking four positions. Jud is in charge of compound security. Jacob here will handle back office surveillance and planning. I need you all to give them whatever assistance they need. You'll likely be pulling some long shifts until Gage and Addy return with their teams."

"A few of the Warriors Path Project participants can probably help fill in gaps," Marcus said. "I've spoken with quite a few. I can see who we can get for secondary support."

"Good. Do it," Jud said.

"Draw Doctor Sinclair into the decision, though. We can't risk any of them regressing," Mary said.

Vi called up HERA's schematics of The Arsenal compound. Green circles appeared on the projection. "These are the active drones and the area they're covering. We can double up, expand outward half a mile around the entire perimeter."

"I wandered around this morning." Jacob pointed to the buildings. "We need sniper positions atop these two buildings, minimum. Uncle Jud could handle one, but we'd be stronger with him fluid in the field. He's a one man army."

Vi wondered how the young man knew so much about Jud's experience and strengths. She couldn't imagine a lone wolf like him sharing much in the way of details. Men like Jud, the silent and deadly variety, didn't have long chats about their strengths and weaknesses. Jud's brows furrowed. Lips thinned, he remained stoic.

"I can help," Bree announced, excited. "I have some new toys. They haven't been field tested yet, but they've fared well in the lab."

"What sort of toys?" Rhea asked, concern evident in her voice.

Sometimes Bree's toys were a bit too complicated for actual execution. The woman had issues dumbing down her ideas to usable schematics. The blonde stood and headed toward the door, but Jud intercepted.

"I need to go get them. It'll take a while to get them set up. They can cover rooftops, though. Two are long range, so they can handle first-line perimeter defense."

Vi bit her lip. She wanted to instill the confidence and experience in Jacob's nephew, but this wasn't a routine exercise. It was grim reality, one she should have foreseen and made better plans to cover.

Like what?

The argumentative voice in her head sounded remarkably like Jud. It was right. The timetable on this entire nightmare was too compressed. She couldn't have gotten secondary teams in place.

"I'll speak with Riley," Marcus offered. "Some locals might be able to come out and pitch in."

Vi didn't like the idea of using locals, mainly because she didn't want any more innocents between her and the bastards determined to kill her. She remained silent, though. This was Jud's play, not hers. She was glad he'd stepped up and taken control of compound security, even if it made the twitchy paranoid part of her uneasy. Hopefully this would be nothing more than a just in case exercise.

"Let's see what we get from the Warrior's Path participants first. Sometimes too many unknowns on a field is more of a risk than having no one."

Vi smirked. Such a typical lone wolf mentality. He'd likely prefer fighting whoever came at them alone. He had a hell of a rude awakening ahead if he thought that'd happen.

"We'll round everyone up and run drills. We can lock everyone in the mess hall if an attack comes. We'll need four guards, but can probably pull those from the Warrior's Path participants," Jacob said. He looked up from the schematics he'd leaned over. Cheeks flamed red, he looked around, then at his uncle. "Right, Uncle Jud?"

"Sounds smart," he replied. "Let's get to it. Bree, why don't you show me those new toys. Jacob and I can help set them up. He'll need to hook them into HERA, right?"

"Oh, yeah." She looked around from where she'd been halted by Jud's presence in her only exit. "Or, I can run them manually myself."

"Pains me to say this since I'm a lone wolf by nature, but we don't need unknown combatants on the field if shit hits the fan. I need Jacob fully aware of the situation so I don't kill friendlies by mistake." He looked over at Vi.

Her pulse quickened when she noted the intensity in his gaze. Heat rose in her cheeks when everyone's attention settled on her.

"You have enough equipment to dole out to everyone? Are there trackers or something where Jacob and I can see who's a friendly? I won't be going for soft take downs if an attack happens."

"Sure." Vi pointed to Marcus. "Marcus and the guys know where the gear is. He can get you and everyone else sorted. We should have enough. Bree and Rhea over order."

"We prepare for any eventuality," Rhea argued.

"Yeah, like armoring the entirety of Texas," Mary muttered with a chuckle. "Vi and I need to get back to the teams. Come back to the theater when you've got the ground teams sorted, Jacob. We'll leave monitors and equipment open for you to use."

"Right. Sure thing, Edge." His voice bubbled with excitement, anticipation.

She followed Mary out and Jud and Jacob continued the debriefing.

"You sure about this?" Mary asked.

"Hell no, but we don't have much of a choice. We should've left one of the teams behind."

"That wasn't an option, we both know it. Marshall and Dylan knew it, too. They weren't pleased we had to delay our application exercise the other day. They'll be chomping at the bit to get it done once this mess is clear." Mary motioned toward the room. "What's up with you and Romeo wolf in there?"

"Nothing," she hedged.

"I heard there was some tonsil hockey over coffee. That doesn't sound like nothing to me," Mary said. "What Dylan and I ran across before that wasn't either."

"Fucking Addy."

"She's worried. So am I. He moves fast."

"He said he's used to making life and death decisions in seconds. He's tired of watching life pass him by while he's staring through the sight lines."

"What about you? You haven't talked to Doctor Sinclair yet. Now we've got everyone we care about in the field and a big target drawn on an almost empty compound." Mary squeezed her arm. "Talk to me."

"I'm okay, scared and more than a little pissed that I screwed up again. I realized we'd be without teams here, but didn't even consider the contract." She lowered her voice. "I didn't think Jud would stay behind. He said he'd trust our teams to get Danny out, that his only mission was keeping us safe."

"Wow."

"Yeah." Wow indeed. "I'm not used to someone wanting to be between us and trouble, you know? It's always been you and me engaging the enemy in the first round. I'm not used to all this."

"All this being Dylan, Marshall and everyone here, too?" Mary asked.

"Yeah."

"It's scary and wonderful all at the same time, like driving a car on a freeway for the first time without anyone else there." Mary hugged her. "We're going to be okay, this is where we should be. This is our home now."

Home. Right. Vi clung to the word, then released it quickly. She didn't have time for foolish notions. She had four compounds to storm and eight teams to get back safe.

To their home.

Which meant it was time to implement one of the many contingency plans she thought up last night. "I want to read Zero D into what we're doing. If things go south, which we know is likely at some point, she's in a unique position to help us."

"Zero D. That's the hacker who helped take down the child pornography rings on the Deep Web a few months ago, right?" Mary scrunched her eyebrows. "I didn't realize you knew who Zero D was."

"I didn't at the time, but the work was stellar enough to get my attention. I did some digging. Zoey Danworth works for the NSA, intelligence analysis."

Mary whistled. "She'd be a good contingency to have at the ready. Let's do this."

Vi was relieved Mary was on board. Reaching out to a potentially new asset was often problematic. There was a fine line between offering enough insight to facilitate a beneficial relationship and sharing too much intel. Knowledge was power and trusting a veritable stranger with anything right now could bite them in the ass. They already had Jud in the mix.

She pulled up the information she'd gathered once they returned to the operations room. Mary scanned the information and nodded her approval as the phone rang.

"Hello?" The hesitant voice sounded from the overhead speakers of the room.

Vi remained standing as she waited for HERA to signal she'd verified the location of the call. Once the system chimed, she responded. "Hi, Zoey. This is Viviana Chambers, though you may know me as Quillery. I'm here with my partner, Mary Reynolds, aka The Edge. We'd like to talk to you about a few things if you have a moment."

"How did you get this number? No, wait." The woman huffed a half-laugh, half-sigh. "You're Quillery. That's how you got this number."

"Sorry, we typically use less invasive tactics to secure a new asset, but we're low on time. My system indicates the number I called is secure. Is that the case?"

"Yes," Zoey replied hesitantly. "I'm at home alone, but you probably already know that. What's up? Is there another perv ring to take down?"

"I'm loving this woman already," Mary replied with a laugh.

Before she second-guessed her gut instinct, Vi offered the woman a brief overview of what they'd uncovered and what they were about to embark on. A couple beats of silence ensued when she finished.

"So you two are leading eight teams through an international four-pronged attack of a drug lord's operations and an international trafficking ring while freeing any hostages or prisoners you may encounter. Did I miss anything?" Zoey's voice pitched a couple beats higher at the end. "I...I don't even know where to begin. You mentioned the FBI, so I'm ignoring the stateside operation altogether. The other three prongs are problematic at best. Have you verified the data with satellite imagery yet?"

"Yes, and we have friendlies en route to recon with drones," Mary replied.

"Okay." The woman dragged the word out. "Why the call then?"

"Contingency," Vi replied. "I'd like to send you what we have gathered so you can verify it with whatever intel you might have access to?"

"You mean the intel you've likely already pulled with that fancy system I'm hearing about?"

"We both know there's always more data than what's buried in surface level data banks," Vi said. "Edge and I are after the blood and bone, not the skin."

"Fine, send it over, but I'm not making any promises. Honestly, you two have lots of people in the intelligence community mighty twitchy, but I admire the hell out of you both. I did before you took those scumbags at Hive down. People are running to ground, though. Lots of letters had themselves tied up with those assholes and they're scurrying to keep out of your wake."

"We aren't hunting for trouble, just taking out the trash after us," Mary said. "If you'd prefer to play it safe, we'll find a new secondary plan."

"But we could use your help. We'll have six teams in harm's way over there, seven if you count the backup team. Most would declare Edge and I idiots for taking this on alone, but the teams are the best around." Vi settled a hand on her hip and gave voice to her concerns. "It's my job to get them back in one piece, but I need your help in case things go sideways. We need someone scanning the chatter, watching for fallout in places we won't have time to worry about. More importantly, we need you keeping our satellite access secure and verifying the data HERA's gathered with what you know. I know you'll have access to more data than we could get."

"Send what you have, the more you share the more I can help. You've clearly looked into me and though we've worked together a couple times, you don't know me. So I'll say this. I won't share what's going down unless I get your permission first. I know things are hot right now, so I'll do what I can. Like I said earlier, I admire the hell out of you for taking Hive down. I know it came with a cost."

Zoey was a hell of a woman. Vi suspected as much based on

the sleuthing she'd done earlier, but the conviction and determination in her voice confirmed it. Mary offered her gratitude and forwarded all the data they'd gathered.

"Thanks, Zero D. We'll be in touch," Vi said as she ended the call.

One contingency plan in place. It was better than nothing.

~

J ud waited until the perky blonde was off the rooftop before he made his call. It wouldn't matter if Bree heard the conversation, but he didn't want to play twenty questions afterward. His skin crawled as he scoped the situation. The teams had left The Arsenal in a hell of a defensible position, one most military compounds couldn't secure. The facility was at the end of a looped road—a road no stranger had a business wandering down. Drones covered every inch of the facility and signaled if any abnormalities were encountered.

Jacob had learned how to switch the sensitivity of the drones and had cranked it down really low. Now something as simple as a cow wandering out of its established perimeter sounded an alarm he and Jud heard. Marcus had recruited five men from the Warriors Path Project with Doctor Sinclair's permission. Rhea had rounded up Riley and her mom and given them a head's up. Together the three women ran drills for getting everyone into the mess hall if the breach alarm was sounded.

All in all, Jud could defend the compound and everyone in it from just about any attack. But he couldn't shake the unease crawling through his skin.

Something stunk. The conversation he'd had with Marla grated his insides. The Collective wasn't going to sit on the sidelines for long because HERA was in play. The more he thought about it, the more he realized they'd make a play to get the system.

And the women behind it.

The line connected. A gruff voice offered nothing aside from, "What?"

Kristof Lavrov was a long-term associate turned friend, the only relationship he'd consistently maintained over the years. The man was the only one he trusted outside family. Though he was in The Collective, he was also a broker like Jian. He was a very sought-after procurement specialist with a unique moral code only he understood. He'd done right by Jud over the years, which was why he deserved a head's up.

"I heard it was going to freeze tonight. You'd best take your plants inside," he suggested. In terms of coded messages, it was pretty obvious, but Jud didn't give a shit.

"I've got all mine covered, man. I'm more worried about yours. You've been busy. Are you sure you don't need help getting yours covered?"

"I should be good, but I'd appreciate a head's up if you see otherwise." He looked around. "I'm in Texas for a while, thinking it's time to move."

"But you're pruning and weeding first," Kristof said. "Be careful. It's a tough job to handle alone, some would say an impossible one."

"Nothing's impossible if you're motivated enough." Jud thought of Danny, the fact The Collective allowed Jian to take him. The fact they probably had more to do with it than they'd admit. "I'm plenty motivated."

"You need help, let me know. I appreciate the freeze warning, man." Kristof ended the call.

He took the stairs down to Command Central two at a time. Jacob was in the midst of whatever made his geek brain happy. He tapped his foot in time to Vi and Mary, as if intentionally mimicking their every move. The three sat side by side in the control room, each working on something for the upcoming missions.

Gage's and Addy's voices filled the overhead as they bantered back and forth.

All teams were in position. The overseas arm of the operation had run through enough dry runs to feel somewhat comfortable to proceed. Translation—they'd run out of time. Sundown yawned over the horizon, which meant the Mason teams overseas would be hitting the camps just after sunrise.

"We're a go in thirty," Vi stated over the com.

Mics checked soundlessly as dots appeared beside the teams. Both Dover teams checked in first. Jud felt helpless as everyone waited. He should be outside, stalking the perimeter, searching for whatever made nervousness settle around him like a second skin. They'd set six of the monitors aside for Jacob. He'd left the farthest exterior drone surveillance up on four of them and alternated between the rooftop drones and the other exterior building drones on the other two. He wondered which of the women had gotten him up and running. Although he sat to the side, both women looked over and scanned his monitors every few seconds, as if preparing to leap to his aid if needed.

"Do we want to know what Bree's new toys are?" Vi asked. She flashed a smile.

"Jesus, you're letting her test new toys while we aren't there?" Addy asked. "Not smart, Quillery."

Quillery didn't have much of a choice. Jud was glad the woman offered them up. He wasn't entirely sure what they did, but the blonde assured him they'd cover the perimeter line easily even though she'd been short on specifics. He hoped to hell so. Neither of the women would leave the room anytime soon and even though his time would be better served ensuring the perimeter was secure, he found himself heading toward the mess hall instead. They needed to eat. His nephew needed to eat.

Riley and another blonde worked alongside an older woman

with the same expressive green eyes as most of the Mason brothers. Their mom. He offered a polite smile as she focused on him.

"My word, you're a handsome one," she commented. "You must be Jud. Everyone around here calls me Momma."

"Nice to meet you, ma'am. Afraid I'll have to stick to Mrs. Mason. My momma wouldn't be too thrilled if you took her place." He motioned toward the plate she handed to him. "Though you're a better cook, but don't tell her I said so. I came to get Jacob, Vi and Mary some grub."

He took the bagged-up plates Momma Mason handed him with a smile and a thank you, then headed back to the computer trip he'd left.

"If I wasn't engaged to the best man in the world, I'd kiss you," Mary declared. "Please tell me one of those is for me."

"It's for you," he said with a chuckle. "Make sure Viviana here eats something. I'll be back later. I'm going to walk the perimeter."

10

"Please, Vi. I need this. I need to see this through. I'm safer in here than in the cafeteria." Riley's imploring gaze stabbed Vi's insides. "All my brothers are out there. I need to understand what they do. They'll never, ever tell me. I'm their little sister. I deserve to know, understand. Mom and I are driving them nuts and they're annoying the hell out of me. They're constantly dodging me at every turn, and I know it's because I don't get what they do. Help me get it."

The Mason brothers had made an art form out of dodging their little sister. She understood their conundrum. And hers. She wasn't the little girl they envisioned, though. She deserved to see how dangerous what they did truly was.

"Fine, but you sit back there and remain quiet. No matter what goes down, you stay quiet. Okay?"

"Okay."

"Come on, I'm observing, too, in case Mary or Vi need me for something," Rhea said. "Bree's on the roof doing something. That alone terrifies me."

Vi smiled. Jud had no idea what he'd unleashed when he'd given her science-minded friend control of perimeter security.

Everyone was in position. Vi looked over at her best friend and recognized the steadfast calm in her gaze. The Edge was in the room. Vi always admired how Mary could summon the lethal calm for an operation. It was why she was the final solution when things went to shit. No matter how bad things might be, The Edge got the teams out every single time. That was Mary's superpower.

Vi...well, she wasn't sure if she had a superpower. She dug, pulled info and data faster than anyone from anywhere. Knowledge was power, especially for field personnel. She hacked into every webcam and video surveillance system within one square mile of the Dover trailer park. Drones flitted overhead and offered insight into the first arm of the mission. Though it appeared the auction itself would take place on-line in one of the trailers, the true target was the large two-story Victorian style home half a mile down the road.

Apparently, Jian was too good to stay in a trailer and had rented the large mansion nearby.

Gage's team would engage the trailers and secure the area while Addy's handled the house. Vi had hacked into the Dover power grid and would kill lights to the area. Both teams had set up frequency jammers that, when combined with HERA's drones, should prevent any notifications from getting through to the three base camps in Afghanistan. Vi studied the latest images she'd just received from the Delta team that'd performed a preliminary recon of all three camps. They'd even dispensed a sand crawler into each of the three camps and left it active.

She shot off the latest intel they'd gathered to Zero D, just in case. They'd already sent her links to the auction site and all data they'd collected so far.

Vi had forgotten the team even had sand crawlers. They were one of Bree's toys, one that passed all field-testing with remarkable results. It burrowed into sand and other fine granular sediments and navigated its way around while it performed a grid-like sweep of the area for IEDs and other nasty surprises lurking beneath the ground. So far, the little monsters had flagged several hot spots in all the camps. She compiled the data and sent them to the team leaders. Fallon's team, as standby, received all data.

You should have left Fallon's team here. You screwed up.

Vi shoved the thought away and focused on the encampments. All three were bordered along two sides by poppy fields. The waist-high opium source was problematic at best and an outright disaster at worse. Armed militants roamed the area, watching over the fields and the workers within them. She zoomed in on the emaciated, barely-clothed people working the crops and snapped images of the restraints. Thin chains around their necks and wrists encumbered movement, but didn't seem to stop their ability to work completely. They were obviously prisoners, but she'd have to dig deeper to determine what kind. Innocents? Possibly. Political prisoners from a neighboring warlord? More likely.

HERA spewed identifications on the captured images of the armed militants and the prisoners. Her gut clenched as she pieced together the evidence they needed to green light the op.

"That's a lot of beeping," Jud commented.

"Beeps are good, right?" Jacob asked.

"Yeah, beeps are very good," Mary replied. "HERA's putting the final nails in this operation. Some of the workers in the fields are from your dad's convoy."

"And Dad?" The boy's gaze moved to their monitors and away from his own.

Vi cursed fate as she studied the images. There'd been six teams spread out to cover the three camps. With no idea what was in each, it'd been a crap shoot at best—one that'd showed fate was a twisted little bitch sometimes. Jesse's team was one of the two in the camp most likely to hold Danny. Jesse and Nolan's teams were in position and ready to move, but she still wasn't sure Jesse had any business in this operation.

She called up his record, reviewed the file of his capture and subsequent rescue. What he endured was unfathomable. The fact he was still out there, doing what kick ass operatives did to keep people safe proved he was a hell of a man.

She keyed in Nolan's personal com and turned the others off so only he'd hear what she said as she fed the images she'd pulled out of the primary feed and sent them to him. "Your site is hot."

"Roger." Nolan's grim voice filled the speakers. He didn't go into detail on what she'd sent.

She felt Jacob's attention on her. Jud approached and put a hand on the young man's shoulder. "Get to work, bud. I need you focused on keeping them safe. Quillery and Edge are working to get your dad out."

"Drone surveillance puts the exfil at twenty-one, three of those in immobile status."

"And the other camps?" Nolan asked.

"More militants, less than ten exfil in each once the dust settles," Mary added. "We need Fallon's team on camp two. There's enough firepower there to light up half the country. I feel like a fireworks display is in order."

"Roger," Nolan replied. "Will send data shortly."

"Data?" Jud asked.

"His team is primary. He'll assess the data I provided and decide who goes where. He'll send his plans to me and we'll program each person into the schematic so HERA can do her thing." Vi motioned toward the schematics. "HERA will do a SWOT analysis of Nolan's plan and offer feedback to his field device. He'll see each person's strengths versus the anticipated skirmish and provide feedback from there. The biggest piece of data he'll have to provide as the battle ensues is the physical and emotional status us his team members."

"You're worried about Jesse. I saw his file pulled up earlier." Jud sat in a seat he'd dragged over at some point.

"He's one of the best soldiers around."

"You're still worried," he whispered.

"It's my job to worry." She focused on the op and tuned out the man looming near enough for her to reach out and touch him. "All camps, we're a go in three. Release drones for first phase clearing."

Team leads in all the camps tapped their assent. Green dots appeared beside their team numbers on the display overhead.

"Power is down in Dover. Jammers are operational. Both teams are a go for entry," Mary said as she stood.

Vi ignored her best friend's standing stance. Mary always stood. When things got bad, she paced. It was her thing. Vi was the immovable force behind the computer. Come hell or high water, her ass was planted in the seat. Drone feeds streamed in, so much between all the encampments, Vi almost couldn't keep up.

Eliminate the unnecessary. Let HERA guide you.

And she did. The system was a genius at dispensing warnings, offering a clue where attention needed to be. Dover was the first problem at hand. There were too many unknown variables in too wide of a space. Unlike the three militant camps overseas, innocents surrounded the two targets stateside. Civilians who had no idea there was a sex trafficker of women and little kids living next door.

She zoomed drones toward lots twenty-eight through thirty, in the back at the top of the horseshoe-shaped park. Audio mics picked up angered shouts. Flashlights flickered back and forth, up and down as the combatants attempted to figure out what was happening. Vi flicked the floodlights on the two larger drones on, flooding the area to offer Gage's team an easier take down. Gunfire echoed from the area as one of the men aimed his semi-automatic rifle at the drones and fired.

So much for a clean take down.

She aimed. Fired. One sleeper dart down.

"They're all yours, Dover one."

"Roger," Gage replied. "We're moving in."

Mary was helping Addy's team penetrate the two-story Victorian, so Vi focused on the overseas teams. With two teams per encampment and enough drones to take on the Death Star, the teams had the situation well under control for the first phase—which focused on taking down as many of the armed baddies as they could before the teams actually moved in.

Drones in the three overseas camps weren't armed with sleepers. Anyone hit wouldn't be getting back up. She focused on Nolan's camp first, helping down as many baddies as she could by taking control of the drones. Once they were out of juice, she flew them toward Jesse's team, who got to work refueling them.

With a few moments to spare, she focused on the second encampment. With two of the best operative teams around involved, she felt relatively confident she wasn't needed. She scanned data from the drones and field operatives. So far so good, but the fight hadn't really started. This was the shock and awe stage—the moment when the other side hadn't figured out they were in someone's cross hairs.

Camp three had a heck of a lot of baddies, almost twice as many as the other two combined. Did they have enough juice? Probably not. Dallas and Dylan had this camp. Mary was already engaged, moving drones into position to take down militants until Fallon's team arrived to assist. Vi shifted her attention back to Dover. Gage's team swept the trailers with precision speed.

Addy's team met resistance.

Vi activated control of two drones and got to work knocking out baddies. One idiot chose to run, but she chased him over a fence and through a neighbor's yard. Spotlight on, she waited until he fell to the ground, hands in the air. There was no running from HERA. She aimed and fired a sleeper dart. She keyed in the coordinates so someone would come and haul the trash away.

"Team two, where are you going?"

"Sweeping the upstairs. I heard movement." Addy's voice was barely discernible. "I'm handling the side mission, Quillery."

Side mission? What the hell?

"I asked her to go up there and get something," Jud said.

"When?" She remained focused on the feeds, alternating between camp one and Dover. Mary had camp two and three well under control, even though the number of red dots at the latter was growing. More baddies were moving in. "Team two, what's your status?"

"Operatives three and four have the target secured in the southwest corner, first floor," Addy said. "Target is immobilized."

Thank fuck. They had Jian.

She ignored the side mission, though anger seeped into her thoughts. How dare Jud order her teams to go somewhere without telling her? And for what? The niggling doubt she'd nurtured grew a bit stronger as she spent a couple seconds figuring out what his objective really was with this entire operation. Why was he here instead of there?

Then she noted the camera feeds from Jesse's headset and froze. Son of a bitch.

"Bravo one, team four has eyes on packages."

"Dad?" Jacob asked.

"Eyes on the monitors, bud," Jud ordered.

The view from the camp was dark, clouded with dust and debris. Gunfire echoed in the distance. Someone beside Jesse flicked their headgear light on.

"We have three DOA and four in critical. Need medical evac. Be advised primary objective has been located." Jesse's voice offered little emotion.

Crap. They'd anticipated medical evac, but she'd hoped it

wasn't necessary. The Delta team helped her secure medical choppers and a couple SEAL teams standing by at the rendezvous. Though having SEALs swoop in and help at the camp itself would be awesome, this wasn't a sanctioned mission. The less they were involved, the better.

Vi switched monitoring of Jesse's view to her laptop. A couple keystrokes later and she was seeing exactly what he was. Son of a bitch. Angry red lines ran along the men's torsos. Untended wounds seeped. Bled.

"You have antibiotics available, team two?"

"Roger, Command." Jesse's voice lowered. "I'm not going to hurt you, sir. I'm Jesse Mason. I'm here to get you out."

"Stay back from him!" an angry voice shouted. "It's not his turn. Take me instead, you son of a bitch. Keep away from him."

"Don't mess with him," another voice shouted. "He's had enough. They both have. Take me."

"Jesus," Jesse let the visual in his headset sweep through the room. Vi studied the situation. Her gut clenched when she realized who the two resistant prisoners were protecting. Chains rattled as the other prisoners surrounded the man Jesse was trying to give aid to.

"Give one of them the headset," she ordered.

The drones were slow establishing identities. Facial recognition scans proved problematic when the person was mired in filth and prolonged, repetitive injury. The first man's identification came through. She closed her eyes as Jesse tried to give the com to him.

"His name's Joe," she offered.

"We're here to help, Joe. I have someone here wanting to talk to you. She'll explain what's going on while I tend to Danny."

"Don't get near him," the other man warned.

"My name's Jesse. I was in a hole a lot like this one not too long ago. Let me get you out. Talk to Quillery."

"Where'd you hear that name? Are you bugging us?" Joe demanded.

"Talk to her and find out." Jesse held the com out.

The man's eyes widened. He snagged the com. "Who is this? Danny mentioned a Quillery, said she was an angel heaven sent."

"I'm no angel, Joe. My name's Quillery. My partner Edge and I are leading this operation to get you and your men to safety, sir. I'm sorry it took so long to locate you and your convoy."

"They separated us, Quillery. I don't know where the others are."

"We have secured the other two camps. I need you to stand down and let my men work on yours."

"Pat, William and Jay didn't make it. I wouldn't let them burn their bodies. They deserve a proper burial. It's been a couple sunrises since the last one went. I'm afraid a couple others aren't gonna make it."

"We aren't losing any more men, not today. Not ever, Joe. Now I want you to stand down and let Jesse work, okay?"

"Are you really Quillery?" The man's voice cracked. "Heard lots of stories about you and your girl."

"I'm sure you have. I'm thinking your pal there made some stuff up to make time go by."

"There was mention of a cape."

"I'll have to add that to my costume. Are you okay to let Jesse take over from here? We've got another couple of camps to help out."

"I'll trust him since you do," Joe supplied.

"I look forward to meeting you soon, Joe." She waited as the man returned the com to Jesse. The second he was back, she finished. "None of the convoy has any known drug allergies. Get them injected and get them out. Medical is standing by at the rendezvous point."

She typed out an encoded message to the SEAL team waiting a

half click away. It must've been hell for them to not engage when gunfire ripped through the sky. But they'd done as requested and hung back, just in case.

Although she wanted to remain focused on Danny as Jesse assessed his condition, she had other teams needing her help. She took over drones in Dover, swept the grounds for any abnormalities. Heat signatures in a distant corner on the lower level in the kitchen looked off. "Team two, we need someone to walk the lower northeast sector, kitchen area. Heat signatures look off on the drone."

"Roger," Addy said. "Sideline package is secure."

Right. Sideline package. She looked over her shoulder and froze. Jud was gone. Jacob's widened gaze regarded her as the chimes from his displays drew her attention.

The Arsenal was under attack.

"Uncle Jud and I have this under control, Quillery. Get Dad and the others home. We've got this." The young man turned his attention back to the monitors. "I'm sounding the warning, Marcus. Jud wants everyone in the mess hall."

Vi's gut soured. The Arsenal was under attack. She needed to help.

She looked at the monitors. Adrenaline surged. A calm swept through her. No. Jud would handle whatever messed with the compound. She and Mary had teams to bring home.

"Team seven, this is command. Come in." Mary paced.

Vi noted the movement as her mind processed the statement. She studied the feed data from camp three and realized Fallon's team never arrived. What the hell? Dread settled into her gut and churned. She did a cursory check of the other teams and camps. Dover was done. Camp one was clear of baddies, but the teams would be there a while assessing injuries and preparing for exfil. Camp two was clear and flagged as moments from heading toward their exfil. Camp three was neck deep in baddies.

The external com line dinged on her headset. She glanced at the number flashing across the display monitors and clicked it on. "I'm a little busy, Zero."

"There's a training camp one point three clicks northwest of the third camp. You need to kill the supply line or you'll never clear that camp."

"Satellite images and recon didn't note a camp," she argued.

Data streamed into her feeds as she allowed Zero remote access into a shared hub.

"It's a pop-up camp, moves every few days. This one came from the eastern region you weren't reconning and set up a day ago," Zero explained. "I only know because we're watching the other group your target's joining forces with. They struck a deal a few days ago."

"Appreciate it."

"Quillery, get your men out and get gone. The group your hitting is connected, the kind of connected I can't talk about." Translation—someone stateside was funding operations or involved somehow. Someone stateside with enough weight to push the alphabet agencies around.

They were neck deep in bullshit and she didn't have time to swim to shore. "Appreciate the head's up, but I gotta cover my teams. If you want to help, find my missing team. Team eight on the data you were sent was en route to camp three and never arrived. I've given you access to HERA's system and the trackers we have on the equipment and the team members. Get me a location and intel."

"On it."

Fuck. She'd just let a stranger into HERA, probably not the wisest decision she'd made but they needed more hands on deck. Mary had to keep the other teams moving toward exfil with wounded in tow. Oh, and she'd also taken over most of the drones in camp three.

Vi forced a deep breath. Mary had assumed control of the exfil on the other camps while Vi had been on the phone and running drones in camp three. She typed in the coordinates of the training camp and sent them to Dallas and Dylan's wrist devices. She studied the satellite images HERA was processing and determined where the biggest payload for explosive ordnance. Weapons caches. A fuel truck.

"I need one of you at those coordinates with ordnance. Team eight is MIA. Intel indicates reinforcements are coming from those coordinates. Neutralize with ordnance at the three zones indicated. I'll guide two zapper drones with whoever goes, but we need to go now."

"I'll go," Dallas replied quickly. "En route."

"I didn't agree to that," Dylan growled.

"You're older and slower, brother."

Vi let the banter go back and forth as she extracted two drones from the firefight and followed Dallas's path to the new zone. Until they got the troop supply neutralized, camp three wouldn't get cleared. Right about now was when she wished they had access to a kick ass military chopper with enough payload to make the freaking camp a sink hole. Sadly, that wasn't on her available armament list today, so they'd make do.

"Camp two is at exfil, two minor injured personnel. Camp one en route with SEAL team accompaniment for medic evac," Mary offered.

Vi kept focused on Dallas's progression through hell. It was the only word that described the brutal pace he'd set, the wake of death he carved out in his path. "I didn't realize you were so good with a knife."

"I took a lesson a long time ago from the best around," he commented. "Someone you just met, actually."

Jud.

Vi held onto the nugget of information as she swept her gaze over to Jacob's monitors. The compound was under attack.

Focus. Keep Dallas breathing. That's your objective.

Neutralize the supply line.

Close camp three.

Find Fallon's team.

Get everyone home. Alive.

11

They'd found Danny. Beaten, tortured, half dead. Rage mottled his vision a moment. Jud took a deep breath and slipped into the mental zone where all bets were off, he'd do whatever necessary to obtain the objective. Today that was keeping The Arsenal secure.

"Uncle Jud?"

"I'm here, bud. Get Marcus to sound the signal. We need everyone secure in the mess hall before I start cleaning house."

"Okay. He's on it. Erm...the weird blonde is on her way up to the roof. Should I let her up there?"

Good question. Bree was a bit stranger than the average person, probably because she had so much genius and not enough brain to fit it all into. "Yeah, let her up. Is she wearing a vest?"

"She's mummified in Flak."

Jud chuckled as he unsheathed his knives. "How many are the drones picking up, bud?"

"Ten so far, I can probably get a couple with the drones if you want. I've been watching Vi and Mary fly them."

"I need you high level, bud. You're my eyes. Let me know where the threats are. I'll neutralize." He thought about the battle ahead. "It won't be pretty, bud."

"War never is. They're after Quillery and Edge. They started it. You end it."

Jud loved that kid. He settled the headgear on, giving his eyes a couple moments to adjust as data streamed by. "I don't want it all, bud. Give me locations and counts. I'll handle the rest."

"Right. Is this better?" A grid of the compound appeared. A huddle of green dots in the mess hall. Red dots moved inward. A few blue dots appeared. Marcus and the others.

"That's perfect, bud. Get Marcus and the others working to clear the ones near the Mason house and the cottages." Jud didn't like the idea of those bastards near where Viviana and the others slept. Where Momma Mason lived. "Keep them out of my way."

Jud studied the other red dots, moved silently through the vacant corridors and waited. Ten operatives was an insult. First phase, the sacrificial lambs. He chuckled into the com as he headed outside and inhaled the fresh air. The scent of death would permeate it soon enough. A knife in each hand, he prowled toward the first set of red dots. The first kills would set the tone— lob the first statement over the bow for whoever watched from a distance, waited.

They'd been warned.

The two men's attention was drawn to the drone circling overhead. He slipped behind the first and thrust a blade into his jugular. The gurgle of blood was music to the raging beast in him, the one that demanded more. He struck the second man, not bothering to catch either as they died where they stood. Too quick. Too painlessly.

"Incoming," Jacob said. "Fuck! Get down."

Jud ducked as a concussive boom thundered from overhead. Blue light struck outward like a ball of wicked lightning. It blasted an area toward the fence line. A feminine whoop echoed from overhead. Jesus, the woman was a certifiable loon. "I think she's got the perimeter handled, bud. Let me know if that changes."

"Right. Okay."

He continued, focused on the next four red dots appearing nearby. Another set of six appeared from the same area. "Need drones over in the southwest zone. They're coming in from over there. Get Bree's toy focused in that area."

"Roger."

A red haze settled over Jud's vision as he struck the group of four. A momentary flash of reality offered one beat of data—he knew these fuckers, recognized the team leader. Jud thrust a knife into his femoral artery and growled. "Warned you to back off."

The man's eyes widened as he fell. One woman managed a kick to his side, but he tossed both knives forward, striking her two teammates as he twisted her neck. The Collective knew better than engage him in hand-to-hand. Idiots.

"HERA's sounding alarms all over. Bullets. I think we have snipers." Sounded about right. Jud went around the corner of the building and crouched as the concussive boom of Bree's toy sounded again. The blue ball shot out, toward the direction Jud had wanted.

Screams filled the air.

"Get more drones out there, give us visuals on what the second string is, bud."

"Roger."

Jud plowed through three more operatives. Blood sprayed, bodies fell. Pain radiated from his ribs. Blood oozed from his side.

"Incoming friendlies from your six," Jacob said. "Marcus and a couple others are moving to help."

"Get them inside. Guard where you are."

"Roger."

Jud worked best alone. Anything with a pulse was a target that way. The only color he saw right now was red. He leaned down and yanked his knives loose, pausing long enough to wipe the blades. Movement from the side drew his focus. He fired off both. Grunts echoed as he moved on. The HERA headset was the perfect companion. It didn't boss, just offered targets. Locations. Numbers.

He fell into the zone, losing track of time as he hunted. He took a deep breath, inhaled the stench of death. His gut soured. He'd dirtied The Arsenal with his carnage.

"We'd appreciate it if you'd leave one alive for questioning." Viviana's voice soothed the raging beast within him.

"No need. They're Collective, recognized the shady bastard leading them." He looked around, noting he'd lost track of time along the way. No red dots appeared in his headgear. Blue hovered around and inside the primary building—well away from him.

Drones flitted about around him. It'd been too simple. The Collective had a massive hoard of teams. Why send so few for a six-million-dollar payday? The situation stunk. "We need to sweep the compound, the grounds and at least two miles around. This was too easy."

"That was easy?" Bree asked into the headset. "I never want to see your definition of bad."

"We took out the second phase, too, Uncle Jud. Drones aren't picking up anything." Jacob's voice rose with excitement. "They underestimated us. They went against the Quillery Edge and the Judge and got punished. Hard."

"Rule one of back office is we never celebrate a perceived victory, not when our teams are still in the field. We assess what's unfolded and predict what could befall them around the corner. It's not a celebration until everyone's home and secure." Viviana's voice tumbled through the com, calm and almost seductive. Confident and cautious. "Let me know when you're clear, Jud. Marcus is inbound."

She knew he wasn't clear, had likely handled men like him a while. Men who embraced the rage and slipped into the killing zone as easily as taking a breath.

"I'm clear."

"Head to the visitor parking area. We'll converge there and assess," Mary ordered.

"And the teams?"

"We had a complication I'm handling right now," Viviana replied. "Mary will help you and Jacob with the compound."

Jud didn't ask about Danny and the others. He needed to keep Jacob focused, in case the next hammer fell. He stepped over the bodies and made his way toward the designated zone, which was marked with a big, green x in his display. He didn't bother hiding the smirk when Mary exited the building with his nephew in tow. The kid's eyes were wider than saucers and he was firing off commentary at a thousand miles an hour. Mary was tapping her handheld tablet. Bree flounced out behind them. Her hair was disheveled as if she'd gone ten rounds with a monster and lost.

"You okay?" Mary asked her.

"Peachy," the woman replied. "I had a few issues with the new toys, but we worked it out. They're listening to Mommy now. We're good."

Mary's gaze narrowed, but she didn't comment.

"It'd be better if we did this debrief inside," he said.

"Sheriff Patterson's on his way with his deputies. I've also alerted the alphabet soup, but I'm not sure which will show up to slap a classified sticker on our party before Nomad sends their crime squad and collects the bodies." Mary put a hand on a hip. "You're a messy one."

Amusement glimmered in her gaze as it settled on him, then swept downward. "Looks like you need a trip to medical."

"I'm fine." For the first time in a long while he realized the words rang true. He was fine. The few hours after a mission were always the roughest, when doubt fed guilt and they chewed away at every move he'd made, every life taken.

Neither moved in and settled in his gut this time. He'd warned everyone to stay away from Viviana and Mary. They hadn't listened.

"This isn't over," he warned the women.

"No. The war just started." Mary crossed her arms and looked around. "You're right. This was too easy."

"You didn't even see the fight. Have you seen how many bodies our one-man army here piled up?" Bree asked.

"They would've known he would," Jacob said.

"Vi, I need your eyes on the situation here. Something's off. You at a holding point?" Mary asked into the headset. "Right, okay. Well I need your eyes on this for two minutes. You're better at assessing scenarios than me."

Mary reached over and pushed a button on the side of his headset. Vi's voice filled his ear.

"One second," Vi said. "I need you farther away before you blow this, Dallas. You're too close."

"She's a bit busy," Mary replied. "Okay, so first and second wave were taken out. Drones aren't picking up a third wave anywhere close. Maybe they're waiting."

"That doesn't make sense," Vi replied into the com. "Dallas, I said farther away, not closer. I'm knocking you aside the head when you get back. So, Jud, I hear you taught Dallas how to use a knife. He's pretty handy."

"Pfft, she clearly hasn't seen your handiwork out here yet," Mary replied.

Explosions sounded through the com line. Jud's insides clenched as silence descended.

"I'll stay here and pick off stragglers," Dallas said. "Get everyone exfiled from camp three. I'll rendezvous with them at exfil."

"Roger," a voice replied.

"Okay, let's look at the compound problem," Vi said. He could almost hear her brilliant mind processing the scenario, running what-ifs. "Call Patterson. Get him and his deputies to back off, stay far away from here."

"Why?" Jacob asked.

"Because they are the third wave," Vi said.

"The crime squad," Mary whispered. Face pale, she motioned Bree inside. "Get up and get your new toys moving. The next wave is about to hit."

Fuck. Of course.

"Command, this is team seven. Come in."

"Where the hell have you been?" Mary's voice was lethal calm but steely with rage.

"We ran into a few unfriendlies needing an education in manners," Fallon replied. "We're en route to exfil. I'm rendezvousing with Dallas at camp four to assist. My team will help with camp three."

"Roger," Viviana replied. "Glad you're okay."

"We'll talk about why we're okay when we return home, Command. We had a big assist."

Jud was glad the teams were all accounted for, but he didn't ask about Danny. He was surprised Jacob hadn't, but he suspected his nephew was still in shell shock over the attack they'd just neutralized. Now all they had left was the next wave. Then the real war would begin.

The Collective made a huge mistake today by ignoring his warning.

~

The external line rang as Vi clicked off from the teams. Everyone was present and accounted for.

"Zero. What just happened?"

"I helped neutralize the problem your team ran into. I'm burned," the woman said. "It wasn't a take down like Hive, but I did what I could to keep good men breathing. I hope it's enough."

"It was. They're en route home, with a few stops to hospitals and military bases along the way." Vi read the subtext behind the woman's statement. "You hung your ass out there for me today, Zero. I won't forget that. Get yourself secure, get out and come down here. Edge and I always have room for someone of your caliber. Come help those good teams breathe every day."

"I'll have fall out from what I did today. I pissed a lot of people off," she admitted.

"Get up and walk out like nothing is wrong. They won't move, not right away. Don't go home. Get in your car and drive to the nearest airport. There'll be a ticket waiting there for you. If you want, I'll send an escort to bring you home. We've got two teams in Dover."

"No. I'm good," the woman said quickly. "I've gotta go home. I have a cat."

Vi couldn't help but laugh as she wondered what Jud would think about the cat. "Stay where you are, in public. There's a coffee shop down the road from the base you're working at. Gage Sanderson will meet you there in one and a half hours. I'm sending you his picture. Don't trust anyone but him. Get to that coffee shop. Edge and I will have you on surveillance the entire time. I've pinged our cell numbers and Gage's to you. He'll help you secure your cat and gear. Okay?"

"Okay."

She sent the data and orders to Gage. She headed outside as she studied the bloody carnage awaiting her. Jud's wake was extensive, and proved what Dallas had said. The man knew his way around knives. Marcus and a couple of the new operatives arrived. The potential team lead's gaze swept over the bodies, then at Jud. He offered a lone chin lift, which was returned. Men. Mary had extra drones heading toward the fence line. The operatives tracked their progression.

"There's still a problem," Marcus guessed.

He was a recruit from Delta, a recommendation passed to Nolan. So far, he'd fared well and all the Mason brothers wanted him fast-tracked to a lead role. Vi glanced up at the rooftop closest to the fence line.

"Potential enemy penetration of the crime scene investigation, or the alphabet soup. We won't know who, if anyone, is a threat," she said.

"Until they are," he finished.

"Me and the guys will take the rooftops. Sal here is a sniper. I can snipe from the roof. Where do you want him?"

Vi studied the area. Before she could reply, Jud was motioning past the entry. "Across the road, where the incline starts. That'll box them in if needed."

"On it," Sal said.

"You should be in medical letting someone tend that wound instead of bossing around my men." She yanked Jud's shirt up and ignored the blood sticking it to his skin.

Most wasn't his. But someone got a hit. She turned him around. Exit wound. Whew. At least there wasn't a bullet wandering around in Jud's body. Heat spread through the palm splayed on his abdominals. She peeked up at him. He stood motionless, mouth tipped up in a slight grin as she molested him like she had every right to.

"You done?"

"No," she clipped. "Get inside and to medical."

"If you think I'm running inside while another squad of

Collective agents comes to plow you and Mary down, you're crazy." His voice lowered, rumbling with a rage she'd noted on the footage. "I warned them off, they didn't listen. I know you're used to being the growly dog in the yard, the one who goes after the bad guy first. But we're in a bigger, badder yard than before, Viviana. This isn't just your fight, not any longer."

"There you go comparing me to a dog again, Judson," she snapped.

"I'm thinking a Rottie with a couple pups," he commented. "An instant family."

Her belly warmed at the thought. She curled her toes in her sneakers and rocked back on her heels. As much as she'd love to argue the merits of cats over dogs, they had a situation to handle. Nomad was the larger town of what locals called the tri-county. Nomad was the north most point of the triangle for the county of the same name. Resino was twenty miles southwest and in a different county. It was fifteen miles west of Marville, which was a dump of a village twenty miles south of Nomad and in a shadier-than-hell town.

Vi let her mind wander to Riley's friend, Rachelle. Trouble of some sort had spooked the blonde and they'd hauled her over to stay at the main house. With things going sideways with their own mess, Vi and everyone else hadn't had time to wade into whatever trouble lurked at their backyard. They would, though, as soon as they figured out what the heck was about to go down. A high-pitched whistle sounded from across the way. Excellent. Sal was in position.

"We have incoming," Bree shouted from the rooftop.

"Let me take the lead on this one," Jud requested. Hand on the small of her back, he leaned down. "Jacob, help them get personnel records for Nomad. We need facial recognition scans on everyone. Hack into their bank accounts, personal data. Make sure there's no abnormal deposits, payoffs, assets moved under their name. If someone paid them off to get them in, there will be a paper trail of some kind. Greed makes people stupid."

Vi flashed a look at Mary, who grinned. It was fun to work with someone more paranoid than them for a change. "Mary, you and Jacob head inside. I'll handle the front line with Jud."

She didn't want her best friend anywhere near danger. She'd endured enough. Fortunately, neither she nor Jacob offered her any guff. Marcus had slipped away, hopefully to take a higher position. She and Jud were alone. Too bad they hadn't at least gotten him a clean shirt or something. He looked like a rejected extra for some *Rambo* movie, but way sexier.

Approach would be tricky. If they gave away their suspicion by being leery, a kill shot could be made from fairly far away. Neither of them wore a bulletproof vest. She made a mental note to get onto Jud for not bothering to try and wear one. It's like he was made of Teflon and shit just slid off him. Her pulse quickened as vehicles appeared. Sheriff Patterson and a deputy exited from the first. So much for keeping the nice man out of their unfolding drama.

"I heard there was a ruckus out here. The boys aren't here?"

"No, they're gone. We had some trouble, but we're handling it." Vi let her gaze settle on the coroner's van and crime scene unit from Nomad. "You'd best head back home, Sheriff. This mess is more in the alphabet soup camp."

"Right." He remained behind the door to his vehicle. "Gary, get on the horn to Nomad, get them on the way."

"But..." The deputy's gaze widened as he scurried into the vehicle.

"We heard there was some trouble," one of the men commented.

"There was." Jud moved in front of Vi. "There is. Take a look around, we've got higher ground advantage on two sides and enough juice in the drones to need a few more bags when the real coroner arrives."

"I don't understand."

"Ready on your mark." The statement resonated confidence Vi appreciated. She hadn't thought too much of Marcus, but he'd gone to the top of her cool list.

"You know I was ready five minutes before the bastards showed up," Mary declared. "Light the bastard up if he reaches for a weapon."

"Roger."

"Roger."

Vi's gaze swept to Sal's position across the road. The coverage was sound. Two snipers and an army of pissed off drones? The bastards moving around her didn't stand a chance.

"You fucked up," Vi stated. She let anger and rage fill her words. "I don't give a shit who you are or who you work for. There's no out for you, not today. Anyone who comes after my crew doesn't walk away breathing."

The man moved his hand behind him, but blood appeared on his forehead. One of the other men screamed. Drones whirred overhead. Chaos ensued. A heavy weight settled atop her as the drones spewed darts. Bullets flew. Sheriff Patterson remained behind the door to his vehicle, returning fire.

But the fight was over. Drones zoomed and darted toward Sal, then moved the direction the vehicles had come. Mary was seeking more prey for the drones. Vi shoved, but the weight atop her didn't budge. It grunted.

No. He grunted.

"Get off me, Judson."

He chuckled as he rose up on his arms and looked down. "You're definitely not a boring cat person, Viviana."

12

"I don't give a damn if you're so important the President wipes your ass. Get in your car and get the hell off this property or I swear I'll dart you and your minions and pile you all in the trunk."

Jud suppressed his amusement, but barely. It'd been four hours since chaos rained down on The Arsenal's front gate. Vi stood with both hands on her hips as she glared up at a suit from Homeland Security. They, along with the FBI and another unnamed guy that stunk of CIA, had shown up and attempted to run roughshod over the situation. That hadn't gone over well.

At all.

"Ma'am, if you don't step out of the way and do as I say, I will have you arrested."

"Go ahead and try," Vi warned. "If you so much as blink in the direction of my compound, I will shoot you."

"You don't have a gun," his helpful partner replied.

Guns cocked around her as Marcus and the operatives aimed. Jud pulled out his knife and sneered at the collection of idiots. At first, he'd suspected the group was another wave of Collective personnel making a downright idiotic attempt at removing HERA from The Arsenal under the guise of evidence collection.

"I tell you what." Vi sighed heavily and pulled out her phone. "I'm going to make a phone call and my operatives are going to stand down. If you want HERA, take her."

She motioned toward the compound. The men looked at one another.

"If you want her, go and get her. All you need to do is bypass her security and remove her from The Arsenal operational theater before the person I am calling sends someone over here to kick your ass so many security levels down the chain, you won't even be able to work as a janitor in Washington." She looked at her phone and punched a few more numbers, then pinned the asshole with a glare. "What the fuck is your name anyway? Badges. Get them out. I'm gonna need them."

When they didn't move to do as she ordered, she stood up on her tiptoes, leaned into his face and shouted, "Now!"

A rumble of warning rolled from Jud when the man's face turned a few shades too red. If the bastard moved to touch Viviana he wouldn't be breathing for long.

"Hi, Bob. I'm sorry to bug you, but we have a situation over here." Her voice softened, then paused. "Yeah, I love it here at The Arsenal. Marshall and the guys are awesome. You should come by for a visit sometime. We're setting up a bunch of new stuff I'm thinking you'd have fun with."

Jud gathered the badges and noted the way the men shifted restlessly as Vi turned her back to them.

"Yeah, we had a critical mission tied to our contract with you. I'm pleased to report things are going smoothly. Or, they were, until a little bit ago. We have some...problems I'm afraid. It seems we have a couple gentlemen from Homeland Security, one from the FBI and a rather strange fellow who hasn't told me yet, but he's CIA. Yeah. I'll ping you their pictures."

Vi looked at her phone, pushed a few buttons, then continued talking. "So, as you are probably seeing, Bob, they're way below their security clearance on this one. I hate to bug you with something this trivial, but I've just come off an op and we have bodies piled all over the place from a hit squad who showed up to neutralize Edge and I and take HERA. And I'm pretty sure we'll have more than a mild dust up because an incredibly brilliant and brave woman working intelligence at the NSA ratted out some really bad operatives who were gunning for one of my teams overseas."

Vi sighed dramatically and rolled her eyes. "Thanks to lots of awesome teamwork, everyone's okay. And we'll handle whatever comes our way, you know we always do, Bob, but I'm afraid my patience is thin, and I may land out with four more body bags to haul off if they keep tap dancing on my last nerve. You don't even want to know how close Edge is."

Vi turned and smiled sweetly at the men, who hadn't moved to accept her challenge of removing HERA themselves. Jud crossed his arms and laughed outright when she held the phone out.

"I think he wants to talk to you," she said. "Come on, everyone. We need to debrief. Bob's handling our unwelcome guests."

She turned and headed into the building. Marcus motioned for a couple of the guys to hang back. Jud remained hot on her heels as she moved silently along the hall, down a corridor he hadn't been in yet.

"Who's Bob?"

"Oh, Robert Mattis," she said nonchalantly.

"The Secretary of Defense Robert Mattis?" Marcus asked.

"Yeah. Bob and I get along way better than me and his boss. That guy's a grade A dick," she said. "Don't worry, I told him so last time he called. He appreciates me shooting straight with him, even though I think he likes Mary better than me. Probably because she hasn't called him the ultimate asshat of all time like I have. Repeatedly." She shrugged and headed through a set of double doors.

Jud froze and stifled his curse as his gaze swept the interior. Medical.

"Well, well, I heard rumors you were around." Logan Callister, CIA doctor and general pain in Jud's ass, snapped on a glove and offered a grim smile. "It's been a while, Judson."

"Not nearly long enough," he returned.

"Wait." Vi froze. Her gaze darted between the two of them. "You know each other. How?"

"Long story," they answered in unison.

"A mutual friend of ours sometimes reaches out to me for favors," Jud said. "The last one was a setup that got me gut shot."

"Didn't have anything to do with that," Logan said. He reached down and pulled up his shirt. "If it's any consolation, a wound like the one I patched up on you almost got me."

"What are you doing here?" Jud cut to the chase. He didn't like anyone tied to the CIA hanging around. He was a bit surprised Viviana and Mary were okay with it.

"I'm out," Logan said. "I got called in when Dylan and the guys pulled Mary out. I'm Arsenal now."

Interesting. Jud studied the doctor. Vi squeezed his arm.

"You're bleeding like a stuck pig, Jud. Let him patch you up," she pleaded.

"It can wait. We need to get a few things handled first."

"It'll wait," she said. "Sit."

"Definitely not a cat person," he muttered.

"Just got word the rescued hostages are being treated. Other than the three casualties before arrival, everyone's going to be okay." Logan looked at Jud as he approached. "Heard one of them is a relative of yours."

"Not sure how that's any of your business," he snapped. Two and a half decades of ingrained distrust in everyone surged forward. "Anyone so much as whispers that connection to him or his kid, they'll eat a bullet."

"I understand you, man," Logan replied. "I'm the same way with my family."

"You have family?" Vi asked. "You've never mentioned them."

"Would you? Do you?" Logan shot back.

Jud wondered what Vi's family was like. He suspected he'd be beating one of them down for the shit they instilled in her head, the need to be perfect. Someone did a number on her.

"He's been favoring his left side, too. I think he has some cracked ribs," Vi offered.

"I'll check it out," Logan replied.

"Should you be up? Aren't you still on bed rest?" She looked around. "We need more staff so you aren't our only go-to-guy."

"Patching up a bullet wound isn't a strain on me, Vi," Logan promised. "Marshall and Nolan are working on more staff for this place."

"Oh, good." Her gaze settled back on Jud. "You're a close quarters ninja. I haven't seen too many of those, maybe one."

He wasn't sure what the term meant, but Logan whistled low.

"The girls don't hand out ninja status to just anyone. I think only Fallon and Gage have it here."

"Not the Masons?" Jud asked.

"Dallas is close. Mary says Dylan is, too, but she's biased." Heat settled in her cheeks.

"What kind of ninjas are Fallon and Gage?"

"Gage is just a ninja. That's like the first level. Fallon is an ordnance ninja cause, well, he's Fallon. He'd make a building blow with just a stick of gum." She rolled her eyes. "It's a hierarchy in progress. The Pentagon has to approve all appointments though, so don't think you're really in."

"The Pentagon?" He couldn't help but laugh at the thought.

"That's her, Mary, Addy, Bree and Rhea," Logan offered.

"Right, the white boarding crew," Jud commented. Jesus, Viviana was an adorable, geeky nut. "Didn't Bree mention something about Riley being in it now?"

"Yeah, she's a new appointment. We were supposed to have an initiation ceremony for her tomorrow night, but I'm thinking we need to postpone." Her shoulders drooped a bit as she moved past the silliness of ninjas and a Pentagon and struck the heart of the matter center mass. "Someone tried to kill us."

"Yeah."

"You said you recognized one. Was he Collective?"

"Yeah, he was."

"So they're in."

"Yeah." They were in. He recalled the op he'd sent Addy on. "I'm sorry I didn't read you in on what I had Addy pull. We ran low on time."

"What was it? I don't like people going behind my back, Judson." She wet her lips. He tracked her tongue as it darted in and out. So sexy. "I'm responsible for every single one of them, for keeping them safe and bringing them back in one piece. Her going off book for you could've been a disaster."

Tension lines appeared along her forehead. He couldn't imagine the tremendous burden she placed on herself—sole responsibility for everyone on a team. Did Mary or anyone else realize the pressure Viviana put herself under every time they took on a mission? Would it matter?

Jud waited a few minutes as Logan treated the bullet wound. He offered a few token care tips they both knew he'd ignore anyway.

"Come on, you need to unwind and rest," he said as he rose. "First, we need to get Jacob and Mary to help us activate the lists."

"The lists." Blood seeped from her face. She yanked her hand away and took a step back. "How do you know about those?"

"Because everyone who gives a damn about someone has them in our line of work, Viviana." He pulled the card from his back pocket, the one he'd put there earlier in the day—just in case.

She read the names a minute. "Judith isn't on here."

"No."

"Why isn't your sister on here?" She looked up. "My family's on mine and I so don't get along with them."

"Judith isn't on there because Danny is. He's been through enough. Seeing the woman who cut him loose the first time he survived hell on the heels of surviving a second time wouldn't be good."

"We'll get her secure somewhere else. We've got resources all over, I just need an address where she is."

"Come on, let's get this done so we can rest."

∾

They'd contacted most of the family. Vi sat between Mary and Jud and stared at the conference phone. Everyone had slipped out to help Gage and Marcus make room for the incoming guests. Family.

"I'll do it," Mary offered. She squeezed Vi's hand. "Let me do it."

"No. They'll take it easier from me, even though it's been a while since we spoke." Eleven or twelve years?

It was the first couple of years she'd worked at Hive, the first security threat. After the first debacle she'd made alternative arrangements for their security, but that wasn't an option this time around. Vi dialed the number she'd memorized long ago.

"Hello." The sing-song voice sounded happy, welcoming. Nothing like what she expected.

"Mom, it's me. Viviana." She swallowed, forcing her dry throat to continue. "There's a situation."

"You have a lot of nerve, young woman." Her voice grew distant. "Harold, it's Viviana. She has another situation."

"What'd you screw up this time?" Her father's voice blasted tension into the room. Jud tensed beside her.

"Hello, it's good to talk to you, too, Father."

"Don't give me that tone, young lady. You don't call, write or visit for fifteen years and have the nerve to phone us now because you've messed up and have a situation?"

Like a used car salesman from Hoboken could take down The Collective and withdraw the six-million-dollar contract on her head. Vi couldn't share details with them. Even if she could, she wouldn't. They'd probably choose the two-comma payday over her if given half a chance. She knew her brother Rich would, probably for way less.

"Captain Mendoza will be by to pick you up and keep you secure until someone can escort you to a private airfield. That will likely be tomorrow around this time, maybe later. Pack enough to stay for a couple weeks."

Marshall and the guys were en route stateside and had insisted on gathering families and bringing them back themselves before returning home. She pitied whoever drew the short straw to collect her so-called family. Captain Mendoza was a veritable saint who rounded them up whenever a threat was serious enough to merit doing so, which had been a rare occurrence. Thank goodness.

"Mrs. Chambers, this is Mary. I'm sorry this is necessary, but it's for your own good and you and your husband will enjoy it out here. It'll be a nice vacation."

"So this is your fault, too?" Her mom's voice rose. "I told her you were nothing but trouble, but she was too smart-mouthed to listen. Always a little know-it-all."

"What the fuck?" Jud muttered.

Vi snagged his arm and squeezed. "Please, don't." She mouthed the words when he leaned forward as if intending to offer his thoughts. The last thing she needed was another opinion when it came to her parents. The more time she gave them, the nastier they'd get.

"We have to go. I'll see you both and Rich tomorrow evening." She clicked off before they could argue.

"Are you okay?" Mary asked, her voice soft and concerned.

"I will be," she said. "We need a list for Zero. Sorry, Zoey." She rubbed her temples as she tapped out a message to Gage. "I offered her a job out here, sort of."

"Good. We need the help and she's good," Mary said. "What'd she do that merits the protective detail?"

"I'm not sure, but it somehow involved her throwing the brakes on whoever was going after Fallon's team. I'm assuming it was a dirty op running that she spotlighted. She's scared and wanting to bolt before the fallout hits," Vi said. "We need support personnel and I was already thinking about recruiting her. It's a win win."

"Marshall wants all footage and images we've gathered from the dust up here sent to him stat," Mary said. She set her tablet down and looked at Jud. "You're a one-man army, a deadly one."

"Was that ever in doubt?" Jud leaned back and crossed his arms. His hair was still damp from the shower he'd recently taken.

The coppery stench of death still tainted her nostrils as she studied his hands. The same hands that had touched her cheek, held her in place while he kissed her, had killed more enemies than she could count. The stray thought heated her cheeks when she noted Mary's raised eyebrows. Best friends were a serious pain in the ass sometimes.

"Thank you for what you did today, Jud," Vi said.

"Are we seriously having this conversation?" He pointed at the phone. "I'd rather chat about what the hell that was. Those were your parents?"

"They aren't winning any parenting awards anytime soon," Mary muttered. "They're like a bad case of hemorrhoids."

Jud didn't respond. The intensity in his gaze rippled through her, a silent awareness he saw more than she wanted him to. He reached into his pocket and slid a hard drive on the table.

"What's this?" Vi pulled it to her.

"Strike one against The Collective," he answered. "A couple years in I realized leverage was important, necessary if I wanted those I loved to keep breathing. I earned my way back into their lives by doing things no one should ever be asked to do, much less agree to. I didn't always know why or for who, but I kept what I could in the way of names. Locations. Anything I could remember."

Holy. Shit.

Shock rolled through her as she locked gazes with Mary, who'd grown pale.

"We need this kept between us. I don't want Jacob involved. If anyone knew I had this, we'd have way more than The Collective after us. It'd be a fallout no one could contain. My graveyard is too extensive and too deep to be exposed. What I asked Addy to get tonight will be strike two. Jian had records of what he's done for The Collective and others."

"Including whoever hired Peter," Mary guessed.

"That's the hope," Jud replied. "Either way, I'm thinking what he has and what's on there should be enough for you to find their Achilles Heel. If they have one."

"They will. Everyone does," Vi said. "I don't even know what to say, Jud. Thank you for trusting us with this."

"Don't thank me yet, Viviana." Regret and embarrassment crept into his expression. "I promised to chase away your nightmares. What's on there will guarantee you'll have even worse ones.

If I saw another way, I'd take that route. Releasing all of this into the world isn't a nuclear reaction, it's a thousand times worse. We need to neutralize The Collective without a ripple effect. You two have been through enough hells lately. We all have."

Jud rose and reached for her, but then pulled back. He took a couple steps backward. "I'm sorry it got so messy today. There wasn't any other way. I promised I'd keep you two breathing. I never promised it'd be clean."

13

Vi set her supplies on the coffee table and plunked down on the carpet facing the door. Jacob assured her he'd escort Jud there as soon as they returned to the compound. He'd run into Nomad to pick up some supplies. Her hands trembled, but she spread the materials out. The thin colored strips of paper fanned out before her soothed the beast within her, the one that sometimes reared its head when an op didn't quite go as planned.

Two new Arsenal agents had suffered minor injuries. All in all, it had been a successful strike.

Except for her almost losing Fallon's team. Oh, and the compound getting attacked because she hadn't thought far enough ahead.

She forced back the thought. For now, she'd reboot her mind, decompress. That's what this time was about.

The door opened. Jud prowled in. His gaze settled on her immediately. Jaw twitching, he sat beside her on the ground. "What's all this?"

"Quillery," she answered. "Most call it quilling today. It's an art of paper filigree."

"That's where your handle came from."

Curiosity softened his voice to a velvety sound. She spun a red strip of paper into shape and positioned it into the teardrop shaper. A squish and a couple tugs with her tool and she was ready for glue. "My mom taught me."

Why had she offered the morsel of information? Few even knew she quilled. It was the one connection to her past she maintained.

"You enjoy it?"

She shrugged. "It soothes the beast, helps me decompress when things don't go smoothly." She swallowed when his hand rested on her ankle. She'd opted for loose sweats and a baggy t-shirt. Heat spread through her as his thumb raked against the exposed skin just above her ankle. She jerked her foot away, but he held on.

"Touch sooths my beast, Viviana," he whispered. "We've both had a long, bad day. Everything went sideways."

"Everyone's okay."

"But not what was expected," he surmised.

"The work we do isn't what you do. We can't pile up bodies, that undermines us with the alphabet soup and everyone else we're working to protect." She smooshed a blue strip next. Another teardrop. The pattern swirled around in her head. She reached for the special pile of papers. The strips she'd made especially for this creation.

"What are you making?" he asked.

"A mandala."

"Your mom made them?"

"No, she..." Vi shoved back the angry retort, focusing on the glide of his fingertips against her skin. Her pulse quickened. "I started mandalas when I got out of college. They soothed me more. Mom started me on this because my brain didn't shut down. I'd have a hard time sleeping. I was always thinking, asking questions. Annoying people."

Annoying her.

The gentle glide stopped. Contact firmed, but she craved the stroke. Like a cat seeking attention, she stretched her foot forward, just enough to get his attention.

"Kids aren't an annoyance, Viviana. I'm sorry she saw you as one. Inquisitive children are a blessing." He whispered the statement as he stroked again, this time further up her calf.

She swallowed and curled the first strip of special yellow paper into a ball. Another teardrop, this one smaller. Subtle to disguise its importance. No one ever needed to know the small secret it held, the piece of herself she left behind.

"Show me," he said.

The second strip of yellow uncurled. She looked up at him. "What?"

"Show me how to do this." He shifted closer. His hand settled on hers. "May I?"

She nodded. Confusion shook off the frustration she'd carted around, the outright anger she'd directed toward him. "Why?"

"Why not?"

"It's boring. I'm boring." She peered up as she squished the yellow paper ball into shape. "Only cat people quill, Jud. It's a rule."

He smiled, the molten one that made her insides warm. Firm, confident strokes moved up her calf, an exposed calf. How the heck had he gotten her sweatpants moved up? Real smooth, Jensen. Real smooth. She stifled the amusement and focused on the task at hand.

"It's important to you, Viviana. Show me why."

"I don't share this. It's for me."

"Fair enough. Then I'll watch." He deepened the contact, shifting attention to her foot.

"Don't tell me you have a foot fetish," she retorted.

"I'm tactile. The quillery soothes you. Touch sooths me." He applied pressure with his thumb on the bottom of her foot and she nearly groaned.

Definitely a masseuse god.

"Whatever," she muttered, not willing to admit how aware she was of each touch.

They fell into a comfortable silence. Time passed, but she lost track of the seconds, the minutes. All that existed were the strips of paper, important interspersed with bright, bold colors.

And Jud's touch. Firm, confident and soothing.

"Mom and Dad didn't like that I was smart. Said I was too smart for my own good." She bit her lip and offered a bigger morsel, one that had built up in her as important to share. "My brother was a sports jock."

"Older," he guessed.

"Yeah, three years. I accelerated past him before he was in the ninth grade. I graduated a year before him, but it should've been two." She curled another yellow and squished. This time she used a different variation of teardrop, one she'd made up. "I went to MIT because they offered a full ride. Mom and Dad weren't pleased, but having me away helped get attention back on him."

"How old were you?"

"Fourteen," she replied. "Mom hired someone to serve as my caregiver. Exceptions were extended by the school. It was tough, but then I met Mary and things got easier."

"Jesus, you were a baby," he muttered. "How old was she?"

"Fifteen. She..." Though it wasn't her story to tell, she offered a morsel. "She came from a rougher background. School was an escape for her."

"And for you."

She froze, startled by his insight. "I had a good upbringing, two parents who loved me."

"You don't have to hide behind the facade, not with me."

And that's what disturbed her even more. She felt comfortable exposing this small part of her she'd kept tucked away. Her insides ached, as if scraped raw. She scooped up the shapes she'd formed and put them in a small box. She'd finish later, after she'd tended to business. Judson Jensen was a distraction, one that'd be gone soon enough.

"We need to look into what all we found at Jian's, make sure his ring is down for good. We probably missed some stuff, so I need to get what that was to the Feds so they can clean up the mess."

"We will, in the morning. After you've rested." He took her hand. "When was the last time you really slept? I'm not talking about in the down room."

Ages ago. Sleep didn't come easy, not anymore. But that wasn't his business. She'd given him too much of herself already tonight.

Oh, and you slept in his freaking arms. God, she was a flaming hot mess.

"Marshall and Dylan want to put you on a team, get you more used to functioning with a team since you'll be here a while. What happened today can't happen again. You saved our asses, but you went lone wolf. I heard the calls. You didn't want Marcus and them anywhere near you because you were worried you'd take them out by mistake."

His jaw twitched. "You're right. I was. Old habits are hard to break."

She and Mary had yet to look at the hard drive, mainly because she'd locked it in a vault and refused. Truth told, she was terrified of what was on it. Terrified it'd change her view of Jud. Terrified of why that view changing even mattered, because it shouldn't. Jud shouldn't be a bullet point in her life. Yet he was.

He'd been so certain she'd judge him for what was on the hard drive. She didn't want to, but her words and actions already did so.

"Today scared me, Jud," she admitted. "I was so focused on the camps and Dover, I got cocky and didn't even consider the compound could fall under attack. I failed everyone here. I'm just lucky you were here to pick up the slack."

"You didn't fail anyone." He cupped her face. "No one's perfect. You and Mary had too much on your plate today."

"Fallon's team was almost taken. I still don't have details, but I had to trust a stranger to keep them safe because I got too wrapped up in the camps and never thought he wouldn't be okay." She forced a deep breath. "I can't get distracted. There's too much at stake, too many lives relying on me to keep them safe."

"And you think I'm distracting you."

Yes. Maybe. "I don't know. You're an unknown in so many ways. I can't take that risk."

Jud glanced at the form. "Is this about the form, or something else?"

"You know what I mean, Jud. But, yeah. The form is important. Mary and I have never placed an asset on a team or worked with one unless we can fill this out." She motioned toward the four-page intricate list. "I tried filling this out earlier. I got past your name and was guessing at everything else."

Jud picked up the list, visibly tightening when he realized what it was.

"Mary and I never work with an operative unless we have at least the first half of this form filled out and verified. The more we know, the easier the op and the higher the likelihood everyone returns breathing." She locked gazes. "You're a threat because you're a phantom, a total unknown."

"Look at me," he ordered.

He cupped her face. Despite her best intention otherwise, she complied. "Jud, don't."

"Not doing anything, Viviana. Tonight's about decompression, nothing else. I won't ever put you or your teams at risk. I'm thankful as fuck you and your crews handled themselves so well through all this. I'm not used to working with teams. I'll adjust."

No. That wasn't the response she wanted, needed.

Adjustment meant he planned to stick around.

"Come on." He stood and held out his hand. "Let's go."

"Where?"

"Bed."

Anticipation wove with desire. Her hand tingled when he took it and guided her to a standing position.

"Not like that, Viviana," he whispered. "Your expressions are so readable when your guard is down."

Hot breath trailed against her cheek when he held her close. She craved the contact.

"You're dead on your feet. Let's get you into bed. We'll figure everything else out tomorrow."

She watched in shock as he carefully gathered her supplies and returned them to the carrier. He placed it under his arm and guided her toward the hallway. She wandered behind him, suddenly bone tired. Her brain was mush, quiet and silent. She welcomed the blissful numbness crawling through her. He set the supplies beside the bed and aimed her toward the bathroom.

"Do what you've gotta do. I'll turn down your bed."

He'd turn down the bed. Vi wandered into the bathroom and tried to remember the last time a man had turned down her bed. Never. By the time she headed back out, the overhead light was off. Pale yellow light shone from the nightstand lamp. She crawled beneath the down-turned covers and moaned. A bed had never felt so good.

"Jesus," he muttered.

"Sorry, I haven't slept in a while."

"Lay on your stomach. I'll rub you down."

The temptation was too good. She remembered how good his hands felt on her. She sighed and surrendered to the offer, the comfort. She closed her eyes as he started massaging her shoulders.

～

There was a special place in hell for assholes like him. Blood surged southward as Jud massaged his way down Viviana's back. Her soft moans and sighs kept him focused on the wrong things, but after a shit day he needed this moment—being nothing more than a man taking care of a good woman, one who'd had an equally shitty day. Security was stretched thin, but Marcus assured him it was under control for a few hours. Jacob was monitoring HERA's readouts and promised to contact him if there was trouble.

"Relax, Viviana. You're too tense."

"This is the most relaxed I've been in years." The pillow muffled her words as she relaxed deeper into the bed beneath them. "You're too good at this. Was this in the assassin training manual?"

"In a way," he admitted. "The better you know the human body, the better you can be at hand-to-hand combat. Using what I learned like this is a lot more enjoyable, though."

"It's hard doing what you do," she stated.

"Yes. The day taking a life becomes easy is when you should eat a bullet. But there's a difference between a distant kill through a scope and close contact."

"How so?" Her voice was soft, but held more emotion and concern than he'd gotten from anyone in a while. More than he deserved.

"It's more personal, harder to scrub from your mind." Knives were a weapon he excelled at, but they created their own demons.

Arterial sprays, walking away from a fight with someone's blood covering you. Though he rarely went into a battle like that unless absolutely necessary, the aftermath was the same. Hot showers and skin scrubs only did so much to wipe away what he'd done—taken a life to save his own. Or someone else's. Every life taken came with a price, a penance. No one walked away from war unscathed.

Jud accepted the burdens of his chosen life long ago, but that didn't make it any easier. "When The Collective allowed me to reestablish contact with my family, I was thrilled at first. I'd been in the dark, alone, too long. I was ready to live, savor family and take a hit of the good I worked to protect. Then I realized it was just a deeper layer of hell."

"Because you weren't out, not really."

"No. I was straddling the line and more alone than ever because I wanted to insulate them from what I did. I'd moved away from the really intense work, but the contracts assigned to me were...complicated."

"Jacob knows more than I expected him to," she whispered. "He's a lot like me when I was that age. Curious and head-strong."

"He's definitely nosy and stubborn." Jud chuckled. "He's why I forced the new deal. Communication with me and my family before then was very rare, but my parents had a contact for emergencies. Jacob hit his rebellious stage early, started hacking and using his skills for personal gain."

"It's hard being a teenager and not fitting in. It's easy to stumble onto the wrong path, especially if there are people around who want you on that path." She arced upward when he stopped massaging, as if seeking his touch. "Mary and I went into our rebellious stage together, started hacking for the wrong reasons our sophomore year at MIT. That's how we ran across the pedophiles and assholes we initially targeted with our first version of HERA."

"I bet they didn't know what hit them."

"It took a while to perfect, but we eventually got a good thing going. We could identify just about anyone and provide law enforcement with their identities and copies of everything they had on their system, where they'd been and who they'd been chatting with. One of the last stings we did our senior year was how we got on Peter Rugers' radar. He recruited us into Hive." Her voice lowered to a whisper. "I should've known he wasn't much better than the assholes we were bringing down."

"You're a beautifully brilliant woman, Viviana, smart enough to understand and accept that not everything is your fault. Things are going to go wrong. It isn't always because you did something wrong or missed something. Even if it is, you're human. No one's perfect."

"You're a lone wolf. A team's only as strong as its foundation, and that's me. If I'm not one hundred and twenty-five percent solid, I weaken their success before the mission is a go. Take today, for example. I should have realized Fallon's team was in as much danger as the rest of the teams, but I didn't because he wasn't striking a camp. A total stranger saved his ass because I wasn't there to do it."

"You and Mary had eight teams to coordinate at once in what most would think was an impossible mission. And that stranger was one you recruited, right? You put her in as a contingency because you knew she might be needed. And she was." He maneuvered from a straddling position atop her and urged her to turn over until she was on her back and looking up at him. "You're an amazing woman, Viviana. But you're wrong."

"I am?"

"The hardest missions are those someone takes on alone. When I'm a lone wolf, I don't have someone to pick up my slack if things go sideways. No matter what might go down, those teams today had each other. And you." He cupped her face. "I wish you could see how fucking incredible you and Edge are. You have no idea. I want to punch whoever made you believe it's your fault whenever something goes wrong, because that's not true, Viviana. When something goes wrong, you are the one who fixes it. You're the solution, not the cause."

"He's right, you know."

Jud vaulted off the bed and lunged for the gun on the bedside table. Mary, Rhea, Bree and Riley stood at the bedroom entry in assorted stages of shocked and amused.

"Okay, that was hot," Riley whispered as she clutched Rhea's arm.

"Uh huh." Bree gulped. "I didn't know anyone who can jump and twirl that fast."

Viviana sat up in the bed. "What's wrong? Are you all okay?"

Jud took in the duffel bags and backpacks each woman held and the assortment of blankets and pillows strewn about in the hallway behind them. He growled his frustration. Viviana needed rest. Then he noted Bree's and Rhea's widened gazes, noted the way they clung to Mary—who looked like she was one scream away from crawling out of her skin.

Dylan was still en route home.

The teams were gone and the compound had been attacked.

The women's homes had been attacked.

The frustration in him eased and he set the gun on the bedside table as he looked down at Viviana. "You girls get settled. I'll grab the gear from the hallway. You all need to rest while you can."

"Addy will be back in a few hours," Bree said. "We were thinking we could all crash here, wait until she gets back."

"That sounds perfect," Viviana said as she patted the king-sized bed. "Come on. Climb on."

"Are we getting massages, too?" Rhea asked.

"Pfft, I think that man has one setting and it's locked to Vi,"

Riley responded as she toed her shoes off and crawled onto the bed. "I didn't do a damn thing today and I'm still exhausted."

"Shock does that." Mary cuddled up against Vi and squeezed her tight. "You okay?"

"No, but I will be. You?"

"No, but I will be."

Jud watched the women nest on Viviana's bed as he tossed pillows and blankets into the room. Duffel bags filled with snacks were tossed haphazardly into the room. The women whispered and chattered as they huddled close and situated pillows around and between them. He covered them up with a couple of blankets and half-shut the door.

Any doubt he'd harbored about whether he made the right decision to protect the Quillery Edge was killed in that room. He'd keep all the women and everyone in The Arsenal safe because, for once, he was on the right path.

Jud wandered back into the living room and sat on the sofa. Pen in hand, he picked up the form and read through it once. Jesus. He'd be an idiot to even consider sharing that depth of information with anyone.

So why the hell was he already on the fourth empty space?

Because him being an unknown put her at risk. She couldn't factor him into security plans and trust him if he didn't take the first step, extend the first olive branch. He'd never shared this much with anyone, let anyone this deep into his world. Each check mark felt like a strike to his soul, the man he'd once wanted to be.

He's operated in the black, the shadows so long he couldn't even smell clean, pure air. Until he'd arrived at The Arsenal. For once he felt good about the stand he was making. He'd never be a good man, but he'd be better as long as he was around.

Which might not be long after today. The Collective wouldn't stop until he was dead.

He glanced down the hall, thinking about the beautiful, brilliant woman sleeping. Trusting him to chase her nightmares away. He would do anything to keep her safe because she'd pulled Danny's ass out of hell. Again. This time it'd been a hell created because of him.

14

Viviana ignored the little man slamming a sledgehammer around in her brain and padded into the kitchen for coffee. She stepped over Riley and Bree. Halted in a bit of confusion when she saw Rhea on the floor a ways away. It wasn't the woman sprawled alone that surprised her. They'd crashed there the past few nights, mainly to keep Mary from climbing the walls since Dylan was gone. It was the silent man watching them all sleep.

"Fallon." His name came out as more of a pained whisper than greeting. She dragged a mug down and filled it with coffee. He made noise as he progressed into the kitchen, intentional on his part since he was always lethal quiet. Not like Jud, but lethal nonetheless. "Coffee?"

"Yeah, black."

Like he'd ever drink it any other way. He'd probably spontaneously combust if he drank it with cream or sugar. She looked around, wondering how long she could stall before he'd get bored and go away. It'd been two days since she'd screwed up and his team had almost paid the price. Although she'd semi-accepted she couldn't have done more, suddenly seeing him in person awakened the almost-comatose guilt.

"I didn't realize you all got in," she said. "Gage and Addy were supposed to wake me."

"We got in a couple hours ago. We decided to crash a few hours before debrief," he commented as he took the mug she offered. "Got an earful from Addy, then Rhea when I came over here a while ago. Seems you and me should have a one-on-one debrief before we all get together."

Her insides churned. She focused on a lone dish in the sink. The water turned hot as it cascaded onto her hand. She wiped the dish, the motion repetitive and hypnotic. If she focused hard enough she could almost pretend he hadn't taken two steps forward and was now within reaching distance. "I'm sorry."

Fallon settled a hand on her right shoulder and turned her until they faced one another. "Before I got an earful from Addy, I got one from Jud. Have to admit that man intimidates me."

Vi couldn't help but laugh at the absurdity. The two men were more alike than any of the others at The Arsenal. Both were private contractors, or had been. Fallon recently signed on and was now a team leader. "Funny. I don't think either of you could ever be intimidated."

"You and Edge did a hell of a good job, nothing you could've done better. The feeds the teams got were only their own, but I got them all. I heard all four strikes. The fact you did all that while the compound was under attack..." His jaw twitched. Lips thinned, he glanced away. "Don't take blame that isn't yours to own. You blaming yourself for that means we all get to blame ourselves for not being here when the compound needed us. You want that?"

No. Talk about stupid. How could they possibly be blamed? They had a job to do and had been in the middle of...

She swallowed the rest of the mental diatribe and narrowed

her gaze. Not even the little voice in her head that blamed Vi for everything could argue with his logic.

"What happened?" She took a sip of her coffee, forcing the liquid down. "I replayed your feed and it was silent. Who got the jump on you?"

"Friendlies, or so we thought. The SEAL team hanging out with us didn't suspect them being anything other than that either. They were CIA contracted, never got the letters behind them. All I know is one minute they were chatting us up and the next they had us taken down. We were outnumbered three to one, but that's no excuse. I trusted them because of who they worked for and shouldn't have. It won't happen again."

So the NSA fed intel to a CIA team and Zero somehow got wind of it. "They were dirty."

"Yeah, they were dirty. We went with them without a fight because we knew we'd get away at some point. I wanted more information on who they were working with and what their end game was." Fallon paused for a sip of coffee. "Before we could make a move, they got a call saying they'd been burned and to pull out immediately. We eliminated them before they eliminated us. We were outnumbered, but not by much at that point. Some of them had left, thinking they had us sufficiently secured."

Big mistake underestimating a SEAL team and an Arsenal team combined. "We knew there was Hive involvement in this mess at some point. I should've had a better contingency plan in place."

"The one you had in place worked. There's a big enough mine field left out there for us to navigate without you throwing this into the mix. We're good. The only injuries were minor and the bad guys didn't walk away." Fallon bumped her nose with his index finger and grinned. "Let's focus on kicking some Collective ass."

Vi was on board with the idea. She and Mary had refocused

everyone's—mainly Rhea, Bree and Riley—nervous, apprehensive energy into an offensive plan. Proactive, not reactive. Not exactly the best motto, but way better than run and hide or cower and cry. They'd spent yesterday holed up in what was now known as the white-board room. At first, she hadn't wanted to involve the other women, but then Mary pointed out the obvious.

They were involved the second this compound was hit. They had the right to fight back. Them helping unravel the data about The Collective was them fighting back.

So, the three women were now neck deep in forensic data mining at its best. Addy had even taken a seat at the table for a change and gotten involved. The hard drive she'd taken from Jian, when combined with what Jud had provided a lot of data—HERA had been processing since late yesterday afternoon. Vi hoped the system would spew data out in time for it to become part of the debriefing, but from what she'd seen so far, she suspected they'd need a third dataset.

"I'll see you later. Chin up. You kicked ass with this one, like always. Don't ever doubt yourself," Fallon said.

"Thank you," she whispered as he drew her into a hug.

"Guess I'm not the only one looking for a shot of sass this morning."

Vi shoved away from Fallon as if he was on fire. The operative chuckled as he took a couple steps back and greeted Jud with a weird handshake and half-hug back slap greeting.

"Just ironing out the wrinkles in her head," Fallon said. "Didn't want another earful from anyone about her falsely taking the blame for what went down."

"You good?" Jud asked her.

"Yeah, I'm good." She busied herself pouring another cup of coffee. "Afraid I'm low on sass, though. You'll have to go sans sass this time around."

"I'm thinking Fallon's not the only one overdue for a conversation with you." He boxed her into the L of the kitchen counter. A hand on each side of her, he leaned in. "And you're never sans sass."

Vi's gaze roamed down Jud's naked torso. Definitely more definition than her code lines. "You have a problem keeping clothes on."

His full lips upturned into the nuclear smile, the toe-curling one. "There's the sass." His words were a husky whisper as his eyes closed.

Jud feathered his lips across hers, the contact so slight if her eyes weren't still open she would've missed it altogether. She settled a hand on his stomach, savoring the ripple of muscle beneath her fingertips. She deepened the contact, fused their mouths together. He tasted of minty toothpaste. A rumble rolled through him.

Images flashed through her mind, her pinned beneath him in a bed. Hearing him rumble as he...

She stifled a shocked yelp when he hoisted her up to the counter and stood between her spread legs. The kiss turned carnal, a downright dirty wrestling of tongues and lewd dances. She wrapped her legs around his waist as his hands slid beneath her thin pajama top. He explored her back, the side of her breasts. He broke the kiss as he grazed her nipple with his fingertips.

Awareness shot through her entire body with the slight contact, an arrow striking the target dead on.

"I have no control around you," he muttered against her mouth. "I'd better stop before I carry you to your bed and keep going."

She was totally okay with continuing.

"We've got lots of fires going, but we're going to stoke this one, see what happens. Tonight," he declared.

"Okay." She wasn't sure what else to say. Her pulse raced faster than a greyhound. Her entire focus honed in on Jud's hand beneath her top, meandering across her skin in a slow, easy manner. There was nothing slow or easy about Judson Jensen.

"You've been avoiding me," he said.

"Yeah," she admitted. "I needed my focus on data gathering. You muddle my brain."

The toe-curling grin returned. Heat rose in her cheeks as he cupped her face. "I'm liking that I muddle your brain. It can be my new superpower."

"You don't need any more of those. Little Penny the Persian couldn't keep up with you if you got too many."

"Penny, huh?"

"Yeah. Fluffy, all white with one of those squirrel-like tails that swishes when she walks. I bet you can train her to walk on a leash."

"Penny the Persian is a hard no. The only sass I need in my life is you," he replied. "Just to say, Viviana, you don't have to toss out Penny to keep the conversation light. I know this is moving fast, probably faster than you need. I'll pump the brakes a few times, ease back into the slow lane."

Vi stared into his eyes a moment as her brain absorbed his words. He'd read her play before she realized she'd even made it. He was right. Penny the Persian was totally thrown out to keep them from getting too intense. She didn't want to analyze why she'd ignored him the past couple of days. He terrified her in every conceivable way, not all of them bad. Most of them were pretty damn good if she were being entirely honest.

"I'm not ready for a NASCAR racer, Jud, but I'm not looking for a grandpa on a Sunday drive either." She put her hand on his chest and swallowed as her eyes feasted on his bare flesh. Jud would never be a Sunday driving grandpa. Her body turned molten as her mind wandered down that trail, the one with the white picket fence and two point five kids. He'd be a fiercely protective dad. She smiled at the notion. His poor daughter wouldn't ever date because no teenage punk would measure up to Jud.

"What was that thought?"

"Nothing," she lied.

"Pains me to admit, but I came here for a reason. The rest of the families are arriving in a bit, probably any minute now."

Dread blasted her insides with the force of an IED. So far, they'd situated Bree's family. Everyone else had required a bit more time to coordinate. Riley and Momma Mason had taken charge of the family portion of their plans, so Vi hadn't been too heavily involved. Marshall and the brothers had arrived stateside early yesterday morning, but had opted to move families after a brief delay—one which gave them time to make sure the families weren't compromised. Mary had coordinated that effort with Dylan and Jesse.

"Come on, let's go," he said, as if sensing she'd avoid it as long as possible. "Get dressed. I'll fix a coffee to go for you."

Her insides warmed. He'd fix a coffee to go for her. Judson Jensen was dangerous to the senses in every possible way.

Vi walked like a prisoner headed to the execution chamber rather than a woman greeting her parents. Anger rose in him with each darted gaze she cast, each nervous squeeze of her hand on his. He looked down at the deathlike grip she'd maintained on him since they'd left her bungalow-style house. He wanted to assure her it'd be okay, but what little he'd seen of her parents nixed the idea. They were likely a real piece of work.

The area outside the compound was filled with people. All the teams were back. Operatives wandered about, interspersed with men, women and a few children. Luggage was piled up. Bree was flitting about with her equally friendly parents and sister. Fallon was glaring at an older couple in an obviously heated conversation with Rhea a ways away. A younger woman about Jacob's age watched, a baby in her arms.

Riley walked over to them, clipboard in hand. "I'd say good morning, but that'd be a lie. Talk about chaos."

"That bad?" Vi asked.

"Oh, you have no idea. Mom is on a tear. She's less than thrilled at Marshall for vacating most of his operatives from their rooms so we have enough space for everyone's families to have some place to stay that's more like a cheap hotel room instead of a barracks-style setting." Riley looked up at Jud. "Thanks for moving, by the way."

"No problem." He'd moved his one bag to the upper level barracks, the one that'd gone unused so far. It was four rows of twelve cots each set. A small chest was at the base of each "bed". A nightstand completed the areas cordoned off with partitions that could be pulled around them to offer a bit of privacy, but not much. Fortunately, the bathrooms weren't toilets and urinals lined along the back wall, but gym style with actual showers. Bathroom stalls.

He'd been in a lot worse.

"We didn't have to move many operatives out, just a few," Riley said. She chewed on her lip. "Your parents are here, Vi. Jesse took them into the visitor's area. They were a bit...irritated."

Jud grunted. He didn't want Viviana exposed to irritation; especially if it was like any of the bullshit he heard when she'd called him. She was already in motion. He wrapped an arm around her, and slowed her progression. "Look at me, Viviana."

Ashen, wide-eyed, she peered up. "I haven't seen them in a while."

"There a reason you let so much time go by?"

She shrugged. "The last time didn't go too well. We had a situation at Hive and I mistakenly had them stay with me at the safe house."

Son of a bitch. "That didn't go well."

"Nuclear meltdowns had less fallout," she commented. "I learned to hole them up somewhere not near me, but this situation is a bit different. We need everyone contained in one defensible position."

The last thing she needed to worry about was parental bullshit. He kept his thoughts to himself. He'd been blessed with a family who loved him, parents who'd rather sleep on the ground under the stars than put anyone out. The door chimed when they entered. Nolan and Marshall bookended their mom behind the reception desk. Both men glowered at the couple Jesse had corralled in the area to the right. A man was asleep on the sofa behind them.

"There you are. It's about time, young lady. What is the meaning of this? We were dragged from our home like common criminals and hauled here like cargo." The woman charged forward. "What have you gotten into this time? I don't understand why you can't have a real job like a normal person. You've been nothing but trouble."

"Hello, Mother. It's nice to see you, too."

"Don't smart mouth me, young lady. You have a lot of nerve dragging us into your mess. We aren't cleaning it up."

"I don't think a used car salesman from Hoboken and his housewife have the necessary skill set to clean up this mess, but good to know where you stand." Viviana crossed her arms. "This is Judson, a friend of mine. I see you've met Jesse. His brothers Nolan and Marshall are behind the desk. This is their place. They've graciously offered to keep everyone safe until everything is cleared up."

"We were perfectly safe where we were, away from your

chaos." The older man's gaze narrowed. "Who are these cretins anyway?"

"I just introduced them, Father. These are my coworkers and friends, the men who will keep you safe."

"Right, the ones probably fixing the problems you caused."

"Everyone, these are my parents, Ralph and Olivia Chambers. The guy passed out on the couch is my brother, Rich."

"Of course he's passed out," the father argued. "He was dragged out of bed."

Jesse stood silent, arms crossed and jaw twitching. He'd clearly had about all he could stomach from the duo.

"Really, Viviana. Are all these dramatics necessary?" Her mother scrutinized her daughter. "You can't even dress like a normal adult. I see you still dress like a homeless person."

"I'd say that's somewhat appropriate given the fact you kicked me out when I was a teenager," Viviana replied.

"We hardly kicked you out, young lady. You were the one who chose to go off and gallivant with those people instead of doing what normal people would do."

"It's called an education, Mother."

"Watch that smart mouth with your mother, little girl. I'm a good mind to..."

"I'm glad you're here safely," Viviana interrupted. "I'll take you to your rooms."

"Don't you interrupt your father with that disrespectful tone. You know better than speak out of turn. That damn mind of yours is always moving and going, making you think you're better than everyone. Smarter. Nothing but disrespect."

"I'm a good mind to..."

Jud had stomached enough. He positioned himself between Viviana and her father when the red-faced man raised his hand and took a menacing step toward his daughter. He squeezed the older man's shoulder until he grimaced. "I'd look around and make a better decision. You aren't getting any closer to Vi."

"The nerve. Ralph, step away." Olivia Chambers grabbed her husband's hand and dragged him back a couple steps. "She's clearly associating with common hooligans."

The couple would likely pee their pants if they knew what all Jud had done. For once he was tempted to share exactly what kind of hooligan he was. Maybe he could scare some common decency into them. His gaze swept the area. The three Masons were one degrading comment away from tossing them on their asses. Momma Mason was red faced and being held firmly between her two oldest sons.

The door chimed. Jud turned and couldn't help the smile that spread on his face. His mother lunged, slamming into him with full-force. He took a step back from the impact as she crushed him against her. Tears trekked down her cheeks as she burrowed against him. She laughed as she said his name over and over in a whispered chant.

"Judson, Judson, Judson."

"Hi, Mom." He squeezed her tight and did the same thing with his father.

The two took turns hugging him tight enough to knock the wind from his lungs.

"He has a couple cracked ribs," Viviana whispered as she gently tapped his mom's shoulder.

Pale-faced, his mother gently touched his sides. "Oh, dear. You should've said something. Judson, Judson, Judson. You're skin and bones."

His father laughed at the outright lie. Only his mom would think that. "It's fine. I'm glad you're all here. Jacob's around here somewhere, likely holed up with the computer equipment. You know him."

"It's been too long," his mom whispered. "Are you okay? Are you safe?"

He was safer and more okay than usual, but far from what she'd deem acceptable. He nodded and smiled as she kissed his cheek and patted his chest. "We'll get through this. We always do."

"Son, we got a call a few days ago. I was going to reach out and tell you, figured it'd come better from you than us, but Danny's convoy." His dad's lower lip trembled. "It's not good, son."

"He's okay." Judson motioned toward Jesse. "This is Jesse Mason. He was one of the team leaders for one of the teams who rescued Danny and the rest of the convoy. Two of his brothers are back there, Nolan and Marshall. That's their mom. The other three brothers are wandering around here somewhere."

"Oh, you look just like Dallas. He was such a nice young man." His mother walked over and patted Jesse's cheek as she looked over at his mom. "You've raised some fine, handsome and polite young men."

"I have," Mrs. Mason replied proudly.

"Thank you for getting our boy back to us," his dad said. "Danny's not blood, but he's a Jensen through and through. We wouldn't be the same without him."

"He's coming home soon. They wanted him and a couple of the others to stay in the hospital a few days, just to be on the safe side. They're in Germany. Once you're settled, I'll take you both to chat with Doc Logan. He can answer any questions you might have."

"I see things are complicated, son." His father looked around. "Dallas didn't say much, just that we needed to be secured for a few days. What can I do to help?"

The difference between his parents and Viviana's was so notable it whipped through the room in an awkward tension. He wanted to introduce the woman beside him to his parents, but knew they'd recognize who she was immediately if he did. She'd been through enough with her parents without adding his family's reactions to the mix. They'd hopped onto the adoration bandwagon for the Quillery Edge long ago.

"Why don't you go and get settled? Viviana was about to grab some breakfast. They've got a nice cafeteria here for the soldiers and operatives. I'll join you shortly. I have something to attend to first."

His mother's eyebrows lifted. "Yes, I see that. Well, if you need help, you know I enjoy a good challenge. It's been a few years since I've taught lessons, but I have a few left in me to dole out."

Challenge wasn't the word he'd use, but he smiled and entrusted his parents to Viviana, whose eyes were wide and expressive.

"I should stay here," she whispered into the silence.

"Yes, you should, young lady. What have you gotten into this time?" Mr. Chambers looked over at his son. "Why can't you be more like Rich?"

Jud touched Viviana's face and forced her focus on him instead of her parents. He leaned down and lowered his voice. "Let me handle them. Show my parents the cafeteria and grab some breakfast. I'll catch up with you soon."

"But..."

"I need to take the lead on this one. Don't ask me to step aside, not for this." He forced a smile as their eyes met. "Save the fight for when it matters."

"Okay."

Nolan entered the fray. He handed a couple badges to her and whispered something in her ear. She nodded.

"Mr. and Mrs. Jensen, we have a room ready for you both. I'm afraid it's nothing fancy. We're still working on getting guest quarters built." Viviana motioned toward the back hall leading into the building. "You're bound to be hungry."

"Jarold, be a dear and get the bags so Dallas can get back to whatever he needs to do."

"It's no trouble at all, ma'am," Dallas replied from the doorway. "I'll get these put in the room for you two."

"So polite," she commented. "That seems to be a trait lacking in some these days."

Jud chuckled at the not-so-subtle jab at Viviana's parents. His mother pointedly glared at the other couple, who'd grown quiet amidst the crush of Mason men now surrounding them. He leaned down and kissed his mom's cheek. "We'll catch up in a few, Mom."

"Oh, take your time. Viviana and I will get to know each other."

That's exactly what he was afraid of.

15

"So, dear, how did you and Judson meet?" Mrs. Jensen lobbed the inquiry out casually as they strolled from the visitor's lobby.

"He's been helping with a job, Mrs. Jensen," she replied.

"Oh, none of that. I'm Jenna, and this is my better half, Jarold." She patted the man's arm. "Waking up to chaos probably wasn't how you wanted to start your day."

No, it wasn't. Vi remained silent, unsure how to handle parents who cared. It was strange. A part of her clung to the insidious dread clogging her insides. Sooner or later she'd have to deal with her parents. Leaving poor Jud and the Masons to deal with them hardly seemed fair. They entered the large cafeteria. The woman beside her gasped. She walked between filled tables and patted people on the shoulders, offering a friendly hello and smile. Marshall would be horrified. It was one of the main reasons he and Dylan wanted their mother to be removed from her volunteer work fixing sandwiches and other meals for the men and women.

Not everyone was ready for socialization on such a personalized level.

She ate up the distance between her and the woman and put an arm around her to keep her from patting someone else's shoulders. "A lot of the men and women here are part of the Warrior's Path Project. It's a nonprofit Dylan and his brothers started to help soldiers leaving the service have a smoother transition to civilian life. Many are former spec ops, and are a bit...unaccustomed to socialization."

The woman's eyes widened. "Ah, I see, dear. My apologies. I should have realized."

"Sounds like a great program." Jarold looked around. "Nice, big setup here."

"The Arsenal is expanding quickly." Viviana motioned toward the large cafeteria area where someone had set up a salad bar, complete with sandwich fixings. Soups were on the end. "If nothing on the salad bar looks good, there's plenty of food in the refrigerators and freezers. Help yourselves to whatever you'd like."

The woman flitted about in the kitchen a bit, then whirled around. "Jarold, you and Viviana have a seat. I won't be long. This is such a lovely set up."

Vi smothered her smile as she and Jud's father sat at a nearby table. He talked about the weather, the trip over and how polite Dallas was. He asked a few questions about The Arsenal, but didn't seem too interested in the details. He'd likely learned not to ask too many prodding questions long ago. Within no time Jenna appeared with three heaping plates. Bacon and eggs with french toast. Vi's stomach rumbled. A few men looked at them curiously as they passed by.

"I'll be right back," Jenna commented as she rose.

Jarold chuckled. "She'll be cooking all day. She loves nothing more than making meals for people, says it's a hug for the stomach."

A hug for the stomach. Huh. Vi admitted her stomach could use a couple hugs. She dove into her plate, then realized they needed something to drink. She flip-flopped over to the beverages and snagged a couple bottles of water and headed back. Jenna was at the restaurant-sized stove in the midst of fixing enough food for an army, quite literally. The doors opened and Momma Mason entered.

Oh boy.

Vi sat at the table and watched as the two women introduced themselves to one another. It was as though they'd been separated at birth. She watched, enthralled as they started yanking enough food out of the fridges to feed the entire state. She covertly pulled her phone out and texted Riley.

"Calling in an intervention?" Jarold asked with a smile.

"Something like that," she replied honestly. "Momma Mason is a lot like your wife. They mean well, but I don't want them doing too much. It's easy to overstep and do more than you should. I'm learning that lesson myself."

"It's always better to do too much than not enough," he offered.

She nodded and continued eating. Jacob and Cord entered, along with Mary and Dylan. The latter looked at Vi and chuckled as they spotted the two older women in the midst of a cooking frenzy. Vi breathed a small sigh of relief. Cord and Dylan would stage an intervention if needed. So far, the people in the cafeteria didn't seem to mind all the strangers fussing over them. Jacob raced to the table and embraced his grandfather, then raced into the kitchen.

"I haven't seen him smile that big in a long time," Jarold commented.

"He's glad to see you and your wife," Vi replied.

"I'm thinking we both know it's more than a couple old geezers showing up. I've put two and two together and am suspecting you're Viviana Chambers, aka Quillery."

Vi's gut clenched. She swallowed the bit of french toast in her mouth and took a sip of water. She offered a brief nod, scanning the cafeteria. Where the heck was Jud?

"I'm not asking to put you on alert. I suspect Jenna put it together, too. I can see you have a lot going on. My son wouldn't have brought us here if it wasn't a life-threatening level of importance, the kind that makes conversations about the past wait." He forked some egg and chewed. Swallowed. "No matter the threat level, I've gotta say I admire the hell out of what you do. You gave our grandson his father back. Twice now."

"I wish I could've done more," Vi whispered sadly.

Jarold took her hand. "I can tell you're a woman with a deep soul, the protector. You've done more than most people would have. I'm proud to have finally met you and get a chance to thank you personally for what you did. You'll never know how much of an impact you've had on our Jacob."

She nodded and got back to eating her eggs and bacon. Her eyes burned slightly. She forced a couple deep breaths. Was this what a normal parent was like?

~

"This isn't working. He's sealed tighter than a nun," Dallas muttered in disgust.

Jud chuckled and crossed his arms. Viviana and Mary had been working the computers, pulling any information they could on Jian and his operations based on the take down. Jian wasn't a lightweight though, he'd played with The Collective long enough to know the strength found in silence. If he talked, he died. It was that simple.

Fallon and Gage both entered the observation room and leaned against the door.

"Now what?" Fallon asked.

"Now I have a go," Jud said as he looked over at Jacob. "Go get my backpack, bud. There's a kit, rolled up brown leather. Bring it and a bottle of water."

Viviana and Mary looked at one another. Marshall glowered from behind them. Jud wanted this mess with Jian done so the two women could do whatever else they needed. Viviana had enough on her plate with her asshole parents in the mix. Making Jian talk would be a fucking pleasure.

He didn't bother waiting for their assent. He exited the observation room and slowly walked toward the hallway leading to Jian's door. Since all the chambers and hallways on this floor were see-through, bulletproof glass, he knew Jian tracked his progression like the scared little piss ant he was. But Jud didn't watch. He paused, knocking on the tempered glass.

The Arsenal had a very sweet setup.

"Sound proof?" Jud asked, knowing the room picked up all sounds via mics positioned along the hallway and in all the rooms.

"Yes," Mary returned.

Jud entered the cell and took a couple steps in as the door sealed shut. Jian's widened gaze was on him. He stood with his back in a corner and his hands in front of him.

"Jian, it's been a while." He smiled and motioned toward the bed. "Sit. You want some water? Staying hydrated is important."

Jian gulped and shook his head. "I'm good."

"You sure?"

As if on cue, Jacob entered with a bottle of water and the rolled up kit. He set the latter on the floor beside a chair and held out the water. "Drink."

Jud sat in the seat, the back to his front and watched as Jian gulped the bottle down like a good pet. He truly loathed interrogating people. It was a pain in the ass when they were stubborn bastards.

"My parents are here, haven't seen them in a long time, Jian.

I'm more than a bit annoyed I'm down here with you instead of upstairs with them." He established eye contact, held it firmly. "You fucked up."

"I-I can explain."

"Oh? You took Danny. You can explain that?"

"No." Jian shook. His entire body trembled. "I can't. That was a fuck up, a huge one."

"You pissed me off, Jian. I've gotta admit I'm not sure what to do with that. I don't get pissed easily." Jud widened his stance, slamming his booted feet down.

Jian jumped. "I'll make amends, Jud."

"Well, I've got six million reasons amends isn't going to cut it. You have any idea what a pain in my ass you created? I told you the Quillery Edge was off limits. You didn't listen."

Jian shook his head.

"Here's how it's going to go. You and I are going to spend some quality bonding time down here. Alone. All nice and sound-proofed. Nice and warm room. Sanitary. Excellent conditions for what I have planned. Then, after I'm done I'll consider whether you've earned the right to share what you know." Jud sneered as the man trembled harder. "Remember Rome, Jian?"

"No, please. I'll talk. I'm sorry. Whatever you want. D-don't." Urine streamed down the man's shorts.

"I'm disappointed, Jian. You know better than to break that fast. What's Marla going to think? Did she tell you to take Danny?" Jud reached down and unrolled his kit. Jian's gaze locked onto the tools he hadn't used in a few years.

Rumors within the shadowy underground he operated within were rampant. Rome was the most talked about, the reason he'd become the infamous executioner for The Collective.

"We needed a way to encourage you to take the contract. It was business," Jian whispered quickly. "She though that'd be the best way."

"The Collective issued the contract on the Quillery Edge?" He reached down and grabbed the first tool, a long, thin blade. He scraped it across the chair. The sound echoed in the room.

Jian shriveled into the corner.

"The contract, Jian. Let's focus."

"She was pissed. Most of The Collective's board didn't want it to go through, but someone with bigger balls than brains demanded it be done. The Quillery Edge was a threat before, but they were curtailed at Hive."

"Because The Collective had Peter in their back pocket," Jud said. "You aren't telling me anything I didn't already know, Jian. That's...disappointing."

He waited through the silence until Jian chanced a glance toward him.

"Remove your shirt, Jian. Lock your hands behind your back and face the bed."

The man crumbled. He shook his head.

"You can't do this. They'll go after you," Jian warned.

"Who will they send?" Jud laughed. "Really, Jian? That's all you have to say. They can't send a terrier after a hell hound."

"What do you want?"

"Who issued the hit?"

"I don't know. All she ever said was it came straight from the top and she couldn't do anything but hope to hell it didn't blow back."

Son of a bitch. Jian didn't know. Jud sat there a few minutes and let the man snivel in his own piss.

"I need names. Anyone and everyone high up in The Collective or associated with them."

"You know more than I do," Jian argued.

"You're in a different circle than I am. Don't piss me off by being a belligerent little bitch."

"Okay, okay. I'll give you what I have." Jian raised his hands. "Are we cool?"

No. They were far from cool. Jud stood. "I'm leaving you be for now, but I want you to answer everyone's questions completely and honestly. Don't leave anything out. Give them anything that will help take The Collective down. If I hear you're being stubborn, I'll be back and it'll be a much more painful experience, one that'll make Rome look like a paper cut."

"Okay. Okay. Okay."

Jud left. He entered the observation room and ignored the tense silence unfurling at his entry.

"I'm seriously wondering what went down in Rome," Gage commented.

"It's about an eighth of what the underground says went down." Jud shrugged and motioned toward Jian. "He'll talk. If he doesn't, I'll carry through with the threat."

"Which was?" Marshall asked.

Jud's jaw twitched as he looked at Viviana, who watched silently. She chewed her lower lip, as if holding back the same question. "I've never professed to being a good man. I have skill sets most don't, talents sharpened out of necessity more than a desire to do so. I moved away from that dark years ago."

"Jian didn't seem to think you'd moved on," Mary commented.

"People see what they want."

"Thank you," Viviana replied. "Fallon and Gage will get what we can, but it doesn't look like he has a name."

"Do you?" Marshall asked.

"You have what I know." Jud looked at Viviana. "I'll see you later."

16

Vi collapsed into her favorite chair in the living room and glanced at the door. All her friends were on their way. It'd been a crazy, busy day at The Arsenal in more ways than one. Families had been settled, which had taken all morning and into the early afternoon. Marshall tabled debriefing until the morning because she and Mary needed to let HERA catch up on processing everything on The Collective.

They'd used the time to question Jian. Fallon and Gage both took a go at the man, but he'd remained steadfastly silent.

Until Jud walked in the room.

The man spewed like a broken fire hydrant as long as Jud was in the room. It was almost funny if it wasn't so pathetic and terrifying. She wanted to know what the hell went down in Rome to crumble a man that quick, but she was better off never knowing. That was a different time. A different Jud.

She believed him when he'd said as much.

She'd endured an awkward, downright stilted lunch with very little conversation with her parents and brother. Then she and the girls had all spent a few hours working with the information spewing from HERA. She'd opted to leave her family to their own for dinner and was now ready to call the exhaustive day done.

But her friends needed an escape, a debriefing of their little niche group. She hadn't been the only one who'd had a rotten day. Laughter tumbled from outside the entryway. The Pentagon entourage entered. Their boisterous merriment felt a bit out of place for a few moments, especially when her gaze lit on Rhea. Her friend was having troubles and hoarding them, like a dragon afraid to leave the lair. That wasn't good, but Vi didn't have the mental energy to ferret out another problem, not now. Riley and Mary plopped down on either side of her. Her best friend had a smile twenty miles wide on her face and, for once, Vi suspected it was because of more than Dylan being awesome and life being better.

She took her laptop and click-clacked away as everyone claimed their spaces. Riley, Bree and Rhea huddled up on the sofa while Mary and Addy took the small loveseat.

"You all okay?" she asked.

"Well, after you left, things in the lobby of The Arsenal got mighty interesting," Mary commented. "I watched with Dylan and the guys. You've gotta check this out."

"Maybe this isn't the smartest idea," Riley said. "He was really intense with her parents."

Jud. She'd wondered how things went with him and her parents after she left, but she hadn't found the time or the willpower to find out via the recorded surveillance.

"Really?" Bree asked excitedly.

"Show us," Addy ordered.

Vi's chest tightened as Mary took her computer and pulled up the feeds. Surveillance footage from the visitor's lobby filled her laptop screen. Jud stood there, his gaze intent and focused on her as she wandered down the hall in all her flip-flop glory.

"Wow, I wish I had a man look at me like that," Bree commented.

"Like what?" Vi asked.

"Like you're dessert and he hasn't eaten in a year," Rhea returned quickly.

The warmth spread, deeper and more intense than before. She delved into the intensity wafting from him as he turned, focused on her parents. "You don't know me, so I'll be polite this one time. This is a one-sided conversation where I set you straight. Then one of these guys, whichever can stand to be around you any longer, is going to escort you to your room and you two are gonna sit in there with your drunk son and think on what I said."

"You don't." Her father froze as Jud took a menacing step forward.

"Shut it," he growled. "You will never speak to Viviana like that ever again. I don't give a damn if she comes in wearing a dress made of bubblegum and her hair is a ratty mess, you will say nothing. You will never, ever demean her and talk down to her the way I just heard you do."

Jud looked back at the guys.

"Thinking they may not know what that means," Dallas commented.

"Right. I'll be specific. You don't ever talk about her making mistakes and not being normal. Every single man in this room, fuck, this entire compound, probably owes their lives to her and her brilliance for one reason or another. I know one man who wakes every morning and thanks God for being touched with her brilliance. She pulled him and his entire convoy out of hell and gave him hope that his boy, who was blessed with the same brilliant light as your daughter, could be like her one day. Then fifteen years later, she guided these good men around you back into another hellhole and did it all over again. She led eight teams on a mission so large and damn near impossible, I doubt anyone on this planet could've done better than her and her partner. I'd crawl through the bowels of hell to protect her and I'm pretty sure every person in this compound would as well."

A couple of the girls gasped at the declaration. Vi's eyes watered.

"I have no idea how Viviana managed to come out of a rat's nest like your world and be so beautiful, brilliant and perfect in every way. I don't know your daughter anywhere near as well as I want to, but I can tell you this. For this last mission alone I'd put a bullet in anyone's brain stem for half the shit you said to her today. I don't know what twisted world you live in that makes her less of a person than the waste of drunk space in the corner, but I do know this. Had I known you'd come into her world, one where every second of her time is so precious she sacrifices her own health and sleep to keep us breathing, and disrespect her like you just did, I would've left you to the vultures."

Oh. My. Wow.

Vi sat there stunned as the silence ticked by through the feed a little while. One of Dylan's brothers whistled.

"Now, to make sure I make myself perfectly clear, you're going to keep breathing because your daughter has made this the safest place on this Earth bar none. Whatever issues you might think you have with her died at the entry to this compound if you want to keep breathing. If that's a problem for you, then I'll take you back to the airport myself. I'm half a mind to do it anyway, because I doubt very much you can keep those viperous tongues in your mouths." He closed in another step. "Since you apparently forgot to pack your manners, I'll kindly request you keep your mouths sealed shut if you can't be civil around my parents. If you think I'm being an asshole right now, you don't want to see what I become if they get even a taste of what you gave your girl today."

Jud turned and stormed out the door.

Mary clicked off the feed and wiped her eyes. "Holy crap. That was so hot."

"Wow."

Addy nodded in approval.

Vi couldn't believe he'd chewed them out. "I-I'm not sure what to say. They didn't even say anything that bad."

"Honey," Riley whispered. "Seriously?"

"It's been too shitty of a day to dreg those waters," Vi said honestly. "But thank you for showing this to me."

"He's got your back," Mary said.

"He's not the only one. I guarantee there's no way anyone will let you be alone with them," Addy stated.

Vi was glad in a lot of ways. Things between them grew worse ever since her sophomore year at MIT, when she mistakenly invited them to a special awards ceremony dinner thrown in her honor. The entire night had been a train wreck of epic proportions. She and Mary had bonded, gotten even closer after the horrid night. They'd declared themselves the misfits of MIT. She smiled at the memory and hugged her friend close. "I love you all."

"Okay, tomorrow we'll conquer the list." Bree narrowed her gaze. "Don't give me that look. We all know you have one and it's probably massive."

She didn't bother denying it. "HERA should be done by then. Marshall has a debriefing early in the morning."

"Do you want to talk about the paperwork?" Mary asked.

"What paperwork?" Rhea asked.

"Jud filled out the profile sheets for us," Mary explained as she pulled them from her bag. "I haven't looked at them."

Unease filled her as she took them. She couldn't explain why, but she didn't want to share the piece of himself he'd offered up. It felt wrong.

"I think our girl needs rest more than she needs to mull over what we already know. Jud is a hell of an operative, one who'd do anything for her. That's all I need to know," Addy said as she stood. "Now y'all get ready so we can watch a movie, eat more crap than we should and drink ourselves into a new day."

Vi hadn't realized how much she needed the support of her friends until she'd already gotten it. Seeing her parents after so long had been a blow, but she'd done the right thing by bringing them here. She might never be the daughter they wanted, but she still loved them. And that'd be enough because she had started to realize it didn't matter if they never returned the love she offered. She had a new family forming at The Arsenal.

~

Someone was in her house. More specifically, someone was in her bedroom. She remained frozen in place, curled underneath the covers and contemplated her options. One loud scream and Addy would handle the rest.

Excellent idea.

She flung the covers back, sat up in bed and...

A hand covered her mouth, stifling the scream rolling from her. She kicked and punched, but an arm wrapped around her, locking her into place with a laughable ease. She blinked, adjusting her eyes to the dark as she heard her name in a husky whisper near her ear.

"It's me, Viviana."

She punched Jud and shoved away. Her breaths rushed in a ragged tempo as he flicked a light on. His half-hooded gaze slid down her briefly, then returned to her face. "What the hell are you doing?"

"I came to make sure you were okay."

"You were worried enough to check on me, so you break into

my house in the middle of the night and sneak into my bedroom? You're scaring the shit out of me to make sure I'm okay?"

"Now that you put it that way..." He stroked her face and offered a faint smile. "Didn't think much past wanting to make sure you were okay."

Okay, that was way sweet. Her anger melted away beneath the quiet honesty layered within his words. "I'm guessing you don't usually do things without thinking ten steps ahead."

"It's not smart," he admitted. "But I did say I was coming, Viviana. Remember?"

"Oh. I didn't believe you," she whispered. She was suddenly too aware of the thin spaghetti top and shorts, the same ones she'd worn in the kitchen when he'd tasted her sass for breakfast.

Was he here to taste her sass again? She licked her lips and remained silent, unsure what to say. Sexy, muscled bad asses didn't drop in to check on her in the middle of the night.

"Viviana." Her name was more of a warning than a plea.

"Sorry, I'm nervous. I'm not sure why. I didn't expect you just to break in and check on me. It's sweet in a totally stalkerish kind of way." She smiled. "You okay?"

"That's my line," he replied.

"I'm better than expected. Seeing my parents again was a shock," she admitted. "I saw what you did. Mary sort of snagged the footage and shared it."

"I figured she would. I was hard on them, probably should've been easier on my delivery."

"No. They don't listen. You were effective, which is way more than I've ever been." Failure. The word summarized her entire existence as far as her parents were concerned.

"You're a beautiful, brilliant woman, Viviana. Don't ever let their stupidity make you think otherwise." He ran his thumb across her lips. "Mom and Dad loved you."

Her pulse quickened. Something in her unfurled at the notion his parents had liked her. The time she'd spent with them had been a bit awkward at first, but once she realized they weren't judging her every little action, looking for reasons not to like her, she'd basked beneath their curiosity and interest. "They're awesome."

He smiled, a full-on smile that hit his eyes. "Yeah, they are."

"Your mom and Momma Mason have a lot in common. If we aren't careful they'll take over the compound, turn it into the world's largest kitchen and feed the universe."

"I heard they started that endeavor," he said. "Mom's got the lay of the land now, understands she can interact with people here, but needs to keep her distance, too. She's good at reading people."

"Is that where you got it from?"

His eyes glimmered in the pale light coming from the bedside lamp. "You're easy to read when you're outside Command Central, Viviana."

"Oh? What am I thinking?" She licked her lips.

"You're thinking it's time for me to take another shot of sass. You're damn near brimming over with it, aren't you?"

"It has been hard keeping it contained. I wouldn't want your parents to think badly of me." The admission tumbled from her. Why their opinion mattered made perfect sense to her, but it wasn't something she wanted to explain to anyone.

She'd already failed one set of parents.

"That's impossible," he declared softly.

"Right, of course. I'm Quillery, the woman who saved Danny."

"No, you're Viviana, the woman who has their son twisted up for the first time in his life."

"You're twisted up?" Her gaze settled on his t-shirt, a snug hunter green number that brought out the gray in his eyes. "Is that good, or bad?"

"I'm thinking it's good." His lips feathered against hers. "Now about that taste."

She grabbed his head and sealed their lips. Mint with a hint of whiskey. She moaned and flicked her tongue across his lips. He opened, took control of the kiss in a carnal fusion of tongues. They wrestled tongues, then bodies as he sprawled her onto her back. His weight against her ignited an ache within her.

It'd been too long.

The kiss turned slow, playful. She growled and grabbed at his shirt. Heat greeted her palms when she settled them beneath the material. All that existed was the fiery kiss and the commanding way he guided the moment, kept her wanton for more while giving her exactly what she needed.

Vi couldn't think, couldn't function beyond relishing the way her skin tingled beneath his fingertips as they ran down her neck, across her shoulders. Heat suffused where he kissed along the same trail.

"So beautiful," he whispered against her shoulder.

She growled her frustration and yanked at the shirt again. "Off."

He chuckled and took it off. She memorized the wounds along his torso. Long gouges along his ribcage. Bullet wounds. Stab wounds. "Shit."

"Viviana." The guttural plea spurred her desire, made her almost believe she really did have him twisted up. She kissed the first wound, just above his right nipple. She meandered south and suckled the bud. She craved his mouth on her in the same way. Would he graze her with his teeth, nibble firm enough to make her gasp? She laved the nub and peeked up through half-hooded eyes as she gave him the contact she craved.

The hungry look on his face almost made her lose focus. Pupils dilated, he ran his fingers through her hair and dragged her away.

"Hey, I wasn't done."

"I see you're part minx," he teased.

"Told you I was a cat person," she shot back. She yanked and tugged, but he pinned her against the bed.

Amusement flickered in his gaze as it settled on her. Breathing labored, she remained still as his fingertips continued the meandering path they'd set upon earlier, the one she'd waylaid with her own exploration.

"I've fantasized about having a taste of you there a long time, Viviana." He tugged the material covering her chest down. Agonizingly slow.

She held her breath and grasped at his hand, suddenly too aware of her imperfections, the bulges of fat on her where only sinewy flesh was on him. The pudges where he had none. The playful glimmer in his gaze stifled the doubts. This once she'd not worry, live in the moment rather than in her head.

"Don't move, minx, or I'll have to tie you up," he taunted.

Pleasure pooled between her legs at the thought. He chuckled, a low rumble of knowing that made her too aware of the barely-there material between her and him. Thank goodness he had jeans on or he'd know how aroused she was.

The wandering hand pulled the material over her breast, fully exposing her. He kissed and licked around her breast, the swell, the side, everywhere but where she wanted the heat of his mouth. She writhed and shifted beneath him, but his other hand worked in tandem with his body to keep her pinned into place, at his mercy.

Heat encompassed her nipple as his mouth laid claimed to her. A moan escaped her. Foreplay hadn't ever ignited her desire. It'd always been a grope here, a pinch there. Nothing spectacular. He repeated the agonizing homage to her other breast. He cupped and massaged while he nibbled and sucked her nipple.

"Judson."

He groaned and dragged her down the bed. Their mouths collided. A battle ensued, one she was too lost in sensation to fully understand. He severed the contact with a lick on her lips. He smiled down at her. "So beautiful and passionate."

Shocked, she watched as he pulled her camisole top back up and stretched out behind her. Spooning? Too confused to speak, she lay there a moment. Her entire body throbbed. Ached for...she squirmed. His hand locked around her waist. Hot breath fanned along her neck.

He'd stopped.

"I hear your beautiful mind spinning a million miles an hour," he whispered in her ear. "Settle down, babe. You need rest."

Rest? Was he serious? Her entire body was a live wire, one he'd turned on and then abandoned. Rest?

He chuckled.

"You're a little hellcat, so passionate." He nibbled her earlobe until she leaned against him, deepening the contact. "I'm not gonna rush this, not with you. You're a gift I'm going to unwrap slowly, savor."

Okay, that was hot. And sweet. Unsure how to respond, she laid in his arms and enjoyed the moment. Being held rocked.

17

Judson looked around at the filled room. They were two hours into the debriefing and he was a minute away from dragging Viviana out. She rubbed her temples and stared at the streams of data coming from HERA. She, Mary and Cord were working to keep up. Jacob had even offered his assistance, assistance quickly accepted.

"I understand Gage has run into a few hiccups securing your new employee," Marshall commented.

"Zoey, aka Zero, was working for the NSA. Her intervention helped Fallon's team, as we all know from the debriefing. Unfortunately, her employers aren't willing to let her go easily. The situation is a bit...problematic," Mary said. "Vi made a call to Bob."

"Right," Marshall said. "Bob called, assured me they'd be wheels up within the hour. Zoey's officially clear and I have assurances from very high up the food chain there will be no backlash from her exit."

"We've completed the first round of Jian's interrogation. The hard drive retrieved from his domicile has been more helpful than him, but we have managed to get some names, locations and account information from him," Vi said. "We should probably hold him a little longer, and try again."

"Agreed," Mary said. "The last item on the agenda is The Collective, specifically kicking their ass for trying to kick ours."

"For the record, before we get in the weeds, I want a say a couple things." Marshall's voice boomed within the room. "Judson, Marcus and Jacob, you three stepped up and did a hell of a job keeping this compound secure against incredible odds. Y'all made a hell of a team."

Jacob beamed. Red rose in his cheeks as everyone smiled. Cord slapped his back and grinned real big.

"Marcus, get with Dylan after the meeting. We're giving you a team. Once we get things down to a dull roar here, we'll move forward with application testing and operative vetting. You can help us if you want, pick your own crew. Dylan and I will have final approval, but I'd prefer you pick your own team."

"Appreciated," the man replied. "Though Jud's the one who should get the bulk of the praise. He was a one-man squadron."

"Yes, he was." Marshall pinned him with a gaze. "If you're willing to pull back those lethal instincts and color within the lines a bit more, there's a place for you here at The Arsenal if you're interested."

"We'll chat," Jud said.

The offer was unexpected, out of nowhere. He'd love to settle down, put his knives away for good and color within the lines. He could almost see himself doing that with Viviana. Here, at The Arsenal. If they'd hire Jacob on...damn. It was almost too much of a good thing to contemplate. Good hadn't had a place in his work world in a long, long time, if ever. He was sorely tempted to accept on the spur of the moment, trust the gut instinct in his head screaming yes. It was the same voice demanding he explore things with Viviana—give normal a shot.

Not that the beautiful and brilliant woman across the room could ever be normal.

"Right. Vi, read us in on what we've gathered about The Collective so far."

"We have lots of data between..." Vi swallowed, glancing at him. "We have a lot of data from two data sets. We've pieced together what we think is a relatively decent chain of command, one with a good chunk of the major players identified."

Images appeared in a hierarchy. Jud nodded. "I recognize a lot of them. How do we take them down?"

"Slowly," Mary replied. "Vi and I went over the options and we think hitting them where it hurts is the best route. Weaken their position by taking their money, a shot of poison to the roots will kill the tree. That's the assumption at least."

"Cutting the money will cut their power," Dallas said. "Most of the lower tier won't work without an instant payday afterward."

"Upper ranks won't either," Jud said. "What do you need to make that happen?"

"Account numbers, the more the better. We got some from Jian. The other data we have had a few."

"I'll give you what I know, but it's old, probably too outdated to use," Dallas said.

"Lots of organizations this massive get lazy, complacent. They likely don't close down their accounts often, just reroute funds. Either way, we can follow the trail, wherever it might lead. There's a digital footprint, even for closed accounts." Vi smiled as she looked at Dallas, then him. "HERA was built on doing exactly this, pulling money from assholes. Once Zero is here, she can help. She's helped me with stuff like this a lot."

"I know someone I can reach out to, get more info from if we need another data source," Jud said. "Kristof has worked with The Collective a while, for some of the blacker ops."

"Let's hold off and see what we can do with the data we get

from Dallas. Keeping this in house would expedite the process," Vi said. "It'll be less dangerous for you that way."

She was worried about him. Something inside him stirred, a restlessness born of surprise and curiosity. It'd been a long time since he'd had anyone in his work world worried about him. Concerned for anything aside from the monetary bottom line.

"Dallas is going to San Antonio for supplies. We've been talking with Marcus and reviewing the security footage from the compound attack." Dylan pinned Jud with an intense gaze. "We'd all appreciate a training session from you on hand-to-hand if you're up for it, Jud. Especially with close quarters and knives. You've got some moves we haven't seen, and that's saying quite a bit given our backgrounds. We respect whatever decision you make."

Jud sensed the test within the request. He was either vested enough in securing the compound and Viviana to train them or not. If he wasn't one hundred percent into the objective, he wouldn't expose himself, neutralize his strengths in hand-to-hand by training other operatives to be as proficient as he was. He smiled at the man across the table and nodded. "Okay, though we might want to contain the lessons to everyone in here at first, branch out to the other team members after you feel proficient enough to assist with training."

"Agreed," Dallas said. "I'll hold off on the supply run until tomorrow if you're up for doing it this afternoon. I can probably help with some of the moves, but I'm a little rusty."

Jud doubted the man could ever be rusty. He'd been far better than most everyone Jud encountered. He nodded his approval, realizing he'd taken one more step closer to the light, the clean. He glanced at Viviana, who offered a knowing smile.

$\sim$

HERA was still working on the bank account hacks. Jud had taken everyone outside to start the hand-to-hand training. She glanced down at the keys on her laptop, the ones which activated the remote video feed. She wanted to see how the training was going, watch Jud in motion, in his element.

But she had no business going down that road, the one which hoped he'd say yes to Marshall's surprising offer. Judson Jensen working for The Arsenal. Vi didn't even know what to do with the possibility. It was too out there in terms of improbable, which was why she'd locked herself in her room and far away from anything that would let her spy on him and thereby feed that dangerous what-if scenario processing in her brain.

She sat at the coffee table and pulled out the strips of paper she'd just printed out and cut up. She organized the quillery supplies and got to work. She didn't bother hiding the important tidbits with useless colorful ones. This message was far too important, too complicated to bother with finesse. She thought about the day and what all they had uncovered. Her mental walls were scrubbed raw and she'd yet to write anything down.

She probably had no business quilling, but hiding important facts in small shapes of colored paper got the gunk out of her head even if it hurt. She pulled out the first bright blue strip and got to work creating the pattern. Minutes flowed into one another as she lost herself in the process. One teardrop became two, then ten. Then twenty. A multitude of colors woven together, the pattern bright. Unlike the message buried beneath, a message no one would ever read.

Her mental purge of the day.

"Viviana."

She startled at the word, but it was the firm hand on her shoulder that made her jump. She blinked. The room was dark except for the lone lamp she'd flicked on.

"Babe, you were a thousand miles away." Jud looked at the desk. Eyebrows raised, he cupped the back of her neck. "How long have you been at this?"

"Since the meeting," she answered honestly.

"The one eight hours ago?"

Oh wow. Time slipped by. Weird. He'd changed at some point, was now wearing a white button-down shirt which stretched across his chest and hugged his thick biceps. Black jeans completed the look. So damn gorgeous.

"Come on. We're going to grab some food and get away from the compound a while." He helped her stand.

Pain shot up and down her legs. His gaze narrowed. "You didn't even get up."

"I zoned."

"I'll be back. I'm going to pull the truck closer so you don't have to walk as far."

She nodded, grateful Jud had left long enough for her to tend to business in the bathroom and make sure she didn't look as terrifyingly freaky as she suspected. Loud voices in the living room drew her attention and pulled her from what she called the quillery haze. She trundled out of the bedroom and slammed into her brother.

"Hey, sis. Still as ugly as always."

"Hey, bro. Just as dumb as always."

"Viviana." Her father's face distorted, as if he'd sucked on a few too many lemons. "I saw that man leave here. We need a word."

"It's probably best to wait until later, Dad. We're headed out and I'm not..." She halted the explanation. They didn't get her why. Not anymore. "We'll talk tomorrow."

"What on Earth is going on, Viviana? We deserve some answers. All we've gotten so far is attitude," her mother said.

"Perhaps if you'd listen instead of whining, people would explain a few things. Or, perhaps if you treated them with a modicum of respect, they'd explain a few things." She rubbed her temples. "You were in danger. Now you're not. There's your explanation."

"Why?" her brother asked. "What'd you do?"

"I'm afraid I can't give you details because of security clearance, but we're working on eliminating the threats."

"How long are we stuck here?" her father asked.

"Long enough to keep you safe. It could be days, weeks." God forbid. "Months."

"We need to have a chat with your boss about monetary compensation," her father said. Vi blinked as he continued. "My time is valuable, too valuable to be wasted here."

"You're a used car salesman in Hoboken, Dad, not the president. I'll make sure your bills are paid if you'll round them up or forward them to me." She rubbed her neck. Sometimes she wondered how she was related to them. Then again, you couldn't pick family.

"This is much nicer than that vile den of inequity they put us in. People tromped up and down the hallway all night, shouting and carrying on. I swear, it's a miracle I got any sleep. Poor Richie didn't sleep a wink."

Probably because brother dearest had been passed out the day before, but Vi kept quiet. It'd been years since she'd endured one of her mom's rants, but she knew the best thing to do was ride it out. Silently. She tuned the droning voice out and focused on getting her purse.

Shoes.

She spotted flip-flops. She toed them on and thanked fate when Jud walked in. He froze in the doorway with a glower on his face. His eyes narrowed. "Are you ready, Viviana?"

"I am having an important conversation with my daughter," her mother replied. "Now, I'm thinking your father and I can take your room. Richie can have the pull out. The sofa's a bit ragged and old, but he can make do."

Addy would string her up by the nearest tree if she let her family stay in the house. She kept her gaze settled on the floor. "We need everyone in one place. The compound's the most secure building around. You'll need to stay there for now. If this goes on longer than expected, I'll see what can be done."

"Nonsense. Ralph, move our things. Or better yet, have that man do it. What was his name? The rude one with the town name."

"Dallas," Richie supplied. "He told me I needed to drink a pot of coffee and grow the fuck up."

"Oh, you poor dear." Mom patted him on the face. "You don't pay any mind to him. You're doing so good. Even your dad doesn't know how you do it. Viviana, Richie has been employee of the month at his Best Buy the past six months straight. We're so proud."

"That's great," she supplied. "I'm afraid we'll have to chat later. Jud and I need to go somewhere."

"Where?" Richie asked.

Anywhere but here.

"There you are, dear. We were worried. Is everything okay?" Jenna Jensen peered past her son and smiled. "Oh, hello. You must be Vi's parents. I'm Jenna. This is my husband, Jarold. Our handsome son here was about to take us all into Nomad for a steak. Nolan and the boys raved about this one place and we're ready to dive in."

Dread struck her in a one-two punch. Punch one was the announcement they were going for steak. In Nomad. Nomad was a slightly larger than pea-sized town twenty miles north of Resino. It was big enough to have a string of national fast food chains along the highway running between San Antonio and Del Rio. There was a hospital and a few banks and other businesses, mostly centered around farming and ranching. The grocery store everyone in a hundred-mile radius used was there.

According to Momma Mason, a trip to Nomad was a big deal, one undertaken by busy Resino residents once a week. Errands were run. Groceries were bought.

Jud taking her somewhere to eat with his parents was a shock. Going into Nomad for said food was on an entirely different level of surprise. She looked down at her clothes, recalled the couple of times Mary had ranted about Dylan dragging her into Resino looking like a bridge troll. At the time she'd laughed, finding it hysterical her friend gave a damn what she looked like.

Now she totally got it. And karma was making sure she got it in a huge way since Jud's parents were tagging along.

The second punch came immediately after the extended offer. Her mom smiled the smile she'd seen a hundred times. She might be the housewife of a used car salesman in Hoboken, but she thought she was the Queen of freaking England.

And Mrs. Jensen was her new quarry.

Damn.

"We'd love to go," her father answered.

Great. Now what?

Vi sighed and peeked at Jud. His jaw twitched. His eyes lit with amusement. What could possibly be funny about this situation? His father had a matching look on his face. She backpedaled toward the hall.

"What are you doing?" Jud asked, his voice soft despite his tense stance.

"I-I need to change."

"Oh, don't be ridiculous. You look adorable." Jenna shoved into the room and wrapped her arm around Vi. "I really need to find out where you find all those lovely leggings, dear. Those skeletons are adorable."

She peeked down at her attire and stifled a groan. She hoped the skeletons weren't predicting tonight's outcome. Jud and his mom steered her out of the house. Jarold herded her dad and brother. They headed down the wide, paved walkway.

"We'll be ready to go in a minute. We're waiting on a couple of people," Jud commented as he put his phone into his back pocket.

"Who's going with us?" Vi asked.

"Reinforcements," he replied. The smirk on his face stifled some of the dread.

Rational reasoning demanded she make the best of the situation. Perhaps Jud and his parents were the padding she needed to have real communication with her parents. Maybe they'd taken Jud's heart-to-heart seriously and were turning over a new leaf.

Yeah and maybe pigs flew.

"There they are." Jenna clapped her hands together. "Everyone, this is Dallas and his brother Dylan. And you already know Mary."

Her best friend flashed her a smile. "Actually, we've never met, Mrs. Jensen."

"Oh." The woman looked between the groups. "You've been friends since you were fifteen. How can that be?"

"No matter," Jarold replied. "Is Jacob coming?"

"Not this time. He's working with Cord," Jud replied. "I'll bring him something back."

"Marshall's calling a large order in, assuming the kitchen can handle it. Mom's going to have our heads when she finds out we went without her."

"What nonsense. We can stop off at the house and get her. There's plenty of room," Jenna declared. "She motioned toward Dallas. Be a dear and go get that sweet mother of yours."

"She's in town at a bunco party with Riley," Dylan explained. "We'll make sure we go back again so you two can visit."

"Wonderful! I had the most marvelous time helping her and

your sister with lunch today. And all those men and women you all are helping. You're all salt of the Earth."

Apparently the plan was to drown her family in kindness. It was an interesting approach, one she was grateful for—mainly because it shifted focus away from her. Since ten people were a few too many to squeeze into one vehicle, Jenna decided she and her husband would ride with Dylan, Dallas and Mary.

Which left Vi with Jud, her parents and Richie.

"You can ride shotgun, Richie. I know you get motion sick." Her mother patted him on the face and looked at Vi. "You can ride in between us."

"Vi rides up front with me," Jud declared. When she didn't move, he nudged her with a hand to her waist. "You want me to lift you up?"

She shook her head and climbed in after he opened the door, a bit stupefied he'd somehow pulled off her riding up front. She looked over at the other vehicle, where Dylan and Mary were climbing into the front. Jud's mom laughed when Dallas lifted her and set her into the back seat. Jarold clapped him on the shoulder and climbed in. Dallas winked at her and closed the door.

Operation Nomad was officially underway.

The large vehicles used by The Arsenal seated everyone comfortably. The trip in was quieter than she expected.

"Are we sure this is safe? Maybe we should just bring Mary and Dylan back something."

"Dylan and I wanted you two out and about getting some recreation. You've been working too hard. You deserve a night out on the town." He reached over and caressed her face. "Sit back and enjoy."

"Jud, I'm not sure this is a good idea."

"It's fine, Viviana." He smiled. "I'm thinking a greyhound is the way to go. We need something fast to keep up with us."

"I just saw the most adorable calico up for adoption," she

responded with a smile. "I think he'll make the perfect playmate for Penny the Persian."

"We tried having a cat once, but Viviana killed it," Richie added.

Jud's hand settled atop hers and squeezed. "What happened?"

"Reckless and I were playing in the yard. I was looking for bugs along the sidewalk and he ran out into the road after a butterfly. A car came around the corner and..." She swallowed and shook off the visual. "I'd gotten him for my seventh birthday three days earlier."

"It was such a disappointment," her mom said.

"Yes, it was." Vi looked out at the road, knowing Jud probably had a couple follow-up questions. He remained silent, as if sensing she needed time to strengthen her armor.

18

___

J ud put the car into park and glanced in his rearview mirror. Viviana's family had been thankfully silent after sharing the cat story. Jesus. He was down for buying her a dozen of the things if they chased away the haunted expression on her face. He'd intended to take her to a nice dinner, catch a movie afterward.

A date.

How long had it been since he'd gone out on a traditional date? Neither he nor Viviana were traditional in any sense of the word, but that didn't mean they couldn't try. Things had gone to hell, though. First his parents wanted to spend time with her. He liked that. Then her parents piled in. No one liked that. So he'd added Dylan and Mary into the pile. Dallas tagged along. The jury was out on that being a good idea.

Her family fled the back of the vehicle and headed toward the restaurant. The mother was whining about something, but Jud didn't listen to much past "that man." He figured someone might take exception to him handling her parents the way he wanted.

Permanently.

He reached over and cupped Viviana's face until she looked at him. Leaning over, he kissed her, lightly at first. She deepened the contact. The desperation in her kiss unsettled him. A new plan formed in his lizard brain. They were alone in the truck. He could haul ass out and let Dylan and Dallas sort out their families. Yeah, his lizard brain loved the idea.

But she deserved better than base instincts.

"Have I told you how beautiful you are?"

"A few times," she whispered. "I'm starting to believe you mean it."

"Good, because I do." He smiled. "Let go eat."

"This isn't a good idea."

"It's going to be okay," he assured her. He'd make sure it was. "Stay seated. I'll come around."

Jud went around the vehicle and helped her out. She was more than capable of handling it on her own. Hell, Viviana could do anything she put her brilliant mind to, but she was short and the flip-flops weren't exactly optimal footwear. Cute as hell, but he didn't want her tumbling, and they weren't exactly the optimal footwear for a fast exit if necessary. No matter. He wasn't leaving her side until they were back at the compound.

"You're staring at my feet again. I'm starting to think you have a foot fetish." She tapped his chest with a playful fist. "Eyes off my toes. You've had your requisite foot time when you gave me a massage."

"I'm thinking I could develop lots of fetishes where you are concerned." He whispered the admission into her ear and wrapped a protective arm around her. "Cute flip-flops, but you can't run in those."

Her eyes widened. She glanced down and wiggled her toes. Pink tinged her cheeks as she looked back up. "I can handle my own in a crisis, Judson Jensen. Don't worry about me and my footwear. Keep your bad ass focus elsewhere."

Cute as hell. He kissed her again, playful and quick. "Let's go."

He turned and almost knocked his parents over. They wore twin expressions of curiosity and amusement. Unfortunately her parents were on the opposite end of the spectrum. Arms crossed, they glared from their location nearer the restaurant than anyone else. Dallas, Dylan and Mary were all either grinning or laughing outright.

"I wish you would have let me change," Viviana stated.

"I've said it before, I don't give a damn what you wear. You're beautiful in anything. You'd make a trash bag a fashion trend."

"I'd be better off in a Hefty bag than this." Her gaze swept the restaurant. "Seriously, Judson, this place is fancy."

"Leave it be, girlfriend," Mary said. "It took Dylan several trips to get me desensitized to this. I finally get it. They'd rather get time away from The Arsenal with us than waste it while we gussy up. Next time we'll make sure you're dressed to kill."

Jud offered Mary a smile. She got what he was saying.

"Besides," she pointed to her leggings. Zombies. "We match!"

The women laughed and headed toward the restaurant arm in arm. He shook his head and chuckled.

"You're good with her," Dylan commented.

"She makes it easy." He regarded the two brothers, then looked over at his parents, who'd quietly followed his progression with Viviana. "This'll likely be an awkward dinner. Her parents are..."

"We know, dear," his mother said. "Let's go."

He closed the distance between him and Viviana as she and Mary made it to her parents. Dallas smirked and opened the door, motioning everyone into the restaurant. He let Dylan handle the seating situation.

"Oh, yes. We have your table ready, Mr. Mason. The order you called in is in works. It should be ready by the time you are ready to leave."

"Appreciated," Dylan responded. He turned and scanned the room as Mary snuggled closer.

The restaurant was a typical layout of several closed off sections, two of which spilled out onto a wraparound porch.

"Oh, miss, we'd love a seat outside." Viviana's mother motioned toward the double-doors.

"Inside," he replied to the young girl escorting them.

"Inside," Dylan affirmed.

"But it's such a lovely evening. The breeze alone is worth being outside." The woman looked genuinely confused.

"I'm sorry, I didn't get your name earlier. I'm Jenna." His mom weighed into the unfolding bout like a prizefighter.

"Olivia," the woman offered. "Don't you agree outside would be lovely?"

"Yes, it would." She lowered her voice and touched Olivia's forearm. "Can you keep a secret?"

The woman's eyes widened, but she nodded at his mom.

"These three men aren't here to take us to dinner. They're here to keep us safe. Outside is lovely, but not secure. Would Prince William have dinner on a restaurant patio without adequate protection?"

Olivia scanned him, Dylan and Dallas. "Very well. Inside, though I hardly see the comparison. I suppose them keeping us safe since we're confined to that compound is a good idea. I'd hate to drag this out any longer."

"Excellent." His mom nodded at the confused waitress. "We're ready."

"We have a private party room," the girl offered. "I'll put you in there and make sure my manager knows."

Jud grinned. The girl had overheard more than was probably

smart, but it'd gotten them inside a secured room. His mother flashed him a wink as they followed the woman to a back corner room. Sitting took a little negotiation. Richie needed an exterior corner, but he, Dylan and Dallas weren't about to give those up easily. Viviana's father relegated the sole end table position to his son and sat on the other side of Dallas. Dylan took the opposite side of the table with Mary at his side. Jud took the seat nearest the wall and pulled the seat beside that out.

Viviana smirked as she sat, but made no comment to the musical chairs. His mother sat on Viviana's other side. By the time the dance was finished, Viviana's parents had been effectively separated at the table. He offered a chin lift of gratitude to everyone.

"This is such a lovely restaurant. I love the lighting. Are those deer antlers up there?" His mom pointed to the wall nearest him.

"Those are moose if I'm not mistaken," Dylan offered as he put a napkin in his lap. "The owner has a restaurant up north as well and hunts up there during season."

Stilted conversation commenced in between drink orders. Heaving piles of dinner rolls were placed onto the table.

"No, thank you." Olivia pursed her lips. "Some of us can't afford to eat that many carbs. It goes straight to our hips. Don't you agree, Viviana?"

"Right." Viviana fisted the napkin in her lap.

Jud reached over and put a roll on her plate. He pulled the plate of butter squares closer. "Dad always taught me real men appreciate a woman for who she is inside, not her dress size. Eat up, Viviana, because you're a hell of a woman."

～

"In case I don't get to say it later, Mr. and Mrs. Chambers, thank you for raising such a brilliant and competent daughter." Dallas looked at Vi, then over at her parents. "She's saved the lives of a lot of people I love and keeps us safe when we're in the field. We couldn't live without her, and we have you to thank for that."

Vi almost choked on her tea. Where had that come from? She peered around the table and wondered if, like Alice, she'd stumbled into an alternate reality, one where everyone had lost their minds. She sat beside Jud and nibbled on her roll.

"I know firsthand how difficult it is to raise a genius. My grandson is a lot like your Vi," Jenna said. "He's nineteen and already working on his master's at MIT."

"That's where Viviana went," her father supplied. "And yes, you're quite right. Raising her was...a challenge. It wasn't easy being corrected by a child because she knew more than anyone around her."

Her stomach soured. She had been a bit...difficult. At the time she'd merely wanted to share what she'd learned.

"Ah, yes, we still have that problem with our Jacob sometimes," Jarold commented. "Then I figured out he wasn't sharing to correct us or show how smart he was. He just had so much in his little brain, he was damn near exploding to share with someone. He didn't make friends easy, still doesn't from what I understand."

It was like Jud's father had read her mind. She breathed a small sigh of relief when no angered retort came from her parents.

"Well, I suppose that is true. She may have been precocious, but she never failed to impress us. Once she got her mind on something she wouldn't stop until it was done." Her mom laughed.

Laughed.

"Mom, Dad, do you remember the trip we took, the one where

the RV died going up the incline?" Richie laughed and shook his head. "I still remember how pissed you were when you came in with that melted cup."

"Oh my word," her mom chuckled and looked around. "I'd almost forgotten. We were going up Rattone Pass and Ralph decided we didn't need a tow truck to haul us up the steep incline. We'd manage just fine."

"So of course we break down about halfway up," Richie said with a laugh.

Viviana couldn't help but join in. The bread in her stomach settled a bit at the levity. "Dad realized he could drain gas from the generator to get us started up again to help the vehicle not die in first gear when going against the sharp incline. It was a great idea. He was always good with cars."

"Right." Her dad cleared his throat. "Obviously I was a bit embarrassed I hadn't just paid the money for the assist up the hill like a lot of the other RV owners were doing. So I march into the kitchen and grab a foam cup sitting on the counter. Viviana looks up and in that fiercely confident tone of hers and says, 'That won't work, Dad. It's going to melt.'"

Vi looked down. Heat crept up her cheeks.

"Dad tells her off and marches out with the cup in hand. I'm sitting there laughing cause I don't understand why it's gonna melt, but I know it will. My sister wasn't ever wrong about science stuff." Richie smiled at her.

She forced a deep breath. She'd always assumed he was laughing at *her*.

"Oh dear," Jenna said.

"Yes, well, I quickly realized I should've probably asked why instead of getting angry," her father admitted.

"That's a lesson we're all still learning," Dylan admitted. "When she or Mary or one of their friends says something, I've learned to accept it as fact and let the why sort itself out."

"Smart man," Jarold said. "When you're in love with brilliance, taking a backseat to it saves the marriage. Take it from me. We're going on thirty-eight years."

"What do you do?" Olivia asked Jud's mom.

"Oh, I'm retired now, but I used to be a professor at our local college." She wiped her mouth. "Mathematics mostly."

Vi smiled as she looked over at Mary. Jud's mom was why he found intelligence beautiful. Because his father did. That was so damn adorable she wanted to drag him away from the table.

"Well, I can tell you, it's not easy being engaged to a bad ass who keeps putting himself into danger. But we'll sort it out." Mary shoved against Dylan, who looked over at her with a big grin on his face. "As for Jacob, I know what he's going through. Being the youngest person on a strange, lonely campus with no family nearby was terrifying. Thank goodness Vi and I had each other."

"Oh, Judson moved close. He's very near the campus to keep a check on him."

"I doubt he appreciates that. He was probably itching to get away and learn stuff," her mom said. "That was Viviana. She couldn't wait to get away, like we weren't good enough."

Vi took a piece of her roll. When was that waitress returning with their food?

"Were you anxious to get away?" Jud asked.

She shrugged. "I guess so. I never fit in anywhere. MIT was like a beacon, a place I'd find people like me. Geeky freaks who were better at math and science than people."

"That sounds like our Jacob," Jarold said. "He's talked nonstop about all his time hanging out with the Quillery Edge."

"What is the Quillery Edge?" Richie asked. "It sounds cool."

"It is way more than cool," Dallas responded. "Your sister is Quillery and Mary is the Edge. They're the most sought after back office operatives in the business. Jacob's been spending time with them, sort of like meeting his favorite superhero."

"Back office operative. What is that? A secretary?" Her mom set her menu down. "I've never really understood what Viviana does."

"Intel is often our most important weapon when we go into missions. Your daughter and my fiancée can find anything and anyone. The knowledge they provide and the quick, decisive actions they take save lives." Dylan put a hand around Mary as the waitress finally arrived.

Vi breathed a sigh of relief. They'd order, then she'd shift the conversation to something a bit less...heavy.

The waitress started with Jud, who ordered a steak with a baked potato and green beans. She cringed when he answered rare for how to cook it.

"I'll have the same as him, but well done."

"Really, Viviana. You can't eat something well done. You lose all the flavor," her father said. "Medium rare is at least acceptable."

"If I don't hear sirens because they burned the kitchen down preparing my meal, then the meat isn't cooked." She swallowed. "I don't like blood. We see enough without it being on my plate."

Whoops. Jud draped his arm around her shoulders. She looked over at him.

"Change my order. She's right. I'll take mine medium well."

"I can handle medium well," she told the waitress.

Conversation flowed, not river fast, but it wasn't as awkward or stressful as she'd expected. Everyone stayed on safer topics. She ate and laughed with her family for the first time since childhood. Her gut still soured when she thought about them, but she'd gotten more insight into what they might have been thinking back then. She hoped they'd gotten the same. It wasn't until the end of the meal when she saw an earbud in Dylan's ear as he kissed Mary that she got the first hint someone other than the people at the table steered conversation.

Dallas excused himself to grab the to-go order. Jud guided her and the rest of the table out of the restaurant. Her gaze swept each table, and spotted her quarry at a two-seat table in the far back corner. Doctor Amanda Sinclair. Surprise merged with a hint of anger. Had the entire night been planned? An intervention?

What part did Jud play in it?

She remained silent as they left the restaurant and got into the vehicles. She'd had a lovely time. It was the first time she'd laughed and enjoyed herself in too long.

With her parents and brother there.

The shift in dynamics was too huge to hold onto the resentment simmering in her. She'd communicate her frustration to Jud and then move on. That was the smart thing to do. Tomorrow they'd likely be moving forward with the plan to take down The Collective. Nothing beyond that was guaranteed. Judson needed to be near MIT for his nephew and there was no way she could leave The Arsenal. Mary.

Her new family.

She noticed Doctor Sinclair heading toward the back where the bathrooms were. Viviana looked up at Jud. "I'll be back in a moment."

"Okay, I'll pull the truck closer. Take your time." He leaned down, kissed her cheek. "You okay?"

"Yes, I'm great. I'll be right back."

Vi scurried toward the bathrooms before she second-guessed her gut instinct to seal off this mental thread without confronting Jud. He may not have had anything to do with this. Besides, it'd gone quite well. She entered the bathroom. Doctor Sinclair withdrew a lipstick from her purse and smiled at her via the mirror."

"I figured you wanted to have a chat," the woman said. "You're upset."

"I'm more annoyed. This whole night was a setup, wasn't it, like counseling for me and my parents over steak?"

"No." She smoothed a layer of lipstick on and ran her lips together. "It was friends having your back by asking someone to help mediate the conversation from a distance. You don't know me, Vi, but I've heard a lot about you from a lot of different people. Everyone is worried about how your parents interact with you. For the record, Jud doesn't know I'm here, and I offered very little in the way of guidance tonight. His parents were quite good at herding your parents."

Harold and Jenna were awesome. Vi smiled conspiratorially in the mirror. The woman had driven to Nomad and eaten dinner at a restaurant alone to help make sure Vi had a good, decent meal with her parents for the first time in almost two decades. "Thank you. That's the smoothest meal I've had with them in a long time. I can kind of understand where they're coming from more than before."

"Well, the important thing is I'm thinking they're starting to see things a bit differently, too." The woman set her lipstick in her purse and turned. "You have a very different career than most, Vi. I hesitate to say most people would be terrified to have someone they love in this dangerous, downright terrifying world."

Vi nodded. "Yeah, I know. But it's me. I fit in here."

"I know, but they don't. Our job is to either get them to see that and respect your choice, or to move you on from them altogether. Your days are too rife with danger and troubles to have a toxic relationship with your parents added to the mix. It's time you do what's right for you rather than avoiding it altogether." Doctor Sinclair took her hand. "You know where I'm at when you're ready. No pressure. Just remember you aren't alone. You're surrounded by a lot of people who love the hell out of you. They're the family you've chosen."

Vi nodded. The woman was right. She'd realized as much earlier. "I'm thinking coming to see you and talking through some stuff wouldn't be such a bad idea."

"Great. I'll see you then." She looked at the door. "You'd best get back. Jud doesn't strike me as a patient sort when it comes to you being away from him. Have a good night, Viviana."

"You, too, Doctor Sinclair."

"It's Amanda." The woman smiled as she headed out.

Viviana took a deep breath, suddenly feeling much happier about the way the night went than before.

19

They exited the vehicles outside the compound. She waved at Dylan, Mary and Dallas as they headed toward the building with large bags loaded with food.

"I'd better go help," Jenna said. She hugged Vi, then Jud. "I'll see you two in the morning. Come on, Jarold. We need to get the rest of the bags so they don't have to come back."

Vi smiled as the two charged off toward the compound. A stiff wind could've knocked her over when her brother sprinted off after the couple to do the same. What the heck?

"We'd best get back, too," her mom said. "I hope we'll see you tomorrow?"

The hope in her voice didn't carry any subtle hints of disappointment or negativity. Vi nodded lamely as she was drawn into a hug.

"You get some rest, sweetheart. Mrs. Jensen was right when she said you looked like you and Mary were both about to pass out. You can't be your most effective if you're tired." Her mom kissed her cheek. "Come on, honey. We may as well stop in at the cafeteria and see if we can help. Jenna mentioned something about she and Mrs. Mason cooking in the morning. I may as well find out what time so I can help."

"Good night, Viviana." Her father hugged her tight, then looked down as he whispered, "Always loved you, princess. I wasn't ever good at showing it, but I love you."

"Love you, too, Dad," she whispered.

Jud took her hand as she watched everyone head toward the compound. "For what it's worth, most of what happened at dinner wasn't planned. Dylan and Mary called Doctor Sinclair on the way, figured she could help if things went too sideways. The doc tagged out when we placed our orders. Everything else was organic."

Everything else was organic.

"I didn't know until we were leaving."

"I had a chat with her in the bathroom. She's a good woman." Viviana chewed on his admission a while. "I should've been warned, but I'm glad she helped. I never thought about what happened back then from any perspective other than mine."

"And they never thought about how hard it would've been for you," Jud finished. "They love you. I didn't see that until tonight, Viviana, but they love you."

Viviana nodded. "Thank you for dinner, though you should've ordered your steak the way you wanted to eat it."

"Come on, I've got a surprise for us." He smiled and motioned to a vehicle pointed toward the pasture roads.

Anticipation and curiosity warred within her as they got into the vehicle and he headed away from the buildings and civilization. She hadn't realized how much land Dylan and his family owned until she'd tried to set up a security grid with the drones. It was an impressive amount of acreage, plenty of land for The Arsenal to spread out however it needed to. She smiled as the vehicle moved deeper and deeper into the country.

"Where on Earth are you taking me?"

"We're almost there," he promised. "I got lost twice coming out here. Dallas and Dylan had to come haul my ass out."

"Seriously?"

"Yep. It was either that or they'd have to send you in with search drones to find me, and that would've ruined the surprise." Full moonlight filtered in through the window and accentuated his handsome smile and the shadowy scruff on his face.

She reached over and stroked his face. She would've been just as happy curling up with him on the sofa. Or in the bed. Anticipation beaded along her skin as her pulse quickened. She'd never been the best at establishing a normal pace in relationships, mainly because they'd been a rarity for her.

"You look pretty intense," he said.

"I was just realizing tonight was our first date."

"I guess it was, though when you found me at Bubba's was technically the first." He laughed and rubbed the hand she'd inadvertently left on his face. "One of these days I'll manage to take you out on a date, a real one with just you and me."

"Where I get to gussy up and look sexy?" She severed contact with him and looked down. "I can't believe I wore skeleton leggings to a fancy steak joint."

"I happen to love those skeletons. I've been thinking about touching each one most of the night," he admitted.

Arousal flared within her at the thought. She clenched her thighs together as he turned off and headed away from the fence line. Shrub and overgrowth gave way to an open pasture area. The vehicle jumped up and down as he headed toward the center of the field. He stopped and parked.

He leaned over and kissed her, a too-quick fusion of tongues. He was out of the truck and around to her side before she could make sense of why they'd be out here, in the middle of nowhere. The door opened and he lifted her out. She wrapped her arms around him and continued the kiss. He groaned and deepened the contact as he walked them slowly toward the back. He put her ass onto the tailgate, which had apparently been down. She'd been so excited about a surprise she hadn't noticed a few critical details.

Like the fact the tailgate had been down.

Like the fact there was a mattress in the bed of the truck.

Her heartbeat thundered in her ears as she severed the kiss and did a half-turn to admire the back of the truck. A mattress. Pillows. A blanket? Holy. Wow. "When did you have time to do all this?"

"I had help," he admitted. "Texts are marvelous inventions."

"Are we..." She looked up at him as he settled his body between her spread legs. On instinct, she wrapped then around his waist. He'd worn a white button-down dress shirt with black jeans. She fiddled with the bolo tie. "You look so country right now I'm thinking an alien abducted you."

"I'm the one doing the abducting tonight," he said. "And to answer your question, this is whatever we want it to be. After the stars."

"Stars?" She peered up and froze.

They twinkled and glimmered in the night sky, each one a wish she'd made over the years. A secret told. She tumbled into the memories, the what-ifs she'd concocted. It'd been too long since she'd visited them. She smiled up.

"Shimmy back onto the mattress, sweetheart. Your butt's going to get cold." Jud chuckled when she looked at him, already a bit dazed at the fact he'd brought her out to look at the stars.

"How did you know?"

"I asked Mary, figured you'd enjoy looking up at them. She got this weird look on her face and damn near cried. Dylan almost pulverized me. Then she smiled real big and said it was perfect." He shrugged. "So here we are."

"She didn't tell you."

"Tell me what?"

"Nothing." Later, much later, right before they left she'd share. For now, she'd visit her friends. Share them with Jud.

She crawled onto the mattress and plopped down. Head on a pillow, she sighed loudly and stretched. "This is the best night ever."

Jud settled beside her. Hand on her waist, he drew her close and spread a blanket over them. Warm in his arms, she realized she'd been wrong moments ago. Now it was the best night ever. She smiled at the thought and pointed upward. "I renamed them."

"Which ones?"

"All of them," she declared.

"You going to share?" His breath was hot against her neck, heavy with possibilities. She angled to face him.

"Maybe, but I kind of like the idea of renaming them with you. Finding our own worlds within the stars."

"I like that a hell of a lot, Viviana." He kissed her, soft and slow, the kind of kiss that made her toes curl. She melted against him.

"We keep kissing like this and I'll forget there's a sky," he confessed.

She would, too. Determined to share the stars with Jud, she turned back over. Now half atop him, clenched beneath the blanket in his arms, she shared her stars. She'd renamed them tons of times, coming up with different arrangements and names depending on her mood. Tonight they were cats. And dogs.

~

"We're not immortalizing a poodle into the star system, Jud. You can't be serious." Vi laughed at the notion and turned to face him.

She'd lost track of how long they'd been there, staring up at the night sky and giving silly names to each twinkle.

"I know you see the poofy curls. Phoebe deserves her place up there. Admit it."

"Never. And Phoebe the poodle. Are you for real?" She play punched him, opting for a palm splay against his stomach instead.

The man was impossibly tactile. He stroked, touched and taunted every inch of her skin he got access to. She'd surrendered to the contact, primarily because it gave her the chance to do the same. She squealed as he started tickling her. Hands beneath her t-shirt, he tickled along her rib cage until she curled forward and kicked her legs in defense. But she was wrapped up in a blanket.

"Unhand me you mangy poodle lover." She growled playfully against his neck as he pinned her against the mattress. Intensity settled in his steely gaze, a turbulent nebula so deep she'd never fully navigate it. "You're an amazing man, Judson Jason Jensen."

"You're pretty spectacular yourself, Viviana Chambers." He ran a hand through her hair and feathered kisses along her temple, across her forehead, down her cheek.

She wrapped around him and moaned as his weight rested fully atop her, pressed against where she craved him the most. "I want you."

"I've never wanted anything more than I want you, but our first time isn't going to be in the back of a truck."

"Why the hell not?" She grunted and growled as she tried to flip them over so she was on top. "Clearly I need more lessons from Addy on how to handle men like you."

Judson kissed her. His tongue swept across the seam of her mouth and plundered like a Viking warrior seeking a treasure. She held onto him, tugging and yanking at his shirt. He chuckled against her ear. "Starting to think you have issues with my wardrobe. First you comment I never have a shirt on, now you're ripping it off."

"Get it off, Judson. I need to touch you." she whispered against his mouth.

"Like for like," he replied.

Her heart banged around as his words sank in. She still remembered how hot his mouth had been around her nipple. The way he'd sucked and... She reached for the bottom of her shirt, but his hand was already there, slipping beneath the material. One hand, then two, snaked beneath on a clear trajectory northward. Her lungs ceased working when he touched her breasts.

"It's like unwrapping Christmas." He licked his lips as he cupped her breasts beneath the shirt. He watched even though he couldn't see anything more than her top. A light squeeze. She groaned. "So responsive."

"Were you one of those kids who spent forever opening every present?" She yanked the shirt off.

"It depends. Some things are worth taking my time." He leaned down and kissed her again as he traced the top of her bra, then cupped her again. Breathless, she returned the kiss and relished the slow, methodical glide of his touch.

Each stroke, each brief contact had her entire body aching, desperate for his attention elsewhere. He separated them. And his mouth was there, foraging the same terrain in molten tongue and slow kisses his hands had navigated earlier. He sucked a hard nipple into his mouth, through the bra.

She groaned and grabbed at his shoulders. "Judson."

The name, more command than plea, was met with amusement. He leaned back and ripped his shirt off.

Finally. Progress.

Yes.

She smiled in appreciation and ran a hand down his chest. Kissed and licked in the same manner he'd used. Then his hands delved beneath her bra and all thought ceased. If he stopped she'd call in a couple sleeper drones, knock his ass out and take matters into her own hands. She roamed southward, paused to squeeze his ass. She writhed upward, rubbing the achy part of her against his prominent bulge.

The bra vanished, leaving her exposed fully above the waist when he rested her on the mattress and repeated the ministrations with his mouth he'd done earlier. This time no material offered resistance. Fiery heat spread through her, from where he sucked her nipple, and fanned outward until her body was one live wire of sensation, a network of desire controlled by Jud, his mouth on her.

He massaged and stroked until her entire body thrummed with raw need. He pulled away long enough for her to wrestle control, taste his hot skin and mimic the hungered exploration with one of her own.

"I love the way you purr," he whispered against her ear. He tugged her leggings, then halted.

Determination and arousal were in his gaze, a heady mix of dilated pupils and narrowed gaze. She'd never had someone look at her with such...need. In that instant she felt like Wonder Woman and Xena rolled into one. She didn't verbalize her response, mostly because she was pretty sure her voice wasn't working. Either that or her brain had forgotten how to talk. His eyes widened when she unclasped his jeans.

She claimed his mouth, demanding the duel of tongues that spread fire through her core and pooled between her legs. A moan escaped her as he removed the rest of her clothes. Hesitation overwhelmed her a few moments. She was so out of her league. Jud exuded confidence, stealthy sensuality in each move, each glide of his hands on her body. His mouth.

Her fingernails dug into his shoulders as he angled downward, licked and kicked an invisible path toward the juncture of her thighs. Awareness crawled beneath her skin, honed in wherever he roamed. She tried pulling him up, but he chuckled and continued until his hot breath fanned along the inside of her thighs.

"Beautiful, sweet Viviana. I've been thinking about this a long time."

Oh God. She squeezed her eyes shut and willed a bit of courage. The last time a man...

She forced the thought aside and focused on the present. This was Jud. He enjoyed her sass and thought she was beautiful. He was a bad ass who did what he wanted and didn't let anyone dupe him into doing something he didn't want to. If he didn't want to...

His tongue laved across her slit. She writhed upward as he plunged a finger into her.

"So wet," he whispered. "I'm going to taste you, Viviana."

And he did. Vi surrendered to the onslaught of sensations. The man was lethal to her senses and she loved every second. One hand roamed, caressed and played with her breasts as the other worked in tandem with his mouth. The flick of his tongue across her clit ignited her entire body, a warm tingling wave fanning outward. Her entire body seized as a cascade of pleasure ignited through her.

She claimed his mouth when he rose above her. Muscles bunched beneath her touch. Pleasure spiraled through her, an explosion of sensations wherever he stroked. He nipped her lower lip as he pinched her nipple. Feather soft kisses along her neck cast a shiver of anticipation through her entire body. The wave of need returned, surging as she writhed beneath his deft ministrations.

"My turn," she stated.

"No, relax. Next time." The seductive timbre stoked her desire as she relaxed against him and sought his mouth.

The man was definitely lethal to the senses. Although she'd been with a handful of men, none had awakened her like Jud, made her want so bad she'd kill if necessary. They hadn't taken the time, hadn't put her needs first. Next time? Like hell.

Hunger turned his gaze molten as he leaned back and undid his jeans. She tracked the glide of the zipper. She licked her lips as she admired his thick cock. He removed his pants with effortless ease, as if they weren't in the back of a pickup truck in the middle of a field. She didn't give a damn where they were, it didn't matter. She wanted Judson Jensen inside her.

Immediately.

She rose up and ran her hands along his sides, tracing the contour of muscles along his stomach. A smile spread across her face as their gazes collided. She wrapped her hand around the hardened length of his arousal and tightened the grip until a groan escaped him.

"My turn," she repeated.

His skin was hot beneath her mouth. He was a live furnace, exuding heat and need so primal, her entire body trembled with the need to satisfy him. She worked his length in her hand and growled when he halted her efforts.

"Next time, Viviana. I'm damn close to losing it and I want to be inside you when that happens," he admitted.

She curled her toes and gulped as images assailed her. Her pulse quickened as she returned to the mattress and watched as he removed a condom from his wallet. "You'd better have more than one of those."

He grinned. "I was a boy scout growing up. I'm always prepared for anything."

Thank God.

He rolled on the condom with an ease that incited Vi's self-doubt. "I'm not very...it's been a while."

"It's been a while for me, too," he replied as he lay beside her on the mattress. He stroked her cheek and studied her a moment. "You're nervous."

Not trusting her voice, she did a half-shrug, partial nod. She couldn't explain the frenzied voice in her head, the one screaming she wasn't good enough. She'd screw something up. She'd battled that bitchy voice her entire life, but never in these situations. She'd never had a man as virile and...

Yeah.

Jud was an entirely different league compared to men she'd been with in the past.

"Look at me, Viviana." He raised her chin with a couple fingers until their gazes locked. "It's just you and me here. Fuck whatever is going through that sexy brain of yours. Nothing and no one else matters, not now. Not ever. Not when it comes to you and me. You're beautiful and I want you more than I've wanted anything or anyone, ever. Don't doubt that."

"I don't even know what this is between us. All I know is what you make me feel. It..." She swallowed and tumbled into the intensity of his gaze. He'd understand. He had to understand. "It terrifies me."

"Good," he whispered. "It terrifies me, too."

He kissed her gently until she relaxed against him. Tension gave way to the desire he stoked easily. He thrust a finger inside her wet pussy and groaned.

"Still so wet for me, Viviana."

"I want you inside me, Jud. Please." She wrapped her legs around his hips when he settled above her. Reaching between them, she stroked his hard cock again and helped guide him inside.

He thrust deep in one long, hard stroke. She cried out, clenching around him.

"Fuck." He groaned. "So tight."

Vi wrapped her arms and legs around him and grabbed his ass with both hands, locking him into place until she was ready for him to move. His mouth sought hers. The frenzied kiss burned away any self-confidence issues she had. A moan escaped her as he moved, rotating his hips.

"Harder," she ordered.

"A bossy little minx." He laughed in her ear. His breath fell along her cheek as he thrust into her harder, deeper. "You feel so good wrapped around me, Viviana. I could spend forever here, inside you."

Yes. That'd be real, real good. She writhed beneath him, met each thrust. Jud grasped her hips and shifted positions. Each thrust went deeper until her entire body spasmed and she orgasmed.

Jud's release followed hers. She relished his weight when he settled atop her. Their heavy breathing mingled. She clenched herself around him where they were still joined and kissed him softly, hesitantly.

He rested his forehead against hers and huffed a few more labored breaths. "That was amazing."

Yeah, it was. Vi curled against Jud and positioned her leg between his. She traced invisible patterns along his side. Her cheeks ached from the massive grin she wore. Heat crept up her cheeks when she peeked up at him. He chuckled and dragged her up, claiming her mouth in a hot kiss. They'd spent the past several hours repeating the same routine. Have incredible, mind-blowing sex. Rest. Repeat.

Her entire body was relaxed. Her mind...well, quilling and created code had nothing on sex with Judson Jensen.

"You're definitely a little minx," he whispered against her cheek.

Vi glanced up at the stars. Such a wonderful night. There was only one thing that'd make it absolutely perfect. Her pulse quickened, her mouth dried. She'd trust him with it. How could she not?

"The semester at MIT was two weeks in when I started. My

parents fought it until the last possible moment. None of the dormitories wanted me there, none of the students wanted a baby as a roommate. Then a resident greeted me and said she had the perfect person for me to share my MIT experience with. It was like I'd met my other half when she introduced me to Mary. Mom and Dad tossed my suitcase into the room and left. No hugs, no wishes for good luck. Nothing."

"Jesus." He hugged her tighter.

"We stayed up the whole night talking, regaling each other with stories about our bullies and home lives. It's better to laugh than cry, right? It was after midnight when we got a crazy idea to sneak up to the roof. We grabbed our blankets and pillows and found the biggest, tallest, flattest roof we could. It took some creativity, but we got up there and spent hours staring up at the stars. I told her we needed to send our dreams up there, turn the stars into a constant reminder of what we would achieve, do. We weren't focusing on what we'd endured, not anymore. We were looking forward and up. Nothing would stop us. Ever."

She paused, kissing his chest.

"Viviana," he whispered.

"That's why she said this idea was perfect, because it was," she said. "Thank you for sharing the stars with me."

"No, thank you for letting me see them with you. You're an amazing woman, Viviana."

"You're a pretty amazing guy, Judson."

"So Phoebe the Poodle is in? All those curls would make a hell of a constellation," he said with a grin.

Vi punched him and squealed as he tickled her sides.

Jud tensed in her embrace as the distinct sound of guns cocking echoed around them. Before she could react, hands grabbed her and Jud. Something punctured her neck.

Darkness descended.

20

Vi jolted awake. Cold air brushed across her exposed skin. Memories flashed through her mind, striking like bullets. She rubbed her neck as she looked around. "Jud?"

Dread settled in her gut as she crawled off the mattress. A lone piece of paper floated on the breeze and landed on the ground. She stumbled out of the bed and fell to her knees. She grabbed the white paper with trembling hands. Shock seeped into her bones. Her entire body quaked.

We'll be in touch. Them for HERA.

They'd be in touch? How? And who the hell was them? Jud. Oh shit.

They had Jud.

And someone else.

Mary?

No. No. No.

She didn't want anyone to be missing, but it couldn't be Mary. Not again. Tears burned her eyes.

Vi scrambled up to the back of the truck bed again and

fumbled around until she found a small cell phone. Likely an untraceable cell, but she'd work her magic when she got to Command Central. She shivered as the cold wind struck her again. The fuckers took her clothes and the blankets.

Her emotions swung a treacherous pendulum. Terror. Anger. Revulsion. Shame. Guilt.

They had Jud.

They'd penetrated their defenses and taken Jud and someone else.

Jud had brought her out here to make the night special and someone...

Someone knocked her out, and...

Don't. Don't you dare fall apart and make this about you. Get your ass back to the compound and find Jud. Figure out who else they took.

Make them pay.

Vi clutched the anger, fed it every pissed off thought she could to shake off the fright. They hadn't taken her. Why the hell not?

Because they wanted HERA.

How had they bypassed security?

Jud had taken them to one of the far back pastures of Mason property, one not in use. But they'd secured the entirety of their land with drone surveillance after the attack.

Fuck. The attack.

Someone had remained behind after the attack, hidden. Waited.

This was her fault. She should have done a head count, scoured every inch of Mason land for heat signatures to make sure no one was hiding. Hot tears filled her vision, but she took a deep breath.

No. There was no way she could've known they would do that. This wasn't her fault, but it was her problem.

Get your shit together. They have Jud and no telling who else.

She crawled out of the bed of the truck. Sticker burrs stuck in her bare feet, but she didn't give a damn. She got into the truck. Please let there be keys. She glared at the empty ignition a moment, then leaned over and opened the glove compartment. She snagged the gun and set it in the seat beside her and rifled past medical gear and extra munitions until she found the extra set of keys.

Too bad there weren't extra clothes in the damn truck.

Vi ignored the fact she was naked and started the vehicle. Her hands trembled as she drove her way toward the compound. Hopefully she'd remembered the route correctly from the night before.

Memories of their lovemaking the previous night assailed her thoughts. Jud was beyond amazing, the best lover she'd ever had. To top it off, he gave a damn about her—really cared. They'd regaled each other with stories between bouts of sex last night. The entire time had been amazing. Then some assholes caught them both off guard and soured the entire experience.

She wasn't sure how long she'd been out. She glared at the phone on the seat beside the gun. She wouldn't use it, not when she was close to the compound. Someone was probably monitoring it, listening. A shudder rolled along her spine.

She needed a plan. No way in hell she'd give them HERA, but she wasn't about to let them keep Jud and whoever else they'd taken. Whoever did this would pay.

Her head ached, her mouth felt like she'd swallowed an entire desert of sand. Relief overwhelmed her when the buildings came into view. She aimed for the compound.

Almost there.

Her mind siphoned through everything she had to do, patterned everything into manageable bullet points to try and organize the chaotic thoughts drowning her. She braked in front of a cluster of bodies, her brain too busy to identify who. It didn't matter. She was back at The Arsenal compound. That's what mattered.

She tumbled from the truck.

"Jesus." The voice rose. "Get Logan out here. Now!"

Vi blinked as the voice became a body. Jesse. Well, this was more than embarrassing. She was naked, a mental mess and all sorts of confused. Other faces fell into view as people clustered behind the man now crouched in front of her.

"Vi. Look at me," Jesse ordered. He grabbed her face and directed her semi-focused gaze. The tremble in her hands intensified. "What happened?"

"Jud. Someone took." She grabbed his shirt and yanked him closer and she forced out the muddled thoughts. "Someone else taken."

"Get Cord on tracking everyone down," Marshall ordered as he crouched beside his brother. "Let's get something on you, sweetheart."

Oh, right. She nodded and mutely held up her hands as the two men put a shirt on her like it was commonplace to dress naked women outside their compound.

"Where were you?" Jesse asked.

"Jud took her out to the northeastern pasture to stargaze," Marshall said. "Dylan shifted patrols to semi-cover the area. He'll know who was closest to the area."

"Dallas," Dylan said. "He's not answering his cell."

"Fuck," Jesse growled. "Where is Logan?"

"En route," someone clipped behind Marshall.

"Vi!" Mary's voice rose from behind the cluster. "Move! Move! Get out of my way!"

Her best friend fell to her knees on the other side of Marshall. Vi returned the fierce hug and sank into the security of everyone around her.

"I think they kept a team, or a couple people, on site after the attack. That was their final phase," she whispered. "They took Jud and someone else."

"Cord's running a roll call. Can you stand? Did they hurt you?" Tears formed in Mary's eyes as she asked the last question.

"No." Vi shook her head fiercely, determined to assure her friend she hadn't been raped, even though she couldn't know since she'd been knocked out. "I'm okay, just dazed. The fuckers left me naked."

"Surprised they didn't take you, too," Marshall commented.

Vi motioned toward the truck. "They left a cell and a note. They'll give back Jud and whoever else they took if I hand over HERA."

The men cursed. Jesse and Marshall helped her stand. Mary wrapped an arm around her waist and guided her toward the building. Although Vi didn't want to waste time in medical, she figured she had a better chance scaling Mount Kilimanjaro than stopping this freight train of concerned friends guiding her toward a checkup. Her heart swelled.

Mary had been right all along. This was her family, too.

Doctor Logan greeted them halfway down the corridor. "I was on my way."

"She's zoning," Jesse said. "I think they gave her something."

"In my neck. I didn't have time to fight. Jud didn't either. He's going to be so pissed they got the jump on us." Vi's voice broke at the last statement.

Jesse hoisted her onto the exam table. Vi was glad the shirt Marshall had removed and given to her was long enough to go down to her mid-thigh. At least things were covered now.

"What can I do? Give me something to do, dang it." The woman's voice pitched higher in frustration at the end. She was short with purple hair with pink tips. A diamond nose ring glinted. Her red lips were downturned into a grim expression.

Who the heck was she?

"Woops, sorry. I'm Zero D." The woman rocked back on her wedged platforms. "Zoey."

Right. Vi had been so busy with everything else she'd forgotten about the newest recruit, the one who'd saved Fallon's team overseas. Something else she'd let slip through the cracks.

"Cord could probably use some help accounting for everyone," Mary said. "Thanks, Zoey. And welcome, I know you got in late last night and haven't been shown around or introduced to anyone. Things are nuts right now, as you know."

"I'm glad to be here. Put me to work."

"Wait. Where's Jacob?" Vi grabbed Jesse's arm. "Is he here? Is he okay? Someone has to tell him about Jud."

"We will, once we know what's going on," Marshall assured. "He's with Cord right now. He's fine."

"Okay, everyone without a medical license, get the hell out," Logan growled.

"I'm not going anywhere," Mary stated firmly as she grabbed Vi's hand.

The doctor regarded the stubborn woman a moment, then nodded. Everyone else filed out. Vi forced a deep breath and steeled herself for Doctor Logan.

The former Army Ranger turned CIA operative slash doctor had almost died trying to save Mary a while back. He had no business working yet, but he was almost as stubborn as Vi and Mary combined. He settled a stethoscope into position and studied her with a half-hooded gaze. Some of the calm she'd felt while surrounded by Jesse, Marshall and everyone else earlier disappeared in the silent room.

"I'll take some blood, to identify what they gave you."

"I'm fine. I'm not the one who got taken."

They'd just spent hours making love. Vi wanted to say fucking, but her brain refused to lie. It'd been way, way more than just sex.

And some asshole tainted what they shared. Invaded their privacy.

Her skin crawled. Had they heard? Watched?

Logan flashed an obnoxious light in her eyes. She squinted and looked away, but he persisted. "How long were you out?"

"I'm not sure, probably not long." She sighed her frustration as he prodded along the side of her head. "I'm fine except for a headache and a dry mouth."

He tossed a glare, but put away the light and went over to a small table. "I'll draw some blood, then you can be on your way."

"No." Mary shook her head. "She was out. She doesn't know what they could've done. You need to check her."

"I'm fine," Vi argued.

"Strangers infiltrated our compound, hid out and waited until they could catch you unaware. They knocked you out and left you naked in the back of a truck bed. What part of that is fine, Vi? Because I'm honestly not seeing anything at all *fine* with that situation."

Well, okay then. Vi glanced at Logan, who'd frozen at her best friend's raised voice. Mary clenched Vi's hand in a vise-like grip.

The phantom screams from Vi's nightmares echoed in her brain, a waking reminder of what her best friend had endured. She grabbed Mary and held on tight. "I was so scared they got you."

"I'm okay. We're okay."

Vi nodded, unsure whether the statement was true or not. It felt as though a part of her had been ripped out and stamped on. Pulverized.

They had Jud.

"Check her," Mary ordered. "We aren't leaving until you check her."

～

J ud woke up suspended from a large meat hook. He wished it was the first time he'd woken up like that, but it wasn't. He kept his eyes closed and his breathing steady as he listened for voices, footsteps, anything to clue him into what the fuck was going on.

The last thing he remembered was Viviana. Losing himself in her. Literally.

He'd spent over two decades in the most dangerous environments on the planet and survived because he never, ever let his guard down. But he'd lost himself the first time Viviana's warm heat settled around him and she locked her arms and legs around him like letting him go was impossible. For a few hours he'd been nothing more than a man making love to his woman.

And there was no doubt Viviana was his.

Once he killed the fuckers who dared mess with her, he'd make sure she knew. Jud was bare chested, but someone had put his pants on. Bare footed.

Voices rose in frustration from the left.

"Where the hell are you? They're both coming to. We're not getting paid enough for this bullshit. Do you have any idea how close we came to dying? Jesus, he went through everyone like they were standing still." The voice paused. "Yeah, well good. Me and Mike deserve triple pay. We need more men here stat. If they aren't here and these two rouse, we're outta here."

"What'd they say?"

"Marla and four teams are en route, three minutes max."

"Good. That's good. That'll be enough, right?"

Fuck. That wasn't good at all.

"Yeah, that should be enough, Mike. Keep watch, we don't need anybody showing up uninvited. I'm going to do a walkabout."

"Yeah, okay. Good. That's good."

Jud was more than pissed off at himself for letting an idiot like Mike get the jump on him. He waited until the thud of the door echoed in the distance before opening his eyes and looking around. Dallas hung beside him, eyes half open and focused on where the voices had come from. He was also bare chested with a pair of pants. Bare footed.

"You okay?" Jud asked.

"A little sore and lot pissed off. You?"

"About the same." Jud glanced up at the handcuffs and chains securing him to the hook. "Fuckers are idiots, but they aren't taking chances."

"No shit. I think we're in San Antonio. I came to earlier than they expected. It took a while to secure you so my drugs must've worn off faster than expected." Dallas's voice lowered. "This isn't going to go well for us, man."

Jud didn't bother replying. The Collective had them. They both knew what that meant because they'd been on the other side, Jud more than anyone. How many people had he detained and questioned for The Collective? Hundreds? Thousands? Probably. He knew what'd go down over the next several hours. They'd start by the book. Beatings. Water boarding. Electrical shock.

Then they'd get creative.

Not that it'd matter.

Jud accepted the fact he'd die long ago. He'd even accepted it'd probably be slow and painful, a last penance for the things he'd done.

That was before Viviana, though.

He hung in the empty warehouse and focused on her, the things they'd shared, the stars they'd named. He smiled when he remembered the poodle. What was her name? Phoebe. Yeah, that was it.

"You are one sick fuck," Dallas grumbled. "We're hanging like meat waiting to get pulverized and you're laughing and smiling."

"It'll throw them off their game."

"If we're in San Antonio, teams will be here as soon as they figure out I'm missing, too. Vi and Mary chipped everyone, like we're fucking dogs."

Ha. Jud couldn't help but laugh. She was totally a pet person, she just didn't realize it yet. A tracking chip meant a rescue would be faster than expected, which meant all they needed was to hold out for a few hours.

No problem.

Jud focused on the high-heeled footsteps clacking against the concrete floor. The bitch couldn't help but show up. She'd likely waited for this moment for years.

Marla entered the room with a smug grin. Twelve men fanned out in the room. Jud personally thought that was overkill, but noted the nervous glimpses between the men as they took a few steps backward. Their gazes remained on him. Jud grinned smugly as he tracked their movements.

"If you wanted a meeting, all you had to do was call," Jud said.

"Funny, you weren't very polite last time we chatted, Jud. You were downright hostile." She strode forward and scraped a nail down his bare chest. "It's been a while, boys. You've both been very busy. And naughty."

Jud looked over at Dallas. Face red, lips thinned, the man looked like he was about to spit nails. To say he had a strained relationship with The Collective handler was an understatement. They'd been hot and heavy the first couple years he came on board, but things turned sour enough for her to order a hit on him.

Marla stood in front of Dallas and slapped him. The strike echoed through the room. Dallas laughed.

"Nice seeing you again, sweetheart. I see you're still a viperous bitch."

"You owe me, Dallas. You were sight lined years ago, but I rescinded the order."

"Funny, I'm pretty sure I rescinded it by refusing," Jud commented. "You can't use The Collective to take out all your boy toys who refuse to play hide the candlestick with you anymore."

Dallas chuckled.

Marla spun and clacked back to Jud. "This is all your fault. All you had to do was take out the Quillery Edge and get HERA. It was a simple request."

"One you knew better than issue as a direct order. No one touches the Quillery Edge unless they want to take me on."

"Well that's hardly a threat right now, is it?"

Jud had several ways to extricate himself from the situation, none of them without a vast amount of pain. Broken hands. Wrists. Dislocated shoulders. The escape strategies listed in his mind, but he remained still. Lethal calm drifted through him.

The bitch wasn't walking away from this.

"Now, Dallas. You and I have some unfinished business. I'm thinking we need to pick up where we left off. Little DJ needs a brother or sister."

Son of a bitch.

Chains rattled beside him. Marla cupped Dallas's cock and squeezed. A sinister smile formed on her face. "Oh, I forgot to tell you about our son. He looks just like you. So precious. Dallas Junior, but I call him DJ for short. He's learning to be a cowboy, just like his daddy. Sadly, little DJ thinks you died. I guess that was a prediction on my part."

Jud thought back to the time Dallas pulled out of The Collective. Marla had been AWOL for a few months before that, operating mostly remotely. Which made sense if she'd been pregnant. *Son of a bitch.* Jud remained silent, let the shock wave of her pronouncement fill the room.

When she didn't get a reaction from Dallas, she continued.

"He's turning four soon and such a smart boy. I don't see him as often as I'd like, but he's well taken care of."

"We have a bit of time to debrief before I expect our guest to arrive," Marla said. She looked around with an amused grin. "Who wants to go first?"

21

Vi sat at the head of the room, foot tapping on the floor as everyone filed in. She hated the fact everyone at The Arsenal was filing in. It highlighted the severity of the mission they were about to undertake. Getting Jud and Dallas back.

Taking down The Collective.

She, Mary, Cord, Jacob and Zoey had spent the past two hours hammering out a rudimentary code that should help with the objective.

"I still don't understand how we're going to get this into their system," Jacob said.

"That's why we're calling the meeting," Cord said. "We hammer out details as a team here. We'll figure it out."

"And we'll get him back?" Jacob asked.

"Yeah, we'll get him back," Vi promised.

She took a deep breath and willed a bit of luck would land in her favor today, but she figured her plan would be an uphill battle —one Dallas and Jud didn't have time for them to argue about.

Not when her way was the only plausible way she could imagine this working.

"Okay, let's get started. We all know why we're here." Marshall's voice was even, but his expression was enraged, like all the people gathered.

One of their own had been taken.

"We confirmed the two unidentified men hid out on the outskirts of our perimeter, which was why we didn't pick them up with our security sweeps. They stayed close enough to watch for an opening, but far enough to remain undetected," Cord said. "Last night was their perfect storm. Jud and Dallas were both on the exterior section of our security grid."

"They want HERA, a presumably even exchange for Dallas and Jud," Mary said. "Obviously we can't do that."

"But we can let them think we are," Vi said. "I have a plan. I need everyone in here to listen and let me get through it before you argue. I know there will be objections, but I know this will work."

"We're listening," Dylan said, arms crossed.

"We give them HERA. She's part one of the first offensive phase." Vi talked through the dissenting replies. "We wrote a virus, one we can spread into their network the second HERA is plugged in. Once it's in, we can dismantle their operation from the inside out, starting with their money. You can't run an organization of that size without money. We take that, we cut them deep. We discussed this in our last meeting."

"And how do we get HERA back?" Addy asked.

"Well, that's where all of you come into the mix," Vi said. "I never said my plan was one hundred percent solid, it's a work in progress. All I know is we take HERA in, or a stripped-down version of her anyway. Something meaty enough to pass their first level inspection. That includes weaponized drones. They'll be the last part of the first offensive phase after HERA's plugged in."

"And who will deliver HERA to them?" Nolan asked.

"I will." Vi made eye contact with everyone as she swept her gaze through the room. "Alone."

"No." Mary shook her head. "Hell no."

"You aren't sufficiently trained in hand-to-hand. Them getting their hands on you or Mary is out of the question." Addy's voice rose. "I'll lock you both up downstairs right alongside Jian before I let that go down."

"I agree," Fallon declared.

So much for them hearing her out. "We have the advantage here. We already know where they are. We can roll out as soon as we finish arguing about what we all know has to be the play. Cut out the emotional and protective responses and think about the facts only. This is the only way to get Jud and Dallas out and cut The Collective's jugular. I know this will work."

"We move in, take out whoever's holding our guys and come back home," Gage offered.

"And we'll lather, rinse and repeat this bullshit again and again," Jesse said. "Vi's right. This will work."

Vi was a bit surprised Jesse was the one who backed her, but she'd take anyone in her corner.

Bree and Rhea sat in the corner whispering with one another. Rhea cleared her throat and spoke. "We agree with Vi. It'll work if we add a few enhancements."

"Like what?" Marshall asked. "I'm never okay with someone going into a situation like this alone, not against someone like The Collective."

"I have a stronger zinger compound, one that requires a lot less to take someone down, which means we can have more darts in each drone." Rhea looked over at Bree. "We're thinking we should replace half the drones with the new formula and leave the other half as they are, just in case."

"Okay, sounds good. What else?" Dylan asked.

"A body suit," Bree said. "It will hide weapons and withstand pat downs and wands from the waist down. The chest area would be hard for Vi because of..." The woman grabbed her own breasts and shrugged.

The woman was a genius, but a bit of a nut at times. Both of the scientists were.

"She's not trained in hand-to-hand with any weapon," Addy said.

"No, but the two men we're getting back are. Assuming they're in reasonable condition, they can fight while the backup teams are moving into position," Vi said. "The drones can handle most of the resistance, but we won't know how many we're up against until we get there."

"They'll likely set the meet at a location they can control," Fallon said.

"So we show up and catch them off guard, move in and take control by switching the venue," Vi said. "It's risky, but better than a known trap."

Mary stood up and left the room. Dylan rose to follow, but Vi shook her head and gave chase. She was sitting in the same alcove Vi had used with Jud days ago. It felt like a century ago in many ways. She sat and wrapped her arm around her friend.

"This is bullshit," Mary gritted out through clenched teeth. "No way in hell should we even be discussing this."

"We'll put a self-destruct on HERA, a safety precaution. They won't get her."

"Fuck HERA. Let them have it." Mary's voice rose. "I'm worried about you."

"I'll be fine. The entire Arsenal will be within striking range. HERA will be in the room."

"You don't know what monsters like that can do," Mary whispered. "Please don't do this, Vi. We'll find another way."

"No, we won't. What would you do if it was Dylan in there?" Vi waited a few beats. "They have Dallas. Mary, they have Jud. I know it's nuts because we haven't been together long, but we connected. He means something to me."

Mary looked over at her. She smiled despite her watery gaze. "We'll need to keep a couple teams here, minimum. And Jacob. He shouldn't go. We don't know what they'll do to Jud and Dallas before we get there. We're an hour and a half away. Even if we load fast, two hours is our fastest arrival time."

Which was what terrified Vi. Every second they wasted arguing over what she knew was the only viable option translated to more suffering for Dallas and Jud.

But running in half prepared was a suicide mission. They couldn't get cocky and assume anything would work. They needed several plans in play, just in case.

"I'll agree on one condition. We scout the situation once we arrive and I have the right to nix your walking in alone plan if I don't think it'll work." Mary held up her hand. "I'll be objective, I swear I will, but I know what monsters like that can do. I don't want you walking into their hands if we can't take them down. It's not worth it. It pains me to say that, but I do because I know that's what Dallas would say if he were here. And seeing how Jud has vowed to put himself between you and anyone who tries to hurt you and freaking has in a huge way, I'm pretty sure he'd be livid you're wanting to do this."

She was not wrong.

Vi hoped he had the chance to be pissed afterward because that meant it worked and she got him out. "We can't let them run roughshod over us, Mary. I don't know about you, but I don't want to live the rest of my life looking over my shoulder."

"You're right." Mary sighed. "It doesn't make it any easier to accept, though."

"You're right. It doesn't." Vi stood. "Let's get back inside."

It took half an hour to load all the equipment and organize the teams into the vehicles. Marshall and Nolan had secured clearance from enough of the alphabet soup to cover their asses for whatever went down. Kidnapping two men wasn't important enough for Homeland Security, the FBI and the Department of Defense to intervene, but the assholes who had them wanted HERA. Someone going after HERA was tantamount to terrorism as far as Homeland and the DOD were concerned. Taking Jud and Dallas was a stupid move. Demanding HERA in return was the nail in The Collective's coffin.

The Arsenal had official permission and a signed contract with three agencies to investigate and take The Collective and anyone associated with them down, the quieter the better.

Cord and Nolan loaded all the electronic gear into the SUV. Mary climbed into the back seat. Bree and Rhea had stripped Vi down moments ago and dressed her in their latest creation. Vi didn't know what the material surrounding her like a second skin was. All she knew was it added several inches to her lower half and hid two KBAR knives along her calves. She'd been shown and forced to demonstrate quick access to said weapons. They were in thin sheaths that'd protect her skin from the sharp blades.

Hopefully Jud and Dallas would be in good enough shape to use them.

Dread settled in her bones as she moved to sit. Voices shouted her name from a distance. Pausing, she turned her head and froze.

Jud's parents were racing toward her. Jacob was behind them.

Jarold and Jenna Jensen were the last people she needed to deal with right now, but she couldn't imagine getting in and driving away as though they weren't running full speed toward her. Both were out of breath and semi-stooped forward by the time they made it to her. Jacob flashed an apologetic look at her as he put a hand on each of their backs.

Tears trekked down Jenna's face as she stood fully and wrapped Vi in her arms. The woman's shoulder's shook, but she didn't wail or sob loudly. Vi gripped the woman tightly a few moments.

"We'll get him back," Vi promised.

The woman pulled back and snagged her husband's hand. The two exchanged determined, angered looks.

"Make them pay," Jud's dad ordered. "I'm tired of them messing with my family."

Vi couldn't agree more. They'd taken Jacob's dad and now they'd taken Jud. Enough was enough.

"I've gotta go. Stay close to Jacob. It may take a while to get back, but he'll have a line into the action from Command Central." She wasn't sure it'd be a good idea for the elderly couple to observe, but she had enough to worry about without micromanaging what Jud's parents did or didn't do.

She turned toward the vehicle.

"Quillery," Jacob called. She looked back. Determination and anger settled on the young man's face, one eerily like his uncle's in many ways. "Courage doesn't come from winning the battle. It comes from looking impossible in the eyes and kneeing his nuts."

She nodded, unsure what to say beneath the intensity in his statement.

"Make them pay," he ordered.

"I will, Jacob. We all will."

She hauled herself into the vehicle and sat beside Mary. Her pulse pounded and her heart ached for the worried family watching the progression of SUVs pulling out.

"They're good people," Mary commented. "It's hard to imagine someone in Jud's profession having such loving parents. Family. That's nice."

"Yeah. It is." Something neither Vi nor her friend were accustomed to, such close ties.

Vi hadn't seen her parents since the dinner the night before.

They probably wouldn't even miss her while she was gone, not that it mattered.

~

Jacob wished he had his dad's patience. He glared at the two people and wondered for the millionth time how they birthed someone as brilliant and awesome as Quillery. "Sit down and shut up."

"Jacob," his grandma warned.

"Settle down, son. If they don't want to watch, they can leave." His grandpa sat. "We can't make them."

"That's where you're wrong." Jacob reached over and locked the only exit from Command Central. "They've wandered around here spewing their hate on everyone like acid. Every word out of their mouths about Quillery is bullshit and I'm sick of it. She deserves their love and respect."

"She has us, Jacob. She doesn't need them," his grandma reasoned gently.

The new woman, Zero D, listened. Eyes wide, she returned her attention back to the display monitors. "She's going in."

"In case you were too busy bitching to notice, two men were kidnapped from the compound last night. My uncle Jud was one of them. Your daughter is about to save their lives. She's saved my dad's twice now. Twice! Now, I can't make you stop being stupid and mean and bigoted and everything else you are, but you two are going to sit and watch what Viviana does. You say she's wasting her time. Well, we're about to see what exactly she does."

"Like they'd have a clue. You should've dragged them in here when she was writing all the sick code being used, the stuff they'd never understand anyway," Zero said.

The woman wasn't wrong. Vi had some seriously sick code in her brain. Jacob had learned so much already and couldn't wait to learn more. He hoped the women would let him stay on for a while longer.

Right now he hoped Vi's mojo was enough to save Uncle Jud, get The Collective off their asses once and for all.

A banging on the door drew Jacob's attention to the security monitor. Riley. He shouldn't let her in, but she was Dallas's little sister. All her brothers were in the field. He hit the button. She surged in. Her lips thinned as she glared at Vi's parents.

"Come, dear. Sit with us." Jenna patted the sofa beside her. "You sure you want to watch?"

"She watched them rescue Dad. That got real ugly. This will be much quicker," Jacob said. "You cool?"

"Yeah. I'm cool." Riley sat. She was pale. Eyes were red. She was far from cool, but he didn't argue. He wasn't very cool either. It'd be their secret.

Teams were in position. Vi paced outside the makeshift command post one mile south of Dallas's chip. As far as The Collective knew, they were en route to the location. Drones provided a layout of their nineteen people, one of which was a woman who was obviously in charge.

Dallas and Jud were...

Vi swallowed and looked over at her quiet friend. Mary hadn't said much since the first images started coming in. Dylan hovered, kept a hand on his fiancée and whispered gently in her ear. Although The Edge was present and ready to kick ass, the fierce woman beneath the honed operative was also present and not quite as ready. Mary had been through hell and what the two men in the warehouse were going through right now were fresh reminders of what she'd survived.

Anger kept Vi focused. Each wound she tracked on Jud, each

growled pain he or Dallas cried out sealed the fate of those inside. They'd observed for five minutes as Marshall and the other teams coordinated themselves for the second phase entry. Vi didn't much give a damn what they did. She knew her part and was more than ready to get in there.

Knock them off their game.

Marla had called half an hour ago and set a meet in two and a half hours twenty miles south, in an abandoned cotton gin outside San Antonio. The location was remote and definitely not in The Arsenal's best interests. Vi walked over to the huddled operatives.

"I'm ready," she said.

"There's a lot of people in there, Vi." Cord looked up at her. "I'm not liking the odds here."

"You and Mary even those odds once you take over the drones."

"Five minutes from when you walk in," Marshall declared. "Then we're moving in."

"Fair enough." She could do a hell of a lot in five minutes.

Hopefully. She hugged Mary and headed toward the vehicle they'd set up specifically for this task. Fallon had enough hidden explosives in it to blow up Resino. Once she drew their attention, he was going to sneak from beneath the undercarriage where he would be hiding and rig the area with said ordnance. Once the final portion of phase one was underway, the explosions farthest from the warehouse would cue phase two where The Arsenal teams would move in.

Vi drove the single mile slowly and parked as close as she dared to the warehouse. There was always the possibility they'd shoot her immediately, but she was worth way more alive than dead. The duffel bag was heavier than she expected when she got out and settled it across her shoulder. Two men armed with AK-47s grabbed her and shoved her against the vehicle. The token pat down was slow, methodical. Her pulse pounded wildly as they found the gun she'd left in full view. No one would come to a situation like this unarmed.

She smiled to herself as they grabbed the duffel bag and dragged her into the warehouse. Voices rose in agitation as they progressed inward. The men huddled closer, weapons drawn.

A blonde stood in front of Dallas and Jud with an electric cattle prod. Her eyes widened a moment when she turned, but she composed herself quickly.

"I see we've hit a snag." She tsked. "It's not polite to show up without notice."

"I've never been known for my courtesy."

Vi's voice drew the two men's attention. Blood seeped from open wounds along their torso and face. A bull whip sat on the table beside them. Water dripped from both men. She let the rage boiling her insides run its course a few heartbeats, then forced her focus on the mission at hand.

"We need to make this exchange quick. I skirted security to get here and make this happen, but they probably spotted my absence five minutes after I left." Vi forced her gaze on the woman as someone set the duffel on the folding table to the left of where they were. A long extension cord coiled beneath the area, which was laden with monitors and computers. A man tapped away on a keyboard like he had a fucking clue how to handle what The Arsenal was about to unleash on his ass.

"I have to admit I'm a bit surprised you're here. Alone." Marla looked back at the two men who'd dragged her inside. "She was alone, right?"

"Yeah, boss. We took her gun. She's clean otherwise."

Right. Zoey and Cord had put a miniature camera in her glasses and on the button of her jeans. So far they hadn't noticed either of the two KBARs strapped to her calves. At least the weird suit Bree and Rhea had shoved her into seemed to be working. Dallas and Jud glared at her. Neither man spoke, but she noted the tension in their bodies, as though they both prepared to strike when given the chance.

"And I'm to believe you'd give HERA up that easily?" Marla walked over to the duffel and nodded for the computer geek to open it. "I'm not stupid, Viviana Chambers. Or do you prefer Quillery?"

"You can call me whatever the hell you want as long as you give me the six million for HERA and release Dallas and Jud." Vi cocked her head toward the bag. "Plug the PC in and I can help you hook it up to your system. The two small cases are the drones."

"Oscar can handle the setup," Marla said. "I never mentioned paying you six million."

Vi shrugged. "It's worth a hell of a lot more than that and we both know it. I'll need money to get away once this is over. I'm sick of the cloak and dagger bullshit. I want out. This is my ticket to a new life."

"Smart decision." The woman approached, heels striking against the concrete floor.

Vi watched Oscar's progression as he yanked the computer out and hooked it up. Her pulse quickened. Hands fisted and unfisted at her sides. He set both cases down and opened them.

Perfect.

"What's to stop me from putting a bullet in your brain right now?" Marla settled a gun against Vi's head. "I could save myself six million."

Chains rattled. Vi held her breath, hoping the two men stayed in place. Too many sudden moves would undermine Cord's and Mary's control of the drones once things got underway.

"You could, but that wouldn't be very smart. HERA won't operate until you have the codes. I'll give you the first set once Oscar has it set up. I get my money, then you get the second set."

"That kind of money will take some time," Marla said.

"Bullshit. If you aren't serious, I'll leave. I'm not here to play games."

"You're here for whatever I say, bitch." The woman grabbed her hair and yanked hard. "What's the code?"

Vi glanced over at the computer and waited until the lights emanating from the shell were white instead of yellow. HERA was ready. She gritted her teeth in mock anger and rattled off the code. She repeated it a few times because Oscar wasn't the sharpest tool in the shed.

"Now." Marla yanked harder. Tears pricked Vi's vision, but she forced a deep breath and ignored the sharp pain. "Give him the other code or you die."

"Nice try," Vi clipped angrily. "He enters that code before six million hits my account and this entire place goes sky high. Between what's packed in the computer and the car outside, they'll be scraping you off concrete for months."

Marla shouted orders at the men to go check the car. She glared over at Oscar, who'd paled and stepped a few feet from the table. "Get to work. Give the bitch her six million. That's nothing compared to what we'll make on it."

"Account's already entered in the data menu," Vi offered lamely. "Let me go. I want to make sure Dallas and Jud are okay."

"I don't think so."

"You want HERA, you'll let me see them. Get them down. Now." Vi clenched her teeth and fisted her hands. "You've had your fun with them. Unhook them now and I'll give you the codes once the money's transferred. After I give you the codes, you can uncuff them."

Marla signaled four of the men to comply with Vi's request. The others closed in, weapons drawn. Vi waited until Jud and Dallas were lowered to the ground. Both men rotated and glared, but neither moved from where they'd been set. Vi closed the distance, careful to remain far enough away not to make the assholes with guns nervous. She huddled her hands near her body to shield the gestures Marshall and Nolan had taught her. They swore Dallas would understand them.

She doubted Jud would.

Dallas's eyebrows furrowed. She repeated the gestures.

"You two okay?"

"You shouldn't be here," Jud clipped angrily.

"You're okay." Vi moved to Dallas. "You good?"

"Golden."

Yes. Marshall said that'd be his response if he understood the message. "Good. I'm going to give Oscar the code, then we'll be out in a couple minutes."

"Money's transferred."

Marla grabbed her by the hair again and dragged her toward HERA. "The code. Now."

Vi pulled back, wanting to stay far away from the drones, especially the newer ones with the super lethal gunk. She figured standing near them was like petting a cobra. Vi tried to do a full turn to give everyone watching a better view of where everyone currently stood, but it was easier thought than done. Vi rattled off the code that'd snap The Collective's neck.

The virus had already snagged their account number and used the data they'd already gathered to cipher access to any other accounts they owned. They'd identified quite a few, but the final bits of data a live transaction offered would seal their fate. Vi almost chuckled when the light of the case turned a light blue. The virus worked.

Marla's gun returned to Vi's temple. "That wasn't very bright, Quillery. Did you really think I'd let you walk out of here?"

"Did you really think I'd give you HERA?" Vi shot back with a laugh. "I'm not the dumb one here. You never should have come after us. I would've let you keep doing whatever The Collective does, but you got dumb when you helped set up Mary's kidnapping. Her torture. You got dumber when you got scared and brokered a hit on us and put a price tag on HERA. But you know what really pissed me off?"

Marla's eyes narrowed to tiny slits. "You think you're so smart. You have no idea you're two minutes from dying."

"That's where you're wrong. You sealed your death warrant when you attacked my home, my family. Going after me and The Edge to get HERA was dumb. Dragging The Arsenal into it was suicidal. I promised Jud's parents I'd make you pay for taking him. I never break a promise. Goodbye, bitch."

Vi sank to her knees and noted Dallas and Jud had followed her suit. Dallas barked an order at Jud, who'd started moving. The second the two men were frozen into place, all hell broke loose. It'd been less than four seconds since she'd finished her statement. Drones whirred into position and fired. Darts slammed into the armed combatants around them. Oscar scurried under the desk. Marla ran.

Stupid bitch.

Explosions rattled the warehouse, the signal for the teams to move in. Vi lifted her pants legs and snagged both knives from their hidden sheaths. Dallas and Jud each grabbed one and went to work.

"Keep Marla alive," Dallas ordered.

Yeah, so not happening. Vi went over to the desk and disconnected HERA, putting her back into the duffel bag. She snagged the other computer and a laptop, in case there was anything important on it. HERA should have established unfettered access to The Collective's systems, but it was possible they'd set everything up in remote segments for added security. If they did it'd take a bit of finagling, but she and Mary would crack it.

"What are you doing, woman?" Jud growled as he shoved her to the floor. "Stay down."

"Mary and Cord won't hit me."

"I'm more worried about the men with the guns hitting you."
He pinned her to the ground. "I can't believe you strutted in here."

"I did not strut," she replied.

Angered shouts and gunfire echoed around them. Vi ran her
hands down Jud's face.

"I'm okay," he said.

Right. Because okay people bled all the time. Marshall and
Gage appeared. Vi rose along with Jud, who kept a protective arm
wrapped around her waist. Dallas was shouting at Marla, who
he'd taken to the ground.

"Where the fuck is he, Marla?"

"You'll never find him," she replied. Blood seeped from her
mouth as she clutched her bleeding abdomen. "You'll never
find him."

"Fuck!" Dallas shouted the statement as he rose and paced
angrily. "Fuck!"

"What's wrong?" Jesse asked.

Jud closed the distance, settling a hand on the man's shoulder.
"We'll find him, man. You know we will. The bitch was probably
lying."

"Lying about what?" Jesse asked.

"No, it'd be just like the bitch to breed, have my kid and never
tell me."

Holy shit. Vi's mouth dried as she stared at the dead woman.
She'd had Dallas's kid?

Holy shit.

She motored forward and wrapped her arms around Dallas.
"We'll find him. I swear we'll find him, wherever he is. Okay?"

"I didn't know."

"Of course not." She squeezed him tighter, then remembered
his ravaged torso. "Sorry."

"I'd rather feel the pain than think about how this could've
gone down. You have balls of steel, woman."

"That's not what I'd say," Jud said. "Mind filling us in on what the fuck this was?"

"A rescue," Vi replied.

"No shit," Dallas said. "It was more. You looked like a cat that ate a cage full of canaries when Oscar plugged the computer in. What really went down?"

"They wired six million to us," Vi said with a shrug. "And the code we wrote sort of took the rest."

"What rest?" Jud asked.

"All the rest. All the data we gathered and what we got via the transfer identified all their accounts and cleaned them out. Any account we could find is gone. It's out first blow to The Collective. They can't operate without funds." Vi rocked back on her heels. "They're going down for what they did."

"God, I fucking love you," Jud declared. He leaned in and kissed her lips.

What the hell? Her entire body tingled. He drew her close and guided her toward the warehouse doors.

"My team and Nolan's will remain behind, assist the investigators. Homeland and FBI have teams inbound. Everyone else, head back to the compound, get on Dallas's problem." Marshall's voice boomed in the area. He clapped Dallas on the back. "We'll find him. Vi and Mary are the best around. They'll find him. We won't stop until we do."

22

Viviana hovered like a chopper caught in a sandstorm. Translation—she sucked at not being obvious. Jud grinned at her as she stood within shouting distance as Logan assessed his injuries. Marshall had wanted him and Dallas to go to a real hospital before they left San Antonio, but Dallas grunted no and Jud was down with getting back to The Arsenal.

His entire body hurt, but he'd been through worse. The entire compound had been sealed tight, in case there was a backlash from what'd gone down in the warehouse. His mind reeled.

His heart still thudded hard against his chest when he thought back to the moment they'd dragged Viviana into the room. He'd aged thirty years in one second. He would've carved out his own heart to get her out of that fucking hellhole. But she'd walked in.

For him.

Jesus.

He expended a deep breath and let the realization he'd fallen head over heels for the woman settle. The man sitting on the exam table beside him was wired to explode. As much as Jud wanted to grab Viviana and finish the declaration he'd uttered in the warehouse, he needed to keep Dallas company. The man had five brothers and more friends and people ready to throw down for him than Jud could count, but that didn't mean he was okay. Jud recognized the haunted, desperate gaze sliding through the room. He was there but didn't fit, not really.

He'd been there hundreds of times after handling a hard target. What'd gone down wasn't a mission, a kill.

That bitch had Dallas's kid and never told him.

He had one card left to play, one move he'd earned. They didn't have a name for who put the hit out on the Quillery Edge and now they had an innocent kid out there without a mom or a dad.

Fuck.

"Need a phone," he growled. "Secure line."

"Is he cleared?" Marshall asked.

"Neither of them should do anything but sleep. But I have a better chance at riding a unicorn than that happening." Logan removed his gloves. "I've done what I can. They're pumped full of antibiotics. Both refused painkillers. I'll fill scripts in case they change their mind. So, yeah. They're cleared."

Jud grunted his appreciation and followed the procession of Masons as they headed toward a debriefing room. Jud didn't want to chat about what'd gone down, but he'd do whatever it took to get things sorted so he could have a few moments alone with Viviana. She appeared at his side. She placed her hand hesitantly on him, as if afraid her touch would hurt. She had no idea. No fucking clue her touch was what he'd focused on, clung to while that bitch did her damnedest to break him.

Everyone filed into the room. Jud didn't want everyone privy to the conversation he was about to have, but he hadn't quite acclimated to the whole teamwork slash brotherhood thing The

Arsenal had going. He'd acclimate because everyone in the room was important to Viviana.

"Are you okay?" She ran her hand down his cheek. "You should've taken the pain meds Logan offered."

"I'll be fine."

"What's our next move? We need to figure out where the fuck my kid's at." Dallas prowled the narrow path in front of the closed door.

Mary pushed the conference phone toward Jud. He dialed the number and raised a hand for everyone to remain quiet.

"You're out," Kristof said. "A few friends and I were inbound to assist your departure, but I see your new friends had it handled."

"Appreciate the gesture," Jud said.

"As I appreciate the head's up. Things would've been messy for me had I not been warned. I owe you."

"And I'm afraid I need to cash in now, the sooner the better." Jud sighed. "Marla had a kid. I need a location. And I need a name behind the contract. I know it was high up the food chain, probably at the top. I need those names, Kristof."

"That is a complicated and dangerous road for anyone to travel. Some destinations aren't worth the effort."

"I think we both know these two are. I'm out. The Collective is going down. I'll vouch for you if you want to have a conversation with someone more in the gray than the black, but I need your assist to finish this. I wouldn't ask if there was any other way."

"Twenty years. We've battled in the dark shadows no one else dared enter for twenty years, watching one another's backs. It's hard to imagine those times are done. I'll admit I'm not sure if that's good or bad. Some demons only die in the shadows, man. Not everything can be handled in the light of day." Caution punctuated Kristof's words. "I'll send what I know, but I've got nothing on the kid. She mentioned a cabin up in Wyoming once. I'll send coordinates in case it's worth checking out. Strike fast on the names. They're scurrying. I'll assist if needed. The man behind Edge's abduction will be there, too. The information recently came to my attention."

The room went nuclear at the declaration, the fact they had finally gotten to the end of the road. They'd have closure for Mary. And Viviana.

"Appreciated, man. Touch base when you're clear, let me know if you need help getting new legs under you."

"I'm good. Go get the white picket fence life you've wanted. And the dog. Name the first brat after me," the man ordered.

Jud looked over at Viviana as he smiled at his friend's words. Kristof Lavrov was the closest thing to a true friend he had while in The Collective. "I'm thinking a cat might be the way to go. I'll be in touch. Breathe free."

"Always. I'll send what you need now. Then we can all breathe free."

The line went dead. Silence ticked by a few moments as Jud looked at the phone. He looked over at his nephew, who'd somehow become part of the caravan of people following him and Dallas. "He'll send the coordinates and data to my secure email, bud."

"I'm on it." Jacob grabbed Cord's laptop and got to work.

"Who was that?" Mary asked.

"A friend, another ghost. He...he and I worked the inner layer of projects for The Collective. What I turned down, he handled, and vice versa. He was in with them a few years before me. He spent the past few years as Marla's personal lapdog after I walked away from the post."

"He was her assassin," Dallas said. "I recognize the name Kristof, but we haven't met."

"Uh, Uncle Jud..." Jacob's voice rose. "There's a whole lot more than GPS coordinates here."

Cord took the computer and whistled. "You're buddy sent a lot of data. Zoey, Jacob and I will get it fed into HERA, let the system process it overnight. The phantom behind Peter's operation is in there somewhere."

"We'll organize teams to move on him immediately once we have a name, location," Viviana said.

"No," Mary said. "Let him sweat. We'll strike him soon, but we need to move teams on the cabin location and track down Dallas's kid. That's our priority. We all want closure on the Hive incident, but the kid is our critical mission."

"And stretching ourselves thin by doing both isn't an option," Marshall said. "We cut too close doing that the last time. Until we're fully staffed, we're not biting off more than we can safely chew."

They were right. It sucked, but whoever the mystery man was would have to wait a little longer. Perhaps not that long. Jud could go in alone and eliminate just about anyone. The fewer involved, the better. It wasn't the sort of op that'd end in a typical manner.

"Good, thanks." Mary rubbed her temples. "Everyone needs a few hours' rack time, then we can figure out our plan."

Dallas pounded his fist on the wall. Nolan and Jesse book-ended him. Jud hoped the two kept close watch on him because Jud doubted he'd be okay with waiting a few hours while everyone caught up on their sleep.

"Cord will run operations on Wyoming. Jesse's team will handle entry. Dallas will go along, but in observance capacity only." Marshall looked around the room. "Wheels up in six hours. Everyone else rest up. We don't know what else is coming our way."

Everyone rose. Jud was grateful for the reprieve from a full debriefing. Addy snagged his arm.

"I'll be at Bree's and Rhea's place. Hurt her and I hurt you."

Jud smiled at the redhead who'd just cleared the way for him to spend some quality time with Viviana. He made his way toward her as everyone filed down the hall and out of the building.

"Judson, Judson, Judson." He took a step back as his mother vaulted into his arms. Roped tightly around him, she sobbed.

Pain radiated from his damaged ribs, but he held the woman tightly and caught Viviana's gaze over her head. He flashed a worried glance at Jacob, who hovered near his grandpa.

"Sorry, I told them you were missing, and they insisted on watching the rescue." Jacob shuffled his feet. "Sorry."

"It's okay, bud." He looked down at his mom when she separated, then over at his dad. "You good?"

"Yeah, son. We're good. Go and take care of Quillery. She looks like she's about to come unglued." His dad smiled. "You picked a hell of a woman. I'm proud. It takes a hell of a man to let his woman be as strong as she can be."

Viviana was a hell of a woman. He smiled at his parents, kissed each of them and then snagged his woman's hand before anyone else could stop them. They were almost to her cottage when his gaze settled on the couple sitting on the steps leading up to the door.

Fuck no. Not even after the dinner. One well-behaved meal didn't justify trusting them.

He positioned Viviana protectively behind him as her parents closed the distance between them. "I'll handle this."

"No. It's okay." She sighed her frustration. "It's been a long day, Mom and Dad. Can we table this until the morning?"

"Please, Viviana." Her father grasped his wife's shoulders. "We won't take long."

Jud wanted to shove them out of the way and lock Viviana away for a few hours, but it wasn't his choice. These were her parents and she needed to decide for herself whether she wanted to give them anymore of herself than she'd already tried to. He didn't pretend to understand the emotional toll of a negative relationship with a parent, but he knew it was extensive.

"It's okay," she said. She looked up at him. "Give us a moment, okay?"

"I'll be inside," he whispered. "Yell if you need me, okay?"

~

Viviana was too mentally exhausted to handle whatever her parents wanted to chat with her about. After today, she honestly didn't give a damn what they thought about her. A man she loved and needed more than anything or anyone was behind the door they blocked. He'd gone through hell today and survived. They'd made a huge dent in The Collective today. Vi wouldn't know how much of a dent until she looked at what'd transpired in the warehouse, which she'd do once they had a plan in motion for Dallas.

A throat cleared behind her. She rubbed her temples and silently cursed the fact she couldn't find a single moment alone with Jud.

"Sorry, I need your help to expedite something, Vi." Marshall offered a polite smile to her parents as he held out a phone. "I'm thinking you'll have better luck cutting through the red tape to get DJ secured into our custody. Mom and Dad..."

The man faltered a moment, shifting restlessly. It was the first time Vi had noted the pain on his face. He missed his father terribly. It was a wound she'd noticed on the other Masons, but never on Marshall.

"My parents were approved as foster parents, if that helps."

Vi took the phone. She had zero clue who to call to get temporary custody over a child whose identity they didn't fully know and whose location was somewhere in the middle of nowhere. She stared at the phone, then up at her parents, who waited patiently. Patience wasn't a word her parents had ever been familiar with, much less accepted into their typical habits.

"Marshall, I..." She took a deep breath. He wanted a miracle pulled out of her ass to make it easier for his little brother to seal off the latest wound he'd taken. "I don't have a name, a county, or anything."

"Can you get the wheels moving and we can fill in the needed data later?"

"I'll see." Who the hell could she even call for this one? She thought back to their latest situations and dialed a number she hoped she remembered. It wasn't like she'd used it a lot.

"This is William." Vi clicked it over to speaker so Marshall could hear.

"Hi, Mr. Persons, this is Viviana Chambers. We spoke several days ago."

"Oh yes, Quillery. You helped take down that horrid sex slave ring. We've been after the Solovs for years. I'm very grateful to you for helping us seal their fate. All the data you and your partner sent over from the computers will lock them away for a long time."

"Great. If you need anything else, let us know."

"Yes. I was just apprised of the San Antonio situation. I trust everyone is okay?"

"Oh yes, and thank you for helping clear everything up. We'll be reviewing the intel we gathered and I'll send briefings to you and everyone else tomorrow morning. I'm afraid I'm in a bit of a bind on a related issue, one that came to light during the warehouse take down. One of the targets had a child. The child's father is Dallas Mason. He didn't know anything about his son until a few hours ago. Needless to say, The Arsenal is extremely focused on securing his son."

"Of course. Do you have a location?"

"Yes. An asset provided coordinates, in Wyoming. We're

wheels up in six hours. With any luck the boy will be there. If not, we'll keep going until we find him. That's what we do."

"I'll make sure a team is there to assist. We'll get everything in order so the boy can be taken back to The Arsenal."

"Thank you, Mr. Persons. The boy's grandmother was approved to foster children. He'll be in a good home here."

"Well, I wouldn't expect anything less from you or anyone in your group. We're in your debt. Let me know if you need anything at all tomorrow."

She clicked off and handed the phone back to Marshall. "That should do it."

"Thanks. See you in a few hours. Get some rest. If you need help, let me know." He glared at her parents, but headed off.

"Sorry about that," she murmured to her parents. "What's up?"

"We owe you an apology," her father declared. "That young man, Jacob. He sat us down and made us watch the rescue. It was rather disturbing."

Holy shit. Vi blinked. Unsure how to respond, she opted for silence.

"I never had any idea." Her mother's eyes watered. "I thought you were plugging in data or that kind of thing, like a secretary or something. I never really listened to what you were saying when you tried to talk about your work. I never had any idea."

The woman crushed Vi against her as she cried. Unlike Jud's mom, though, the crying jag only lasted a couple minutes. Long enough for Vi to grow uncomfortable. She wanted a real relationship with her parents, but she couldn't navigate from their toxic one to a normal one. The path mystified her.

"Jenna mentioned there was a lovely counselor here, Rebecca Sinclair. She suggested that once things calm down maybe the two of us could go see her, maybe we could do a session or two with you," her dad said. "I'm not proud of the things I've said to you, Viviana. I'm sorry."

"I'm sorry for not trying harder recently," she admitted.

"We love you, dear. Don't ever doubt that." Her mother patted her cheek. "And we are proud of you, more than you'll ever know. I was so worried about you outshining Rich I'm afraid we suffocated you entirely."

"No, you didn't." Viviana let the partial lie settle between them.

"We'll talk more in the morning, or whenever you get this sorted. I know things are up in the air. We're going to start pitching in around here and helping out. It's the least we could do." Her father motioned toward the cottage. "He's a good man. You have a good night. We'll see you tomorrow."

"I love you." Viviana said the words she'd held onto for a long time.

"We love you, too," her mom said.

Misty eyed, Viviana entered her cottage. Jud snagged her at the waist and hauled her into his arms. She gasped.

"Put me down, Jud. You're injured. You can't be lifting me."

"Nothing will ever stop me from taking care of my woman."

Her insides warmed, her pulse quickened. He carried her toward the bedroom. "I was terrified out of my mind when I woke up and you weren't there."

"Did they hurt you?"

"No. No. I'm okay," she assured him. She wrapped her arms around him as he settled her on the bed. "Make love to me, Judson. I need you inside me."

Pleasure ignited through her when they kissed. She yanked his shirt off and he followed suit with hers. His touches were frenzied. She softened their kiss, settled her hands atop his. "We have all night, Jud. We're together and home. Safe."

He licked and sucked his way down her body, paying special attention to her hardened nipples. She moaned and begged him for more. Jud rose off the bed and made quick work of removing the rest of their clothes. Her gaze focused on his ravaged torso. The bitch had died too quickly for hurting him.

"We shouldn't. You're hurt."

"Nothing will ever stop me from making love to you, Viviana. Nothing." He took her mouth and positioned himself between her legs.

His weight pressed there ignited her need, quickened her pulse. "Let me love you this time, Jud. Let me show you that you're mine."

Intensity gathered in his gaze. He moved onto his back, but pulled her down enough for their mouths to fuse once more. Now that she'd gotten him relaxed on the bed, she could pick up where they'd left off. And his ribs were safe. She kissed along his chest, grazing his skin. She bypassed the wounds, made note of each one so she could make sure they healed properly. Her man was one scar after another.

Not anymore.

She wrapped her hand around his hardened length and flicked her tongue across the tip. Jud's body writhed beneath the contact. She hummed her approval as she took him into her mouth. He wrapped his fingers into her hair and helped set the pace. His groans filled the room, making her feel like a freaking super hero.

"Ride me, Viviana."

Hell yes.

She reached over and grabbed the box of condoms some sly roomie had put in there. Jud chuckled at the super-sized box. "Someone's feeling industrious."

"I'm thinking you're up for it." She worked his length with one hand as she undid the package with the other and her teeth.

Thankfully Jud took it from her. Her pussy muscles clenched as he rolled it on. Deft hands massaged up her thighs. He stroked her pussy and thumbed her clit. She writhed against the contact, so close to an orgasm she growled in frustration when he stopped.

"I want us to come together," he whispered. "Ride me, Viviana."

His long, thick length filled her fully. She sank down onto him, relishing the way he felt inside her. He grasped her hips. She was unsure where to put her hands so as not to hurt him. God. His back.

She'd forgotten about...

"Stop worrying about me," he ordered.

She leaned down and kissed him, letting the fusion of tongues and mouths convey the words lodged in her throat. She'd never fully understood how Mary got so lost in Dylan. Now she understood. The world started and stopped with Jud. Pleasure beaded along her skin, from where Jud sucked her nipples down to where his other hand rubbed her clit.

Her entire body tensed.

"Judson." She cried his name and rode the wave of white-hot pleasure igniting within her.

Vi continued to ride him until he came. He melted into the mattress and she carefully curled beside him.

"You okay?"

"I'm perfect, Viviana." He cupped her face and kissed her mouth. "I love you. There's nothing I wouldn't do for you. You're the most amazing woman I've ever met and I'll spend each day proving that to you."

"I love you, Judson. I've never had someone like you in my life, someone who saw the real me and didn't give a damn that I'm not perfect and never will be. For once I'm okay with who I am and wouldn't ever change a thing because it led me to you."

"Did it go okay with your parents?"

"Yeah." She chuckled and stroked Jud's chest. Your nephew has a secondary career as a psychologist if he wants it. He sat them down, made them watch the rescue. I think your parents were there, too."

"Yeah, he admitted my mom and dad were there, but he hadn't mentioned yours. I'll have a word with him."

"No. It's okay." Vi sighed as he covered them both with a sheet. "I'm going to see if we can expedite his father's return stateside. Now that things are calming down, I want them reunited so Danny can start to mend fully. Jacob, too. He's been through a lot."

∾

Viviana couldn't sleep. Her mind buzzed. A million thoughts marched through like lost soldiers with no direction, no compass. She sat on the floor near her bed and looked up at Jud. He slept hard, as one would expect after surviving kidnapping and torture.

She'd put on a brave face for him and everyone else, but him getting taken cut too close to the vein. It was too much like Mary. She couldn't lose him. Whatever the future held, he was a vital part of that as far as her heart was concerned.

Tears filled her vision as she typed out her fears, her dreams.

I've never been so scared in my life.

I want to spend the rest of my life wrapped up in you.

You are my heart and soul.

I love you.

Time shrank beneath her determination. The thoughts lulled. The fear subsided. Silence ticked by. She spun the tiny strips of paper and added them to Jud's mandala.

"Hey, you okay?" Jud's voice startled her. She glanced at the clock and noted the two-hour loss of time.

She contemplated his question before nodding. She wouldn't ever keep something from him, not when every secret was a potential threat. They'd survived enough adversities without throwing in unnecessary risks. "Yeah, I'm good now. My brain was just needing decompression time."

"That's a big mandala. It's beautiful," he said.

She looked down at the dark and light blue interspersed with white and pale yellow strips. She took a deep breath and held it out. "I made it for you. It had to be big because I had a lot to say."

She didn't expand on the latter statement. Baby steps. Sharing her secret messages was something she'd sworn to never, ever do. That was her decompression, her off loading of her most intimate thoughts.

But she loved Jud, which meant those belonged to him now. They affected him. She was all in for whatever was going on between them.

"I love you," she whispered as she flicked off the lamp and crawled back into bed. She curled into him.

"I love you, too." He kissed her softly and wrapped an arm around her as he held her gift with his other hand.

She closed her eyes and surrendered to exhaustion.

J ud knew the moment she fell asleep. She gave him all of her weight, trusting him to keep whatever demons had roused her at bay while she slept, like she had that one night.

It had to be big because I had a lot to say.

He'd watched her spin the small strips of papers, had even asked her questions and tried it himself a few times. He looked down at the beautiful woman sleeping beside him and realized giving this to him had been a huge step. The fear and indecision had been evident on her face. The absolute trust in the end had undone him.

He loved Viviana Chambers more than anything.

Which was why he needed to figure out this mystery, make it

okay for her to not have to explain. He slowly extricated himself from the bed and padded into the other room.

The pale light from the corner lamp spotlighted a corner of the coffee table enough for him to study the beautiful creation. He gently undid one of the blue strips and unraveled it.

Nothing.

He removed a white. Unraveled.

I want to spend the rest of my life wrapped up in you.

It was one of the pieces she'd added tonight. He'd watched her for a few moments before drawing her attention. Jesus.

How many other pieces held messages? What did they say?

He wanted to rip every piece off and figure out the mystery beneath the beautiful creation, but this was a gift. Something she'd made for him. He wouldn't ruin it, not if he could be careful and piece it back together.

"What are you doing?"

Jud jumped.

"Was going to stay away, but Dallas said her parents were yapping about showing up here early, having a word. I thought I'd head them off if they showed up."

He glared at the door. "Appreciated."

"What are you doing?"

"Nothing."

Addy smirked as she padded into the room wearing a long t-shirt and a loose pair of men's boxer shorts. She sat beside him and picked up the white piece of paper. He damn near ripped it from her hand, but he didn't want to wake Viviana up by throwing down with her friend.

"Huh." Addy set it down and headed into the kitchen.

How the hell could she read that and just say huh, like it didn't matter?

Like it didn't rock the entire world with its fierceness. Love.

She popped the top off a couple beers as she sat. Handing one to him, she motioned toward the mandala. "Go get her box of supplies from under the bed. I'll help you so you don't ruin it."

"You aren't pissed I'm violating her trust?"

"Did you steal this from her?"

"No, she gave it to me."

"Then she was ready for you to know." Addy shrugged. "She's been quilling for years, ever since I knew her. I didn't realize the significance until we moved into this place and I realized she only did it when she was having emotional problems. She quilled a lot right after we got Mary back."

Jesus.

"I investigated one day, found the messages." Addy's gaze narrowed. "She doesn't know I know. I doubt she's ever told anyone, but she's going to tell you soon if this is evidence. She's never given any of her stuff away before. They're all buried in the back of her closet in a locked chest."

Jesus.

He looked down at the mandala and felt a moment's guilt for not waiting for her to trek the rest of the road. She'd entrusted him with this much. It was time he manned up and went the rest of the way.

"Let's get to work."

~

Wyoming was a bust. Evidence of at least one child residing there was present—strewn toys and children's clothing. The FBI had helped comb through the cabin and had swept a twenty-mile perimeter.

Whoever Marla had entrusted the child to was in the wind, but not for long. They would find DJ. For now, focus was on getting Danny and the other men back from their overseas nightmare.

Vi found her quarry in Command Central, which should have been her first place to look. Jacob was shoving his laptop into the backpack. He halted his efforts when she entered.

"Hey," he said, his voice more a whisper than expected.

"You okay?" she asked. "Things have been pretty intense around here."

Jacob nodded, too quickly. She sat, waiting him out. He fell into the chair beside hers.

"How do you keep control of the calm? You and Edge are always so calm."

"I wasn't very calm when I woke after they took your uncle," she admitted. "I spent a lot of years thinking I needed to be perfect, collected at all times. Then I finally figured out the truth."

"What's that?" He looked at her with wide, hopeful eyes.

"It's okay to feel, to react to what's going on around you. It's not possible to be stoic and calm all the time. We remain in control when it counts by giving the chaos to someone, letting them hold us up when we need a break. That's what family does." She smiled and took his hand. "I learned by watching Edge with Dylan."

"You've got Uncle Jud," he said.

"Yeah, and you have all of us," she whispered. "You're an amazing young man. You have no idea how well you've done, how strong you've been through all of this. I remember when I first started at Hive. Mary and I were a freaking mess."

Jacob smirked. "I can't believe that's true."

"Well, it was. Trust me. Heck, ask her." Vi let the silence fall a few moments.

"I was so scared," he admitted. "I cried like a baby after Jian called saying he had Dad. Uncle Jud held me, gave me the time I needed."

Vi's heart swelled. Jud was a good man, he'd be an excellent dad one day. The thought made her smile. "I was terrified when I woke up in the field and he was gone."

"I felt helpless. I didn't like feeling that way."

"Me neither," she admitted. "But we got through it because we have each other. It's taken me too long to figure out we're stronger as a team than we are alone. It took a long time for me to figure that out. I did because of your uncle. And you."

"Me?" Jacob looked at her.

"You." She squeezed his hand. "You and I are a lot alike, Jacob. I'm thinking it'll take both of us to keep your uncle out of trouble."

"Probably." He grinned. Red tinged his cheeks. "I was thinking. Things keep going the way they are with you and Uncle Jud..."

Warmth spread in Vi's stomach as her mind meandered down the trail Jacob's words hinted at. She waited him out, let him form the words her heart already had.

"I'm glad you are part of the family," he said.

"I'm glad, too." She smiled. "I love you, Jacob."

"I love you, too, Vi."

She dragged him into a hug, and finally pulled away because she suspected there'd be a manhunt for them both soon if they didn't get to the vehicles. "Come on, everyone's waiting. I'm sure your dad's anxious to see you."

The one and a half hours to San Antonio had never felt so long. Thanks to Marshall and Nolan's contacts in the Delta and SEAL's squads, a good chunk of the red tape had been burned away. Vi suspected the phone call Marshall had made to Washington had a bigger impact, but she doubted he'd mentioned that to anyone. Dylan had taken his team and Jud overseas to handle security for the transfer. No one was taking any chances when it came to The Collective.

Either way, the freed prisoners were all in the military hospital in San Antonio under heavy guard, despite the fact none of them were military. An investigation would be underway to determine what role, if any, a certain government agency may have played in their imprisonment. Riley was sprawled out in the third row of seating. She'd insisted on coming along, but hadn't slept much the past couple of days.

She was going to kick some serious Mason man ass when she saw them. They'd all dodged her. They didn't have any idea how impacted she'd been by seeing two of their ops. Mary had finally managed to get Riley to catch a few hours' sleep by dragging her out to the barn of all places. Vi had found both women snuggled under a blanket in an empty stall next to the adorable horse named Peanut.

She pulled up into a parking spot near the door and threw the vehicle into park. As planned, Jud was outside. Long legs crossed, he looked like a weary traveler in need of a few days' rest. She was more than willing to keep him company while he did so. She moved into his arms and kissed him hungrily.

His whiskers rubbed her face, but she didn't give a damn. He tasted like home.

Love.

"Missed you," she whispered. Six days. He'd been gone six days.

"Missed you more," he returned. "He wants to see you first."

"But Jacob's here and..." She halted when Jud put a finger over her lips.

"He's still in rough shape, Viviana. He wants to talk to you first. Give him that play, for me."

She nodded and looked over her shoulder at Mary, who was wrapped up in Dylan. They both nodded and Dylan did the man chin-lift thing in Jacob's direction. They'd make sure he stayed clear until Danny was ready.

Vi couldn't imagine what the man had endured. He'd yet to be debriefed. It'd likely take weeks, if not months for him to be fully cleared medically. Dehydration and malnourishment had been concerns for all the prisoners, but he'd suffered far more extensive torture than the others.

The doors to the hospital swooshed open. Cool air struck her face as the entered. Her boot's heels clacked against the light-colored flooring. Each step took her closer to him.

"What's this conversation about, Jud?"

"I'm not sure."

Vi shook off the nervousness as he knocked on a partially open door. Nurses flitted about in the hallway. Their not-so-subtle gazes tracked Jud's progression. No doubt they'd been drooling over him since Danny arrived.

"Hey, man," Jud said. "I see you're still playing the sick card to get extra pudding cups."

The man's lips cracked into a smile. Tubes came from his nose and both hands. Monitors beeped and chimed from both sides of him. Bile rose in her throat.

"I finally get to meet the infamous Quillery," Danny said. He patted the bed. "Come. Sit. I don't bite."

Vi sat down on the side of the bed. He grabbed her hand and squeezed.

"I never got a chance to thank you the last time." His voice was low, barely discernible over the beeping monitors. "You saved me, changed my life. My boy's life."

"No." She shook her head. "That's all on you. You're an amazing dad. You've raised a brilliant young man. In a couple years he'll be giving me and Edge a run for our money."

He laughed, held his sides and smiled through the obvious pain. "That's my boy. Always told him if he wanted something he'd have to be tenacious, just like you."

Danny had built up his memories of her, created a super hero to battle whatever troubles his boy came across. "Did Dylan and the guys tell you about the Warriors Path? I'm thinking you'd be a good fit. I know you aren't military, but you may as well be."

"Yeah, Dylan's fitting me in. He thinks it'd be a good fit, a good chance for me to get on my feet. He said you and Mary gave my boy a job, a place to belong."

"He's a tremendous help. He's shown us a lot, improved some of our coding."

"I heard you got Jud away from The Collective and helped take them down." Tears filled his eyes. His lower lip trembled. He thumped his chest. "You're in here deep."

She hugged him close and whispered her reply. "You're the one in deep, so deep you healed me when I didn't even know I needed it. Thank you."

Danny had been the catalyst long ago, the one who'd returned the favor by thrusting Jud into her life. If he hadn't remembered what she'd done so many years ago, Jud wouldn't have intervened.

Vi sat up and swiped the tears from her eyes. "I've stolen enough of your time. We'll have plenty of chances to catch up once you get to The Arsenal."

She looked back at Jud, who nodded and leaned into the hall. "Come on, bud."

Jacob ran in with the force of a hurricane, straight to his dad. The young man, the future back office operative, disappeared. Tears streamed down the two men's faces. Vi stood, leaning into Jud's weight as he wrapped a protective arm around her.

"Love you, Viviana."

"Love you, Judson." She looked over at the father and son. "Let's go outside, give them some time alone."

Jud led them outside and clicked the door shut. A man hovered nearby, shifting from one foot to another. His gaze moved from Vi to the floor, then down the corridor. Her grip on Jud tightened, but she offered a smile in greeting.

"Hi." The man's voice cracked. "Danny said you were coming. I wanted to thank you for coming for us. Dylan and his brothers tolerated my gratitude well enough, so I figured I'd wait out here. I'm Joe. Thank you for saving us, Quillery."

He was younger than she'd expected in appearance. A light salting hair along the temples and atop his head of otherwise dark brown hair was the only hint of his age. Forty-three was far from old, but she figured the man felt at least thirty years older after what he'd been through.

Vi closed the distance and wrapped the man into a big hug. Tension radiated from him a moment, but he relaxed and returned the hold. "I'm glad you're back and safe. I hear some of you are coming to stay with us at The Arsenal."

He flashed a smile. "Yeah, Dylan said it'd be a good way to acclimate, find a new path in life. I got out of the service a few years back, thought contracting overseas would be a good fit. Guess I was wrong."

"Sometimes it takes a few stumbles before the real journey starts. I'm glad you'll be joining us."

"See you around, Quillery."

"Later, Joe."

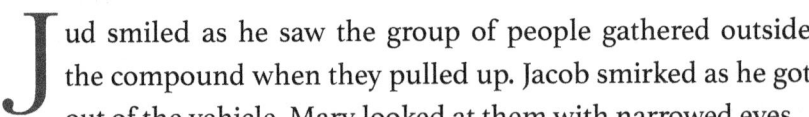

Jud smiled as he saw the group of people gathered outside the compound when they pulled up. Jacob smirked as he got out of the vehicle. Mary looked at them with narrowed eyes.

"You two are up to something," she said.

He kept his focus on Viviana as she exited the vehicle. He'd spent the past several days planning the surprise. He hoped the woman wrapping her arms around him liked it. Nervousness swarmed his insides like an army of crazed bees. He'd been in thousands of deadly situations and never experienced the emotional rollercoaster assailing him.

"Jud?" She squeezed him. "Are you okay?"

"You always sense my mood swings. I spent decades as an emotionless machine. No one ever noticed my emotional shifts. They never cared."

"Well, I do. What's wrong?"

"Absolutely nothing, Viviana. For once, I'm looking ahead and seeing nothing but good. That's because of you. I love you." He kissed her lips softly, then smiled. "I hope you love me enough to forgive me quickly if this goes sideways."

"If what goes sideways?"

"Holy shit. No way!" Mary declared from up ahead. She peered through a small space between Bree and Rhea. The two women were laughing and smiling so big their faces almost split in two. Even Addy was smiling. Dylan glanced in the same direction and laughed.

Jud's parents and hers were there. Everyone was there.

The moment was upon him. Which surprise did he spring first? The one everyone knew about, or the impulsive one he'd made alone without anyone's input.

Fuck.

He'd rather take on a third-world country's army than have either of these things go sideways.

"I realized the other day I'd been looking at our pet debate the wrong way. It's not about what you like or what I prefer, not anymore. I don't want to go through life focused on differences, not when we live each second like it could be our last because we know it might be." Jud looked at Bree and Rhea and nodded. The two women jumped up and down as they moved out of the way.

A solid white kitten and German Shepherd puppy bounced forward, as if sensing how important the moment was. Tears appeared in Viviana's gaze as she looked at him, then them. Mouth gaping, she fell to her knees as the two shaking babies sniffed her.

"Judson."

He laughed to himself at how the two surprises transitioned into one another so easily. Everyone surged forward. Bree and Rhea appeared in his vision. Mary joined them. Addy crouched nearby, not committing fully to the girly girl act of loving on kittens and puppies.

"Judson spoke with a very nice man in town, he was a doctor. Riley mentioned he'd helped patch Mary up a while back. He's a rather handsome fellow. Brant. Isn't that a lovely name?"

"I'm not sure she needs those details, Mom," Jud said with a laugh.

"Well, we were eating at Bubba's and he had a seat and we were telling him all about the stuff going on out here. Jarold mentioned you two were so cute, arguing about a cat versus a dog. Brant chuckled and said he could solve that problem. He told us about these two little cuties and we called Judson."

"They've been raised together and are the best of pals," Riley said. "They're perfect for you two."

"Yes, they are." Viviana threw her arms around him. "Thank you. I love you, Jud."

"I love you, too." He kissed her gently, but was cut short by the puppy when he hopped up to get her attention.

Viviana squealed and started rubbing him down. Everyone's attention was on Viviana and the puppy. The kitten was scampering toward her parents, who'd approached with cautious grins. He slid his hand into his pocket.

And locked gazes with Addy.

Ever observant, always protective Addy.

The woman's eyes widened a bit. Her gaze turned watery and she smiled and nodded. The bees turned into buzzards cawing as the nervousness crawled into his throat and broke his voice.

Jesus.

He was going to fuck this up.

"I figure we'll let them get a bit older before we have our first child. I want a boy first because I'll need help kicking punk teenage ass when they try and mess with my little girl." Jud opened the box. "There's not any wine and roses, but you've got my heart and soul. I love you, Viviana Chambers. Marry me."

"Holy shit!"

"Oh wow!"

"Yes!"

Guffaws exploded around them. He smiled as Viviana leaped atop him.

"Yes, I'll marry you, Judson Jason Jensen. Yes."

Vi looked around the large dining room table with amusement. The Mason men weren't very happy they'd been wrangled into a "conversation" with their little sister. If the glowers, glares and outright growls were any indication, they were less thrilled they'd been "escorted" to said "conversation" by Addy, Fallon, Gage and Jud. The latter chuckled and wrapped his arm around her. Life with a man at her side was awesome.

Mary slid into a seat beside Dylan as Riley entered from the kitchen. She was weighted down with a thick portfolio, rolled up documents and other stuff. Dallas was the first big brother to toss aside his supposed frustration and help her out. Vi exchanged a glance with Mary, who smiled back. It was about to get interesting at The Arsenal because little sister Mason was entering the fray in a huge way.

It'd been two weeks since their standoff with The Collective. Danny was faring well and had been unofficially enrolled in the Warrior's Path Project with some of the other men they'd freed. Most of them had already returned home, a move Vi wasn't sure some of them had been fully prepared for. Transitioning from something that horrid and back into a normal life wasn't easy, or so Doctor Sinclair had assured her.

She and the doc had a somewhat amicable relationship now. Vi went once a week and had started opening up about some of the darker recesses in her skeleton closet. She'd talk about whatever went down with Jud afterward. That particular conversation always left her feeling loads better than the one with the doc.

He'd admitted he figured out the mandala messages. The fact he'd taken such care to read every notation and put it back together exactly how it had been made her love him even more. It was proof he loved her enough to treat every word, every thought she ever had with utmost care.

Jud had closed down his new operation and had moved in with her and Addy. Addy promptly packed and took up residence with Rhea and Bree next door.

The search for little DJ continued with little success. One lead opened another each time, though, so Viviana was optimistic. As long as there was a trail she'd follow it.

The trail for Peter's betrayal, Mary's abduction and the entire Hive catastrophe ended with one man—a high-ranking executive with The Collective. By all accounts, Bradley Upton was a narcissistic prick and general scum of humanity. Viviana couldn't wait to take him down, but Jud made her swear she'd let him handle it whenever the time came.

She and her man would handle segments of that mission themselves, once the dust had settled a bit. Letting Upton think he'd gotten by, maybe sweat a bit and look over his shoulder was the perfect foreplay to what'd be an epic fuck you for the bastard who'd hurt her best friend.

Her family.

Based on the intel they'd received from Jud's friend, Upton was the man behind The Collective weighing in on what they referred to as the "Quillery Edge issue." Bastard. He'd sanctioned a six-million-dollar hit on them and forced pawns into place to get Jacob's dad taken.

So, yeah.

Taking him down was huge, a move she couldn't make alone because she hadn't been the only one affected by the bastard's decisions. For once, however, she wasn't going to let vengeance or the need for justice control her, not now.

For now, she'd breathe free and enjoy a new chapter in her life, with her new man. Vengeance could wait a few days. Bradley Upton sure as hell wasn't going anywhere she couldn't track him down.

Jacob and Zoey had taken to The Arsenal like proverbial ducks in water. They were official employees, with the understanding Jacob would complete his course studies at MIT.

And The Collective was weakened. Significantly. HERA had procured more than ninety-five percent of their liquid assets, according to the Deep Web and data crawls she and Mary had done afterward. The contract was kaput since the payday couldn't be funded and Jian was in a federal prison awaiting trial. For now, there were no fires burning, no enemies to quash.

Except Bradley, of course.

They could breathe easy.

"Riles, I know you mean well, but..." Marshall halted his sentence when Riley held up a hand.

"The first part of this agenda isn't a two-sided conversation, big brother. It's a you're all going to sit your bad ass butts down and listen or my peeps are going to kick your ass until you do kind of presentation." Riley took a breath and pointed to Addy, Fallon, Gage and then Jud. "Now, to make your ears work better, I'm going to start by saying I'm sorry."

The brothers glanced at one another. No one spoke.

Riley looked down at the thick, black portfolio. "I still

remember the day you six sat Mom and Dad down and told them you all planned to enlist. The way Dad swelled with pride when you looked him in the face like the young men you were and said you wanted to give the world a slice of the peace and safety he'd given you."

"Riley." Cord choked the word out as a quiet warning.

"I had no idea," she stated.

"You came back, got out when you could so you were closer to Mom." She looked around the table. "Me."

"Riles," Nolan said.

"You gave up a piece of your dream to keep Dad's going for me and Mom." Riley sniffed, keeping her focus on the folder to keep attention from her watery eyes. If Vi noticed, there wasn't any chance in hell the woman's six older brothers hadn't. "I've been nagging you like an old woman to help folks in Resino. Marville. I figured you were home, doing whatever you were doing. I thought it was simple protection details, guarding politicians when they headed overseas or something along those lines. Then you all went in and got Mary and I got my first clue."

"Think we need to fast forward a bit," Marshall replied.

"No, Marsh. This needs to be said because you all won't ever sit still to hear it from Mom. He would've been prouder than hell of you. Every single one of you." Tears flowed from her eyes as it swept each brother. "I wish you could've heard him at Bubba's, around town. He didn't know where you were or what you were doing most of the time because that's how it had to be. He was prouder than hell."

"Jesus." Dallas adjusted himself in his seat like he was about to run. Gage moved and shook his head. "Jesus."

"My eyes are open now. I see what you are juggling. You're out being commandos, kicking ass and saving people like you told Dad you would. But now you're doing it from his land, the ranch he and Mom loved. You're trying to keep it running, thriving."

Riley took a deep breath and shook her head. "Saddens me to say he wouldn't be proud of what you're doing now. He'd be up in your faces telling you how it's going to be because Dad wouldn't want you stretching yourselves this thin, especially not with what you are doing. Where a second of hesitation because you're too tired from rounding up cattle or whatever means you get shot. Or killed."

"Riley, enough." Jesse's face distorted.

"No, Jess. Dad's not here to speak straight and tell you how it's going to be, so I'm doing it and you're all going to listen. I'm not asking for permission or approval. Most of this is already in progress or finalized, so you're going to accept what I'm laying out or I'll have you laid out." Riley opened her folder. "I'll make this quicker because I can see sitting six bad asses down for more than a minute's tantamount to walking on water."

Vi chuckled.

"Right. First off, the Mason ranching days are done. I've had a meeting with the tax folks in Nomad. They gave me numbers, how many cattle we still need to run. It's about a fourth of what we've got now. Juan and his boys are handling foreman duties. So, from this point forward, aside from braking if a random cow gets in your way, your cattle days are done."

"That's not our call, Riles. Mom's the one who needs to make that decision," Dallas argued.

"And she has. Trust me, she'd be in here up in your faces if I'd let her. I figured it'd be tough enough to talk sense into you six without adding her to the conversation. Again, I'm not asking for permission. These are check marked items on my agenda to get your shit sorted." Riley took another breath. "So, Doctor Sinclair and I had a conversation. Horses and dogs are good for the Warrior's Path Project. Therapy animals and training of them is a good sideline to add to that project. I've had a conversation with Brant's uncle, the vet one not the doctor one. He's making some calls so we can get that going. He knows someone who'd be a good person to oversee starting a therapy dog training program out here, one some of your Warrior's Path folks could help with while they're here. That is the one and only item I'm leaving for you all to approve. You know what'll help those men and women better than me. Horses are a good idea, but I respectfully suggest we stick to dogs. Peanut is particular about who she befriends. We don't need a bunch of strange horses running around."

Dylan cracked a smile. Cord laughed outright.

"Now, onto the bigger items. Mom's done in the mess hall. She and I have been taking turns fixing meals and keeping the cafeteria supplied. I keep my head down and mouth shut when I'm in there, but you know Mom. She's been in those people's faces mothering and carrying on. I had my suspicions that wasn't what she should be doing, and I've had confirmation from both Logan and Doc Sinclair, so she's done. I've hired Rachelle to handle the cafeteria. She's a good cook and she needs a better job than the one she's got. Starting tomorrow, she's The Arsenal's official Food Manager. I'll think of a better title later, cause let's be honest. That's a shit title. But it'll do for now."

"That's a good idea," Nolan commented.

"Great. I'm glad you're on board because the next three items are in your wheel house." Riley leaned back and crossed her arms. "Consider this a coup. I'm taking over front office operations for The Arsenal. You and Marshall are bad asses. You need to be doing whatever it is you do. Front office is a train about to go off the rails, so I'm taking over. Effective a week ago."

"Really?" Marshall smirked. "Exactly what are you taking over?"

"We have a new Office Manager. She's starting tomorrow. She'll handle appointment scheduling, accounts payable and receivable, purchasing, schedule coordination and basically keeping your shit sorted. Now, I know she's the perfect fit for the role because she'll keep her mouth shut in town, but I've had Vi and Mary both vet her for security clearance. I figure she'll be more in the know on your bad ass goings on than anyone, so she'd need proper clearance. They both approved her, so Ellie Travis is the new Office Manager."

"Okay." Marshall crossed his arms. "We were going to hire someone. Eventually."

Riley lost a bit of her bolster beneath her brother's approval, which radiated in his voice and on his face. "Okay, good. We're switching up the visitor's building, too. The meeting rooms in the back are a good idea, but the lobby is bullshit. Bad asses don't need lobbies. It's not like you've got tons of people coming out here. Ellie will coordinate your schedules and visitors whenever you have them."

Silence fell. Vi knew what was coming next because the woman's hands fisted. Jud had given Vi a head's up last night after he'd finished talking to Riley.

"You all are too busy and too bad ass to help with the troubles going on around Resino and Marville, but folks still need help. I'm opening shop. The visitor's lobby will be a perfect office for the operation. Now, before you all can argue and give me shit about this, listen to the plan. Then I'd love to have your input because I love you and you're great at what you do."

"What's the plan, sweetheart?" Dylan asked softly.

"I'm getting my private investigator's license. Jud has one, apparently. Who knew bad asses got licensed? He said some others around here are, too. Anyway, he had an operation he'd just opened up in Boston. A modern-day Equalizer, the kind of place people went to when their backs are against a wall and they're about to drown in bullshit they can't fight alone. I pitched my plan to him. It was complete shit, so he tossed it out and gave me a better one. A wicked awesome one where he and I go into business together, based here. Ellie will be our office manager, too. I'll field potential jobs as they come in and handle the petty crap while I'm getting licensed. He'll handle the not-so-little stuff, the ones needing a bad ass because he's way closer to one than I am. When we need a real bad ass, we'll call one of you or your crew in."

Dallas raised his eyebrows at Jud, who grinned and shrugged. Vi chuckled. Mary laughed outright. Poor Riley had no idea what Jud's background was. He was probably the most lethal person at the table.

"Vi and Mary have agreed to help and give me access to HERA, as long as said access doesn't get in the way of Arsenal operations." Riley looked at Marshall. "I can keep Resino and the surrounding area safe while you handle the rest of the world."

"A couple things," Marshall said. "First, I know you've already started training with Addy. You work with Nolan or me on weapons and Dallas or Jud on hand-to-hand. Addy's great, but you need to go up against men bigger and stronger than you so you get practice taking them down."

"I'm down with kicking your asses," Riley replied.

"Jud will make a good partner for you. The idea's solid, but I want you turning briefs over to Nolan and Jesse on what you are both working on. We maintain the right to pitch in whenever we feel it prudent to do so." Marshall looked at Jud. "Goes without saying what we're expecting from you on this one."

They'd have his ass if he let anything happen to their little sister.

"Understood," Jud replied.

"I'll get a system set up once your new office is ready, make sure you've got a line straight to HERA," Cord offered.

"When things get hopping for you two, we've got plenty of licensed operatives who can pitch in," Dylan stated. "There won't be any shortage of assistance possible. Coordinate with me, Jud.

Nolan and I will make sure the team rotations leave people open to help."

"Appreciated," Jud commented. "I'm focusing on Marville first. I've had a conversation with Riley's girl, Rachelle. She's settled out here and away from the threats she was getting, but we're going to find out why she was getting those threats and shut it down."

"Jacob's taking a couple semesters off from MIT so he can stay here with his dad," Vi commented. "He's got some big plans to get you two hooked up."

"Which leaves the last couple of items on the agenda, ones I know you're probably going to have some problems with, so hear me out first. Okay?" Riley looked around the table.

"I think we've been pretty good so far, Riles. Keep going," Jesse said.

"I had a conversation with Brant's brothers, the ones who own Burton Construction. They did us a solid by getting the small houses Vi and the girls are in done so quickly. Anyway, I have an idea, one I got a couple weeks ago when I was talking to Vi. The biggest problem I see with Warrior's Path is the housing."

"What do you mean?" Dylan asked.

"They're in a dormitory-style environment, one step up from military barracks. That's not how real life will be. We need transitional housing, something like halfway houses." Riley grabbed one of the rolls, removed the rubber band and spread the papers out. Dallas and Cord took the ends. "The Burtons came out a couple days ago, did some surveying of the back pastures, the ones we won't need for the cattle anymore since we won't have many head left. I got these back from them this morning. I started naming the little roads, but that was more for fun."

Vi smiled. Warrior's Path was the main road leading to a neighborhood of homes. The smaller streets were named in similar ways, but all started with Warrior's. The houses were nestled in cul-de-sacs. Two different playgrounds were between the different areas. And a swimming pool.

"Wow. How much land do you all own?" Mary asked.

No joke.

"They think they can get a total of thirty homes in and leave plenty of room in between. Doctor Sinclair and Logan sat down with them, gave some insight into what sort of things we'd want to have." Riley chewed on her lip and pulled out the second scroll. "This one's the one they're pushing for, saying we may as well go big or go home. I agree."

Dylan and Jesse helped her position the other blueprints on the table. "The first section is an exact duplicate of the first ones. This one expands the neighborhood into the acreage we acquired, the old homestead next door. It's flat terrain and can be bulldozed easily. The Burtons think we could fit another twenty homes. They've got a company out of Nomad that can expand our perimeter fencing quickly so everything remains secured."

"Riley, this is impressive. We'd love to do this, but it's a huge undertaking. I'm not sure the finances are there for something this large," Nolan said.

"The Burtons are willing to do it for ten percent above cost. They're thinking we can round up quite a few people to help from out here, like we did with the houses that just got finished." Riley shrugged. "It'll take a while since they'll have to put focus on any real contracts that come through, but they're making it a priority until something comes in. They're slow."

"And money's not an issue," Vi said. "Our latest...incidents have the Deep Web coffers very full."

None of the alphabet soup wanted to deal with the hassle of tracking down which seedy bastards the money she'd taken came from. Like every other government agency out there, The Arsenal had an under-the-table blessing to do whatever they wanted with the funds they'd procured from The Collective.

Vi and Mary were working on tracking down some of the owners. Any funds illegally stolen or obtained would be returned anonymously, but they would be left with a fat bank account no matter how much they returned because the underworld didn't keep books. Cash was virtually untraceable.

Marshall grabbed the paper clipped to the edges of the largest plan. He scanned it, then passed it to Nolan.

The two men did some chin lift grunt thing.

"Fifteen over cost," Nolan said. "We don't undercut anyone that much, not even if the project is worth it."

"Agreed," Marshall added. "What size are these places? Same as the ones we just did?"

"Most, yes. This one area in the back of section two will be bigger. Three and four bedrooms. They're settling those closer to the playgrounds. We're thinking some of the soldiers with kids and families could transition to those, bring their families out for a few weeks. Doc Sinclair said it'd be a great step before they go home."

"Hell of an idea," Dylan commented. His fingers ran along the edges of the blueprints. "Never thought this big, not with everything else in the mix."

"Well, that's why I'm making decisions. Each thing I've mentioned today is a passion one of you has held close to the vest. Us letting some stuff go means you can each have your own piece of happy. That's what family does, and in case you haven't gotten the memo, we Masons have a helluva big family." Riley rolled her eyes. "The cousins are willing to help however they can."

"This'll take years to finish," Cord commented.

"Pft, you clearly forgot what Brant's brothers are like. Those men don't mess around. They're saying eleven months for the first phase, with another six for the final piece."

"That's impressive," Gage said.

"That's Resino," Riley replied. "Folks hear what's going on out here and the timeline will compress."

"Can't have a lot of town folk out here wandering around," Jesse said.

"What do you think about opening the old entrance from Grandpa Mason's place? The one two miles south of the main entrance?" Riley pointed to it on the blueprints. "It'd mean an extra security detail, but we could fence off the construction zone so anyone who comes out to help doesn't have any reason to come near the compound. That'll help keep the soldiers away from the curious people, right?"

Dylan smiled up at his sister. "Yeah, sis. That'll help."

"Pretty amazing plans. You've been busy," Dallas said.

"That happens when I have six big brothers actively avoiding me."

"Sorry," Cord offered.

"Things are going to get smoothed out around here so you all can focus on Arsenal business, whatever that is."

"Nothing is more important than you and Mom, Riley," Marshall said.

"Damn straight." Jesse thumped the table. "Don't take this all on by yourself. We'll help."

"I'll break stuff into small chunks. Divide and conquer. It's how you eat an elephant." Riley nodded.

"Speaking of elephant, I've got something to throw into the pile while we're overhauling." Cord looked around the table. "What do you ladies think about bringing someone in to create a virtual interface simulator?"

"Oh. My." Mary breathed.

"Wow." Vi leaned back in her chair. "Like one that'd take HERA's data?"

"Yep. We could have a couple simulation warehouses to use since we'll need lots of space." Cord motioned toward the plans.

"Figured I'd mention it in case we want to work them into these blueprints. It might not be a good idea."

"It's not a good idea." Mary crossed her arms. "It's an excellent idea."

"Heck yeah it is!" Vi grinned at Cord. "Have you looked into the cost?"

His shoulder's drooped. "Afraid you don't want to know."

"I'm thinking they already know," Marshall commented.

"Like I said, we're covered," Vi said. "And I can always clean the Deep Web."

"I don't want you taking risks," Nolan said.

Vi nodded dismissively. Her mind was already planning how to make it happen. Three-dimensional simulators the teams could use to do practice runs through ops? With real specs fed into it by HERA? It was the wet dream of all wet dreams for geeks. "How the hell did you keep this idea to yourself?"

"Wasn't sure it'd work."

"We'll make it work," Mary said. "You have an idea who to hire?"

"No. We'll need to vet whoever it is, obviously."

"Okay, so nerds are one thing I didn't even understand." Riley clapped her hands. "Now. Let's tackle the last agenda item. Mom. I need help bringing her back to reality. She is out of control with the wedding plans."

"She is?" Mary paled and looked at Dylan. "What does out of control mean, exactly?"

"Last I heard she had over a thousand people invited. That doesn't include what she calls Resino proper." Riley looked at Mary. "I know you and Dylan don't care. You'd already be married by the JP if you had your say, but this is a big deal for Mom and she's going overboard in a big way. I can't talk her down."

"I'll have a word," Dylan commented. He took Mary's hand. "Thanks for the head's up."

"I want to talk to her," Mary whispered back. She moved Dylan's hand to her stomach. "I'm thinking we can refocus her on something more important."

Shock rippled through Vi. Joy exploded in her, across her face as the weight of her best friend's words struck in the room like a live mortar round. Guffaws, whistles and back slaps filled the room. Dylan's eyes were saucer wide. Pale, he looked down where his palm was spread across her lower stomach.

"Surprise," she whispered. "I was going to tell you tonight, but I couldn't imagine a better way to tell you than while surrounded by our family."

"Holy shit." Riley repeated the two words in an endless loop as she collapsed in the nearest chair, which was already occupied by Jesse. "She's gonna freak. She's finally getting a grand baby on the heels of finding out about a secret one we're still looking for. Crap, the rest of you had better get busy or the kid Mary pops out will be spoiled rotten."

A flicker of remorse settled on Riley's features as she looked at Dallas.

"It's okay, little sis. We're going to find DJ soon. No one can hide from the Quillery Edge for long," Dallas said. "I'm glad he'll have a little cousin to play with soon."

Jud chuckled and nudged Vi. Hot breath fanned her neck as he wrapped a hand around her middle. "I'm not a Mason, but I'm thinking we should get busy with a little rugrat. We need the next generation of the Quillery Edge growing up together."

Holy cow. Vi couldn't breathe. Had he just...

"Did you just?" She stared down at the ring on her finger. She'd barely recovered from his proposal and being the future Mrs. Judson Jensen. Or having a future Mr. Viviana Chambers.

"I want our kid raised here, alongside Mary's. If you're ready, I sure as hell am. I've wasted enough of my life alone to know I've got a damn good thing here and I'm ready to go all in."

Vi smiled and leaned her head against his shoulder. "Go big or go home, huh?"

"Damn straight. What do you say?"

"I get dibs on naming the kid. We aren't having a Judson Jason Jensen Junior."

Jud's laughter echoed through the room. Vi joined in. Life was good. For the first time in a long time, she stared through the sight lines of life and knew she'd hit happy center mass.

~THE END~

Thank you for reading Sight Lines. Please consider leaving a review. I'd love to hear what you thought about Vi and Jud's story.

The Arsenal series continues with Blood Vows, releasing May 2018

Do you want the latest news and exclusive content? Sign up for my newsletter!

ABOUT CARA

Born in small-town Texas, Cara Carnes was a princess, a pirate, fashion model, actress, rock star and Jon Bon Jovi's wife all before the age of 13.

In reality, her fascination for enthralling worlds took seed somewhere amidst a somewhat dull day job and a wonderful life filled with family and friends. When she's not cemented to her chair, Cara loves travelling, photography and reading.

Newsletter|Facebook|Twitter

www.ingramcontent.com/pod-product-compliance
Lightning Source LLC
Chambersburg PA
CBHW051409170626
46809CB00006B/2082